GOD
FATHER'S
DAY

LYNDA REES

GOD FATHER'S DAY

By
Lynda Rees

Email: lyndareesauthor@gmail.com
Website: http://www.lyndareesauthor.com

Pinterest:
https://www.pinterest.com/lyndareesauthor/pins/

Goodreads:
https://www.goodreads.com/author/show/17187400.Lynda_Rees

Twitter: https://twitter.com/LyndaReesauthor

Facebook Fan:
https://www.facebook.com/lynda.rees.author/

Original Edition
978-1-7323116-3-3
Publisher: Sweetwater Publishing Company
6612 Ky. Hwy. 17 North, DeMossville, KY 41033
sweetwaterpublishingcompany.wordpress.com
Copyright © 2018 by
Sweetwater Publishing Company
Edited by Melinda Williams

Characters and locations in this book are fictional and figments of the author's imagination. Characters, locations or events portrayed fictionally associating or interacting with fictional characters in the story portrayed in ways feasible. However, their experiences are fictional and of the author's imagination. Similarity of fictional characters or events in this book to actual characters and events is purely conjecture on the part of the author, for the sake of entertainment only.

Email: lyndareesauthor@gmail.com

Website: lyndareesauthor.com

Facebook: @lynda.rees.author

This book is dedicated my father who courageously

brought his family out of a desperate situation

into a volatile area during a time of

change and turmoil,

searching for the American dream of a better life.

You were the bravest and one of the smartest men

I've ever known.

Everything I've done and have become,

my successes and achievements,

my drive, work ethic and values I owe to you.

I miss you every day of my life.

Lynda

CHAPTER 1

A long ten-hour shift at the hospital had Becky Watkins-Simms dragging ass as she parked and walked to the mailbox at roadside to collect today's delivery of junk mail and bills. She walked to the porch, glancing through the envelopes mentally sorting so she could toss trash in the can by the door she placed invoices in the drawer to be paid. A strange envelope snagged her attention.

Hair on the back of her neck stood, and foreboding oozed in as she reached the house. Instead of entering, she sat on the swing and slit it open with a short-cropped nail.

Damn, the paper cut hurt.

Peeling thick stationary from inside, she unfolded it and closed her eyes tilting her chin slightly asking for heaven's grace. Forcing her focus to the page she read the short notice deliberately, absorbing every word's meaning. It wasn't easy the way her hand trembled.

Finally able to take a normal breath it seeped

out as a loud sigh. She managed a couple robust gulps before convinced she wouldn't hyperventilate. The hollow in her gut wasn't from hunger though she had been famished a few minutes earlier.

It didn't matter. Like always, Becky must move forward balancing whatever bullets life threw her way without hesitation or dropping the ball. Too much at stake. She blinked twice, stood pushing her shoulders back and forced her head high as she shoved the offending note into a sweater pocket. No time for a pity party or worrying about implications.

Becky dragged herself into the house. "I'm home."

A four-foot munchkin rushed at her with arms wide. She scooped Evan into a bear hug and spun him around with a genuine grin on her face. "What has my little man been up to today?" She settled the tot onto his feet and taking his hand led him toward the kitchen.

"Something smells scrumptious in here." Her brows rose in a grin at her son.

Cheerfully Sadie smiled from the range and provided a much needed dose of comfort. "Welcome to the nut house, sis." Sadie Watkins' refreshing wit and musical laughter ruled the house with her contagious jovial manner.

"I've been practicing tying knots while Aunt Sadie cooks." Evan climbed onto a bar stool and displayed two knots he'd evidently learned well.

Leaning over him, Becky inspected them. "Great job, Evan, those are mighty handsome knots." She soaked in the much needed fortifying love of family.

"Guess what we're having?" She never tired of his sweet chirp of a voice.

"Mmmm, let me see. We're having pumpernickel pickle sandwiches." She tossed her head putting her hands to hips dramatically, making a production to entertain Evan.

"No, silly; Aunt Sadie is making my favorite—spaghetti and meatballs. I'm starved."

"Awesome, I could use spaghetti and meatballs. The garlic bread smells yummy." She rubbed her tummy exaggeratedly.

"It's done." Sadie pulled a salad from the refrigerator, eying Becky curiously. Had she detected something?

Becky set the table and poured her son a glass of milk then filled iced tea glasses for herself and Sadie. Sadie loaded plates with steaming pasta, meat sauce and garlic bread. Becky said grace giving special thanks for her son and Sadie. The sisters exchanged knowing looks when Evan dug into the meal. Sadie cocked a curious brow at Becky, but didn't ask.

Things had been tough with Becky a divorced new mother and the girls devastated by the loss of their parents in a car accident. Clinging together, depending on and taking care of each other had been an effective arrangement. Sadie loved Evan as much as Becky.

Thank God Becky had summoned strength to run for her life vowing never be powerless again. She didn't need a man. The beast couldn't be trusted.

Life was good and their little family happy

together.

Becky chuckled checking out Sadie's latest thrift shop fashion find. "Sadie, you're a fashion rebel or a genius. I can't decide which. Only you can pull off wearing the strange get ups you put together."

Head high Sadie proudly placed hands on hips and swayed shoulders back and forth, modeling her latest discovery. "Thanks, Becky. I get a kick out of vintage threads." Today's delight was a bright yellow and orange sleeveless tent dress with white go-go boots with stacked, square heels. A silky scarf tied around her slim neck matched Sadie's brunette bias-cut with a pink side streak.

"Quirky outfits have become your trademark." Becky adored Sadie and loved her wacky hair and clothing. "You look sweet and approachable—not what you're going for—tough and edgy. Whatever, it works for you." She winked at Sadie's pretended frown.

"Whatever and thanks, I guess." Sadie shrugged.

Evan stopped eating staring at his mom then Sadie. "Why would Aunt Sadie want to look tough? She's the nicest big person I know."

Sadie patted Evan's hand. "Thank you, little man. You're special, too." She winked. Satisfied he dove back into his food.

Becky envied the rebel in her sister, tending to be the stoic responsible one. "You're right, Evan. I'm proud of my little sister. Sadie is exceedingly cool."

The feeling was mutual. Sadie wiped a tear

from the corner of her eye with a napkin, careful not to disturb her dramatic eye makeup. "Thanks, Becky. You make me proud, too and inspired me to become a nurse. It's truly my calling. I'll never be able to repay you for all you've done for me." Smart and studious, Sadie worked hard, did well in school, and aced the nursing exam.

"No need. We're family. We stick together. Besides, your help with this one is the best thanks you could give me. You're good with our boy like a second mom." She ruffled Evan's hair. Becky quiet and reserved contrasted Sadie. "Your bubbly spirit and constant laughter helps make this place a home."

Evan chuckled between bites. Red sauce drizzled across his chin. "Aunt Sadie's the life of the party."

Becky swiped a napkin across his jaw. "She certainly is. Sadie's personality comes through loud and clear spreading fun wherever she goes. She's hard to resist." Sadie lit a room, giving to a fault.

"Aunt Sadie knows how to love. She's not bashful with hugs or kisses." He gave Becky's sister a toothless grin, and Sadie swiped red sauce from his chin smiling proudly.

Sadie rose to the challenge kissing his cheek, forehead, and neck until he was in a fit of giggles. "I have to tell my people how much I love them at every opportunity."

The sisters realized time was precious.

"We're glad you're still living with us, now you're a successful cardio nurse and can afford your own place. You're a ray of sunlight around here and

welcome as long as you want to stay. We love your company, but I don't want to hold you back."
Sadie's constant help with the house and with Evan made Becky's life easier.

With a snide smirk toward his mom, Evan laughed. "We'd starve to death if Sadie moved out."

Becky tweaked his cheek. "No, we could live on peanut butter." He giggled and dug back into his noodles.

"What fun would living alone be? I'd miss my main man." Sadie ruffled her nephew's hair again. "Besides, I'm grateful for everything you've done for me. I'm to find anything I can to ease your burden."

"Don't be silly. You've never been a burden. I need you more than you need me."

As a cardio surgery nurse for a private practice, Sadie worked with a team of doctors in practicing at the hospital where Becky worked. Highly respected, those close to Sadie saw her heart of gold—not taking much seriously, but dead serious about patient care.

"I can hardly believe Evan is seven already, and in kindergarten, excelling in reading and math. You inherited the big brain from your mommy and me." Sadie grinned at Evan.

"Your soccer game is at six Saturday. T-ball is at ten. It's going to be a full day with lots of sunscreen for your tender skin. Isn't there a race car building event coming up with the scouts?" She winked at her son, who squirrelled his mouth up and shrugged.

"Yeah, but it's a dad and son thing. Moms

can't participate." His shrug and the sad look on his face made breathing difficult for Becky as she gulped a huge ball of regret. But there wasn't anything she could do about it. Neither she nor Sadie had a man in their lives to be a substitute dad for Evan at the races.

His blonde hair, deep brown eyes, and sturdy build resembled his grandpa, Sadie and Becky's dad. Inheriting his dad's natural athletic abilities, Evan learned fast and enjoyed team sports—the only good thing the jackass had done for the child.

Blossoming in his family's love, the happy, well-balanced child did well in school and made friends easily. Fortunately inheriting Becky's slow, even temper the sweet child was easy to love. He didn't get it from his dad.

Luckily she escaped when she did. Life turned out well despite hell the Brent put her through.

Later doing dishes while Evan took a bath, Sadie washed and Becky dried in the tight kitchen. Hip-butting Becky, Sadie stood at the sink with suds to her elbows. "All right, the munchkin is out of range. What's wrong?" A brow raised, Sadie handed her a freshly rinsed plate to dry.

"How do you sense something's bothering me? You're as psychic as Mom. She sensed when something was wrong."

"Don't change the subject. Spill it. And yes, I inherited Mom's sixth sense. I read your moods."

"I received a notice. Brent is free."

"Damn, I hoped someone would put a *shive*

in the bastard before he received parole." There was truth in her joke.

"Nope, he acts decent around the male population. He only gets off on roughing up women. He was probably a model citizen in prison."

"Too bad." Sadie shrugged.

CHAPTER 2

Justin Martin slid a hand up the slit in the elegant gown of the stunning woman seated beside him. Yancy's bare leg was smooth as satin and hot like the woman.

She gave him a wicked grin. "Down, boy, you've had enough pussy to do until after Daddy's gala.

"You take my breath away. Your exquisite body looks deliciously voluptuous in that gown. You can't blame me for being your willing victim." She was everything he wanted in a woman. "The word beautiful doesn't do you justice; you're downright spectacular."

She didn't pretend to blush, only patted his hand with a knowing smile.

Without regret, he sought out Yancy's type since college—elegant, classy, vibrant, fun to be with, and glamorous—a fantasy come true. She fulfilled every sexual fantasy, so it wasn't a sacrifice doing her bidding; showing her off at these functions. He devoted attention to her needs and a presence in her social life—and her bed—all she required and fine with Justin. What more could he ask for?

She didn't tax him emotionally—also fine. As long as he attended to her desires, she required nothing on a deeper level. The way Justin rolled—a shallow affair held appeal, essential in fact. She acted satisfied with what he willingly gave. Yancy, loved playing the spoiled rotten handful, and Justin, a lucky sucker with her on his arm, were a perfect match.

He'd learned his lesson at sixteen. Love hurts. Don't go there or have expectations.

Street lights glistened on her golden tresses pulled into a curly chignon at the back of her flawless head. Diamonds he gave her for her birthday dangled from her ears catching the glow. A matching string cradled her slim, aristocratic neck—a gift from *Daddy*.

The forest green silk gown fit to perfection—of course, created by a famous designer he couldn't recall the name of when she flew to France on one of her yearly treks to refresh her wardrobe. A strapless bodice displayed enough tantalizing cleavage to make a weak man drool. Justin wasn't weak, by no means, tough as they came.

He'd panted for Yancy earlier at her condo when she'd given him the best head ever. Soon as he'd come Yancy returned to the role of a lady. A sensual kiss on the mouth then she straightened her slim skirt and patted her curls impeccably into place. As she strode toward the bar to retrieve her purse, slender hips swayed seductively.

Damn, she's something. He couldn't take his eyes off of her ass as she slinked away. "You sure get off on torturing me."

She wickedly grinned then winked.

Panties gave the impression she was *commando* framing a perfect behind deliciously in slinky material. Tossing him a sultry, knowing smile over a shoulder, she reapplied red lipstick watching him tuck his cock into his trousers. *Geez, it must be painted scarlet.*

"Thanks Baby, I enjoyed it. Let me do you." He wrapped her in his arms and nuzzled her neck. Her personal scent, an expensive perfume designed for her in Paris, combined with his odor on her breath made him woozy with longing. He enjoyed leaving his mark on this woman.

She liked it too. She laughed and licked her lips closing her eyes.

Enough play time.

Yancy pulled a tissue from a box gently dabbing excess paint from her mouth. Shaking her shoulders signaled to release her. Snapping her handbag shut, she grabbed a fur wrap and strutted gracefully past him toward the door. Saucy heels clicked against marble as her hips swayed exaggeratedly, and thin cloth clung like a second skin displaying her attributes perfectly.

"Not now, baby, later. Daddy is expecting us. We mustn't keep him waiting."

Of course not, nobody kept Landon waiting.

In the car Yancy began lobbying for a more permanent relationship. She might not want depth emotionally, but she wanted marriage. Justin tuned the familiar chatter out. She'd ramped her marriage campaign after their four-month dating anniversary, talking incessantly about her friend Macy's wedding, and pouring on the pressure.

Yada, yada, yada, whatever. Justin didn't listen.

He could handle a full diet of Yancy, but had to keep his sanity. She never noticed, or pretended not to. He got the general message. Good enough for her—she'd get her way, like always.

Marriage brought advantages providing profitable opportunities for his career. Her never-ending string of wealthy, powerful friends meant money-making business for him worth investing in. She'd get what she wanted. So would Justin.

Yancy wasn't stupid or naïve. With the best education money could buy, smart with no interest in commerce, marriage with a home of her own was her career goal, high class fashion, and never-ending shopping—the only things of interest to her.

Of course, Yancy was insatiable and expected lots and lots of sex. *Good for Justin.*

She'd expect her husband to maintain the style she was accustomed to. Was Justin up to the challenge? It depended on his firm.

"Did I tell you I'm up for partner?"

"You said you hoped to be. It's good. Making partner comes with criteria. A partner is supposed to exude stability—meaning be married."

Of course she honed in on points to push her agenda. No problem.

"I have no problem bringing in billable hours." Marriage to Yancy would fulfill the obligation.

"You work hard, harder than most at the firm and bring in more billable hours than other attorneys, except maybe the partners. You've been there only five years, but they owe you partner. As a partner you'd be expected to entertain. I love hosting parties. I'll be an asset to your career. We'll make perfect partners." It sounded like a done deal—a business transaction. It practically was. "I have connections to make your career successful."

She wasn't wrong. Yancy would make a great partner's wife. "You're a fabulous hostess. I've kept my nose to the grindstone. We'll see how much it helps." A beautiful dangle on his arm with no career ambitions of her own, she brought everything he needed in a wife. "And you're sexy as hell." Why had he been delaying the inevitable?

They met through a senior partner at his firm. Harry introduced them in the office, and Justin rode the elevator with Yancy. Justin asked her to lunch. It stretched into dinner then breakfast and a long weekend shacked up in her penthouse.

"I love the incredible view of the city from the bed in your condo. After our first night together I've never looked at the Nashville skyline quite the same way. It gives me a stiffy remembering it, and I'm still as hot for you." She didn't pretend to blush.

Yancy didn't care she was way out of Justin's league. They both realized it. The spoiled princess, only daughter of multi-billionaire developer, Landon Bridges, who shamelessly catered to her every whim, she had the best of everything and expected no less. She wanted Justin, who'd proved to be the best suitor according to *Daddy*.

He wasn't from her side of the tracks. Their past drastically differed, though he made a decent living, nothing like Landon racked in. "What do you see in me, Yancy?"

Justin wasn't sure, though sometimes ladies heads sometimes turned when he entered a room, so he mustn't be unpleasant to look at. And he'd never had complaints about his performance in the bedroom.

She shrugged gazing out the side window. "You're well-built. You work out and are always groomed impeccably. You're good looking with your black, wavy hair and green piercing eyes. You drive a nice car."

Justin gifted himself his treasured Jaguar after his first year with the firm. "Thanks."

She shrugged in his peripheral vision. "You've made a name for yourself in corporate law. Your attention to detail makes you in great demand. You perform well in court and provide strong cases with valid evidence and persuasive arguments. More often than not, you convince competition to settle out of court. When you take a case to the judge, you're deadly—a formidable litigator. That's why you seldom lose." She sounded proud, but she talked about business and his appearance—not about the man he had hoped she would have noticed in him.

"I've got attention from the senior partners, and I'm a viable candidate, but competition is tough."

"Nonsense, you're on the road to being one of the most sought after corporate attorneys in Nashville, and in the state of Tennessee. It's a matter of time before they offer partnership. Those fuddy-duddies don't want to lose you."

Even with that, he didn't make enough money to keep Yancy as she was accustomed to. Her own money aside, she'd assume her husband would foot the bills. Yancy didn't understand not everyone lived the way she did. She took much for granted.

His spoiled princess, at least for as long as she'd have him, maybe a lifetime, and he intended to make the most of it.

No matter the lady she portrayed in public, in the sack she acted wild like an animal ready for anything—definitely appealing. She was lovely, fun to be with, and sexy as all get out. So he'd go with the flow.

"You never tire of your daddy's parties. Landon enjoys showing off his desirable women." As assets, Landon's women acted as one more thing inspiring admiration from associates.

"It's expected an affluent, powerful man have at least one supportive woman on his arm. Daddy's no exception."

"Landon is a force to be reckoned with in development and real estate—a tycoon of the highest power."

"Yes, Daddy's responsible for deals making the city and state what they are today."

Landon had friends and associates in all areas of powerful positions. His frequent parties proved instrumental in bringing contracts together. Not only social functions held for fun, but functioning meetings with liquor and fine dining combined with strategy and goals. Blending a perfect mix of people empowered Landon to achieve whatever he had in mind.

Justin generally enjoyed the events. "I find them entertaining and highly profitable. I've acquired business contacts through these parties and brought in multiple clients to the firm as a result. I enjoy networking and observing Landon-the Master at work. I admire him and his way with industry. He never misses a beat, unique and in a league of his own. I'm happy for the opportunity to learn from him."

Yancy graced Justin with an appreciative smile and patted his hand, still resting on her naked leg.

"Daddy does decorate a crowd with celebrities from all walks of life, providing entertainment, and bringing an engaging aspect to an evening."

"He does. I wonder what celebrities will be in house tonight." It could be network executives, movie stars, sports figures, writers, designers, artists, race car drivers, Kentucky Derby winning jockeys or breeders to name a few. Anyone famous could be on the invite list.

"I'm not sure. There'll be at least a half a dozen celebrities in the mix with the usual developers, real estate tycoons, government officials, bankers, financiers, investment brokers, etc. Daddy's a genius at putting together the right mix."

For achieving his current objective. Justin pulled off the highway onto Bridges Drive into Yancy's family estate—aptly named Bridges Way. He felt like a chump having tuned Yancy's droning out earlier; but *damn*, she droned on and on about weddings realizing he wasn't listening. Her disappointed glare with the particular pout showed when not getting her way. Marriage, a topic near to her heart, determined to get him matrimony bound. He'd give in sooner or later. He might as well get it over with.

Yancy is so sure of me. She'll consider my proposal an unnecessary formality.

Maybe he'd ask her tonight, alone in bed. First, they'd exhaust their needs. She'd be hot-to-trot after impressing *Daddy*. Her daddy fixation didn't bother Justin. *Whatever.* It got him laid, with the best sex he'd had.

His shoulders snapped back as he adjusted his posture, pulling into the long, tree-lined driveway leading to a monstrous house. The majestic mansion sparkled like an enormous gem. Rain blanketed the well-manicured lawn with water beads transformed by headlights into a sparkling diamonds sea—a fitting prelude to the elegant evening.

He parked, and a uniformed valet caught the keys he tossed. Justin circled to where another attendant assisted Yancy from the car. Lifting his arm, she took it and they strutted toward the house. In princess mode, her pout disappeared, mentally prepared to be *Daddy's perfect lady* again—a role she cherished and acted well.

She'd make a wonderful wife.

Each time he pulled into the stately drive the manor house stole his breath. The fabulous residence wasn't a real home. Nothing intimate or homey about the glamorous, brick monstrosity, it may as well be a business building—indeed it was, only masked as a home.

Landon had created an intimidating residence sending a clear message. His palace bore witness. Landon acted the master of his kingdom. Modern grandeur of the three-story, sprawling white stone displayed lots of glittering glass depicting a traditional plantation look with huge columns flanking hand-carved doors.

Never in Justin's wildest dreams had he fit into a scene like this.

High heels clicking marble flooring echoed in the enormous lobby as they entered. A spectacular stairway with carved banisters graced the center. Built in the Tara tradition, it swung wide, narrowing as it ascended the three-story domed ceiling, which sported a mural. The enormous chandelier sparkling from the center must've cost more than Justin made in a year.

A tuxedoed servant wearing tails and striped trousers bowed and took Yancy's wrap and purse, depositing them with a crisply uniformed maid. Yancy took Justin's arm, and he led her into the ballroom where the butler announced, "Mr. Justin Martin and Ms. Yancy Bridges." He bowed and backed from the room.

Justin laughed to himself each time this happened. Who would've thought he'd attend a party and be formally announced? Leave it to Landon to require the royal treatment. This pompous ritual had the desired effect, clearly showcasing Landon's supremacy—nothing if not shrewd.

The place hummed a low beat—an electrical current of unleashed power. Justin couldn't wait to work the room.

A multitude of flowers provided a heady aroma. Ada, Landon's current wife, designed the floral arrangements herself and had overseen the huge event in their impressive ballroom ensuring every detail cared for to perfection, so the night would benefit her powerful husband.

The *royal couple* greeted them with mock-hugs and cheek kisses. "So glad you came, Justin. You brought my favorite person." Landon winked.

Ada glanced away but her expression never changed. *Ouch.*

After the brief obligatory chat they sauntered off to circulate. Justin and Yancy made the rounds talking with people then split apart. Each spoke with acquaintances—networking for business sake. Drinking, dining, and dancing fueled data exchange and bargains made in this world.

Justin and Yancy occasionally danced together. Attentive to her needs, he kept a watchful eye from across the room and ensured her glass stayed full of Kristal, her favorite. Justin preferred bourbon on the rocks.

At the bar getting a refresher, Landon met with him. "Got a minute for the Old Man?"

As though I could refuse.

"Old Man—my ass; you're fit as a fiddle. You could take any man in the place, including me. What's up?"

Landon exuded power from his core and acted the role of industry baron. His tux, created by his personal New York tailor, cut from the finest material money could buy, showed off his well-honed physique. Everything about him spoke of power.

"Let's adjourn into the den for a cigar." Landon led the way. Once there, he handed Justin a fatty. "You'll like these. They're hand-rolled and imported."

At least fifty dollars apiece.

Landon eased his commanding frame into a square tufted chair in the center of the room. Arms outstretched over soft, brown leather of the man-sized seat. He motioned for Justin to join him. He sat across from Landon.

The room teemed with extravagance and oozed testosterone. A scent of rich upholstery and warmth of polished wood combined with cigar aroma and intoxicated the brain. Before taking a sip, Justin appreciatively inhaled the heady fragrance of the best bourbon money could buy.

Yep, this is the life.

"How's work?" Landon studied him casually drawing on his stogie—odd because Landon never did anything for the fun of it.

"Very good, sir, I'm swamped with interesting cases, bringing in billable hours and productive clients to my firm. They're considering me for partnership."

"As I suspected." Landon knocked embers into a crystal ashtray. "I've been observing your career and checking on you. I'm impressed with what I've seen." Landon studied him critically. Justin didn't flinch, used to operating under scrutiny. "You brilliantly handled the Market Street case. You have a powerful presence in the courtroom. Are you happy at the firm?"

"Happy? I suppose so. I've worked my ass off achieving goals I set for myself. I'm proud of what I've done. So yes, I guess I'm happy." Justin took a draw on his smoke, growing uneasy about what might be on Landon's mind. Whatever, it likely benefitted Yancy. He chose to be flattered Landon cared, even if it proved self-serving, as expected.

"Son, maybe you haven't set high enough goals. You're capable of more. You should reassess what you want from life. Reach for the stars while you are young enough to jump." He'd recently started calling Justin *Son*. Everything Landon did had purpose—even that.

"I'm not sure, sir." *Where are we going?* "What exactly do you mean?"

"It's no secret. My daughter fancies you. She's quite taken and apparently serious."

"I adore Yancy, as well, Sir." *Here we go* — "Yancy lives a life of luxury accustomed to the best."

"Yes Sir, I'm aware she enjoys the good things in life."

"If you and she are to have a future, it's important you prepare and be capable of taking care of my little girl." Landon took another long pull and blew smoke circles eyeing Justin, giving him time to react.

"Sir, Yancy and I haven't made a commitment, though we've talked. If *we decide* we're meant to be together, it is between her and me. I'm sure you get my meaning." He didn't want to offend, but didn't care for Landon mixing in his love life—even with his daughter as the object of affection.

The older gent laughed bawdily. "I'm sorry, Son. Don't take offense. I respect you for it."

"Thank you, sir." Justin sniffed.

"Let's talk reality. You understand. Yancy's my only daughter. She will never be without. It is a fact." He pronounced each of those four words separately, giving emphasis to them. "If you want to be part of it, and if she wants you, you'll find a way to provide what she desires and needs. It's simple."

Justin chuckled admiring the tenacity—remarkable—simply unstoppable. The meaning clear, Justin resented interference, but logically expected no less.

Landon wasn't finished, pausing letting his words soak in. Justin sat quietly waiting—reigning in the wrath Landon's interference stirred in his gut. His profession required disguising his opinions and emotions. No different.

"We take care of family. If you're to become part of it, you must be brought into the fold. Yancy's my only heir, inheriting everything. She fancies you." He paused heavily. "She has no interest and certainly no head for business. She's not and never will be in a position to assume the helm of my empire. So, I must assure she marries someone capable of managing it for her, someone with strength, drive, intelligence, and balls. You're the man. She needs you, Son. It works well if you'll let it. You and Yancy will have a good marriage."

"Sir, are you giving your blessing or asking me to wed your daughter? It sounds more like you're offering a job?" Flabbergasted, Justin stood and paced with hands in his trousers.

Landon chuckled. "I love a man who meets a bull head-on and roars in its face. Son, you have a great future. I hope it will be with us. I'm not asking you to marry Yancy. If the two of you are inclined to, you have my blessing." He sipped his bourbon.

Justin wore his court face waiting.
"Justin, I'd like you to take a job with my firm. As you know, I have a team of the best lawyers money can buy. You have potential to out-best them someday. I'm offering a beginning position with my team. If it works out, and it will, you'll move to other roles in my company learning from the ground up and all angles. I'll prepare you to manage my

empire, and I'll be your mentor. If Yancy wants you for a husband—she's as much as told me she does—you'll be ready to take the reins someday. Not only that. Working for me you'll be able to support my baby the way she should be. If things don't work out with her, you still have the best career possible as a top man in my firm." Landon took another long puff on his fire stick and put it out. He swigged remaining bourbon from his tumbler. "Consider it, Son. You have it in you. I can turn you into a business mogul like me. Think hard on it. Make the right decision."

"Thank you, Sir. I'll consider it." Justin couldn't be more thrilled had he hit the lottery. His innards jumped to Landon's beat.

"Let's return to the party before the women send a search team." He slapped Justin on the back as they ambled together.

Shocked, proud and eager about the amazing proposal, also appalled Yancy's dad meant to manipulate her marriage along with a trade score. In his heart Landon thought this aided his daughter's well-being. It also helped boost his ego, satisfy his concern, and secure his legacy.

I get it—just not sure I like it. Then again, I love it. How it worked in their world became clear. The rich and dominant manage power by guarding it and keeping it in the family. Justin's golden ticket would morph him into one of them—a mover and shaker—the future Landon.

His chest expanded, and shoulders rocked back as his chin shot up. Flattered, not having grown up in this world, he hadn't known how high was high, so had fallen short in his expectations. He could learn to control Landon's kingdom and excel at it. The tremendous opportunity sounded grander than he'd ever considered. He was up to the challenge.

He'd need to swallow whatever was stuck in his crawl about interference in his relationship with Yancy, and accept the strange offer. He could fit in as Landon expected, but would he thrive in such an arrangement? Could he live with the strings attached and be happy?

Did it matter if he became happy? What the hell was it about anyway? He'd be successful and prosperous in an over-the-top way. It should make him complete.

Wow. Torn—giddy on one hand and apprehensive on the other, he had considering to do. But not tonight, he needed to stay in the present. He'd think it through later—alone.

Ada and Yancy chatting about clothing and designers hadn't missed their men in the least. Only four years apart in age, instead of resenting each other they got along famously—another odd thing about their sphere.

They could be clones, but total opposites with Ada's darkly exotic beauty and Yancy's blonde sultry. Apparently Landon fixated on a type. Ada's lengthy locks piled high and her silver, backless gown appeared to be painted on her curves, showing off her ass-cheek-outline, and leaving one to wonder—thong or commando?

Landon made his own luck and fortune. Women flocked to men like him, and he could have any he chose. He'd selected a lovely trophy serving him well.

"Where have you boys been?" Ada pretended to scold, though she'd never do such a thing.

"Man talk, Darling." He kissed his wife on the jaw she offered, groped a butt cheek with his hand and wrapped a possessive arm around her waist staking his claim.

As Justin slid an arm around Yancy's petite shoulders his dad's special ringtone chirped. He created it so he'd never miss a call from the old man—the only family left.

"Sorry, Sweetie, I have to take this. It's my father." Answering and smiling he backed away and walked toward the atrium, seeking a quiet location to better hear. "Hey, Dad, how's it going?"

Instead of his father's baritone a soft, efficient voice spoke. Hairs on the back of his neck stood.

"I'm sorry, Mr. Martin. This isn't your father calling. I have bad news. Mr. Martin is in the hospital in critical condition. He suffered a major heart attack and arrived in an ambulance. He has been in surgery and is stable. However, it's not good. I recommend you come right away."

Justin leaned against the nearest wall steadying his self. The hand holding the phone trembled, and breathing became thick and erratic. He tried making sense of it, but must've been in shock.

"Of course, thank you for calling. Where is he?"

"St. James Hospital in Louisville. May I tell him you're on your way if he regains consciousness? How long before you arrive? I'll inform him and his physician."

"Of course, I'll leave now and should be there in about four hours." Justin clicked the line dead as his insides numbed. He shook his head to clear it and rushed to find Yancy stepping onto the dance floor with Landon.

"Hon, I have to leave. There is an emergency with my dad. I must go to him right way. It's serious." Yancy looked stricken and initiated her pouty face. Justin ignored her obvious lack of concern sulking at being abandoned, and he couldn't care less.

To Landon he extended a hand, which Landon shook amicably. "Sir, can you see Yancy home safely? I apologize, but I must run. Please, excuse me."

"Of course Son, go. My limo driver will take Yancy home. We'll talk later."

Justin kissed Yancy's cool, scowling lips. She didn't resist but didn't respond either. Poor Yancy, her evening wasn't ending as planned—too bad. He spun and left, never giving another thought to her *problem*. His dad was his only priority. Mentally he was already on the road focused on getting to him. With a quick stop at his condo, Justin ran in and tossed his tie aside. He threw a few things into a duffle bag, grabbed a bottle of water for the road and sped to the car hoping he had what he needed. If not, he'd buy it when he arrived. He had no idea how long before he'd return home.

His stomach churned with foreboding. What would he find at the hospital?

Oh, God, a hospital—

CHAPTER 3

Worried, he hadn't noticed as miles speed by. Justin made great time, pulling into the parking lot at 3:30 a.m.

A hell of a Saturday night.

Nerves had about all they could handle, and he ran on caffeine and adrenaline. Clenching the steering wheel, he hesitated staring at the eerily quiet brick building.

Why did his gut wrench in fear? Doom all but smothered him. He massaged hammering swelling in his temples as the beat echoed through his skull assaulting his senses. Bile rose and he feared he might barf.

Raging memories rendered him incapable of quieting thoughts penetrating his armor. Fear gripped his soul, awakening tormented recollections he battled reluctantly. Labored breathing came in ragged gasps. He struggled to draw a deep cleansing gulp, fighting the sensation, unwilling to allow panic to rule. It sure gave him the battle of a lifetime.

It lived in his mind, but he couldn't help aching, recalling his last visit here. This edifice had stolen the only woman he loved—Mom. It had murdered childish dreams, stripping the happy-ever-after scenario from his life. Disillusioned, loss tainted his perspective since the day forward.

Aware the structure didn't possess actual power, simply a construction of steel, brick and mortar, but it didn't prevent the involuntary assault engulfing him, or wrenching in his gut making him tremble, suppressing a gag.

One night long ago youthful innocence had perished in the benevolent place. As it withered, he had forged a future incapable of intimacy and sworn to avoid its weighty ramifications and substantial cost. He'd lived by the vow.

Dad was the only person he loved. Undying commitment to Dad forced Justin to defy anxiety riveting him and forge forward. Obligation to the man who'd given him everything was more than sheer responsibility. Dad had molded Justin into this dedicated man.

Get a grip. A hospital was meant to be a beacon of hope and healing—not the essence of torture and desperation.

Closing his eyes the bond with Dad embraced him. In a life void of sentiment, their mutual affection stayed a blessing. Justin would face the devil for Dad. He'd survive this. Hopefully Dad would, too.

Get on with it.

Adrenalin surged through Justin's veins. Steeling himself, he reluctantly hurled from the vehicle forcing each step, surrendering to the future—whatever it held. As he strode toward the entrance, a petite woman with a mop of bouncing, chocolate curls ending below her ears strolled out wearing nursing scrubs lovely but looking fatigued.

As she exited the revolving door, a man bolted around a dark corner heading her way. Panic blanched her face. Shock registered there. Her mouth hung open and she back-stepped uncertainly. Her arms flew in front of her as if to fend the bloke off. A tall, bulky uniformed guard shot toward the door noticing the interaction.

The stranger reached the nurse and grabbed her arm jerking her close. Her hand slid between them, and she emitted a meek squeal like a mouse caught in a trap. Justin's heart sank at the sound.

The guy pulled her toward a darkened area he'd appeared from. She attempted to stall movement by bracing her feet and bending. Resistance proved ineffective. The tall, muscular fella tugged hard. No match for the large, well-honed man's strength.

Distance between Justin and them, proved too great to prevent the guy dragging her. Clearly she wanted nothing to do with him. Her eyes held terror.

Justin bolted toward them in a run. The assailant gripped her arm keeping her from running away. It felt as though a bag of sand hit Justin's stomach watching the dude manhandle the defenseless woman. She shouted and slapped at his hands trying to get free, but nothing she did helped. By the time Justin grew near enough to do anything, she'd become full-blown panicked. Tears rolled from her eyes.

Justin snatched the man's forearm and yanked hard. Releasing the gal, he spun sideways facing Justin. "What the hell?" He looked confused.

"Let go of the lady, Mister. She obviously doesn't want to go with you." Justin clutched the stranger's shoulder whipping him backward. He stood few inches taller with musclebound shoulders and a slim waist, but it didn't deter Justin. Fury had him working on adrenalin as he spat words. "Take your hands off her."

The strange man backed slightly and hesitantly eased his grip. Red imprints remained on her arm, angering Justin more. She meekly twisted it away from her assaulter then slid uncertainly behind. using Justin as a barrier.

"Stay out of it, you son-of-a-bitch." The thug spat the words.

"Is this man bothering you?" Justin peeked over his shoulder.

She nodded. "He is. My restraining order says you aren't to come within three hundred feet of me, asshole." Her voice trembled at the screeching shout.

"Who the hell do you think you are?" Justin barked feeling steam rush out with his words.

"Get lost. This is between my woman and me." The unfamiliar dude's face flashed red.

"I don't give a damn, you SOB. Leave the woman alone. No one has the right to maul a lady, especially her man, who should cherish, not hurt her."

"It's none of your business, stud. So leave— now." The red faced fella blurted then spat the sidewalk beside them. His chest expanded broader with each breath. "Ah, Becky, honey, I only want to talk. I mean no harm."

"You can't be here. Get lost and leave me alone. I mean it. I won't put up with your crap any longer. Go back to Cincinnati and stay away from me. Or I'll have you arrested, and you'll end up back in prison."

Quiver in her voice made Justin ache inside. "Look, dude, the lady doesn't want to talk. You best get lost, or be arrested." Justin tried reasoning.

"Becky, you can't keep me from a medical building."

"Are you seeking care or visiting someone?" Justin eyed him critically. She heaved huge breaths of air acting as though trying to get her bearings. "You okay?" She nodded unconvincingly.

"I'm here to talk with my wife." The angry fellow threw his shoulders back and put fists on hips.

"Absolutely not—not anymore. I'm not your wife." Glaring at her assailant she spoke through gritted teeth. "Brent, you're dead to me. I don't owe you anything. Go, and leave me alone." Her voice cracked speaking between sobs.

Justin's hands fisted and moved to the front instinctively readying to fend off a blow. He tried leaning around Justin, but Justin adjusted his stance providing a barrier.

"But, Becky, honey, I'm sorry. I want us to be together and make a clean start. Let me make it up to you." He peered over Justin's shoulder pitiful pleading, as his face sagged and eyes drooped pathetically. "Let's go somewhere and talk, honey. I'm sorry." The bulky dude's shoulders slumped as hos shrill voice begged.

"Not on your life. You can make a clean start if you go now. Otherwise, I'm sending you back to a hole where you belong." Her petite hand lay on Justin's shoulder using him as a safety wall. His chest filled with pride, and his shoulders stayed back. He felt taller suddenly.

"Is there a problem, Miss?" The hulking guard asked standing between Justin and the pissed off intruder. One broad paw trained on his club and the other on his radio.

"Yes, officer, thank you. I have a restraining order against this man. He's trying to drag me away."

"Do you want him arrested?" He grabbed the assailant's hand wrenching his arm behind his back. A pained grimace came over the stranger as his knees buckled. He slumped sideways trying to ease the grip. Justin gave him credit. He didn't try to fight the guard.

"No, but please hold him until I'm safely gone. I don't want him to follow. I'll report the incident to the police myself once I'm home safely." She glanced at the officer's name tag.

"Are you sure, Ma'am?" He looked doubtful.

"Yes, thank you. Thank you both."

"Provide the police my name, Ma'am. I'll happily back your story up, if they call." Suppressed anger at the guy accosting the poor woman pulsed in his veins. His palms itched as he balled fists dangling at his sides, wishing he could quell the urge to punch the fella's face.

She nodded, and her warm palm slid along Justin's arm. She squeezed his hand then ran into the parking lot. The officer dragged the angry dude inside and shoved him into a seat.

Justin mentally prayed for her safety, wishing she'd asked the officer call the police. The warmth of her hand remained on Justin's shoulder as he observed, making sure she drove out of sight before going in. He wanted to ensure the culprit didn't get released too soon.

The attacker waited on a bench, as Justin finally lugged himself inside. The uniformed man released him. He glared at both men then spat the floor by Justin's feet. "Stay out of my business, you bastard."

"Apparently she's not your business, asshole. Get lost." Justin gave him his meanest glare then headed toward the elevators.

The duty cop laid a hand on his weapon. With another on a tiny bat-type instrument hanging from his belt, he gave the angry jerk a glare showing he meant business. His shoulders shook and he sauntered toward the parking lot in no hurry.

CHAPTER 4

Justin located the Pulmonary CCU Unit and a duty nurse buzzed him in. In his room, Richard rested peacefully, heavily sedated. The nurse on duty explained the on-call doctor was in charge. She didn't anticipate his cardiologist returning until Monday, unless there was an emergency warranting his presence.

God forbid. Justin could wait for Monday. *No more emergencies.*

Still not understanding what he was dealing with, he hesitated at the door of his Dad's room. Antibacterial cleanser and antiseptic odor overwhelmed his senses. Only a hospital had power to manufacture the particular stench. He hadn't spent much time in them, but the few times he had recalled a stink one never forgot.

Justin forced back memories. He must focus now on Dad.

Enough wallowing.

He braced for what awaited inside still shocked. If he hadn't known he wouldn't have recognized Dad. Frail and helpless, with more silver than before, he'd grown thinner and aged years in a few months.

Technology ruled the room. Steady tunes hummed from contraptions monitoring bodily functions. Wires protruded from beneath covers in all directions. Tubes secured with tape to arms connected to beeping bedside machines. Numbers on monitors meant nothing to an untrained eye. A hospital gown draped over Richard like an apron and tied behind his neck. A thick tube protruded from his mouth connecting to a loud wheezing instrument breathed for him. The eerie sight oddly reassured him—a sign Richard still lived.

Where there is life, there is hope.

Man up. Get a grip. The old man needs you. Don't let him down.

Lifting Richard's frail arm countless purple bruises became obvious from needle pricks on unusually slick, thinning skin. Brown age spots dotted the tops of his limp hands.

Dad has old man skin.

It hadn't occurred to Justin his dad aged. He'd been too wrapped in creating his own life to consider how time might change his only surviving relative.

"I'm here, Dad—it's Justin. Don't worry. Everything's okay. Rest. I've got this." He wiped tears with his sleeve. "I love you, Dad. We're going to take this one day at a time, as it comes." His whispering voice told lies hoping to reassure the sleeping man.

With the contraptions connected to him, Richard appeared resting quietly. There didn't seem to be anything Justin could do—except be there. He made himself semi-comfortable in the only chair in the room.

Richard's hand lay limply in his, feeling lifeless but warm. He tried without success to recall the last time he'd held it. Probably on his last visit, when they had said goodbye, shook hands and hugged. It seemed ages ago.

Machines kept a steady round of beeping, assuring systems stayed under control. Slow, erythematic breathing the equipment aided Richard's efforts. The constant noise comforted Justin. Things appeared stable for the time-being. The gadgets would alert any threat.

He should catch a nap so he'd be alert when doctors checked on Richard. Sliding into the stiff-backed chair, he crossed extended feet and pulled his ball cap over his eyes.

He must've dozed, because he woke with a start. Sun shone through a window. An aide with her back to him checked machinery as it tooted steadily. Richard slept still out cold.

"Morning." The pleasingly-plump aide smiled sweetly. Probably middle aged with a mop of brunette curls wrangled into a messy bun beneath a nurse's cap. "I tried to not disturb you." Her badge read Cindy.

"No problem, Cindy, I needed to get out of this miserable position anyway." He straightened and rubbed his stiff neck, aching everywhere.

The bright day made the situation appear starkly worse than the night before. Justin wanted to cry watching his helpless dad sleep. Extremely pale, his puny body appeared feeble hooked to all the gear.

Cindy acted satisfied the apparatus' performed properly. She made notes on Robert's chart, refilled a bag of clear fluid hanging by the bedside connected to Richard's arm by a tube then left silently.

How long would it be before his dad regained consciousness? He stared out the window at a brilliant day. How could the weather be so lovely when Justin kept dying in side? He needed to find out what was going on.

He stretched then gazed at the view from a picture window. An adjoining building's rooftop air-conditioning system sat on the flat, graveled roof. Sides of a garage and another hospital wing spanned the remainder of his vision. In this place it would be easy to forget what the outside world looked like—easy to become overwhelmed, wrapped in the misery of it. At least the portal provided natural light.

Things aren't always the way they seem.

He stretched then dialed Yancy. "Hey, Baby."

"Hello, Justin." Her formal tone proved she was pissed.

"I wanted to make sure you made it home all right."

"Of course. Daddy sent me home with his driver." Her icy mood shot to hostile and accusatory.

"I apologize, baby. It was out of my control." *Didn't I make sure she had a way home before leaving?*

"Is it so?" She wasn't buying it.

"Baby, you have to understand. Dad is in critical condition and alone. He needs me."

"I need you, Justin." *And we're back to pouting.*

"It is debatable. You're fine. He isn't. He's the only family I have. I need to be with him. Yancy, if Landon was in the hospital you'd be hurting too; and you wouldn't leave his side."

She quieted for a while—obviously not wanting to admit it, because she didn't want to give Justin an inch. "You're not coming home? We're scheduled to attend the art museum opening tonight. I need an escort. Maybe I'll ask Harvey." She sounded thoughtful—a poor trick to get her way, intending to make him jealous. She'd never make it as an actress. Harvey was an old flame from high school.

Landon didn't approve of Harvey, though the young man sprouted from old money. He acted weak and lazy without drive or ambition. Yancy needed someone she could trust to control her fortune—someone Landon trusted. Harvey would never manage Landon's empire. Justin had nothing to fear from him.

Justin suspected Harvey was gay, which might be why Yancy allowed Landon to push away from Harvey toward other men. Harvey would've been a safe date for a high school virgin. He wouldn't have pressured her for sex. Now she' decided to give it up as a grown woman, and became insatiable in the sack, Harvey couldn't satisfy her.

"It's a good idea, baby." Agreement was the opposite of what she wanted.

"Humph." Pissed—her ploy back fired.

"Yancy, I need to go, but it is good hearing your voice. Have fun with Harvey. I'll call tomorrow." He waited for her click before hanging up. Mad, she didn't bother saying goodbye.

He walked to the on-call nurse. The station surrounded by Cardiac Care Units similar to Richard's, enabled them to keep a close eye on patients and monitor conditions from the desk. A familiar petite brunette clad in pink scrubs sat behind a dashboard where several computers produced constant readouts of feedback about each patient. The girl accosted in the parking lot last evening.

"Good morning." Becky greeted him with a sunny smile. "Oh . . . it's you. Thank you, by the way, for your assistance. Are you related to Mr. Martin?"

"Yes, I'm his son, Justin; and you're welcome." He hoped she'd seen the last of her husband. No ring graced her finger when she shook his hand. Her name tag read Rebecca.

"Rebecca, could you tell me Dad's condition?"

"I will tell you what I can, but it's not much. His vitals are off, but not alarmingly so. He suffered a severe heart attack and underwent emergency

41

surgery investigating and getting him to stable. He's resting comfortably. His doctor ordered medication to keep him heavily sedated so he can rest and heal. He went through a lot. The on-call doctor will check on him when he does rounds this morning. He'll give you an update then report to Richard's cardiologist, who will be in likely on Monday—unless Richard takes a turn for the worst."

Her sympathetic smile showed she understood this wasn't all he wanted to know. "I wish I could tell you more. It's all I have. You'll get the rest from his team of doctors as they filter in. Is there anything I can get you?"

"Thank you." Justin rubbed his stiff neck. "I could use a cup of coffee and maybe a place to brush my teeth."

Maybe she could direct him to where he could buy a cup, without needing to be gone too long. He should run out and retrieve his toiletry bag from the car, but hesitated leaving his dad.

Rebecca reached behind her desk and handed him a new toothbrush with a tube of toothpaste. "Use the bathroom in your dad's room. There are fresh towels in there. I'll get your coffee. How do you take it?"

"Thank you, Rebecca." He hadn't expected actual help—just explanation where to buy a cup. "Black would be wonderful, thanks."

Rebecca entered Richard's room as Justin emerged from the restroom feeling better with a clean mouth. She placed a tall mug of steaming liquid on the table beside the bed.

"Thank you so much." Justin took a

fortifying sip of the scorching brew. "This is thoughtful, Rebecca. I don't want to risk missing the doctor by leaving, no matter how bad I need it."

"Not a problem. In fact, anytime you want a refill, a bottle of water or a soft drink, let me know. I have a tiny kitchenette with drinks for this purpose; and call me Becky." Lovely, especially when she smiled, she acted confident in her realm— unlike the woman he'd encountered outside.

"Thank you. I needed this." Justin's muscles relaxed. It must be comfort of the strong, warm drink. However, the beautiful nurse had a definite calming effect.

"You slept in the chair, didn't you?" She wore a look of disapproval.

"I must've dozed. I arrived super late, so caught a cat nap in the chair. I won't leave Dad, at least until he's in a better state."

"We need to do something about it." Pointless to argue, she sped from the room on a mission retrieving security to remove him from the grounds.

Let 'em try.

He must've breached a hospital rule— sleeping in a patient's room. He refused to harbor guilt about the infraction. If she thought to make him leave, she was sadly mistaken. He wasn't alarmed, just determined.

Becky bustled into the room deliberate in her mission, a triumphant look on her face. Instead of dragging a guard to toss him out or set him straight, she pushed a rolling chair with a high back inside.

She slid the chair he'd slept in to the other side making space for the larger one beside Richard's bed. She smiled at Justin with a glow of satisfaction then zoomed out and returned in a couple minutes with a sheet, pillow and blanket. She placed them inside the closet and faced him with hands on her slim hips.

"This should make you a bit more comfortable while you watch over your father. See how this one lays back into bed position then pull out the bottom." She demonstrated. "It becomes a single-person bed. It's not the Ritz, but it's cozier than sleeping the straight-back chair." She beamed.

Justin gazed, floored by the unexpected kindness. "Thank you, Becky. Thank you so very much."

Beautiful even when she didn't, but he preferred her smiling. Becky seemed real and genuine. It had been a long time since anyone had cared for Justin's needs—except for in the bedroom—or gone out of their way for him. A foreign concept, not used to being on the receiving end of nurturing, he couldn't remember a time when he felt so pampered—not since Mom passed.

"You're welcome. I better get back to my duties. Let me know if you need anything else." She sped away to take care of other patients.

Justin marveled at the sheer sweetness of Becky's nature. She instinctively understood his needs; and without being asked cared for them. Becky looked lovely in a natural way, possessing a totally endearing, unusual charm. Inspired by her grace, he became humbled and grateful.

She fascinated him. The imp of a woman's inviting spirit filled the atmosphere around her. Her unusual charm amused and intrigued. Her presence brightened the room and helped cheer and reassure him, even in the dismal situation.

♥♥♥♥

Late afternoon the on-call doctor checked on Richard. He introduced himself and shook Justin's hand then propped against the window sill.

"His body has been through extreme trauma in the last twenty four hours. Without sedation he'd be in extreme pain. It would agitate and make him miserable. We must keep him calm and pain free giving him recovery time."

"How bad is he?" Justin sat on the edge of his chair.

"Richard suffered a severe heart attack causing extensive damage to the heart and valves. He is in critical condition. He is resting well, considering. We'll watch him closely for the next twenty four hours. If his cardiologist agrees it is warrantied, we'll start reducing meds to bring him to consciousness early next week. His cardiologist will be in on Monday. Until then, it's in Richard's best interest we continue this semi-coma condition."

"This is all you can tell me? What are his chances of recovery?" Justin expected more details He wiped his forehead with exasperation.

"I'm afraid so. Test results will be in by Monday. We'll know more and a prognosis should be possible. I'll check on him this evening and tomorrow." He patted Justin's shoulder. "Hang in there, Son. Your dad needs your strength. I'm sure he's glad you're here." He cleansed his hands with antiseptic by the door.

"Does he know?"

"I believe so. Talk. Your voice should sooth him."

Justin's head spun. He wiped a tear from his face with his sleeve. He'd morphed into *Alice in Wonderland*, having fallen through a rabbit hole. He'd plopped into an alien world and needed to find his bearings.

Justin spent the rest of the afternoon by his dad's side. Sandy, the nurse on duty, told Justin she'd call his cell if anything changed. He walked to the cafeteria to grab a meal. A dry hamburger on a steam-shrunken, rubbery bun lacked taste, but would provide the necessary nourishment. He tossed the trash and left on automatic pilot.

Needing a semblance of normalcy, he retrieved his bag from the car then washed and shaved in Richard's bathroom. He dressed in sweats and climbed into the makeshift bed figuring he'd spend another sleepless night. Instead, he rested comfortably. Becky had been right.

Sunday morning he showered, shaved, put on fresh underwear, and a clean shirt. He felt like a new man.

"I thought you could use this." Becky entered with a steaming cup of black coffee. She checked Robert's vitals writing information on his chart. Her smile lit the dreary room.

"I sure can. You make a good cup of coffee, Becky. This was thoughtful of you. Thanks." He sipped steaming brew allowing it to fuel and strengthen.

With no change in Richard's condition, the day dragged similar to the one before. He looked forward to Becky's frequent visits and serenity she brought each time she entered the room. She was a welcome reprieve from boredom and anxiety.

♥♥♥♥

Justin finally called Yancy late afternoon. "Hi, Sweetheart, how are you?"

"I'm fine. Where are you?" Tension made it sound like a demand.

"Kentucky, with Dad, we're still in the hospital. He remains unconscious. I don't expect his cardiologist until Monday to learn more."

"When are you coming home?" Her pouting was more than he wanted to deal with. She didn't ask about Richard or inquire how Justin felt handling the situation. Her focus as usual, stayed on Yancy.

"Not sure. Not soon."

"We have tickets to the opera tomorrow."

Justin rolled his eyes at Yancy's self-centered whining.

"I supposed I could ask Belinda." She fished for him to give in, but he couldn't—not this time. He wouldn't.

"It's a good idea. You do that."

"I miss you." Yancy sulked at not getting her way. She didn't actually miss him, only the attention he lavished her with. Her selfishness grated on his nerves. He didn't have patience to deal with it now.

"Yeah, well, I'll let you know when I'm coming home—when I know. I'll stay in touch. Have fun at the opera. Thank Belinda, for me." This time he clicked off first.

Justin hated it. Yancy didn't care enough to pretend interest in his or Richard's situation. Amusing how easily he could be substituted for. Her only concern inconvenience caused by his absence.

It got old.

He called his secretary and asked her to send Belinda flowers with a thank you note. He also asked her to arrange for a bouquet to be delivered to Yancy. Hopefully it would pacify and soften her attitude. He wasn't in the mood for all this self-pity crap. Justin requested his secretary ship a fruit basket to the nurse's station in Richard's cardiac care unit. The least he could do. Thanking her, he told her to take her husband and herself out to dinner on his account.

Hopefully Belinda would enjoy the opera. He'd thank her personally when he returned to

Nashville. He despised opera and only attended to make Yancy happy. She enjoyed it.

What in the hell have I signed on for? I'm planning to marry a thoughtless, insensitive woman.

When happy, Yancy acted normal. He tried keeping her that way, but began realizing she was unbearable when unhappy. He didn't like this part of her.

A long term commitment might prove unbearable. Maybe he should reconsider.

Not now. He had enough on his plate.

CHAPTER 5

Monday finally rolled around with Richard still unconscious but continuing to rest well. Justin slept better. The one-person bed proved not a long-term substitute. He missed his expensive California king-size foam mattress.

At least today he'd talk with the surgeon and cardiologist. He grew more eager for his dad to wake and anxious to take him home from the dreadful place.

A short, middle-aged, balding physician in a white coat stepped into the room. His eyes lit seeing Justin. "Hello, I'm Dr. Mason, your dad's surgeon."

Justin accepted the man's warmer than expected hand. Dr. Mason studied Richard's chart getting up to speed on how he'd faired through the weekend. He checked vitals and looked at the machines. Finally after a suspenseful five minutes, Doctor Mason looked Justin in the eye.

"Our patient did well this weekend, better than expected. The on-call doctor probably told you. To kick-start the healing process, it was best to keep him heavily sedated for a couple of days allowing him to rest comfortably, recuperate from trauma of surgery and the attack, and spare him a great deal of pain."

Sitting quietly the words rolled around in Justin's head struggling for clarity. He wanted to take advantage of this time with the doctor to ask pertinent questions. Time became precious.

"I'll sign off on weaning him slowly from sedation over the next couple days until he gets to a bearable state where he's cognizant without major discomfort. It's the cardiologist's call to determine how and when, but he has my consent to move forward."

"It's great news, Doctor Mason. Thank you. I'm anxious to talk with Dad. It's difficult taking it in. I figured my old man larger than life and invincible. I expected him to live a strong, vital life forever." His sheepish grin showed he'd been naïve.

"We think that way about our parents . . . until something like this happens; and we learn they're human like us." The physician prepared to leave.

"Thank you for understanding and for taking care of Dad."

"You're welcome. Richard's a dear friend. I'm sad for him. I'll check on his progress occasionally." He patted Justin's shoulder.

"Unless an unforeseen issue results, I'm considering surgery a success. Dr. Greenburg is in charge of Richard's care now."

Thank you, Lord.

Relief washed over Justin at the word

success, any progress welcomed. Mopping sweat from his face, he pushed aside a wisp of hair falling across his forehead. He sat forward with closed eyes and rested his chin atop closed fists. Elbows on knees he braced to think.

He stirred as someone entered. Drained and mentally exhausted, he wasn't sure how long he sat that way. Only morning, he had more to face today.

"Hello, young man. You must be Mr. Martin's son. I'm glad you made it." Bright blue eyes lit a pudgy face on a grey-haired man. His fuzzy eyebrows possessed a mind of their own. The gent extended a stout hand, and Justin shook it. "I'm Dr. Greenburg, Richard's cardiologist and an old friend."

"Justin Martin, I'm pleased to meet you, Sir." Justin backed away leaning on the window sill, allowing the doctor time to peruse the chart.

"This is good." Dr. Greenburg smiled. "Richard did well over the weekend. I figured as much since no one called. I asked to be alerted immediately in the event something went wrong. Dr. Mason has been in and signed off. We're making progress."

"Yes, I met him a short while ago. Surgery was successful, and he's released Dad to your care. He told me you'd decide how to withdraw medication bringing Dad around."

Dr. Greenburg took a seat opposite Justin. "Yes, we'll begin right away, but it's important we do it slowly. Richard has been in major discomfort. We need to control it. I'll provide the nurses a plan for withdrawal before leaving the ward. He'll become conscious gradually. He will be in and out and won't remember any of today. Talk calmly with him, but don't expect much. He may not make sense when and if he speaks. He may be anxious or frightened as he wakes. Try comforting and reassuring him you're here, and he is being cared for."

"How long will it take to get him fully awake?"

"By late tomorrow he should be on a pain push he can administer himself as needed. He'll be groggy. You may need to assist with it today. He'll be able to talk and remember most of what is going on by tomorrow. The next day we'll discuss issues and plans for moving forward with him."

"Sounds good; so how is he really doing?" Justin stood vulnerable with arms crossed.

"Not good. I wish I could tell you different, but I won't lie. He's in bad shape. We cannot fix him. Two prior attacks did major damage. Though he has been in my care for the last three years, he's continued going downhill. The stint put in after the first attack is holding, but he never alerted me when he had the last one. Richard must've been home when it happened and simply waited it out. Test results show it created considerable damage."

"I don't understand. Dad never told me he suffered one heart attack and never mentioned surgery or a stint." Justin's agitation welled, and he grew further concerned the more he learned. *How could Dad keep something so important from him?*

"I find it often with older patients. They believe they have it under control and don't want to bother family. They minimize their condition and hide it from loved ones. I'm sure he didn't want to worry you or interfere with your life, with what he considered a minor issue."

"Minor, huh? Wow." Justin wiped sweat from his forehead. "If the surgery he had Friday was a success according to Dr. Mason, what do you mean you can't fix Dad?" Justin returned to shock mode. He didn't understand. Wringing his hands, light headed, he leaned into his seat for support.

"Surgery went well. Dr. Mason put a couple stints in opening flow from a clogged valve and artery." He produced a diagram of the heart pointing to two locations. "Unfortunately Richard's heart suffered irreparable damage. A good part of the muscle is dead. Valves have thinned to useless. They shred at the touch. Only a transplant would help. What we did will allow him to live longer, but without a new organ, he doesn't have long. Even with a suitable donor arteries to the heart wouldn't withstand surgery or adhere well to a replacement. Chances are he wouldn't survive surgery."

"How long is not long? How much time does he have?" Tears welled, taking over, and he was losing what control he'd strived to maintain.

"Son, your dad has been on the transplant list. We've covered it with his insurance. It's not simple. Thousands of people go on this list every day. Donors are fewer than demand. Compatibility is difficult in the best of cases. Your dad started at the bottom like everyone else, but he's not a viable candidate. Anyone above him will get a heart before he does. Priority is given to young victims and favors healthy people likely to survive and thrive. It is not Richard. His age and health work against him. He won't receive a new heart even if he lasts until his name rises to the top."

"So he just goes on waiting to die?" Justin choked the words out.

"Richard could suffer another attack at any time, and I doubt he'd survive. How long? There's no way of knowing. It could be days, or it could be two to three months." He hesitated for Justin to digest the information. Hatred for this part of his job showed on his face. It must be worse in this situation since Richard was his friend. "What I'm saying is should he have another attack he'll likely die before reaching the hospital. If he were viable, he probably won't live long enough to make it to the top of the transplant list. He's not a good candidate, so his prognosis is not good."

Justin quietly soaked it in trying to control tears gushing from his eyes. He wiped them with his sleeve. "You're telling me he's going to die, but you'll keep him comfortable. Right?"

"His heart may not meet his body's demand. He may slip away." Dr. Greenburg scratched his head revealing how he hated to deliver the dreaded news.

"Will he leave the hospital?" Justin's voice cracked. "Tell me he won't spend his last days in a hospital."

"Our goal is to get Richard to a manageable, tolerable pain level on oral medication, so he can return home. Once there, he should do nothing physically taxing or exerting. He needs to avoid stress. He will be short-winded, weak and will tire easily, so needs considerable rest. Emotional stress is to be avoided if possible. Of course, this is going to be traumatic and emotionally taxing. He'll need to face dying and come to grips with it. So will you. It's going to be agonizing for both of you."

Justin grew numb. His brain couldn't take much more.

"My advice is, take him home. Spend time together. Make memories you will cherish. Talk and get anything unsaid out in the open. Be honest and let him be the same. You need each other. This time is a gift. Don't squander it." Brushing his slacks he extended his hand once again with a hearty shake.

"Thanks, Doc. I appreciate your bluntness. Not sugar coating this will enable me to prepare. I'll take your advice to heart. Thank you for caring for Dad."

Justin wasn't sure how long he stared blindly at Richard before his phone buzzed. Time became irrelevant, watching him breathe. It appeared to be late afternoon from sunlight painting bland, yellow walls. His phone showed four thirty p.m.

"Hello, Yancy. How are you?" He didn't especially care. Words came out in rote. He had more important things on his mind.

"I'm okay, but I miss you. You're still in Kentucky. Right?" she whined.

Justin rolled his eyes. "Yes, I'm at the hospital. Before you ask, I'll be here however long he needs me."

"What about your job?" *Refreshing new*

tactic.

"I've put in for a leave of absence. I can be out as long as it takes."

"You have—without telling me? This could damage your career. What about partnership? This could delay or end it for you." She laid it on thick but couldn't care less about his career.

"Yes. It could be delayed. It depends on how long I'm out. This won't ruin my career. I've worked it out with the firm. They're anxious to have me back whenever I decide to come."

Justin spoke at length with the partners earlier. They had assured him he should stay and told him to take whatever time necessary. They temporarily moved pending cases to other associates.

"There are more important things to consider." She expected to be number one on his priority list. This wouldn't settle well with her.

Too damn bad.

"It's awful. You should be more concerned." The drone in her tone grated on his nerves like nails scraping across a blackboard. He winced.

"Since when have you cared about my livelihood?" She simply tried to have her way as usual. What she wanted became less and less important to Justin.

"I care about you, Justin, Sweetheart. I'm aware how important work is to you." She laid it on thick. Words came out sweet as molasses. "I want you home, Baby. I miss you. We have plans. The State Heritage Museum benefit is tonight. The symphony is on Friday. Daddy's party is Saturday, and he's counting on you being there."

He pictured her pouting expression in his mind. "Find someone to escort you to those events, Yancy. I don't care what's on your calendar, and Landon has parties constantly. He doesn't need me there." Justin tried keeping the edge out of his voice, but nearing his limit he grew angrier by the moment.

"Daddy expects you, Justin. He offered you a position and wants you to take it. He plans to announce your appointment on Saturday. You're accepting his offer. Right?"

Damn.

He'd forgotten Landon's offer. She was right. Had he not rushed to his dad's side, he'd have accepted—no longer. "I'll call Landon and explain, but I'm not accepting the offer."

"Justin, you should reconsider. Daddy can do amazing things for you. It would be good for us and our life together." This time her voice registered actual shock.

Too bad.

Surprising how much she understood about business, though she hated it and didn't want to be involved. Aware of Landon's motive, Yancy had her own agenda for Justin. She and Landon probably formulated the plan together, to bring Justin into the fold. Resenting their attempt to manipulate him, he had enough.

He hadn't actually admitted it to himself, but he didn't want any part of their plans. He was his own man. Not a toy soldier for Landon to mold and move around a game board. He wasn't a Ken doll

Yancy could dress and toy with.

He'd make his own way in the world. He didn't want or need their management of his life. He could create his own success. Time came to end the charade.

"Yancy, find another escort, and someone new to occupy your time. I'm not the man for you. I can't give you the life you require. You're not the woman I need. Maybe there isn't one; but if there is, she's not you. I need more in a relationship. It's been fun living in your world, and I thoroughly enjoyed being with you. But it is over. You and I are finished. This sounds cruel. I hate doing it over the phone. Under normal circumstances I'd tell you in person, but there's no choice. This can't go on. Have a good life, Yancy. I wish you well. We're done."

She softly cried, not for losing the love of her life, but for losing an easily maneuvered boy toy. "Justin, you're making a mistake. We're a good team. You're confused because we've been apart too long. Nonsense about a hearts growing fonder is ridiculous. We need to be together. We have a wonderful life, and I make you happy. Daddy can give you the occupational experience you deserve. We'll table this discussion until you return home."

"No, it is over. I won't pretend. I don't fit into your life or your plans. I don't know what the future brings, but it doesn't include you or Landon. Yancy, we had fun. You're witty, exciting, and the sex was good between us. But it's all there was. We deserve more than enjoyable and convenient. It wasn't love. It's over, Yancy. Get it through your head. Goodbye." He clicked off and slipped the phone into its case.

In the bathroom he washed his face then dialed Landon's private number. "Hello, Sir."

"Son, I expected you."

"Yes, I figured. Yancy called." No response needed.

"Of course; she's distraught concerning your conversation. My daughter wants you. It makes me certain you should be working for me. Let's forget the nonsense." It sounded like a command.

"Sir, with all due respect, I have no future with Yancy. You could do great things for me. I appreciate the offer." *No matter how self-serving.* "However, I respectfully decline."

"Don't be hasty, Son. Everyone suffers a lapse in judgment occasionally. It is what has happened here. Normally I give no one a second chance to disappoint me. I'm making an exception. You're under tremendous stress. Dwell on it for a week or two. When you come to your senses, we'll pretend this never happened."

"Thank you for your understanding, Sir. Sorry to be a disappointment." Usually good at control, he pointedly held back fury taking hold of him. This thing with Dad proved the exception, beside himself with worry. "I appreciate your patience, but it's misguided. You've interfered in my private affairs with your daughter. So I'll be blunt. I don't love Yancy. It's become exceedingly clear. I'd never take your offer under false pretenses. You're brokering wedlock the way you would any other deal. Marriage is not a transaction.

I don't wish to marry Yancy. I'm not right for her. She deserves someone who worships her. She isn't right for me. We don't love each other. She and I are done. I'm respectfully declining matrimony to your daughter and joining your organization."

Landon cleared his throat. He spoke slowly and matter-of-factly. "You're making a mistake that you will regret. I'm starting to lose patience, but will give you the benefit of time. I hear you. I understand. I also know, even if you don't love her, Yancy wants you. In time you'll grow to be happy with her. What's this nonsense about love, anyway? Love has nothing to do with it. You will be a worthy husband and can provide the future Yancy desires."

For real?

Justin's mouth gaped open in awe at the gall. Her father suggested he wed Yancy explicitly to gain access to her money and power. He could hardly believe Landon condoned a loveless life for his daughter.

Did one surrender life's foolish notions to gain power? Was love one of those? Did you settle for less to gain more? Maybe the rich and dominant lived this way.

Whatever.

He'd planned to wed Yancy previously for those reasons . . . before her self-centeredness honed in and gave him a migraine. It had never bothered him before. He could no longer live the best life money could buy with a woman he didn't love.

Landon bore no resistance or response.

"We'll revisit this when your head is clear. Don't do anything rash, Son. Take this time to get it together. Let's talk." Landon got what he wanted, like his daughter. He wasn't surrendering easily. He wanted the final word, determined to have it.

Let them do what they want. It's not worth the battle.

Justin had finished, regardless. Life proved too brief to waste. He wouldn't squander his on Yancy. Time wouldn't change his mind, but he couldn't influence Landon and didn't want to argue any longer. He didn't have the strength—too exhausted from worry. Richard his main priority, this argument could wait.

"Goodbye, Son." Landon ended the call.

Justin stared at the phone shaking his head. He understood and admired Landon's audacity, but found it inexcusable. At least, he survived the initial conversations with them. He'd follow through soon. It wasn't over. He'd been straight with them—all he could do at this point—all he had energy for.

CHAPTER 6

Justin stood at the window staring blindly, struggling to calm his fitful breathing and deep in reflection, trying to formulate a plan. Soundlessly Becky entered. The air thickened difficult to breathe.

She worked quietly as though trying not to disturb Justin. Checking Richard's machines and adding data to his chart. When nearly done, Justin tried to smile. Her eyes filled with sadness viewing moisture in his threatening to burst into full-blown tears. Despite efforts to appear otherwise, he must've looked pitiful.

"Tough to take, isn't it?" Becky grimaced.

"Yes, very."

She walked closer and took his hand. Warmth of her gentle grip jolted his senses, and he became intensely drawn to her. Silky skin comforted and intrigued him. Long, lean fingers exuded calming energy straight to his core—an alien sensation in no way sexual. An aura of purity surrounded Becky. She radiated serenity piercing painlessly through his armor. Nothing like women in his past, and nothing like what he expected from a female.

Sweet and simple, yet ultimately beautiful.

She handed him a cup of crushed ice and a bottle of water. "You can use this." Her voice mellowed soft, like a breeze on a warm spring day.

He inhaled easier with her sharing the oxygen. "Thank you. It's considerate." He accepted the bottle. He stared at it trying to absorb any energy she'd left on the container.

A short French manicure on delicate hands emitted strength as though easily capable of holding his troubles. Nothing pretentious about the woman, real as they came, open, honest and decent, he nearly believed she held power to lessen his throbbing, aching heart.

Becky reminded him of someone. This woman he hardly knew understood him instinctively without effort. She recognized what he required, and for a strange reason wanted to provide it.

Usually the giver, Justin rarely landed on the receiving side with the opposite sex—a new experience. He needed her strength, patiently waiting for him to release her once he no longer required the innocent connection. Without asking or either of them uttering a word, she remained there—for him. Finally feeling calmer, he pulled away and smirked meekly with embarrassment.

Her whisper sounded soft like her hands and heart. "Can I get you something? Anything you need? May I call someone for you? You shouldn't be alone."

She had other patients and families to care for. Justin felt guilty monopolizing her time, but couldn't resist indulging in Becky's care. He'd never been so vulnerable . . . not since losing Mom. He needed someone to be strong for him. It sure as hell wasn't self-indulgent Yancy. Becky nursed Richard; so their relationship doomed to be fleeting. For the time being Becky was there for Justin.

Humbled at her kindness and compassion, he'd forgotten how it felt being cared for. He struggled to recall the last time someone had helped shoulder his problems. No one had cared enough— not since Mom. Why Becky reminded him of Mom. She possessed the same giving nature.

Dad was different. He'd suffered along with Justin, losing the woman he loved more than life. Agony of watching them lower her into the ground had been excruciating. Justin told himself he would never love so intensely. He wouldn't risk agony of losing a love so powerful.

He had no right asking anything of Becky, but he'd taken what she offered. He desired it— from Becky. Unreasonably he didn't want to share her though he must. She had huge responsibilities. Here she lingered with him—and he wasn't a patient.

Drawing fuel from her presence, abnormal sensations began controlling his body. Radical, foreign emotions bounced around inside his heart. Used to being in control of his mental state, it felt alien.

Compelled to be with Becky, he yearned for her companionship, instinctively accepting her comfort. The gut-wrenching ache became sedated with Becky's smile.

"No. There's no one to call. It is only me. I don't know how to thank you."

"I'm sorry." She appeared taken aback. "There's certainly no need to thank me. It's my pleasure. Let me help you."

When she grinned sunshine filled the space and softened tiny wrinkles at the corner of her tender eyes. He longed to touch them. The beautiful creature opened to Justin offered support.

Petite, much shorter than Justin, her feminine features gave her a fragile appearance. Yet she proved exceptionally solid as though she could effortlessly carry the weight of the world. The urge to let her grew strong. Defenses he had built over the years and taken for granted gradually slipped away, melting in a pool at her tiny feet.

Blue non-descript scrubs hung slackly over Becky's slight frame. Her feminine, graceful gait and perfectly proportioned body swayed gently as she moved. He made out the shape of her tiny bottom, loosely concealed by the uniform. A longing to cup his hands around the petite mounds and snuggle her against him surprised Justin.

Where did it come from? He shook his head. *Man, you are losing it.*

How could someone as tiny have such a huge personality with so much to give?

"Would you like coffee? I brewed a fresh pot at the nurse's station. You take it black. Right?"

"It'd be nice. Thank you, Becky." He hadn't realized how dry his mouth had grown. He took a long swig of the bottled water.

Becky quietly left, returning minutes later with a tray. She placed it on the bedside table. "I thought you could use nourishment." She smiled and left.

"Thank you," Justin muttered watching her stroll away. Captivated, he couldn't take his eyes from her. Her magic worked on him, and Justin calmed considerably.

She's sweet. He hadn't met anyone as thoughtful, not since being a kid. He shook his head to clear it.

Sweet, caring Mom.

Her second sense about people evidenced in her actions showing how much she cared, never expecting praise or thanks. She found joy in doing a simple kindness.

God, I miss her. With Dad in this situation could Justin bear it without her?

He perused the tray. Bottled water, a cup of ice and a straw—delightful smelling hot coffee aroma released as he removed the plastic cap. Fruit and pudding cups, a plastic-wrapped breakfast biscuit sandwich, a mini-box of bran flakes, a tiny container of milk, and plastic utensils wrapped in a napkin—Becky thought of everything.

She knew he hadn't eaten.

Justin hadn't realized his hunger, but the delightful fragrance ignited his stomach rumbling. It was odd, experiencing something so normal—how could he be hungry facing disaster? Justin unwrapped the sandwich and unleashed spicy sausage odor. The pit of his hollow gut yearned to consume it.

How had Becky known? He hadn't realized. Again, she had seen to his necessities without him asking.

He bit into the soft biscuit savoring the tasty combination of eggs, cheese, sausage, and bread—delightful. His noisy stomach became indebted.

Finding it empowering doing something as ordinary as eating. Maybe one required normalcy in the face of harsh reality. Justin must create a semblance of normalcy for Dad.

Making quick work of the sandwich he moved to the cereal, polished off the fruit and pudding without hesitation then leaned relaxed in his chair enjoying the last of the java. A server stepped into the room retrieving the empty tray and handed the water to Justin. "How're you doing, man?"

"Not bad, under the circumstances. The food helped. Thank you."

"No problem, but I didn't bring it. Becky ran to the cafeteria herself and picked out the best she could find for you. You're in good hands. She's the greatest."

Justin nodded. The guy was right.

"Here's a menu for lunch. Mark what you want. Someone will pick it up in an hour. You'll be charged for a meal whether he's conscious and can eat or not." He left with the tray.

Justin selected lunch and placed the menu on the table, then laid his head back and fell asleep.

♥♥♥♥

Justin Martin didn't react when Becky entered to check Richard's vitals. He cutely snorted as he slept. She giggled out loud the first time she heard it. But he wasn't sleeping now, only day-dreaming in deep meditation.

The lean, attractive man's wavy, black hair fell loosely over a handsome, tanned forehead. She longed to lose her fingers in the thick mane. His deep green eyes hypnotized her and were sexy regardless of agony flowing from them.

Sadie would call Justin a hunk. Becky laughed to herself. Not wrong. *Hunk* fit the stunning man though there appeared more than a pretty face to Justin Martin.

He resembled his dad. The elder Martin stood shorter and stockier, the way of aging men; but Richard looked younger than his years. Richard remained handsome with shocks of grey decorated black tresses above his ears adding character; but his son was a knockout.

Their tragedy and what it did to them broke her heart. Pain glistened in Justin's emerald eyes and played out clearly on his face.

She ached to take the misery away. But it wasn't for her to do. It was theirs. They owned it and paid dearly for the right to emotions tied to it.

It didn't stop her from having compassion and concern. She vowed to do whatever she could to lessen the burden. She tried not to disturb him, soundlessly checking machinery then adding data to Richard's chart.

He appeared deep in thought, in a world of his own with moisture pooling in his eyes, pitiful despite efforts to appear otherwise.

It broke Becky's heart. She ached to wrap him in a hug and let him cry on her shoulder, surprised at how intensely she yearned to sooth him. It felt the natural thing to do—only it wasn't. Not for Becky.

No reason to make it worse. He had no cause to be embarrassed. He had a right to his emotions. Her gut was heavy with sorrow as she tried not to disturb him.

Fighting sorely netted tears, despite his efforts to appear otherwise, he looked pitiful. She hoped the weeping helped. A good cry went an astonishingly long way toward reestablishing one's equilibrium. Too bad many men tried avoiding it.

Becky clearly felt attracted to Justin. She didn't understand why. She usually avoided close contact with men, even gorgeous ones—no entanglements, no affairs. Something different about this man and for once, she didn't bother resisting a male's appeal. Justin's anguish and vulnerability strangely affected her soul.

He became her priority, and she put him first . . . because he needed someone to care. She cared; it amazed her how much. He invaded her every thought.

As a seasoned nurse in the CCU her patients remained critically ill, many terminal. She routinely handled family members, but not this way. As a professional she kept personal feelings out of the workplace. She nurtured, but maintained distance.

She didn't have the power to do it with Justin. His uncanny pull forced a link between them and a sensation she wasn't used to, but couldn't avoid.

His shocking revelation floored her. How could a man so fine be alone in the world?

She left quietly with a heavy heart filled with sorrow for him. He'd aided her in the parking lot and never mentioned it again, sparing her dignity.

She promised him help, and she meant to give it. Justin would not be alone—long as she was round.

Becky winced recalling the tragic night resulting in her becoming a single parent. She had never regretted it for a moment, though it had been a long eight years. Everything happened, good and bad, resulted in bringing Evan, the best thing ever happening to her.

She hadn't always been so confident. Becky married her high school sweetheart after graduation. She attended nursing school, and Brent Simms enrolled in college. They lived in a tiny apartment close to the university in Louisville where they studied. Graduating with honors, she became a cardio nurse at the hospital and loved her work. A year after taking the position holy hell wrecked her life.

Becky was doing well at the hospital, having achieved a promotion before the incident. Brent should have been proud. Instead he resented her advancement.

Now she had ten years at her present job and enjoyed interacting with patients and families. She made the lives of doctors depending on her easier, and she took excellent care of their patients.

Becky's devoted sister brought joy into her life. Her adorable son made it worthwhile. And she did it all—without Brent—despite him.

♥♥♥♥

As usual, Evan cleaned his plate then asked permission to go out before bath time to hit balls in the yard. The sisters watched from the kitchen window while washing dishes. The youngster placed ball after ball into a t-ball stand and hit them into a net Becky had erected for practice.

Sadie acted distracted. Something was up.

"Great dinner. Thanks. You look tired. Why don't you relax while I finish the dishes?"

"Nah, it's okay. I'll help. I enjoy this time with you. It's hectic around here in the evenings. This is peaceful." Sadie handed her a dish.

"How's work? Is something wrong?" She dried the plate and stacked it on a shelf.

"Friday's my last day. I'm transferring patient files to the doctors taking over while Ben is in Europe. I can't stand hanging out with nothing to do. I like being busy and having responsibility. I've been considering how to spend the time while Ben's traveling." She sighed heavily.

"Anything interesting?"

Sadie gazed thoughtful. "Not really. Ben will be lecturing off and on for four months at medical institutions across Europe. It is a long time. He and Marcia will sightsee between gigs to make it a vacation. He doesn't care what I do. Ben wants me back when he returns to practice. So I can't take a regular job while he's away. He has been more than generous, giving me full pay and benefits during his absence. I don't have to work, unless I want to."

"Do you have any options?" Becky started formulating ideas in her head.

"I'm not sure. I could volunteer or work at one of the other doctor's offices, but I'd be intruding. Or I could take a paid vacation and simply chill, but I'd be bored out of my gourd. I don't want to travel alone, and I don't have anyone to join me."

"Oh well, give it more thought. You'll work something out." Becky had a notion, but didn't want to push it on Sadie.

"You acted stressed when you first arrived home. Did something happen at work?"

"Nothing drastic, just a long day; I'm troubled about a patient. Actually I'm concerned for both him and his son. They're in a bad way. I wish I could make things easier on them."

"I'm sure you're doing everything possible. You're a fantastic nurse. They're lucky to have you." Sadie gave her shoulders a quick hug.

"Yeah sure, medically speaking, but it's more. I wish I could find a way to relieve their stress."

"Why? What do you mean?" Sadie tilted her head with confusion on her face.

"The dad, Richard Martin, is dying from a fatal heart condition. He'll go soon, no matter what's done for him. They can't fix him, so they'll make him comfortable and help him function enough to leave the hospital. It will enable him to spend what's left of his days at home with his son, Justin."

"Wow. Awful. How's Justin taking it?" Sadie leaned against the sink drying her hands.

"He's pitiful. What he's going through is awful. Love for his dad is written all over his face. It makes me want to cry. I wish I could ease his burden." Becky took a seat at the table.

"It's good he's loved and has someone to care for him in his last days. He won't die alone in a hospital."

"Yes, but Richard's passing will be devastating for Justin." Becky wiped a tear with the dish towel.

"Justin, hum? You like this guy." She tilted her head studying Becky's face.

"Yes. I like him. He's nice and extremely vulnerable. It never occurred to him this could happen. He isn't ready to lose his dad—not anytime soon. Richard should be in the prime of his life, but we know how it works." She blinked tears back, still not over her own loss.

Sadie gave her a quick hug. "We've been through it, so understand the gut wrenching agony. Mom and Dad's deaths hit suddenly and brutally." Sadie wiped a tear from her eye with the dishtowel.

"How can I help Justin through what I haven't been able to recover from? Maybe no one gets over losing a parent." Becky blew here nose and blinked back tears.

"How old is this Justin?" Sadie glared sideways from peripheral vision sitting beside Becky at the table.

"I don't know; probably a couple years older than me. Why?"

Sadie studied Becky curiously. "Is he good looking?" One perfectly cropped brow rose above Sadie's elaborately painted eyes. Purple shadow matched the steak in her hair.

Becky timidly admitted. "I suppose so." Her cheeks grew hot. "Who am I kidding? He's gorgeous."

Sadie grinned. "As I thought; you're taken with this guy. I'm glad he's a hottie."

Becky smiled embarrassed. "He is." She laughed swatting Sadie with a dish towel. "I wouldn't say I'm *taken* with him exactly. He's a swell guy who happens to be going through an awful time. He acts desperate, miserable and terribly alone." Once voiced her words sounded lame—even to her.

"Yeah, he's hot; and you want him. So, what does he need? How can you help?" Sadie pulled her feet into the chair wrapping her arms around her knees.

"I'm not sure. He wants to take Richard home to spend what time he has left with him. I don't see how he can handle it alone. It's a major undertaking caring for the critically ill. It will be difficult enough watching him grow weaker and weaker before finally giving out. Richard's medical needs might be more than one untrained man can handle."

"He'll need a nurse, maybe fulltime," Sadie observed thoughtfully.

Becky considered for a few minutes. "You could be right, Sadie. Maybe I can find a nurse to help them. I could recommend someone from hospice. Know anyone available?"

"I do actually. With Ben taking off for Europe Friday, a certain cardio nurse will be at loose ends with no clue what to do for four months. I could help your friends." Sadie smiled broadly.

"Wow it is a great idea." Sadie would force-feed vitality into Richard and Justin's home.

"If you want to discuss it with them, you're free to recommend me."

Becky hugged her sister tight. "Awesome. I can't thank you enough. You're exactly what they need—a breath of fresh air. I can't be sure they'll go for it, but you may be the answer to their prayers. You can handle the medical care and bring sunshine into their worrisome lives. You have a way of making people happy simply by being around. They certainly can use it. I'll ask them to consider it."

"You may enjoy it if you take the job. They live at some type of resort. It might prove to be a working vacation for you."

"It would be good. I love my job, and Ben's great, but I've been bored lately. I'm edgy like I'm ready for a change, but have no idea what I want."

"Ben's whirlwind tour and your four months with no routine have you feeling antsy. It will ebb with time. If you take the job with Richard and Justin, it will be a change of pace, exactly what you need."

"I suppose. I don't know what the future holds. But I'm excited at the prospect."

CHAPTER 7

Justin awoke holding his dad's hand the next day. Richard fell in and out of stupor. His eyes glassed brightly at seeing his son. "You're here. They called you? I'm so sorry. You're busy. I don't want to be a burden."

"Hush, Dad, you're certainly not a burden. Of course they called me. Rightfully so, I need to be with you." Justin gently wiped beads of sweat from Richard's forehead.

"Okay." Richard groggily struggled to keep his eyes open. "I have to help your mom bring in the groceries—," he slurred and dozed off.

Justin laughed. Dad enjoyed happy dreams in his drugged state. Mom eased his anxiety. He woke a couple more times during the day and continued drifting off after a few minutes. Sometimes he understood. Other times he rambled nonsensically in a world of his own.

The wonderful brain had the ability to protect itself, thankfully so. The next morning Richard could carry a conversation.

"Thank you for being here, Son. I didn't

want to bother you, but I'm glad you came." He struggled into a sitting position. Justin hastily adjusted the bed.

He encouraged Richard to eat so he'd have strength to recuperate. Richard washed down broth and green gelatin for dinner. He continued acting guilty about having dragged Justin away from important work *unnecessarily*.

"Dad I don't want to be anywhere else. I belong by your side. You didn't let me help the last time you became sick. A heart attack and stint are serious. How could you keep it from me?" Justin wiped a tear with the back of his hand.

"It didn't amount to much, over and repaired quickly. No cause to worry you for nothing. I hate the concern in your eyes."

Richard's demeanor showed he understood his error in judgment, so Justin let it drop. No benefit in making it worse. His dad didn't need the stress. They had worse things to deal with.

"Let's forget the past and concentrate on now." Justin took his hand, and Richard squeezed it, further discussion pointless.

"Yes, let's focus on getting me out of here. Once I'm on my feet, you can get back to your demanding life. I'm so proud of you and what you've accomplished. You've built an impressive world for yourself. I can't wait to meet the woman who captured your heart."

"Dad, you're the most important part of my life. I'm not going anywhere. You need me. The rest can wait."

"The young lady won't wait forever, Son. If

you're serious about her, bring her to meet me. Get on with it. You aren't getting any younger. You know?"

Justin began understanding brevity of life. He had no intention of bringing his dad and Yancy together.

He hadn't heard the last of Yancy. He had tried setting her free, but she refused to listen. He hated having left things hanging and needed to settle them. It grew more and more clear. He didn't want to spend the rest of his life with her. Their fling had run its course. The life had no appeal any longer.

Tenacious, Yancy would be in contact sooner or later, probably waiting for an advantageous time. Much as he wanted it ended, he dreaded further confrontation. He didn't want to hurt her pouting at the truth. He hated the way they'd left things. Loose ends irked him, not part of his makeup. It wasn't fair. She deserved better. He must make her see.

Justin wanted to keep Richard in the blind about his prognosis as long as possible fearing knowing might impede his ability to grow stronger. It could wait. Tomorrow would be soon enough. Maybe the doctor would break it to him. He couldn't do it.

The next day when Dr. Greenburg arrived, Richard acted stronger but not enough to walk. He'd enjoyed a sponge bath and shave, and his hair slicked back. He sat in bed eating breakfast and smiled when they shook hands, acting like his friend came to tell him he could resume a normal life.

"Good morning, Seth. Thanks for taking care of me. I understand you've met my son, Justin." He beamed proudly toward Justin sitting near the window.

"Yes, we met Monday. You have a lot to be proud of, Richard. Your boy has grown into a fine man."

"I sure do. Thanks, Seth. So, when can you spring me to escape this joint?" He laid his spoon aside giving the physician his attention.

"Richard, I'm here to give you an update on your condition. Yes, you'll be leaving soon, but give us a couple days to get you on your feet first. I want you ambulatory before you leave."

"Awesome, it can't be too soon. I'm anxious to return home. My business needs me; and Justin needs to go back to Nashville and work."

"Dad, don't worry about the business. It should be the last thing on your mind." He nervously rubbed the sides of his jeans and met the doctor's eyes with a plea. "Do you need me for this? Has anything changed since we talked?" Justin didn't want to be there when Richard learned the truth. He couldn't bear watching his face.

"No, Richard is basically the same. Why don't you take a walk while Richard and I have a chat?" He acted as though he understood.

Justin shook hands with the cardiologist, thanked him and left the CCU. Safely in the deserted hallway he leaned his backside against the wall. Emotionally spent, his body shook as tears fell uncontrollably. He gripped his fists and shook them as though he could pound despair from his life.

Electronic doors of the CCU swished open, and Becky entered. She paused seeing him silently crying alone in the deserted hallway. He wiped at tears turning away attempting to hide his emotions. Too late, she'd halted seeing he lost control.

Usually good at hiding his mental state, Justin had perfected the knack essential to a skillful attorney. Somehow the ability deserted him. Helpless and embarrassed, he straightened and stared at the ceiling trying to regain composure.

Becky walked to his side without a word and put a hand on his arm. "Justin, I'm going to the cafeteria courtyard for lunch. Why don't you join me? I'd love your company. I hate eating alone." She squeezed his arm, walked quietly away, and boarded the elevator at the end of the hall.

How does she know? She gets me, understanding what I need. An angel? He laughed at his silly musing. It would be a blessing if angels existed.

Justin stepped into the washroom and splashed water on his face. Feeling stronger he followed signs to the café searching for Becky. He craved time with her and couldn't resist the draw of her offer. He bought a coffee and sipping it entered the courtyard.

Pleasantly surprised, the courtyard had benches and tables scattered in the abundant sunny space. Geraniums bloomed in clay pots helping scent the air with a heady aroma. A cool breeze fluttered through flowering plum trees. Their blossoms added another layer of fragrance, completing an enjoyable spot for a meal with good company. Becky sat at a picnic table beneath a canopy.

"I'm glad you could join me. I need company. In fact, I hoped you might be free for lunch. I made you a sandwich—meatloaf."

Justin accepted a plastic wrapped sandwich with a surprised smirk. "I love meatloaf. Wow, did you make this yourself? It's been years since I've eaten homemade meatloaf, or homemade anything. Is there ketchup on it?" He removed the wrapper and took a bite. It tasted like sheer ecstasy.

Becky smile. "You should see your face, looking like you're savoring filet mignon or something as special. Of course, there's ketchup on it. Is there any other way? But no, I didn't make it. My sister Sadie does most of the cooking at our house."

His belly did a flip at her beaming smile. "Were you sent from heaven to bring me strength? I hate the way you saw me earlier." He couldn't hide the flush of color reddening his cheeks. He touched the heat, closed his eyes, shook his head then opened them again.

"You've nothing to be embarrassed about. I understand what you're going through. Losing a loved one is the toughest thing you'll ever face." Beautiful, sweet Becky's bright green eyes shone like emeralds catching sunlight. He could gaze at them all day.

"I guess so. I've never gotten over losing my mom. Now this . . . I'm having a problem handling it." What compelled him to share? He never talked about Mom and certainly never shared his deepest hurt with anyone, let alone a woman. "You must be my guardian angel."

"Not so sure about the angel part, but I might be of help." She smiled and patted the top of his hand. Tiny sparks of heat teased his skin with each tender connection. He wished she would lay her hand there to stay.

"You've been helping me since the minute we met, anticipating my needs before I realized I had them. What more could you possibly do for me?" He rubbed tension in his neck and stretched his back.

"Well, you'll soon be taking Richard home. It's a huge undertaking in his condition, and you might need professional assistance caring for him. Have you considered hiring a nurse?"

Shaking his head in wonder he eyed her in awe. She'd done it again. "I hadn't thought about how we'll handle things once we arrive. I've been focused on getting Dad home. I'm clueless how to care for him." It hadn't dawned on him Richard might need specialized nursing.

"I can help you with it." Becky beamed.

Justin hand an urge to scoop her into his arms and hold her tight against his chest, soaking up the power the petite woman exuded. "You have a job."

"Not me. I know a cardio nurse who is free this summer and might be available to you."

"It would be amazing. Thank you. I appreciate the recommendation." He finished the last of his sandwich. "Who is this person? How do I make arrangements?"

"Actually it is my kid sister, Sadie. Her employer is out of town for four months. She's free. She might be willing to work for you as Richard's private nurse if the three of you like each other and come to an agreement."

"Awesome. Can she come to the hospital so we can meet her? If we hit it off, and Dad's agreeable, we'll talk about the arrangements. She'd need to stay with us. Dad owns a fishing resort about an hour away with cabins, campgrounds and a marina. Sadie will have her own cabin while she cares for Dad. Would she consider it?"

Becky nodded. "She will love it. Sadie enjoys being around water. Between you and me, it would be good for her to be on her own for a while. Sadie has lived with us since our parents died when she attended in high school. Too young to be on her own, I took her in. We've taken care of each other since. Now she's grown, and I fear she is giving up independence she's earned, because she's so devoted to us." Pink rose on her cheeks. "I don't understand why I shared it. I usually don't. You're easy to talk with, Justin. But please, don't tell Sadie. I don't want to embarrass her. She's a great person, very responsible and a fabulous cardio surgical nurse. You'll be lucky to have her. You and Richard can discuss the rest with Sadie in person. Why don't I ask her to stop by later today, after her shift? Today is Friday, so her last day at work. Explain it to her, and the three of you decide."

"Perfect. I'll talk it over with Dad first. If he'll consider it, you can call her."

She glanced at her watch. "Great. Well, I better get back to work. My break's over. Thanks for the company."

"Thank you for the fabulous food; for the recommendation and for the hope. Being able to do something to make this time with Dad tolerable is a huge help. I appreciate your kindness. I'm sure Sadie is what we need."

"You have no idea." Becky laughed and walked away.

Justin couldn't help noticing the graceful sway of her petite hips striding toward the elevator. The strikingly beautiful woman had a fantastic body and a natural, subtle, sexy way about her. So much more than a beautiful body, she acted unaware of her appeal. She proved to be a woman of substance—a *real* woman. He'd forgotten the sort of female existed.

He began to realize he'd instinctively avoided such women in the past. He'd tended toward sexy ladies lacking ambition and admittedly not much upstairs. The gals he chose expected little from him. He hadn't sought relationships taxing him mentally or emotionally. He wanted the basics—a beautiful sexy siren on his arm; and a warm, eager body in his bed. He had stifled himself emotionally when it came to the opposite sex. After losing Mom, he'd allowed himself to become an emotional cripple.

He laughed at the thought, but it proved true.

He shook his head to clear it then wiped hair back from his face with a hand. His firmly established belief lasting love didn't exist revealed as a bill of goods he'd sold himself. Long-term relationships were doomed in today's world—in his warped mind. He'd been lying to himself, and allowed himself to believe the falsehood.

Consequences of not going along with the deception seemed too great. He swore on his mother's grave he'd never be hurt as severely as Richard had been—or as he'd been when they lost her.

It had become so for him. He didn't want a *real* woman—not one who'd expect more than he willingly gave. Scarred, suffering a horrendous blow of losing her, he'd done everything possible to avoid it happening again. Falling in love no option, he denied its reality. Protecting his heart, he'd constructed an invisible wall against such evils.

Had he lied to himself? In his heart he knew. He could be wrong. The defensive shield slowly started to crumble.

Without trying a sweet beauty had waltzed through his armor. She hadn't realized she did it. Without permission she penetrated a barrier years in the making.

The funny thing; he didn't resent it. It didn't scare him. Relieved, maybe even happy—freer than he'd been in years, tightness in his chest he never noticed before started softening—an invisible constraint being eased—a burden lifted.

Odd.

She didn't mean to, unaware of her

unintended impact. Being her generous, caring, open self, doing what she did for any wounded person, Becky gave without being asked, kind beyond reason, compassionate and sympathetic without condescendence.

His permanent beliefs about relationships were facts. *Right?* Did he fool himself? Apparently his convictions were not so strong after all. Suddenly he no longer cared to settle for less. He wanted more. It was irrational considering experience, but he couldn't resist the itch to further investigate and find out.

The threat of losing Dad hurt to the core, making a living without meaning no longer appealing. Worth it, he deserved more.

Suddenly Justin yearned for someone to cling to, to love and be loved by. His ban lifted. . . . permanently. He opened and welcomed love in. He wanted it.

He no longer wanted someone to live with. He wanted someone to share life with.

Justin laughed out loud. No guarantees; but given the chance, he'd accept the risk, put himself out there and allow someone in. He'd wasted too much time playing dumb and running from something he hadn't considered real.

Fool.

Becky had worked this miracle. He had no choice in the matter. It happened, ready or not. Without realizing it occurred, knowing he wanted it or was willing to try, Justin fell in love.

Sap.

With her around, he leaned in for a whiff of

her hair scented of honeysuckle shampoo, a fragrance as sweet and pure as her personality.

Yep, he was a goner. He couldn't turn away if he wanted to. She acted as a magnet drawing him to her; and he wanted her, so wouldn't resist the force.

She'd captured his heart, but he wasn't sure what she wanted. She wasn't a flirt and hadn't tried to win his heart. Becky had done nothing indicating she cared for him this way. She treated him the same as others encountered in her job.

Justin needed to learn more and to understand his competition, because he would never interfere with a marriage. She had a husband. Had she gone back to the asshole who accosted her in the parking lot? She'd mentioned Sadie took care of *them*. Sadie lived with them. She didn't wear a wedding band. Maybe she had a live-in boyfriend. What if she didn't want Justin's attention?

He didn't dare scare Becky away with unwanted attention. He would tread lightly and play this slow and careful.

Becky was a different animal; not like his normal gal pals, so much more.

Suddenly other women he'd been with became insignificant, inconsequential parts in his life, a waste of time. Yancy no longer tempted.

Justin had apologized for showing what he considered weakness in front of her. He had nothing to be embarrassed about. His emotions and tears

GOD FATHER'S DAY

were sorely earned. Becky hoped they helped ease his suffering. Astonishing what a good cry could do to establish ones equilibrium.

Becky tried not to disturb Justin quietly checking machines Richard hooked to and adding data to his chart. Tears appeared ready to burst from Justin's eyes, despite his efforts to appear otherwise.

Concern for the fine-looking man broke Becky's heart. It surprised her how much she yearned to wrap him in a hug and let him cry on her shoulder. Yet it felt natural. Only she realized how far from normal her yearning was.

Becky hadn't been attracted to a man in years, but she mooned over Justin. Why bother to resist it? She couldn't if she tried.

Justin's suffering and vulnerability penetrated her very soul. She made him her priority, putting him first now . . . because he needed someone to care. She cared—clearly and felt shocked how deeply.

A seasoned nurse and true professional with critically ill patients—many terminal; Becky normally handled this sort of thing adequately. She kept personal feelings out of it and nurtured, but kept a distance.

She didn't have the power to do it with Justin. He held an uncanny pull for her like a force connected them, a sensation she didn't understand, but didn't want to resist either.

How could it be? How could the lovely man be alone in the world? She had been stunned by his answer, and it made her more determined to help him.

Matching them with Sadie might be the best thing she could do. Sadie would work her magic on them.

♥♥♥♥

Justin returned to his dad's room. Richard stared out the window with a blank expression on his face. Justin sheepishly knocked before entering, having no idea how his dad would react to the shattering news. "May I come in?"

"Sure, come on in." Richard choked out the words and wiped tears away, unable to hide them. "You know?"

Justin came forward taking Richard's frail hand. It chilled his and trembled. Justin patted it gently and nodded. "Dad, they don't know everything. Medicine is a *practice*. They're only guessing. They could be wrong."

"Not this time, Son. I'm sure the diagnosis is accurate. My heart says it's my time." He wiped a tear away.

Justin sat near the bed. "What now?"

"We get on with living, at least while I can. I go to be with your momma, and you live your life."

"Yeah? How in hell do I do it?" Justin wiped tears springing from his eyes unashamed.

"Son, if I can go on after losing your mom, you can certainly go on without me. You're strong, independent and young with a full life ahead of you. You have everything to live for, much yet to experience, and love yet to give. I've lived my life fully—some of it bad, some good. I've loved deeply, and had more excitement than I dreamed possible. I'm okay with this. Or at least by the time it happens, I will be." Richard shook his head as though clearing it. He blinked getting control of his weeping.

Justin glanced away out the window. "I can't stand this. I'll never be okay with it." His voice barely audible, like his throat had gravel in it. An otherworldly sensation, one that he didn't want to deal with.

"It's hard, Son; but we'll get through this . . . together. No one is ever ready to go. I witnessed it with your mom. The advantage of knowing she was dying gave us special time together. I'll never regret experiencing it with her. I cherish every second of it." His words choked as they rolled off his tongue. He cleared his throat. "We're fortunate to have this opportunity to say important things. Let's not waste time whining and crying about dying. Let's get on with the process of living in the moment–together. Justin, let's make a bargain."

Justin faced him feeling more hopeful.

"Let's grieve today. We let it go. That way we won't waste a minute of priceless time mourning what could have been. Okay?" Richard's eyes pleaded.

How could Justin refuse him anything? It was the best offer he could hope for. "Sure, Dad, first of all, I love you. I promise to be with you until the end." Justin hugged the man who raised him, so small and frail in his arms. He mentally memorized the moment. They would make memories Justin could carry with him, long after Dad passed.

A server brought Richard's lunch and broke the spell. They recovered from their teary conversation. Richard made a feeble attempt to eat.

"It's weird. I can't taste food—must be the meds. It doesn't matter. My body needs nourishment to sustain itself. I'll do whatever necessary enabling us to spend more time. I adore you, son." His eyes filled with moisture.

Words sounding hokey days before now were vital to be spoken aloud. Conversation unnecessary, sometimes silence spoke as loudly as talking. He vowed to commit to memory this and every experience with his dad from here on out and to never forget a moment of their time together.

After lunch Justin told Richard about Becky's idea and recommended they consider hiring Sadie. With Richard receptive, Justin asked Becky to call Sadie and arrange for her to stop by to meet them.

His son acted different, something subtle Richard couldn't put his finger on. But it was there, a definite change in Justin. He'd visited a few months earlier, and they talked regularly on the phone. Justin appeared softer, more sensitive and open, rawer emotionally, as though wearing his feelings closer to the skin. It might have to do with his dying, but likely not. Whatever, it was seemed positive.

Justin shut down ardently after his mom's

death. He became reserved, closed off and; as much as it pained Richard to think it, shallow.

Maybe Justin fell in love. A good woman could soften the hardest man. The last few times they spoke on the phone, Justin mentioned his girlfriend. Rarely had Justin mentioned women. Great if Justin had finally allowed a gal close to him, but Richard couldn't recall her name. He wasn't sure Justin had mentioned it.

Richard had invited them to the resort, so he could meet her. But Justin had refused the invitation. Now seeing the change in Justin, Richard grew more anxious to meet the doll who'd made this remarkable transition in his son.

"Invite your girl to visit while you're staying with me."

Justin didn't act like a man in love. He avoided a meeting, or for the matter, talking about his woman more than in passing. "No, she's got a full calendar. She won't be coming to the resort." Justin issued bland excuses whenever Richard had asked about her. Now was no different.

"Why so hesitant? I'm eager to meet her, especially if you're serious about Yancy, Fancy, Dancy or whatever it is."

"It's Yancy, and she won't be visiting." No explanation or reasoning as his voice droned the words. Love should be exciting. His indifference strangely bordered on agitation.

Falling in love might spur the healing process in Justin. Worrisome, how little Justin allowed himself to feel. Yancy could be the reason for the difference in Justin's attitude, but something was amiss.

Richard wanted Justin to find love and happiness. Hopefully Yancy would provide Justin children. He longed for grandchildren, but would never live to meet them. Raising a family became the most fulfilling thing Richard had done. Justin deserved the same joy. He wasn't ready to hear it yet. Best not dredge up the subject.

Maybe my ghastly condition is opening Justin's heart. At least something good came of it.

Becky knocked and walked quietly into the room followed by a tall, lanky young woman. Her shocking, black, bias-cut hair hung shorter on one side than the other. Bangs hung over her right eye. A jolt of bright pink striped through the center of her bangs.

She must've been going for a *take no prisoners, don't mess with me* vibe. However, the striking hair doo failed in the respect. It had the opposite effect. Her brilliant personality flared immediately. The combination gave her a fun, approachable appearance.

The peculiar mop of hair framed Sadie's adorable face. Glistening blue eyes sparked in the light when she smiled. Her deep complexion tanned to a light gold, and her makeup bold. Her flashing smile framed by bold pink lipstick. Chartreuse scrubs suited the carefree, happy-go-lucky lady acting friendly and sociable.

Justin smiled meeting his dad's grin. Richard straightened in bed and eyed the captivating beauty curiously. Even in his condition and age, Richard had an eye for a pretty female, and this one intrigued him.

Both attractive, Sadie drastically differed in stature and coloring from her sister. However, resemblance was apparent. Sadie missed the splattering of freckles Becky's light complexion sported. Their similar smiles came easily. Noses and mouths were the same though coloring differed, and eyes shaped much alike made them recognizable as sisters.

His son's demeanor when Becky entered the room changed, similar to a drowning man suddenly snagging a lifeline. His face lit into a striking smile, and he greeted the ladies enthusiastically. No mistaking which sister Justin fancied. He could barely take his eyes off Becky.

Curious, since Justin was involved already. Maybe things weren't how they appeared.

"This is my sister, Sadie. Sadie is a cardio surgeon's nurse, with lots of experience. She is well thought of; and though she's available for the summer, her employer is anxious for her return to work in four months." They shook hands. Once they settled in, Becky left them to discuss business.

They chatted amiably with Sadie for an hour. She explained her free summer, provided background, references, and answered questions with a light-hearted openness. Soon they learned everything they needed to know.

"Sadie, you're perfect and more than qualified to be my home nurse." Richard held her hand warmly, and Sadie smiled compassionately. They offered her ample salary, and she agreed to move to the lake with them when Richard was released.

"I'm excited about living on a lake. It sounds lovely."

"You'll have your own cabin near ours."

"This will be a first for me. I've never lived alone. I love new experiences. I'll take good care of you, Ricky. Thank you for the offer."

Becky anxiously watched through the opened door from her station.

"You're very welcome, Sadie. You'll be perfect for our needs." Justin shook her hand.

At Richard's open arms, Sadie bent to hug the older man as though they'd known each other for ages. "Bye, Ricky, see you soon." Sadie chirped.

♥♥♥♥

Becky walked her sister out, and Sadie briefed her on the interview. When Becky returned Justin waited leaning on her desk.

"I don't know how to thank you. Your sister certainly is a hoot. Dad already loves her. I'm excited she can help. Sadie's what our household needs and will definitely keep our spirits up. I'm sure she won't allow us to grow sober while she is around."

As though he couldn't help himself, Justin grabbed Becky in a bear hug and spun her around with her feet off the ground. A quick, friendly embrace held no personal undertones; but left her breathless.

Becky surprised herself and welcomed the warmth of his arms enjoying a faint hint of spicy aftershave and chocolate mint on his breath. New to her—normally she didn't hug. Sadie and Evan provided the exception, of course. Having Justin hold her close felt like coming home, a feeling of belonging. Surprisingly she wasn't in the least threatened—far from it. It left her warm with a happy glow having enjoyed his arms around her.

How would it be resting her head against Justin's strong shoulder?

The more she was around him the more Becky liked the man. He seemed special and produced no fear in her. She trusted him. That alone was remarkable.

Becky enjoyed Justin's company. Smart, witty with a good sense of humor during the worst of times, Justin proved easy to talk with, even about difficult things. She'd opened to him without hesitation, talking about things she never discussed.

Strangely, she wasn't concerned. She wanted to know more about Justin and longed to share things about herself with him—a new one for her as well.

"You're very welcome. And yes, Sadie would never stand for it. She is all about enjoying life."

"It's certainly what we need."

"She's a God-send and made my life easier over these last few years."

"She lives with you and your husband?" He glanced at her bare wedding finger.

"She lives with me and my son, Evan. Sadie is a great help. I'm not sure what we'll do without her. She's got us spoiled. But this will be good for

Sadie. So we'll manage."

"You and Evan? What about his father? Doesn't he live with you?" Justin cocked his head sideways.

"No, Evan's dad died in a car accident when Evan was a year old." She winced at the lie, hoping he didn't see through it. With years of practice she'd gotten used to quoting it, but the deceit burned her gut as she lied to Justin.

"I'm sorry for your loss." Justin's eyes fell sympathetic.

"We weren't together when it happened. But thank you anyway. We divorced before Evan's birth. He never met his Dad." The rest of the story—lie.

"I'm sorry." Justin acted sincere.

"I never told my son. Evan doesn't need the details. It's bad enough he lost his dad. But he's never had one, so I doubt he misses it." She hoped.

"I understand you wanting to protect Evan." Justin appeared thoughtful.

"Sadie's had a lot of responsibility for a person her age. She spends too much time worrying and taking care of us. She is young and needs to be independent and free, to think about herself for a change. Being on her own will be good for her. She'll be safe with you and Richard. You'll look out for her."

"She wears responsibility well." Justin acted surprised Sadie carried so much on her young shoulders.

"Sadie told me she's excited about it and agrees it will be good for all of you. It won't hurt

Evan and me either, learning to live without her. She can't always be there for us." Sadness filled her, and she ached inside. It was for the best.

Justin studied her face as she pretended to work, glancing at monitors and charts.

"Is there any chance you and Evan could come visit? We'd enjoy having you, and Sadie stated that would be a treat for her. She said so when we talked."

For the first time since she met him, Justin produced a genuine, glorious smile. She wanted to revel in it all day. Her heart gushed with longing to reach and cup his chin in her hand.

Eagerness showed in Justin's eyes.

"It's a sweet offer. Thank you. We'd love to. Evan will be over the moon. It will be a vacation for us. Thank you for the invitation. We'd happily pay our way. Let me know how much a cabin is." She felt herself beaming from the inside out.

"Fantastic, and for goodness' sake, no payment please, we'll be thrilled having you. There's room in Sadie's cabin for you and Evan. They're three bedrooms. Can we expect you when you get off work on Friday?" He thrust a folded note into her hand.

She nodded. "Thanks. We should arrive around six o'clock." She confirmed gazing at the directions he had written. "Thank you again."

"Great, come hungry. The grill will be hot when you show up. Prepare for my fantastic cooking." He walked toward Richard's room providing a view of his tight fanny in expensive blue jeans. Her heartbeat drummed with adrenaline.

CHAPTER 8

The following day a tall, older gentleman with a thick shock of silver hair and matching mustache entered the through the front sliding doors of the hospital. The petite brunette nurse pushed a wheel chair carrying a familiar face. The man stepped aside and glanced in another direction. The man and woman chatted laughing. Neither noticed him moving out of traffic's way. From a hidden corner of the plate glass wall, he observed.

A younger version of his old acquaintance stepped from a pricy Jaguar. He rounded the vehicle and opened the passenger door for the older man. The nurse talked casually with the two as the young folks made the old gent comfortable. Though his face tilted away, his ear leaned toward the constantly opening and closing doors, so he caught parts of the conversation.

"Nice wheels." The nurse whistled at the beautiful Jag gleaming in the morning sun.

"Yeah, nice, Son." The older man's voice sounded weak. "Hope this thing rides smoothly. I'm not sure how much bumping around I can stand with these staples in my chest." He winced adjusting his seat in the luxury machine.

"Guess I should've brought along your beat up, old pickup jalopy." The younger guy appeared to be joking.

"Yes, now there is a ride. I love the old 1977 Chevy four-wheel drive, three-quarter ton pickup. She is a *beaut,* and she looks brand new."

The nurse bent to hug the older man. "Behave yourself, Richard. Take care. Be safe."

The nurse waved watching them drive away. She blew a kiss at a gothic clad woman in a tiny red foreign job. "See you Friday. Take good care of them, Sadie." She shouted before going indoors. The gothic gal waved and sped off appearing to follow the Jag.

The show over, he headed toward the elevators eager to meet his new grandson.

A silver-haired gentleman leaned against a wall in the lobby as she wheeled the chair around. He appeared to be waiting for something or someone then strode off.

So many people worrying about loved ones
—

A sight she never lost compassion for. She pushed the empty wheelchair in the doors eager to return to work. The stranger stepped onto the elevator as she jogged to catch it.

His eyes blazed toward her as though watching curiously from behind. It gave her an ominous feeling. Thrilled, she left the guy carrying a limp teddy bear with a red satin bow. He'd sent chills through her, though she hadn't gotten a good look at his face. She shook off the feeling, knowing better than to ignore her instincts.

Good thing he headed to another ward.

On the drive home Richard and Justin discussed the resort. "I hired Sam Baker to help out at the marina."

"Isn't she the cute, freckled girl with braided pigtails who helped her Mom clean cabins?"

Justin liked the skinny girl with a big smile. Samantha acted uncomfortable with her blooming womanhood. Her tiny breasts began to perk to attention; she had attempted masking them with over-sized men's shirts somehow making her appear more feminine.

"It would be her. Sam was a few years behind you in school. Her Mom still cleans cabins. Sam runs the marine store, handles reservations, and the website. She also does ordering and marketing. I do maintenance, mowing, banking and books." Richard shrugged. "At least, I used to."

"It's a good arrangement, but we need to make a few changes. You can't do maintenance any longer." Justin tried to make it sound less brutal than it was. But it was a reality they had to face—

among many.

"Sam has been wonderful. She's a beautiful young woman, no longer has a face full of freckles, and grew into those long legs."

"Now, Dad, no match-making." It was a warning.

"Not my intention." Richard held hands high. "Sam is happily married. Her husband recently got out of the service. He was wounded in Afghanistan and suffering from PTSD. He is doing pretty well with it, considering. Therapy seems to be helping. He's looking for work, but it must be difficult in his condition. He has an income from the Marines, but Sam worries. He needs something to occupy his mind more than anything. People became reluctant to hire him learning of his PTSD."

"Why don't we ask if he'd work for us at the resort? He could take over your jobs. Do you think he'd be interested?"

Richard's eyes perked brightly. "I'm not sure, maybe. I'll talk with Sam. Garrett is a good guy. If he's willing, he could be a help around the place."

"Great, let's ask Sam tomorrow. We'll invite Garrett to come in so I can meet him. We can talk about it if he is interested."

"Garrett might be perfect. He and Sam married when they graduated before college. Soon as he got out Garrett joined the service. It's when Sam moved back home." Richard gave a satisfied nod.

"You might remember Sam's husband from school. He's a year older and played high school football. His name is Garrett Mason. Sam is now Samantha Mason."

"Oh yeah, I remember Garrett. He was a nice guy in school and made good grades for a footballer. He won a full scholarship to play at UK. I can't imagine the Marines changed him."

"No he hasn't changed much, older I guess. Garrett is a super nice man, considering. Sam hasn't changed much either. She's a sweetheart. They make a good match."

"Let's invite Garrett in and offer him the job. Hopefully he'll take it." This idea must've satisfied Richard, and it sounded like a blessing if it worked out. It took a load off of Justin's mind, freeing him for Richard.

CHAPTER 9

Impressed, Sadie rolled her window open to better take it in. A half mile gravel drive flanked with blue spruce pine trees welcomed her to Shady Pines Resort. Oak and magnolia trees in full bloom provided hypnotic fragrance scattered randomly through the camp. Sadie breathed deeply enjoying fresh air and her favorite flora.

Individual distinctive cabins nested among trees, small but quaint and well cared for. Each displayed a porch facing the lake. Large windows provided breath-taking views. Each white cottage sported a unique pastel colored trim. Matching lounge chairs claimed focal position on expansive porches, and chairs cushioned with coordinating hues. Grills and picnic tables located nearby so guests could enjoy a cook out or lounge and appreciate the lake view. Air smelled of charcoal, and meat on the hot grate, as guests gaily cooked dinner.

The delightful sight made her giddy inside. What could be better than living on a lake having a wonderful stay with her gracious employers? For their sake hopefully it would be a long one. Secretly she hoped the same for herself. Who knew what the summer had in store?

At the main cabin, Sadie set to work helping Justin settle Richard. Exhausted from the drive, he laid down without protest. Justin put Sadie's bags in the cabin next door. He left her to unpack.

Her new home was adorable. Love at first sight—the delightful white cottage trimmed in pink could not suit her more perfectly and was all hers.

Two bedrooms separated by a bath formed the back half of the house. One long front room with a wall of windows faced the lake. Sadie's stomach fluttered happily as she took in the view from every angle.

She could snuggle with a throw over her legs and a good book curled on the cozy couch. A loveseat and easy chair defined the living room side of a great room. A round oak table and chairs provided cozy eating space. Ample countertops and a bar separated the open kitchen. Sparkling, stainless appliances and lots of cabinets provided a haven for the homemaker in her conjuring delicious meals to create.

A covered porch spanned the width revealing the beauty of the lake. Two pink, wooden rockers separated by a matching table with a floral umbrella filled one end. A broad, pink swing graced the other, and a floral cushion ensured the seat would provide a comfort spot to enjoy leisure time—assuming she'd have it. This created a delightful area for entertaining friends.

How long would it take to make friends

here? She knew only Justin and Richard, yet she'd fit in. Before long she felt new friendships forge. The idea comforted her, and she welcomed the prospect.

Sadie loved to cook and thrilled finding the cabin fully stocked with dishes, pots, pans, and linens; and a bookshelf lined with games. She couldn't wait to cook for someone in her very own home.

She gazed happily at her living room. She did a happy dance in a circle, glancing outside to make sure no one observed.

How fun.

A house all to herself—privacy—something she enjoyed little of, though it never bothered her. She thrived in their loud, busy home; but this was a treat.

She'd miss Becky and Evan, her only family, used to being with them continually. But they'd be fine without her for a while. It would be good for them and easier now Evan was older and involved in sports and scouts. He wasn't a baby any longer.

Besides, they didn't live in another country. They were an hour away; and visits with each other would always be in the making. She looked forward to exploring the lake with them the following weekend. Her spare guest bedroom room with twin beds perfectly house Becky and Evan when they visit.

Missing them, feeling strangely alone, but also wonderful, this was a good thing. Something magnificent would come of this job. It had already started. A transformation was happening.

Sadie unpacked her possessions and placed a photo of herself with Becky and Evan in the living room and one of their parents on top of the entertainment center. Finished unpacking, she rang Becky to tell her she'd arrived safely.

"Hey Sis, how's it going? We only now settled in." Sadie flopped on the comfy couch and sat her iced tea glass on a coaster on the end table.

"Great. Thanks for calling. How was the drive?" Becky stopped washing dishes and leaned against the sink.

"Easy with hardly any traffic. I'm so excited. This place is fabulous. It's quaint and lovely. Cabins are darling cottages. The setting is breathtaking. They plopped these sweet houses into heaven. We're surrounded on three sides by woods, so birds sing constantly. The sound of wind through the trees could lull you to sleep. The air is thick with floral fragrance. It is so beautiful. I can't wait for you and Evan to see it."

"It sounds adorable. I'm glad you're enjoying it so far. How's Richard?"

"Exhausted—he headed straight to bed."

"And Justin?" She sounded tentative. Could she be taken with the good-looking attorney?

"He's good, a gracious host. He made me feel at home."

"Is it clean?"

"The place is immaculately kept. My cabin is fully furnished. Sam, the gal who works at the marina stocked my refrigerator and pantry—beyond welcoming. These guys are amazing. Ricky is so

111

funny. He gets me and approves of my macho. He cracks up at my strange sense of humor. He's a cool guy. He laughs at my nickname when I call him Ricky. No one ever called him that before, but he finds it funny and is letting me."

"Well you're fitting in perfectly, as I suspected. I'm glad you're happy and in good spirits." Becky laughed. She enjoyed Sadie's joking around. Apparently Richard and Justin did also.

"Justin is a sweetheart. It's beautiful the way he dotes on his dad. He oozes love for Richard and is a genuinely kind man with a good heart. And he is smart. No wonder he's a successful lawyer."

"Yes. I found him bright and liked him as well."

"Yeah, and he doesn't hesitate getting dirty either. He got on his knees outside crawling beneath a bush fetching a ball for a kid while he unloaded our bags. He's a gentleman. He wouldn't let me carry anything heavier than my purse. What a super nice guy."

"It's great to hear. Otherwise, I would never have recommended you take the job. I'm glad hearing I haven't entrusted my sweet, baby sister to a couple of maniacs."

"No way, Sis, these guys are the bomb. I'm stoked being here. I'm safe. They'll take care of me, and I'll take care of them."

"I know you will, Sadie. You're a wonderful person and a great nurse. They're lucky to have you."

"I miss you guys. I'm glad you're coming this weekend. I can't wait to share this place with you. Evan will flip. The kid will freak out. The guys have all sorts of ideas for things they want to do with the two of you. They're excited to have Evan around, as much as I am."

"It's good to know. I don't want to be a burden or in the way."

"You deserve this, Sis. It will be your first vacation in years. It's a treat, if only for a three day weekend." Sadie worried Becky didn't rest enough and never treated herself. Everything she did was for Evan and Sadie.

"Please don't let them overdo. Richard is in a precarious situation with his health. Don't allow him to exert himself on my account."

"Seriously, they're anxious for your visit and to meet the little guy. Richard had hopes of being a grandpa by now. He probably won't live to meet his own grandchildren, given his condition. Justin seems to love kids. You should've seen him with the children here at the camp. And I'll make sure Richard gets plenty rest and won't let him overdo. Don't worry. Come and enjoy yourselves. Richard and Justin need the distraction. It'll be good for them."

"If you're sure . . . we'll see you Friday. Love you."

"Love 'ya back." Sadie grinned ending the call.

Sadie checked on Ricky and gave his evening meds. The three of them had a light dinner of tuna fish sandwiches, pickles, and macaroni salad Sadie whipped up.

After Ricky rested, Justin and Ricky drove

the golf cart to the marina to talk with Sam. Sadie came along. "It's nice to meet you, Sam. Thank you for your extreme thoughtfulness stocking my kitchen with food."

"No problem, Sadie; and you're welcome. A pleasure, I shopped for Richard and Justin. It wasn't much additional effort to buy for you at the same time. I hope you like it here." The gorgeous, tiny woman had a hearty shake. Her long, blonde ponytail swayed with movement surrounding a face amazingly perfect without adornment. Darkly tanned in a tank top, frayed cut-off jeans and tennis shoes, the only jewelry Sam wore was a slim gold band on her ring finger. Her bubbly, welcoming personality would be difficult to dislike.

Sam was the perfect match to her handsome husband with the strong back and bulging muscles. His slight limp and short blondish brown hair attested to a recent stint in the service. A warming smile made him instantly likeable.

The men had spoken earlier with Sam on the phone about hiring Garrett. Sam agreed, so she called Garrett. Intrigued, he met them at the marina to discuss it. Before leaving they made a fitting arrangement for everyone.

Justin and Ricky acted happy having the problem solved. Justin could've done the work, but didn't want to take on a full-time job. His time was better spent with Ricky. He didn't mind the work. He didn't want to be continually tied up. He would however, have lots of time to himself during Ricky's much needed down time. He required lots of rest, meaning frequent naps.

"My brain may atrophy," Justin confided to Sadie while helping with her bags. "I'm not the kind of guy to settle down with a book and be happy. The resort bookkeeping will be minimal not taking more than a couple hours a week, and I can do it while spending time with Dad. I may require more stimulation. I'm used to being challenged."

"I'm sure you'll find something to fill your time." She hoped so because caring for Justin was part of her job.

"I'm surprised how good it feels being home; home—what a funny word." Justin had told her.

Why would anyone leave a place like this?

♥♥♥♥

He'd called the resort home earlier, referring to his place in Nashville as his condo, never his home. His condo was temporary and unimportant, never a home. It lacked a homey essence.

Justin had lived away for a long time. First college then a job offer his senior year, he moved to Nashville where life became exciting. He'd forgotten comfort home provided. Now he remembered he became determined to relish his time at home with his dad.

Dad had tons of messages from concerned friends and acquaintances. He returned calls reassuring friends he was still kicking. He didn't explain the extent of his condition, however, except for a select few of his closest confidants. Dad made coffee and lunch dates for the next week with pals.

The entire community appeared eager to visit with him.

He arranged a get-together at home for his closest contacts, his poker buddies. Normally they traded hosting weekly games and had missed Dad. It wasn't his turn, but he decided to host this week's game, anyway. Anxious to be together and knowing Richard's precarious health they agreed to play at his home.

Justin frowned. "Dad, you up to all this socializing?"

Richard grinned happily unconcerned from his easy chair, "Son, I've still got living left to do. I'm not going to letting his *death threat* keep me from doing it. My buddies are an important part of my life. It's not about to change for some *illness*."

Finally Justin relented with a sigh. "Okay, Dad, have your poker party."

"You're invited to join. Sadie too, if you want, girl." He glanced her way.

"Thank you, Ricky. I'm happy to shop and cook for you boys. But I have no interest in intruding on your *testosterone bash*."

"Okay, but you're in if you change your mind. I'd appreciate you making grub for the boys. I can have it catered if it's too much trouble. I don't want to overload you."

"I would love to cook for you, Ricky." Sadie winked.

His dad's eyes showed Sadie's offer touched him. "You're a great cook and would create a spread I'd be proud to serve, but I don't want to put you out."

"Nonsense, Ricky. I'd adore cooking for you and your buddies." She tweaked his cheek causing him to blush. Justin couldn't recall his dad blushing before.

"Thank you, darling. It has taken you no time to become indispensable around here. You manage this household with ease as though its second nature to you. Controlling my schedule and medications is complex enough, but you go way beyond, cooking and doing laundry. You make sure the cleaning lady does a thorough job. Sadie, you run our lives with ease. Pretty lady, you're a force of nature."

"Absolutely, Sadie, we didn't mean for you to become a homemaker and nurse when we hired you. But we appreciate everything you do." Justin touched her shoulder lightly producing a quirky smile on her adorable face.

"Someone needs to take care of those things, and it might as well be me. I enjoy taking care of you boys." She winked at Richard.

The glow on Richard's face said it all. "You have an unusual perspective on life. It makes you a stimulating companion. You've got to admire a gal who thinks out of the box. I admire your insightful take on world events, and you're a tough competitor at chess, checkers, and cards. You're beyond competent and skilled, striving for perfection."

Dad wasn't fooling anyone. He got a kick out of her calling him Ricky and loved it when she kicked his ass at games.

"Dad enjoys spending time with you. It's great you like watching baseball with us. It's refreshing you know a lot about the league. Dad's a fanatic fan, and you seem to enjoy the game as much as he does." Well-read and smart, her quick wit constantly kept them in stitches. Her spirited attitude was refreshing, and her character admirable.

A brow cocked as she glared along her nose wickedly. "Are you calling me anal, Ricky?"

He waved her joke away. "Hell no, you're a damned perfectionist, sweetheart. I love how you cut to the chase and take no prisoners." He slapped his knee laughing. Possessing an astute intellect, she wasn't intimidated by truth, even when it hurt.

"I try not to be harsh, Ricky. When the truth hurts, I try to tempered it with kindness and cloak it with love." She winked.

Justin enjoyed her company, too. "Becky must really miss having you around all the time. Her loss is definitely our gain."

"I miss them too, but they'll be fine, and we'll see them this weekend." Sadie bit the side of her lip.

"I admire your spirit. Younger with a good heart, I'd chase you all over these hillsides. Those outrageous outfits you call costumes keep Justin and me guessing what you'll come up with next, but you are delightful." Richard patted her hand affectionately.

She wagged her shoulders teasingly, and her unusual hair cut exaggerated her keen personality. "I like to be creative in my wardrobe. Clothing represents my nature."

"Well, you're immensely amusing. It's unusual to find a gal game for anything, as comfortable watching news on television, as she is curled up with a good book. You didn't hesitate to play touch football with the resort children in front of the cabin, or romp with them in the swimming pool. Baby, you radiate vitality, and it's something to watch. I wish I could do all of it with you."

"I've gained five pounds from your wonderful cooking. We're getting spoiled."

"I love cooking for my people, and you boys are my people."

CHAPTER 10

The evening of the poker party Sadie pulled hot wings from the oven as the first guest arrived. She assumed Ricky's friends would be his age or older. *Not so.*

A gorgeous mountain of a man towering over her five-foot-six-frame knocked then let himself in lured to the kitchen with its enticing smell. He leaned over Sadie's shoulder getting a whiff and seeing what wonders provided the tempting aroma. His scent exhilarated her senses. Her nose tilted into him blissfully.

"Umm, hot wings, my favorite. I hope they're spicy with blue cheese dip." The hunk grinned—not a leer, but a sweet, appreciative, pleasing smile. His intrusion on her personal space somehow comforted seeming familiar though they'd never met.

No hat topped his thick shock of short, black hair framing a chiseled face. Slim hips held an empty leather holster belt over a navy-blue police uniform. Short sleeves exposed powerful arms and bulging muscles. Massive hands bore no ring.

Sadie liked this sexy, hard-to-forget man with a unique face, broad jaw and dimpled chin. He could likely be intimidating if it was his intention, maybe downright scary. The friendly guy acted genuine and warm.

His demeanor tender and sweet, he turned attention toward Ricky, grinning like a possum from his easy chair watching Sadie and his bud get acquainted. The man obviously had been worried and cared a great deal for Richard. Wiping hands on a dish towel she observed their greeting and bear hug.

Who would've thought a police officer would give her heart palpitations? *Mercy. Country life is good.* She couldn't wait to meet the others if this was a sign of things to come.

The tall stranger's immense smile was friendly as he extended a hand when Ricky introduced them. Straight, white teeth enhanced his appearance. Sadie immediately liked and wanted to know this man.

"Sadie, this is my friend, Chief of Police Jack Barnes. Jack's friends call him JJ. This is my devoted friend and nurse, Sadie Watkins."

JJ took Sadie's hand in his manly one and held it as though handling a precious gem. She felt feminine and delicate in his broad grasp. Warmth radiated from JJ, and she tried absorbing as much as possible. He held on longer than necessary as though reluctant to release her. Sadie sensed heat flowing from him as though his firm, gentle caress offered protection from an unknown threat. As he let go, she clasps them together somehow lonelier without him.

Mmmm, chemistry, he's attracted to me too.
"Nice meeting you, Jack."

His smile radiated warmth as he beamed, and she became enchanted. "Please, call me JJ. I've heard wonderful things about you, Sadie. You're taking good care of my man here—not simply the nursing care. It's a great thing you're doing. This house has been too long without a woman's touch."

"Thank you, JJ. I'm enjoying Ricky and Justin's company. This is a lovely place to live." She stepped away as heat flowed from her heart shooting south, and the pit of her stomach fluttered joyfully.

A beautiful specimen of manhood.

It had been a while since anyone stirred her senses, and JJ did it effortlessly. No denying sparks flying between them.

An interesting summer, more than expected.

Others began showing up. Ben Franer, the city attorney with a private law practice in town, was a sweet older gentleman about Ricky's age. Short and balding, he had a slight middle paunch.

Gary Lang, owner of Lang's Grocery, strode in like he owned the world. Tall and thin in his early fifties, Gary's great sense of humor showed in his costume. A pink golf shirt with pink, yellow and green plaid slacks showed Gary liked being the center of attention and was used to it. Reveling in laughter his outfit initiated. The guys got a charge from kidding Gary, and he took it in stride acting cocky and parading exaggeratedly across the room. Even as a newcomer, she understood he received the reaction he sought.

Barry Anderson, owner of Gas & Bass, the local bait and tackle shop, stood six feet tall with a powerful, lean build, probably in his mid-sixties. Stylish, thick blonde hair fell across his handsome forehead.

"Barry, who cuts your hair? I need a good, local stylist." Sadie joked but was serious too.

Barry grinned and shuffled through his wallet; then handed her a business card. "Connie will take care of you. Tell her I sent you." Clearly Barry enjoyed fine things. Pricy navy slacks and a matching tailored, short-sleeve shirt fit perfectly. A woven belt and soft, suede moccasins with no socks gave him an elegant casual appearance, distinguished but friendly and down to earth.

Bait and tackle treated Barry well. Who would've known selling worms was a lucrative venture?

Circuit Court Judge Mike Stands stood tall, round and jolly. Balding on top with a warm, friendly smile which focused when listening, making one believe you're the only person in the room.

A fitting trait for a judge.

Leslie Cord, owner of Suthern Kumfert Resort along the shore from Shady Pines Resort arrived last. Leslie drove a new Cadillac SUV donning well-worn work boots, denim bib overalls and a plaid flannel shirt with sleeves cut off fraying at the shoulders. His Rolex® watch and Bulgari® sunglasses pushed atop of his bushy head were obvious signs his resort was a moneymaker. His comedic style proved him comfortable in his own skin.

A brawny guy, with broad shoulders, slim hips, and a pleasant round face, scraggly black hair greyed at his temples. The unusual character was showcased in a messy, shaggy manner. But his well-spoken way showed he was highly educated. Ricky had told her Leslie chose his career, versus ending with it out of circumstance. Friendly and uninhibited, the sort comfortable in any setting, he laughed and joked with spontaneity acting as though he cared for his friends and had been worried sick about Ricky.

"It's a pleasure meeting Richard's friends. Thank you for treating me as though you've known me forever and going out of your way to welcome me into your home."

"Nonsense, we appreciate your efforts making our evening pleasant and fun." Leslie shook his head. They thanked her endlessly for all she had done for them.

She especially enjoyed the twinkle in JJ's eyes when he thanked her. He made a point to touch her arm. When she didn't withdraw from his touch, he pulled her into a quick hug. The tingle zipped all the way to her middle and between her legs.

"We're a hugging sort here in the sticks. I hope you don't mind." He winked.

Stilling her quivering heart, she smiled. "I like it fine, thank you." She straightened her shirt and moved to the kitchen.

Sadie finished putting food out and prepared to leave them to their game. Besides a tray of hot wings with blue cheese and ranch dips, she served meat-heavy nachos, a crockpot of chili and plated a tray of veggies with dip. A pitcher of homemade lemonade, a jug of sweet tea and a coffee pot sat ready to brew in case they wanted it. And Justin lugged a huge cooler full of iced beer and bottled water onto the deck in front of the sliding glass doors.

"The spread looks awesome, and we sure appreciate your cooking and hospitality." JJ stood closer than needed talking in a sexy, deep voice rolling off his tongue, melting her heart like honey on a hot biscuit.

"Sure beats the grub Richard usually serves." Mike play-punched Ricky's arm being gentle with his buddy, teasing Ricky endearingly.

Leslie rubbed his hands together studying the banquet. "Anything beats Richard's culinary skills. Sadie, you've made the old geezer proud. This smells scrumptious."

"Thank you, gentlemen." She curtsied laughing as she went to her cabin so the fellas could enjoy their evening together. She curled up in the comfy porch rocker with a cup of honeyed green tea and *Catching Air* by Sarah Pekkanen, ecstatic at the luxury.

A couple hours had passed when JJ approached his cruiser fetching something he brought Ricky. Noticing Sadie next door reading, he waved. "Hey there, how you doing?" He strolled forward and leaned on the railing.

"I adore this beautiful evening. Peace and quiet of this lovely place is overwhelming. What a view." She pointed toward the lake.

"Yes, we're used to it, and take too much for granted. You've certainly improved the view. I'm enjoying it." He blushed at his impulsive comment, but his eyes never left her. "I'm sorry. I shouldn't be so forward." Stepping onto the porch, he propped against the railing.

"It's okay, and thanks." She flirted tilting her jaw, eyeing him sweetly as she folded the book in her lap.

"I rarely meet such a beautiful woman hanging out with my old buddies, especially a gal who can cook." His slow, sweet drawl emphasized the words, and the sound delighted her senses. She could happily listen to him recite the tax code.

"Beautiful hum?" Sadie cocked an eyebrow coyly. "I'm glad you're enjoying it. I love to cook. I don't get much chance to feed men, not until I came here caring for Justin and Ricky. I hope I made enough."

"There's plenty, but it's hard to believe. A woman as stunning as you should have men swarming her like bees honing in on honey."

She laughed at the example. "Don't get me wrong. I date, but don't bring men friends home to cook for them. I live with my sister and cook for Becky and her son Evan. It's not a place to bring a man for a romantic dinner."

"Well, you've got space of your own now. I'd certainly entertain the notion of dinner with you. I'd love the chance to get to know you better. I'm willing to cook if you don't want to. Have dinner with me. We'll go out if you'd, rather. Can we make it a date?" His sensual grin and the glint in those smoky eyes proved more than she could resist.

Sadie suspected JJ had come outside on a rouse as an excuse to find her. The way he invited himself over amused and pleased her, making her belly gurgle.

"I'd enjoy it. How about tomorrow evening? I should have Richard and Justin settled with dinner by six. I can make a nice dinner here. How do you feel about meat? Beef, pork, chicken or fish?" She laughed.

"You have got 'ta love a woman who eats meat. Honey I'd eat anything you cook. I'm sure whatever you make will be delicious. The company will be delightful. I get off duty at six. How about I show around seven? It'd give me a chance to shower, shave and change."

"It's a date." *Hot dog.* Her belly did a happy dance.

"Red wine okay?"

"We can make it work."

He winked before going back to his friends with a soft wave. Sadie settled back into reading, but her mind busily crafted a menu to impress JJ.

The future's getting better by the minute. She smiled at the fluttering butterflies taking over her midsection.

During breakfast Ricky shared disturbing news with a concerned voice. "Ben Franer told us last night he's having medical issues. The old fart has lung cancer but never smoked a day in his life. His lungs have started failing, anyway. He's scheduled for chemo and needs to reduce his workload during treatment. In addition to being the city attorney, his law practice is thriving." Ben turned to Justin. "Son, it's a lot to ask. Is there any way you could help him out for a while?"

Justin hesitated. "I don't know, Dad. I don't want to commit to anything with you ill. Individually each of your pals asked me the same question last evening. You and your homies persistently present a valid case."

Richard eagerly studied Justin's face. "You wouldn't have to be away much. You can work from here much of the time. His assistant will bring your work and pick it up from you here. I sleep a lot, son. It would give you a stimulating outlet while I catch up on rest. I'd sure appreciate anything you could do to help."

Justin swiped a hand through his hair and shook his head giving up. "Okay, Dad, if it will make you happy I can work two to four hours a day from home. I can take occasional appointments in the office with clients, but only as needed, and only if you're otherwise occupied."

"It would be awesome, Justin. I'd be eternally grateful. You'd need to appear in court once a week for about two to four hours. I could make arrangements with friends in town during those times."

"Okay, fine. I'll arrange a workable schedule."

Ricky beamed. "This makes me so happy, Justin. Thanks for helping my pal out. It won't cut into our one-on-one time. I promise."

"It is fine, Dad. I needed something to fuel my brain and challenge me while I'm here anyway, but only when you're tied up."

"Sure, Justin, this should keep you from becoming bored to death with quite lake life. Without engaging work, you'd soon suffer withdrawal. You're a workaholic and would go stir-crazy with your *type A* personality. This should help you as much as it does Ben. It provides an opportunity for you to contact friends and neighbors you've lost touch with since moving away." Ricky dug into his oatmeal, seeming delighted at the solution.

"Sure, it will be fun." Justin scrutinized his father, smiling at Ricky's newly robust appetite.

Sadie drove into town for groceries and a lunch date with JJ. Justin and Richard relaxed on the deck soaking in the sun's warmth. Richard warily broached a subject. "Tell me about the woman you're involved with in Tennessee, Yancy, Fancy or something like that. Right? Is she the one you want to spend your life with? When do I get to meet her?"

"Her name is Yancy. Yes, I would've married her, but I've changed my mind."

"I'm sorry hearing it, Son. If she wasn't right for you, better now instead of later. I hope you have an opportunity to find the right gal. I want you to experience the sort of love your mom and I enjoyed."

"You know, Dad, I never believed in love. Every relationship was doomed sooner or later. Either the person turned out to be something you didn't expect or people grew apart, or died like mom did. Love being temporary could only to be enjoyed for a while."

"You have never been so wrong. Your mom and I would be together today and forever, had we gotten the opportunity. Nothing could've kept us apart. The love of my life became a completely unexpected part of me. I never thought to be valued that way, and I didn't deserve it. However, she cared for me, anyway. If she lived, she still would today like I will always love her." Richard gazed wistfully.

"You might be right, at least where you and Mom are concerned. I've seen so many ugly divorces in the law business, I'm wary. Marriage doesn't make it. I had this idea I'd settle down with Yancy. She's sexy and passionate, and she brings connections and power to the table. What marriage should be, it would replace anything lacking, and my career benefited from it. "

"Son, it's the dumbest thing I've heard. It makes marriage sound like a business arrangement. Wedlock is tough enough when you're head-over-heels in love. It'd be a disaster with someone you're not nuts about. You'd be doomed to unhappiness."

"Arranged marriages have worked for certain cultures for centuries. Why not now? But

I'm starting to believe you could be right. I broke up with Yancy while at the hospital with you before you woke. I can't imagine a lifetime with her. I may not find a love like you and Mom had, but I certainly don't want the marriage I envisioned with Yancy. I've learned recently due to what is going on with you, life is too short. I want more than a marriage of convenience. At least, I'm open to the idea of falling in love."

"Son, this transformation in you makes me happy. Don't block the wonder of it from your life. Keep an open mind. Be receptive. It will find you, probably when you least expect it." He beamed.

Justin wasn't sure or pleased, but deeper in turmoil at odd ends with his life. At least before he'd had a plan and worked it. Now, he acted lost like a stray puppy, wondering about this love nonsense.

"I better take a nap. I'm worn out. Beating you at chess drained me." Richard stood on shaky legs. Justin rushed to assist, bracing an arm around his shoulders. "Why don't we take the bass boat out for a while tomorrow and see how they're biting?"

"It's a great idea, Dad. Let's do." He helped Richard to bed.

♥♥♥♥

Sadie prepared the dinner table and checked the freezer. "We're low on ice. I'll run to the marina for a bag before dinner."

Justin smiled back at her from a game of checkers with Ricky at the table. "Take Dad's golf cart. It's parked next to the cabin."

Ricky grinned. "It's the one with the name tag on it, Big Daddy."

"Sure thing, Big Daddy, I'll be right back." She left them to their game and hopped into the red cart which hadn't been used in a couple days. The engine revved, and she sped along the gravel lane toward the dock. Halfway she tapped the brake to slow the cart before hitting the steep incline toward the tall bank surrounding the gangplank. Nothing happened. She tapped it again several times as the hair on the back of her neck popped to attention. Nothing. Slamming the pedal to the floor she began to panic as the increasing incline forced speed to pick up.

Glancing around with wide eyes, she searched for a solution. A few cars parked around the launching area. The boat ramp leaned steeply toward water's edge. The gangplank blocked by a couple of trees preventing carts from driving onto it, flaked a blue plastic outhouse beside the trees.

Swerving slightly one way then the other, she attempted to slow the vehicle. It worked but marginally. She chose the target of least financial value and allowed the car to slam head first into the two trees.

BANG.

Sadie flew forward. Her forehead bounced off the plastic windshield. Her neck snapped backward. Her skull slapped the back windshield as she slammed against the cushioned seat with force. The sound of crunching metal rang out, and the golf cart thudded to a sudden stop.

It bounced sideways from impact. The right side collided with the portable potty. The stinky structure tilted wildly until it flipped off its pallet and fell headfirst over the embankment. It screeched its way across boulders covering the bank and screeched to a stop on its side halfway between parking lot and water's edge. The air filled with an odorous stench.

Fishermen pulling their boat into the dock stopped to gawk. Campers raced from their cottages to discover what the noise was. They laughed and pinched their noses, some making *pwewing* sounds. One man rushed to help Sadie from the dilapidated golf cart.

"You okay, Miss?" The pudgy gent in flannel and jeans held onto her arm as she climbed safely to ground.

Sadie rolled her head stretching her neck and rubbed where it ached. She blinked a couple times and took a long, fortifying breath. "I think so. Thanks." She walked around the cart. "The brakes were out."

"Smart of you to slam into the trees."

"Yeah, I figured the golf cart would be the only victim. I didn't foresee killing the toilet." She grinned wickedly, and the guy chuckled. "I didn't want to hit someone's car. It would've been expensive."

"Smart thinking, you could've been hurt badly if you'd gone over the edge. Falling on those boulders wouldn't be good for the body." He shook his head as if in wonder.

"You've got it right."

♥♥♥♥

"You ready for a day on the lake, Son?" Richard asked the next morning over breakfast.

"Sure." Justin patted Richard's hand across the table.

"Did you find out what happened to the cart yesterday, with Sadie?"

"Dad, I took the damned thing apart last night. From what I see the brakes were intentionally tampered with. Cables weren't frayed or worn, but clipped with a clean cut. I checked the other carts but only one had an issue."

"Seriously?" Richard appeared confused. "Damn, we've never had trouble with vandalism here before. People don't mess with other folks' things."

"Well, something has changed." Justin stood to clean the table. "We're lucky she wasn't hurt badly."

"This irks me. Sadie could've been badly injured." Richard acted apprehensive, like he mulled over the situation.

♥♥♥♥

After breakfast Justin packed a cooler with water, ice and live bait from their marine store.

"It's a glorious day on the water." Billowing clouds lightly dotted brilliant blue sky. "The low wind is enough to ripple the water, and should make the fish jump into the boat." Richard swallowed morning medications Sadie doled out and surprisingly didn't invite her to go along.

"You and Justin have a lovely time. I'm going to catch some sun. It's inviting reflecting off the water." She glanced out the wall of windows toward the glistening lake.

"Yep, it's a perfect day for lake lovers." Richard picked up his favorite rod and reel.

"I grew up here." Justin entered having prepared for their excursion. "I'd forgotten how much I enjoyed the water. This place provides a familiar sense of peace. I'm glad to be here, Dad." He felt giddy inside, like the first time Richard let him drive the boat as a boy.

The men climbed into a golf cart Justin had inspected earlier, making sure it was in proper running order. Richard drove them to the marina's wide dock, parking the cart outside the scarred trees and out of the way of the guests.

Air again smelled fresh and clean, and stench created by the flipping outhouse the previous night had drifted away on the wind. The rental company replaced the damaged structure with a fresh, blue toilet standing proudly where its fallen comrade had met its doom.

Justin noticed things he'd taken for granted as a child. The bird feeder flocked with blue jays, each patiently waiting a crack at seeds, doing a delicate dance circling and taking turns eating while others munched on spillage on ground below. A blue heron guarded the end of one boat ramp. His keen eyes trained on water searched for unsuspecting prey swimming close to the surface—

an easy fishing day for him with the crystal water. Sea gulls cawed overhead periodically diving beneath the surface for a fish meal. A family of wild ducks swam toward the back of a cove. The mother led, followed by six ducklings in a row protectively followed by a doting father.

They waved to Sam who pumped gas into a pontoon tied to the dock. "Let me give you a hand, Dad." Justin helped Richard aboard then stepped onto the boat. It tipped slightly with their weight. Justin grabbed Richard's elbow. "We sure don't need you falling."

"Thanks, Son. Things are bad enough. We don't need an accident. Why don't you put a couple dozen minnows in the bucket and a carton of worms?"

Justin collected gear from a locked shed. He filled the minnow bucket and handed it to Richard. He selected foam cartons of night crawlers and placed them in the bait cooler.

Richard had secured their fishing poles to hangers on the side of the boat by the time he returned. "Everything is loaded. Let's roll. I hear bass calling my name . . . Ricky . . . Ricky."

His laughter welled Justin's heart as he memorized the moment. Richard had wiped boat seats and console while Justin selected the bait. He proudly perused the bass boat as metal-flaked emerald green paint caught the sun's rays. "I love how this boat glides over water once I get her on a plane. She's a great ride, and I've got her decked out with the best of equipment. This fantastic machine is my pride and joy. I'm happy spending a day on her with you, Son."

"Me too, Dad." Justin choked on the tears he swallowed. How many opportunities would his dad have to enjoy his beloved boat?

Richard pulled out a couple life jackets and laid them on a seat. He did a quick check ensuring they had a whistle and other necessary gear. He laid a flat throw cushion on top of the live well. "We're good to go, aligned with legal requirements. Let's hit the water." He took the driver's seat. Justin untied the craft and hopped onto the grey carpeting and reclined in the comfy bucket seat beside his dad. Richard put the boat into gear, and they cruised off.

The breath-taking day wasn't too hot or humid, and water lapped fairly calm with enough chop to be perfect for fishing. "This is a lovely place. I can't believe how much I enjoy it here." Richard's smile took on a sly quirk listening to the joy in his son's voice.

There was no need for conversation. They rode silently enjoying the peaceful experience.

They eased past the no-wake zone. Richard kicked the motor into high gear, and the boat responded lifting atop waves settling into a comfortable float on the plane. They sped out of the wide cove where the marina was located and onto the main lake.

"I'd forgotten how massive, Kentucky Lake is, spanning from the middle of western Kentucky south into Tennessee."

"Yep, she's one of two sister lakes. Barkley is nearly as enormous making the distance spanning into Tennessee as well. They appear slim on a map, but these bodies of water spread over a mile across at any point and one-hundred-eighty-four miles long with over a hundred and sixty thousand acres of water." Richard gazed around proudly. "Remember when you were young, and we hunted deer in Land Between The Lakes?" He pointed east toward a narrow stretch of land between Kentucky and Barkley lakes.

"How could I forget? I got a kick out of camping in a tent. Its brilliant how the state keeps the preserve primitive for sports and nature lovers."

The wide channel grew rockier than the cove but not so rough they couldn't fish. "Some species bite better with a current. Walleye prefer a bit of chop on the water." Richard slowed to low gear barely moving south in the channel.

They grabbed their poles and secured a couple of lures on their lines. Richard expertly guided the craft at a crawl along the right side of the strait. Knowing the lake like the back of his hand, he kept the boat in the deep pool for trolling, yet drifted close to the bank where fish would be feeding. They tolled for a while, stopping occasionally taking their catch off their lines.

"Damn, I forgot how thrilling it is hearing the yell—*fish on*." Richard cut the engine at the familiar signal. The one without the hookup managed the net. Once the fish played out and swam close enough to the boat, he netted it.

"I like keeping only a few decent sized fish we can eat. They taste better than larger ones." Richard grinned netting a sizeable walleye for

Justin. "This one is awful fat. Let's take a photo and return him to the deep."

Justin nodded, posing as though kissing the fish in the mouth getting a hearty laugh from his dad. Most he gently released into the water.

After a couple hours of trolling they crossed to the other side of the main lake and located their favorite catfish hole. Richard pulled the boat carefully near a plastic jug float serving as a buoy during summer pool. "Watch for the rocky high spot beneath the surface where the house sat before the area flooded." Richard warned.

Justin leaned over the bow scanning the depths for a rocky mound holding a set of concrete steps visible above water only in winter pool. The lake was created in 1944 by the Tennessee Valley Authority creating the lake.

Catfish flocked to the spot, feeding abundantly. "Considerable numbers of bait fish swarm thick cover of these boulders." Richard cut the engine and raised the motor so it wouldn't bump. Justin set the anchor. They baited hooks with night crawlers using floats so the bait wouldn't sink and tangle in rocks. "Floating bait works best here enticing huge cats out of hiding." Richard gazed at Justin tentatively. "Why did you break it off with the Tennessee gal?"

Justin shrugged, uncomfortable discussing it with his father. "I didn't love her."

"Was there more to it?" Richard wasn't letting him off so easy.

"Yancy was beautiful—stunning actually— well educated with no ambition or inclination toward work. Into taking care of herself—shopping, traveling and enjoying life, rich and spoiled, she wanted to continue being so the rest of her life, all about her. I liked her—a lot, but didn't love her."

"It wasn't important for you before. She cared for you though self-centered and selfish. Didn't she?" Richard eyed him quizzically. "You sounded serious about her, ready to make a long-term commitment. What changed?"

"She cares about the life she pictured us having together. I presented a good choice for her, and would've made her life easy. I could take care of her. And she liked me well enough, I guess. But I doubt she loved me in the sense you mean. I recently realized she enjoyed me but is capable of loving no one but herself." There's no pain in the truth. Yancy had every right to be herself. "I wanted it in a wife — fun, exciting, dynamic with incredible business connections, wealthy beyond imagination and destined to inherit Daddy's empire. She would be a powerful wife, the perfect trophy, a pretty piece of candy on my arm and a sexy, warm body in my bed. Her dad offered me an amazing opportunity with his firm. He planned to groom me to take over his empire someday. I wanted it. I enjoyed Yancy's company, the sex, and I liked her. I didn't mind her obsession with herself."

"Is it my fault you broke up? Be honest." Richard's face didn't harbor guilt. The simple question sought an honest answer.

"I started seeing things differently. It's not your fault, but your illness put things into perspective. I began realizing I'd never be happy or satisfied with Yancy. If I wanted a woman at my side, I wanted more than Yancy could give. A life with her would be settling. Life's too brief to settle."

"Well, I certainly agree with it. Too bad she wasn't the one for you. Marriage to the right woman can be an incredible high, and surfaces emotions you never considered you had in you."

"Is that how it was with Mom?"

"Absolutely, she was it for me. I never expected to love anyone the way I did her. I wasn't worthy or deserving. I didn't believe it existed until I met her. Boy, was I wrong?" Richard's face took on a soft dreamy appearance.

"It's what I thought until lately." Justin's words may've reached him, but Richard became lost in a long past day with his wife. Wonderfully, the mind replays scenes from the past reliving them. Sensations rush back vividly like being there again.

"Is it so? What made your feelings about it change?"

He heard.

Justin hesitated, not wanting to upset his dad. "I love you and Mom; but I've never loved a woman before. I've seen many screwed up marriages. I didn't believe in love."

"Oh, it exists all right. You'll know when it knocks your socks off." Richard chuckled slapping his leg.

"If it or anything similar exists, I might want it." Justin grew pensive, not wishing to share his fascination with Becky with his dad—not yet. "I wasn't open to it in the past. I didn't want it and blocked it out. Forever love may not exist, but I want at least a for now love." Justin wondered at the possibility.

"Son, I'm here to tell you, ever-lasting love exists." Richard wiped a tear with his sleeve.

"Why weren't you worth loving, Dad?" The comment puzzled Justin. "It seems odd."

"It's a long story, and a question you could ask of yourself, Son. If you're up for it, I'd love to tell you about my past. I've kept it from you for too long. Not today, Justin. I'm totally spent. Let's talk about this tomorrow."

"Sure, Dad, whatever." *What the hell?*

CHAPTER 11

After a delightful fish dinner of grilled walleye, hush puppies, potato wedges, and coleslaw, Sadie washed dishes and readied to retire to her cabin. "Ricky, I'll return in a while to administer your meds and help you to bed. You boys have fun this evening." She waved gaily as she sped out the door.

Justin helped Richard to his easy chair and plopped on the sofa. Before Richard could click the boob tube on, Justin halted him with a puzzled expression. "Dad, you can tell me. I'd love to hear about your past. Now would be a good time."

Richard steeled himself for the discussion. "Okay, Son, you're right. I've waited too long because it will hurt and will change how you look at me. I owe it to you to level with you now or never thought everything will change between us. I'm not the man you think. I'm far, far worse."

Shocking, how could a good man have misgivings about himself? Probably nothing, but whatever . . . he deserved the opportunity to flush it out of his system.

"It's hard for me to believe; but sure, please tell me."

Richard grew stiff and pale as he dredged up memories. With a cold expression he braced for something awful, obviously dreading revealing his secret.

Willing to listen, Justin tried to ease his mind. Richard, his rock, his safe haven, his teacher, and mentor, had ensured Justin experienced a wonderful childhood. Together they engaged in character building activities. Actively involved in Justin's raising, Richard had provided a proper education and supported Justin's endeavors—a loving, amazing dad.

Justin couldn't picture anything warranting fear or would change his opinion of his father. Anguish in Richard's eyes physically hurt Justin. He leaned back chocking himself up for whatever came next.

Hands clenched, elbows on knees, Richard stared at the coffee table, avoiding Justin's eyes. "It's hard to admit. I was once a very bad man who didn't deserve your mom when I met her. When I learned she loved me, I tried to push her away; but she wouldn't allow it. She saw something in me no one else did. I wasn't worthy, but I wanted her. Finally I came to grips with it, determined to become the type man she rated, a better man, one she could be proud of."

"Dad, Mom was proud of you. So am I. You're wonderful and have been an incredible father and husband. You provided us a great life. You're respected with tons of friends. Why?" Justin leaned against the sofa sipping his beer dreading what sounded like a defining moment in his life.

"Let me start at the beginning, so you'll understand. I won't beg forgiveness because it's too much to ask. But at least maybe you will understand."

"Ridiculous." Justin insisted wiping hair back from his forehead adjusting the camouflaged cap he wore. "You couldn't possibly have done anything I wouldn't forgive. I know you. You're a good man. You couldn't do the unforgivable."

"We'll find out soon enough." Richard winced obviously under substantial stress, making Justin worry for his condition, but the doctor advised to say the unspoken while time allowed. "How about I tell you everything from the beginning? We can see what happens." Clearly Richard had important things weighing on his chest.

Justin nodded taking a long swig of beer. He sat back listening quietly and giving the respect Richard deserved.

"Born in Newport, Kentucky to a beautiful but weak woman—a drug addict, my mom prostituted for drug money. We lived in a shady neighborhood in a third floor walk-up reeking of urine. I never left the building while Mom lived."

"She pushed me into the hallway while entertaining Johns. A tiny, terrified child with no clue what was happening, afraid of those men, I knew not to antagonize Mom. Apparently guys don't want a toddler watching them have sex."

Justin's heart sank into his gut. He was heavy with grief for the youngster in his dad's story.

"I cowered on the filthy floor beneath the stairwell lying in peeling paint chips among other disgusting refuse. I cried myself to sleep many nights, sometimes freezing with no blanket. More times than not, she passed out and forgot me. So I spent the night there. On lucky evenings when she was sober enough to remember, she brought me in once they finished with her; and we slept together on a foul, lumpy mattress on the floor."

Justin turned to hide wiping a tear away. Richard batted back tears at the sight of his son response from this grief. No backing away now and no saving them from the ugly truth.

"She loved me, at least as much as she was capable of. She lived for and only truly loved her needle. But when somewhat sober and alone, she acted kind and tender, speaking with a soft, calming voice quivering as though in pain. Now I realize she needed a hit." He paused and swiped a tear. "She had a beautiful smile. I loved it about her. Long, stringy blonde hair blanketed her shoulders, dirty and matted much of the time. It would've been lovely if she cared for it." He smiled.

Justin saw, Richard loved her despite how the woman neglected him. It didn't seem real—more like a bad fairy tale or a movie tragedy. How could it be true? And how could Richard love his druggie mother despite her treatment of him? He didn't interrupt to ask, having vowed to hear his dad out.

"There was never enough food for both of us. She didn't eat much, due to the drugs. She didn't care about food; so she let me have whatever was available. Sometimes she brought homemade bread and peanut butter. I learned to feed myself early on when food was accessible."

"Mostly I stayed hungry. A lady on the second floor checked on me when she could. She'd sneak me to her apartment when she found me in the hallway and take care of me. I'd get a bath and a full belly. She'd wash my clothes and watch over me while I slept."

"Sometimes she snuck food into our apartment while Mom lay passed out. She put extra in the refrigerator for later too when she could. She bought me clothes once in a while from a thrift store. I loved the sweet old lady." Richard sighed deeply.

"Mornings I slept with Mommy until she woke up. Sometimes I could wake her, and she'd play with me for a few minutes or fix whatever was available to eat. Other times she growled at me to leave her alone, and I foraged for myself." He shook his head sadly.

"A pitiful soul with torn, stained clothing; deep, dark wrinkles; and circles framing her eyes, she was too young to have them. Drugs made her old. I suspect she was in her early twenties, but appeared considerably older. At her worst she lay drooling with dried spit and slobber on her face. It was all I knew—familiar, and it made me sad." The truth exhausted Richard who emitted a loud sigh.

"One morning when I was around four-years-old, I couldn't roust her. She was cold. I finally gave up, scared and confused not knowing what to do. I found something to eat and sat playing on the floor. Days dragged by, and she didn't wake. I ran out of food and drank water from the faucet filling my aching belly, but I grew weak and sickly. My gut hurt from emptiness. I slept next to her body at night, and during the day tried to pretend she'd wake soon. In my heart I realized it wasn't the case. She was gone for good."

Justin wiped his eyes. Richard cringed guiltily, having caused his tears. Richard sat with elbows on knees and head down, staring at the floor without seeing it. Justin's heart broke at the story making his stomach roll and sour.

How could someone be so cruel to a child? Dad actually survived it.

"After a few days and nights two cops showed up along with the old lady from the other apartment. One officer hoisted me into his arms and told me. It will be okay, little man." I never forgot how kind his voice sounded. The other one checked on Mom and shook his head. I understood what it meant. We walked to the old lady's apartment to wait for others to arrive. The sweet old gal cleaned me and fed me while the policemen asked questions. They asked how long it had been since Mom was awake. Too young to tell time, I held three fingers and said it had been that many nights. They shook their heads. One turned away trying to hide his tears."

"Eventually a woman from Child Protective Services showed up. She told me I didn't need to worry. I'd be fed and cared for. She took me to a place called Holly Hill, a child's orphanage and school. I'd never seen anything like it. Of course I'd never been outside our building. The immaculate two-story brick with sprawling wings had a huge yard, a ball field and playground. Like a park complete with swings, teeter totters, monkey bars, and lots of other things to play on. Compared to where I'd been it was heaven. The second floor barracks for boys neighbored one for girls on another wing. A cafeteria provided three delicious meals a day—something I'd never had. A walkway connected to a church where we attended classes. I loved the old chapel, having never seen anything so ornate. I found comfort in the ceremony, pomp and circumstances of the service. I was happy at this place, with its schedules, routines, studies, and, simple chores. I belonged, a part of something, so I studied hard and obeyed the kind, caring nuns, and teachers. They provided clean clothes, plenty of nourishment, and a clean bed."

Richard stared through the window at the lake blinking for a few seconds. His eyes shot to the floor.

"People visited, shopping to adopt. The nuns dressed us and usher us through interviews with prospective parents. A good child, healthy and not bad looking, I never understood why no one chose me to be their son. It was emotionally dramatic, but I tried not to be hurt by rejection. Of course I was, but I was happy with the nuns. Completing eighth grade, I passed the age to live at Holy Hill. They transferred me to the foster home system and relocated me into a foster home. People received payment to let me live with them as their own child would. And they don't need to love you in the temporary situation. The first home worked out fairly well. Four boys lived there, with me being the youngest. The kind middle-aged couple never had children of their own. They helped us with homework and gave us chores to do around the house suitable for children. They fed us, kept our clothes clean and actually cared. It wasn't so bad, a decent arrangement."

He shook his head and sighed heavily as though gearing for something worse.

"After a couple years my foster dad's job transferred them to Chicago, so they dropped out of the system. We split up and relocated. Things went downhill from there."

Justin studied Richard's gaze as he glared at the carpeting, head slumped with a blank stare. Justin wore his lawyer expression, doing his best to hide his broiling emotions because Richard needed to finish the sordid story without interruption.

"My next placement was another middle-aged couple. They *were not* caring or kind. Six foster children, four boys and two girls provided their labor force. They took in kids simply for money and manpower. Girls did housework. Boys did all other manual labor. We lived on a farm outside of Alexandria where they raised vegetables for market. We worked fields for two hours before school and after school until dark. We did homework late at night. Many times I slept four or five hours. Gruesome for a youngster, I had a hard time keeping up. They were never satisfied that I worked hard enough in the fields, harping because I couldn't make better grades. Not concerned for me—it drew attention from authorities, and they didn't appreciate people butting into their business wondering why I didn't do better. We ate only beans, cornbread, and water. It didn't matter. I liked beans and cornbread and had lived with less and worse. They reserved milk from their cow for market, minus what they drank themselves. Any kid caught sneaking a sip received a strong back-hand and no dinner. It was tough. The older boys bullied younger ones like me ganging up at night knocking me around. They pounced on any weakness shown. I learned a few tricks from them though. I could take care of myself unless more than one at a time attacked me. One day returning from school the couple sat us down and told us our foster dad was ill. They could no longer care for us." Richard took a breather sipping his iced tea and staring at the lake. He was in a dream-like state, obviously reminiscing and gathering strength to persist.

Pity soared through Justin's veins. Richard wouldn't take the sentiment lightly, so Justin kept it to himself. His dad needed support, not pity. So he sat quietly waiting for Richard. Why hadn't he been more curious about his parents' lives growing up? Did kids assume parents existed only after their birth? He was disappointed in his foolishness.

"Social workers relocated us. I won the prize for the worst next home. My couple was early fifties, and heartless. They took in a few children to help on their pig farm during the notorious time. Nearby wild Newport, a bustling metropolis and booming gaming town filled with illegal gambling and prostitution run by mobsters. Pigs' sole purpose—they masked stench of home-brewed liquor from a still atop the hill. Roaming freely over the hillside, the creatures buffered the odor. Trucks delivered loads of stale bread and food scraps as slop from Newport restaurants and dumped it for the swine. It stunk to high heaven. So did the critters. Aroma so rank no one distinguished mash cooking farther up the hillside, scent deterred hunters, and neighbors avoided walking along the road. Trucks returned to Newport gaming clubs and casinos loaded with liquor. The productive business earned the old couple a substantial living though they had to cower to gang men they served. Wads of money were paid when drivers picked up the brew. The cash business avoided income tax, and the stingy couple didn't waste dough feeding kids. We salvaged bread and meat enough to keep us alive before dumping slop to the hogs."

Richard hesitated as Justin cleared his throat thinking the lump in it would suffocate him.

"Saying they treated us poorly is an understatement. The hardest job was fetching water because we had none at the house. We walked a few miles to a spring and filled jugs and buckets we lugged home for dishes, baths, and drinking—the easy part. Hauling several loads every day to the top of the hill for the still was worse. It took two of us pushing and one pulling a wagon loaded with heavy pails. As a puny thing when I arrived, let me tell you, after months of it, I built muscles. The old folks worked us hard from sun up to way past dark. Without electricity a pot belly stove in the living room heated the place, but they shut the upstairs door so heat wouldn't rise there, keeping the downstairs warmer. The kitchen stove put out heat, but the drafty shack wasn't insulated and had no upstairs vents, so we didn't benefit from minimal warmth there was. Doing homework by a dim oil lamp light in our frigid attic was difficult, but I enjoyed it. Dressing in layers, wearing what few clothes we owned helped, and we crammed together in a bed under a stack of thick army blankets. I could see my breath in cold night air but we survived. In summer we spread pallets on the floor. The bigger boys claimed the bed. I didn't fight for it. I'd slept on the floor in worse places."

Justin shuddered, and his stomach grew sour.

"As their money ticket and free labor, they feared we'd run away. It had happened before. So they locked us upstairs at night. The mister was especially mean when he went on the bottle. We avoided him because he enjoyed giving a beating when he was drunk. The old gal disappeared those times, but we couldn't avoid him. If he couldn't find the old gal to punch around, he unlocked our door and picked a child to take frustration out on. I tried being inconspicuous and prayed not to be noticed, but occasionally I found my turn at battle. He broke my nose, and another time busted an ear drum. I've not heard well out of my right side since. I had a concussion from a beating with a weeklong headache. I couldn't sleep fearing I might not wake up. At seventeen, I swore I'd never let him hurt me again. The old gal saw him stagger downhill and took refuge with a neighbor. He tired of searching for her banging around downstairs. Cussing, he stomped downstairs screaming a pig with a litter had died. Hearing him unlock the attic door we tried to prepare for the worst. Tension felt pliable. I forced my breathing slow and quiet pretending to sleep. Fully clothed wearing my shoes huddled beneath the covers I hoped he wouldn't choose me. He reeked of liquor and sweat. Eyes closed feeling his piercing stare I lay still hoping he'd move to the next bed. He jerked my covers off and grabbed my arm shaking me so violently my ears rang as he spit the words. You little piss ant, where do you get off sleeping when there's work to be done? A dead pig needs attending to. You and me are gonna' play. I'll teach you a thing or two. You'll drag the nasty-assed sow to the burn pile. He pulled back his fist preparing to punch me in the face. I didn't know what to do, but determined he wouldn't hit me again. No one was. I picked up the only thing within reach—a chain found in the old barn hung on my bed. I reached behind and swung with all my might toward his face. It caught him by surprise. He didn't expect a fight. I screamed. "No, you old bastard, I've learned enough from you." I hit him again and again. Red drizzled from his nose as it hung crooked. His hands swung in front of his face trying without success to grab the chain. I kicked him in the balls, and he doubled over. I hit him over the head with the thick cable again. Blood spurted from his skull. He fell and passed out still breathing. Afraid, I didn't check his pulse. If he came to and grabbed me, I'd never live to see another day. I stuck the chain in my overalls and ran. The others shouted for me to go. I kept running along the road for a ways then into the woods in case he followed. I climbed over the hill and across the other side to another road then kept walking and walking until I came to a town."

Justin ached for the poor kid who had beaten the old farmer in self-defense. He took slow, even breaths. He avoided his dad's eyes, afraid he'd break into tears. They didn't need it. His dad needed patience and understanding, and for Justin to remain silent. The least he could do for the gentle, kind man he knew Richard to be. He had never seen him raise a finger in anger, or lose patience with anyone.

A nightmare or a depraved movie plot—too awful to be real, but Richard didn't make it up. Why would he? How much more horror had he faced?

Richard eyed him. "You okay, son?" He laid a hand on Justin's hand.

"I am, but I'm shocked you could be so normal after the nightmare you lived as a child."

Richard coughed to clear his throat. "I'm beat. Would you mind if we table the rest of this story until after the weekend? I need to get to bed now. Becky and her son are coming to visit.

Justin took his thin, cool frail hand. "Sure, Dad. Let's get you to bed. We can fish next week alone and if you're up to it, you can tell me the rest of what you want me to know."

Richard nodded and moisture pooled in his eyes. He swallowed hard.

"Don't worry, Dad. It's going to be fine. I love you."

"And I love you, Son. Witnessing what a

wonderful man you've grown into makes everything worthwhile."

On cue Sadie walked in to help Richard to bed. "How's my favorite patient?"

"Is it all I am to you, Sadie? I believed you were falling for my charms." Richard winked.

She stepped beside him, helping him out of his cozy chair and walked him toward his bedroom. "Now, Ricky, I'm hopelessly in love with you."

A satisfied grin on Richard's face gave Justin a chuckle inside. His harmless flirting with the spunky nurse fueled his system. And Sadie encouraged his humorous banter, like she enjoyed it as much as Dad.

Richard smiled adoringly. "I'm exhausted. My chest aches like a massive weight rests on it."

Sadie popped a pill into his mouth. "Put this under your tongue. It will open blockage and relieve pressure and pain." He did as asked.

"Is he okay?" Justin followed standing in the doorway as Sadie helped Richard change into his pajamas.

"He'll be fine. Ricky needs a good sleep." She winked as Richard slipping his shoes off. She unbuckled his belt and slid his trousers off. She pulled the top over his head and slipped the trousers up, yanking them to Richard's waist.

He lay back smiling. "Thanks, sweetheart. You're a blessing."

Sadie kissed him tenderly on the forehead and covered him with the blanket. "See you in the morning."

"Goodnight."

♥♥♥♥

They quietly left the room. Sadie closed the door and stopped in the kitchen to record the episode and medication in a journal. Afterward she joined Jason on the deck. His head hung between his knees—hands on the back of his head. His body visibly shook.

"You okay Jason? Can I get you anything?" She placed her hand on his back.

He didn't attempt to hide tears. He reached out to her, and she drew him into a hug. Head on her shoulder, his body racked with pain as he cried unashamed. Once spent he regained control, pulled away and wiped with the handkerchief she handed him.

"I'm sorry, but thanks for your patience and for taking care of Dad. You're wonderful with him."

"No worries. You've nothing to be sorry about. Vast emotions go with this situation. A good cry is the best medicine. I understand what you're going through. Becky and I lost our parents when I was sixteen. It's tough. What you're feeling is normal. I'm sorry you and Ricky are going through this. I wish I could do more."

"Believe me. You're a godsend. I don't know what we'd do without you. Stress got to Dad today talking about unpleasant stuff. We weren't arguing, but he shared things he wanted me to know. Dragging up old memories upset him terribly. It's understandable, now I realize what he experienced."

"I see. Stress is hard on his condition. However, it's good to get things off his chest. The same goes for you. Anything you want to say, do it while you can." She laid a gentle, friendly hand on his cheek.

"Is he going to be okay?" His voice broke.

"Probably, he weakens by the day. Ricky has life left in him. We'll take it one day at a time."

"Thanks Sadie. Thank you so much." Life drained from his body. Justin went numb and limp.

"Of course, it's why I'm happy being here for you both. You're exhausted. Why don't you take a shower and hit the sack?"

"Great idea." He headed to his room as she left the cabin.

♥♥♥♥

What a nice man he is. He cares desperately for Ricky. It's beautiful to watch. Her heart quickly filled with love for both of them.

Sadie spent a quiet evening on her porch reading and watching the sun set. Chirping birds helped themselves to meals from feeders placed throughout the resort as they sang happily enjoying the lovely evening. The calm lake appeared flat as a gleaming satin sheet. Massive sky splattered with sparkles without a cloud to mask stars. A sliver of moon hung low over a pine-studded horizon.

This resort owns more than its fair share of heaven.

Life was good, and she was fortunate

occupying the idyllic setting on a stunning, glorious night, cherishing every moment of precious life.

CHAPTER 12

Richard and Justin sipped their last cup of morning coffee while Sadie washed dishes bustled about doing laundry and straightening the cabin.

Justin hardly slept after their discussion, struggling to understand how the man who raised him could be the tortured child in Richard's story. It changed nothing between them.

"Tell me, Son. You sounded hot and heavy with the Tennessee gal before you broke up with her. You hinted she didn't believe the relationship over. Is she waiting for you?"

"I hope not, but probably. She thinks I'll come around after a while. I won't. I'll need to deal with Yancy at some point, but not yet. I'm letting her cool off. Maybe she'll see I'm right and will go on with her life."

"Yeah, sure, you know how reasonable women can be." He snickered. "You didn't love her?" Richard eyed him sideways.

"I had lust with Yancy, not love. I've never loved any women. I enjoyed them. We had fun. But I never considered a permanent relationship. I courted the sort of gal who didn't want permanence either. Yancy came along when it was time to settle down. My career would benefit from having a wife. I'd have married Yancy and made the biggest mistake of my life, if I hadn't gotten my head on straight."

"Don't you want marriage?"

"I did, but only because of the benefits involved. It feels like a lifetime ago. Tennessee is a fuzzy dream at this point. I hit the pause button, like when you're watching television and need to pee." They laughed.

"You're returning to Tennessee to finish the dream—when this is over?" Richard eyed him curiously.

"Not so sure; maybe, but not with Yancy, the appeal has faded. I don't know what I want. I *don't* want to dwell on it—not now, anyway. My career was fun. Even with the success I wasn't fulfilled." He shrugged watching his dad's reaction. "Yancy's not my future. We're over. So is the partnership with her father. It would've never worked for me. I realize it now."

In his quest to make his mark on the world, Justin had been a fool. He had discounted the idyllic location to do it in.

He stretched breathing fresh, country air letting it exhilarate his senses. Lake air was invigorating. Peace and quiet worked its magic. Simple, slow country life started healing Justin from outside in.

"What do you want now?" Richard cocked his head one way then the other.

"Not sure, Dad. I'm happy here living in the moment. I'm surprised how intrigued I've been, working for Ben Franer. I like helping people with their troubles. It's different from corporate law, more personal. No corporation gifts you a jar of homemade jam, a loaf of zucchini bread, a bucket of green beans or fresh eggs when they come for consultation." They laughed, but Justin became serious.

"People are considerate, nice and don't treat me like a shyster lawyer. They act like I'm a friend helping in a time of need. It's great."

"It's about career. What about personal life?"

"Who knows? Maybe love will find me, like you said."

"It sounds like you've found your calling." Richard knew better than to push too hard.

Justin felt him holding back, impressed at the lack of pressure. "It's something to consider."

Richard changed the subject. "Sadie's sister sure is a sweet thing. Don't you think? She treated me well at the hospital. Sadie will be happy having her here this weekend." Richard glanced sideways without turning his head. He appeared to try not to laugh but couldn't help it. "You should see the smile on your face."

Justin laughed. He hadn't realized Richard could read him so easily.

"Becky will be here around five o'clock tomorrow. I plan to grill and show her around tomorrow evening. I can't wait to meet her boy. She sounds like a good mother and is extremely proud of Evan. She talks about the boy constantly."

Justin's insides quivered jumpily thinking of Becky, like he'd swallowed a school of minnows swimming around in there. The chance to know her better filled him with anticipation and wonder. He was keen to explore whatever might happen between them.

Strange getting a chance at something wonderful, when my world is shattering.

Friday came quickly. Time flew at the resort while Richard and Justin struggled to make the best of it.

For Becky the week drifted slowly, anxious to see Sadie and Richard, and more so to see Justin. He had captivated her. Justin was special. Unintentionally he cast a spell capturing her willingly, like a magnet she couldn't resist. Great on one hand, but on the other, it scared the bejeezus out of her.

She made a promise to allow whatever happened between them to develop naturally. New for her, she usually avoided entanglements. Tired of mourning her history and being a recovering victim, she readied to enjoy a life free of baggage the past saddled her with, open to new experiences, and maybe love.

Finally Friday rolled around, and she drove with butterflies fluttering a silly dance in her stomach. More excited than she wanted to admit, she giggled like a schoolgirl as she pulled into the resort. Evan gawked animatedly chattering about his hopes for their visit.

"We're here, Mom," Evan squealed. Peeking across the dashboard his head spun from side to side taking it in. "Look. They have a pool and a playground with a tree house. There's a beach at the lake with a float in the water."

A sign welcomed them to Shady Pines Resort. This vacation provided an opportunity to know the men better, especially Justin. His intense draw akin to how bees being lured to honey instinctively.

Becky never considered welcoming another male into her life. She kept telling herself she wanted to be Justin's friend—a lie. She vowed to stop denying an attraction like none she'd experienced, not with her husband. Giddy inside like a teenager, she felt carefree.

Justin treated her as though worthy and whole, and she felt strangely safe. She owed herself the opportunity to explore what so obviously pulsed between them. Scared out of her wits, it might be more than she could handle. She couldn't turn away and forget him. She needed to see where her strange longings led.

Go with the flow. Relax and enjoy it.
Easier said than done.

Evan acted nearly as excited. "We've never been to a lake. Will we go out on the water in a boat?"

"I don't know, Evan. It's gracious of Richard and Justin to invite us. It's a wonderful gift. We couldn't afford a vacation like this. Money is too tight."

"I know, Mom. It's okay. I don't mind. But this should be fun, right?" Joy in her sweet son's eyes filled her heart.

"It should be fun, but I don't know about the boat. We'll do whatever they have planned and not ask for more. I expect you to behave while we're here." The worst could happen—they'd have an awful time.

She ruffled his hair fondly. "I bet Sadie is mad to see you. I'm sure she has missed you terribly. She told me so whenever she phoned." Becky patted his leg reassuringly, more for her benefit than his. She trembled inside.

Parking beside the cabin number Sadie told her about, she unbuckled her seatbelt. Sadie ran from a bigger cabin across the lane. Misgivings and fear evaporated as she greeted her sister with a brilliant grin and stepped from the car into Sadie's waiting arms.

"So glad you're here. You made great time." Sadie beamed, looking contented and joyful.

"Yes, little traffic in this direction."

Sadie rounded the car opening Evan's door. "Give me a hug, Little Man." She picked him up and swung him in circles.

Justin rounded the corner toward her. Becky couldn't explain a sudden shock of heat burning her cheeks and rushing southward, settling in her core. *Wow,* this guy affected her like no one had, and she yearned to be close and touch him craving his delightful essence. But she controlled the crazy impulse and smiled casually.

"So glad you came. I've looked forward to it all week. So has Dad." For the first time she noticed slight dimples and wondered how it would taste running her tongue across the tiny cleft in his chin.

Earth to Becky — "Thank you for having us. We're thrilled being here. Evan has been anxious for this weekend overjoyed about the lake. It's not often we get to the country."

They circled the car, and Justin extended a hand to the boy. "You must be, Evan. I've heard a great deal about you and am eager to get acquainted."

"Thanks, Mr. Martin." Evan shook his hand confidently.

Justin appeared noticeably impressed. "You can call me Justin . . . if it's okay with your mom." He glanced at Becky, and she nodded.

"Mr. Justin, thank you for inviting us."

"It's great having you. We have a fun-filled visit planned. I hope you have a great time."

Justin led them toward their home. "Come meet my dad. You can call him Mr. Richard if you want." He glanced across his shoulder for Becky's approval, as she and Sadie followed. She smiled and nodded.

Firm mounds of Justin's behind in tight jeans and his broad, muscular shoulders in a tee shirt made her mouth water. An image of running fingers across those strong shoulders massaging muscle beneath made her involuntarily shiver with delight.

Oh, I've got it bad. Sadie must've noticed her train of vision. When their eyes met, Sadie winked and grinned.

At the deck Justin halted. "Becky, I'll take your bags to Sadie's cabin while you introduce your son to Dad." She hit the clicker unlocking her trunk.

Richard waited elatedly on the deck with arms open for Becky's hug. "I'm so glad you came. We're thrilled to spend time with you and meet your son. This fine man must be Mr. Evan." He winked at Becky.

Richard extended a hand which Evan shook briskly. "Impressive manners and a firm grip for a boy your size. Becky, it's not surprising your son is a champ."

"Nice meeting you, Sir. You can call me Evan. Is it okay for me to call you Mr. Richard? Mr. Justin said so."

Richard nodded. "Perfect." He patted a chair next to his, and Evan took it.

"Thanks for letting us come, Mr. Richard."

"My pleasure, Evan." He patted Evan's knee.

Justin sprinted the two steps to the deck joining them. The air smelled somewhat sweeter as he arrived.

"Becky your bags are in the bedroom on the left with two single beds. Everything you need should be in the cabin. If you need anything else, let me know." He strode to the grill and placed meat on a sizzling burner.

"We're having rib eyes. Sadie said you enjoy steak. How do you like it?"

"Steak sounds wonderful—medium-well, please."

"Evan, what do you want? Do you eat steak? Or should I cook you a burger or a hotdog? I have both in the fridge."

Sweet—considering Evan's needs. Justin didn't appear experienced with the younger set, but he was a natural with her son.

"Steak is good, but no blood. Blood is gross on a plate. I can't eat a big one. So maybe cook me half of a steak. I can't eat as much as a grownup." Becky welled with pride.

"I will make you a whole one. Your Mom can cut the amount you'll eat. We'll put the rest in the refrigerator for breakfast."

"Good idea, if you have enough." Becky joined Richard and Evan at the table. "Can I help?"

"Sit and relax." Sadie told her, comfortable as mistress of the house. "Justin and I have everything under control. We'll eat when the steaks are done."

Sadie entered the house retrieving a tray of plates, bowls, napkins, silverware, and a bowl of salad. Ice filled glasses sat on the table beside an icy pitcher of lemonade.

"Becky, if you want to dish out salad and pour lemonade that would be great." Sadie asked, right at home. It pleased Becky seeing her sister becoming more independent.

Sadie returned to the kitchen and reappeared with a bowl of butter and a couple bottles of salad dressing. Justin started loading plates with a steak, baked potato and garlic bread. They chatted gaily savoring a delightful dinner.

"The steak was cooked to perfection. Thank

you so much." Becky hoped she didn't appear a babbling idiot.

"My pleasure." Justin stood to clear the table.

Sadie jumped to attention. "You guys relax while Becky and I clean up."

"Thanks, Sadie."

Once the table was cleared, they were alone in the kitchen where Becky washed while Sadie dried. "It was nice of them to welcome us here." Becky handed her sister a plate with a smile.

"They're good people, and I'm glad you suggested working with them. They treat me like family and care a great for each other. It's beautiful watching them together. I love it here at this fabulous lake. I could easily become a small town country girl." Sadie gazed blissfully out the window from the sink. From every angle lay spectacular countryside or water.

"You've met someone. Otherwise you wouldn't say it. You have the sparkle in your eyes." Becky eyed her suspiciously.

From first glance something new about Sadie got her attention. She'd chocked it up to newfound independence. But it seemed more. There was a man involved.

"Justin is friends with everyone. It's the type place where people know everything about the others. Sam, short for Samantha, works at the marina. Her husband, Garrett Mason works here too. They're friendly, though he's shy. Garrett is taking over Richard's chores. He's disabled ex-military with PTSD. They hired him in particular to help him settle in, now he's out of rehab. His condition made it hard to find employment. It's sweet and thoughtful of Ricky and Justin."

"It's swell of them; but not what I mean. There's a single male shaking the bushes around my little sis." Becky laughed at Sadie's vagueness and cocked a brow staring pointedly. "I want the poop." She dried her hands and propped them on her hips.

"Well there is someone, maybe." A dreamy haze came over Sadie as she appeared to be picturing the guy and wondering how much to confess. Her sister had good instincts, so if she chose not to share, fine with Becky. But it didn't quell her curiosity.

"Richard hosted a poker party. I figured it to be a bunch of old geezers. But great guys of all ages are part of the group. Jack Barnes, the police chief, is called JJ by friends. What a hunk." The silly expression on her face and way she laughed told more than words.

"Tell me more. I assume you're now friends, so you call him JJ. What happened with this hunk? Tell all time, Sis—spill the beans. I want juicy details." Becky leaned her backside against the sink.

"Minding my own business after leaving them to party, I sat on the porch enjoying the evening breeze reading. JJ came outside to retrieve something. Honestly, I believe it was a ploy to see if I was around. He wanted to talk. After getting something from his car he strolled over to chat and started flirting adorably. He's really cute, blushing, sweet, and eager. I liked him right off. His wacky sense of humor is similar to mine, so we laughed and talked a while. It was fun. He asked me to dinner the next night, but I invited him here and cooked him a meal."

"So, what happened on your date with JJ?" Sadie wouldn't sleep with the guy right away.

"We had a wonderful evening, talked, laughed, and flirted. We kissed. The way he looks at me makes me feel beautiful and cherished. It's great."

"Did you sleep with him?" Saying it outright was Becky's style. Why beat around the bush?

If Sadie didn't want to fork over information, she wouldn't. Not anybody's fool, she wasn't a naive child. Sadie never gave Becky reason to worry, being fairly discerning; proving to be a competent, responsible adult who could take care of herself.

If Sadie became serious about this man, their lives may never be the same. Good or not—no way of knowing. One thing for sure, Becky's love for Sadie would never waver. Sadie's happiness was the important thing.

"Of course not, JJ's a perfect gentleman. He treats me like I'm a precious, rare gem. He touched my face gently like fragile porcelain he feared dropping. It was awesome. Guys hate it when you call them sweet, but he was. He's too much a man to be stereotyped. It threw me for a loop. I've never experienced such an intense moment. I fell limp. If I'd been standing, my knees would've buckled. We kissed and petted, but JJ never pushed, though I could tell he wanted me. He wants to take it slow like he's afraid rushing might destroy something special. He's waiting for the right time. When and if we make love, it'll be perfect."

"Wow. He sounds like a heck of a guy. I approve of your JJ, at least for now. I reserve the right to change my mind if he doesn't live up to your expectations. I can't wait to meet him."

Sadie beamed. "You're getting the chance tomorrow. It's his day off, so Ricky invited him to join our outing. Justin and Ricky have the whole weekend planned. They're considerate and eager to entertain you and Evan."

"It's great. Yes, they're wonderful. I can't thank them enough for their hospitality. I don't want Justin and Richard going to a lot of trouble on our account."

"This is a difficult time for them, but they're dealing. It's stressful when everything is out of your control. They've had good and horrible times this week. They need the distraction and want you, Evan and me to enjoy this beautiful lake. They're exceedingly proud of the place and love the water. Let's make sure this time is fun for them as well."

"Yes, it's a deal. There's no way to change their situation. I'm sad for them. Let's make this a great weekend for everyone."

Sadie glanced at the deck, and Becky's eyes followed. Evan spent much of his time with women. He reveled in attention of the two men—a rare treat bantering. It was powerful watching him delight in their company.

Evan needed to be exposed to good men. She didn't intend on denying him such an experience. It had worked out that way so far. Sadie worked her magic on the men as Becky predicted. Everyone received a benefit from this arrangement.

"They're probably wondering what's keeping us. Let's check on them. I hope Evan isn't being too much trouble." Becky led toward the deck.

Richard laughed at Justin and Evan playing Frisbee and having a blast in the front yard. Justin taught Evan to toss the disk, and the boy was a natural.

"Hey, Becky, Sadie, join us?" Justin waved.

"Not on your life. You guys are too good for me." Sadie sat beside Richard.

"Why not?" Becky shrugged taking the steps.

They played for an hour and had great fun. Finally exhausted from leaping in the air and running circles, Becky patted her belly laughing. "It's been about ten years since I played this game. Thanks, Justin, for keeping me humble and a great way to helping me work off the calories in that delicious steak."

Justin put his arms around her and Evan in a friendly hug. Warmth shot electricity from his body surging through Becky's and finding a home between her thighs.

Whoa. Hold on, Girl; no ideas.

It had been eons since she desired a male. Justin was a nice guy being hospitable. He didn't mean to cause the reaction in her.

He sure is sexy as hell.

She tried chasing thoughts from her mind.

♥♥♥♥

Justin ached to touch her since first laying eyes on Becky today. Cupped beneath his arm, it was all he could do to keep his hug light and friendly.

His mouth watered with the urge to taste those beautiful lips she constantly tantalizingly licked without realizing she did it. It drove him wild. Would she taste of honeysuckle? She was as sweet.

Struggling to control baser urges was new to him. This wasn't a girl he could toy with, not the type he normally dated.

He didn't dare scare her away, and his inside voice told him she'd take her heart and run if he wasn't careful. Nothing evidenced his sentiments were reciprocated. Becky had no such ideas concerning Justin. She came to see her sister, give her son a vacation, and nothing more. He respected that and must keep it light.

"Let's walk to the marina for dessert. There's hand dipped ice cream. I need something sweet after the workout." Justin laid a hand on his flat tummy. He hadn't been to the gym since leaving Nashville.

Getting soft.

"None for me." Sadie shrugged.

"Me either, I'm full from dinner." Richard smiled fondly. "Justin's got a sweet tooth."

"I could use a cone, Mr. Justin. Thanks." Evan hopped to Justin's side and slid his hand into Justin's.

"Not sure I want ice cream, but I'd love the walk. I can meet Sam."

Eager to walk, make a new friend or spend time with Justin? He hoped the later.

She took Evan's other hand, and they set off laughing and chatting along the lane to the marina. Becky was easy to talk to, and he enjoyed listening to her soft voice like a summer southern breeze. Every word came from those pink lips sounded important to his eager ears. He wanted to know this woman, to learn everything about her, but treaded lightly so he wouldn't spook her. She was worth the patience. The more they talked, the more captivated he became.

They cordially met and greeted Sam and selecting icy treats. When Becky wasn't looking Sam caught Justin's eye and wagged her brows saucily, obviously approving and reading his intentions toward the young mother. He smiled, laughing internally. He was easily read, even with his lawyer straight-faced training.

On their walking tour of the resort, Becky licked her cone driving Justin to distraction with longing to taste her perky little tongue. *Good grief, what's wrong with me? Am I that horny?* It hadn't been that long since he'd had sex. Patiently answering Evan's many questions provided a welcome distraction from lusting after the child's mother, and Justin enjoyed the banter.

"Evan has a keen insight for someone so young. His curiosity is thought-provoking. It's going to be stimulating having you around this summer. You do intend to come often. Right?"

Becky didn't curtail her son's inquiry. Her smile was shy as she answered. "I suppose, we could come whenever Evan doesn't have sports events on my days off."

Returning them to Sadie's cabin, the boy ran inside to update his adored aunt. Becky lingered. "I can't tell you how grateful I am for your way with him. It's rare Evan spends one-on-one time with a good man." One by one her reserves fell away, and her manner toward him softened.

"I'm glad you think I'm a good man." The lump in his throat thickened, making it difficult to swallow. "Evan is smart and quick. I was as engaged as he was. I rarely get the chance to see the world through a child's eyes. It's refreshing. Dad is having the time of his life with the boy here. We're getting more out of this visit than you and your family. We appreciate you being here. We'll never be able to thank you enough for all you did for Dad, and for you bringing Sadie into our lives. Dad's crazy in love with her. She's good for us, like a ray of sunshine."

"Evan's over the moon, and I've never seen Sadie as happy. Guess I better go in. It's been a long day. We need to make an early night of it."

Justin couldn't resist the urge, so his hand briefly caressed her arm. His thumb grazed her skin and memorized the innocent touch he would recall all evening long.

"Good night, Becky. Sleep well. See you at breakfast."

"I will. Fresh air and sunshine work magic on the body. Goodnight, Justin." She tiptoed, and her lips pecked his jaw. She sped into the house.

His hand lifted to his face as though protecting it, not allowing the sensation of her soft lips and warm breath to dissipate. It wasn't the air working a spell on Justin.

CHAPTER 13

After a restful night they met for breakfast at the main cabin. Sadie rose early to administer meds and help Ricky get ready for the day.

"I can get around by myself, Sadie." His voice muffled by the bathroom door as he showered, and she made his bed.

"I know, Ricky; but I'm more comfortable being nearby, in case you weaken or needed help. I don't want you overexerting. You must conserve energy so you can enjoy your company."

"I certainly intend to. Evan is something special—reminds me of Justin at that age—full of spit and vinegar, asking how everything works. He's a joy."

"He surely is." She laid his clothes for the day on the bed. "Justin walked to the dock to prepare the pontoon for our outing. He packed a cooler and took it already. We should have a fun-filled day on the lake."

After Ricky dressed, they found the rest of the gang waiting. Breakfast was ready.

Richard never missed an opportunity to

brag. You'd think Sadie was his daughter. "Sadie baked coffee cake, fried ham, egg and cheese omelets and we have fresh fruit for breakfast. I hope everyone came hungry. My mouth is watering, and I'm starved. Sadie's the best cook I know. I gain weight looking at her food."

"Thank you, Ricky." Contentment and pride filled Sadie listening to her patient friend boast. Fulfilled by frequently vocalized appreciation, she had quickly grown to adore these men; and they'd become family.

After breakfast they loaded beach gear into golf carts for a short drive to the dock. Sadie could hardly contain herself, feeling her insides go squirrelly sighting JJ's cruiser parking in the marina lot. Sadie hadn't reacted this way toward a guy since high school, resisting an urge to giggle and jump around clapping.

"I can hardly wait for you to meet him, Becky." Her voice muffled low so the others wouldn't hear, and she tried keeping it steady but the words vibrated slightly. Sadie valued Becky's approval. Powerful emotions for JJ swirled inside making her light-headed, where normally she'd act restrained. The persona melted away at JJ's adorable grin as he peeled his long frame from the police car. She smiled and waved.

"JJ, I assume?" Becky laughed whispering, playfully shoving Sadie's shoulder bringing her out of her daze. "So this is the hunk."

Sadie nodded and grinned. JJ smiled adoringly when his gaze locked on Sadie. He jogged the gang plank toward them and gave Sadie a conspiratorial wink.

"Morning, Ladies." JJ showed off gleaming straight molars. "Miss Sadie." He nodded his head toward her.

"Morning, JJ." Sadie extended a hand. He took it and held it tenderly, first eyeing it then slowly, sweetly brought it to his lips for a kiss. The touch sent Sadie aquiver, and a tingle shot to her core. JJ stepped forward and snuggled her tight against him under one enormous arm. "Hey, Babe." He grinned into her eyes, and she felt precious.

"Becky, this is JJ, Chief of Police Jack Barnes. JJ, meet my sister, Becky Simms." Sadie's voice had a slight crack in it, filled with emotion and longing to snuggle closer into his arms.

"It's a pleasure." JJ extended a hand to Becky.

Becky's brows rose, and she half-smiled as though measuring how to respond. She cleared her throat. "It's nice meeting you, JJ. Sadie speaks highly of you."

"It's good to know. She sure misses you two. Sadie talks about you and Evan all the time. I'll tell you right now, I'm nuts about your sister. This spunky, little gal could charm a snake right out of a bird's nest. I'm glad she invited me to join ya 'all today."

JJ's southern twang delightfully rolled off his luscious tongue—a favorite appendage Sadie had recently become acquainted with. He gave Sadie a peck on the cheek. Her face fired hot and her eyes fluttered. "I've been eager to meet ya 'all. Richard and Justin swear you're an angel sent from heaven."

His charming drawl and open nature was winning with her sister, bowling Sadie over more by the minute. The more time she spent with him, the more addicted she became. "JJ, this is my nephew, Evan. Evan, this is Police Chief Jack Barnes."

Evan's eyes grew wide and his mouth opened. JJ extended his hand. Evan shook it solidly. "Good morning, Sir; it's nice to meet you." Evan eyed him curiously.

"Good to meet you too, Evan. I've heard wonderful things about you. Miss Sadie adores you, so you must be special. Ya 'all please call me JJ. My friends do."

"Mr. JJ, you're wearing a cowboy hat. Where's your police hat?" Evan cocked his head sideway questioningly examining his waist. "Where's your gun?"

JJ guffawed properly tipping his hat in salute. "Good observation, Evan. My cap is in the cruiser, and my weapon is locked away in the trunk. It's my day off, so I don't have to wear it today. This hat will protect me better from the sun, and I don't expect to run into criminals on the lake."

"Oh." Evan shrugged and nodded, satisfied.

"Well, I best help the boys out." JJ strode toward Richard and Justin as they finished loading the boat. "Thanks, Guys, for inviting me along. I don't get on the water much, but I enjoy it when I can. It's a treat spending it with such a beautiful family."

"Absolutely, man; we're glad you could join

us." Justin slapped JJ's back companionably.

"You're welcome anytime. The glint in your eye, staring at Sadie showed interest in her. You and she had a nice date earlier this week." Ricky eyed him critically.

"Indeed we did. She's quite a woman—your Sadie." JJ glanced her way, and she waved.

"You be good to her, JJ. She's special." Ricky warned acting like a proud daddy.

"I intend to, Richard. Rest assured." He nodded at the older man and took the minnow bucket from Justin to fill with bait fish. Justin put four containers of night crawlers in a cooler with an ice bottle to keep them cool and alive on the hot day. Their gear loaded onto a lovely pontoon with two Bimini tops for shade. Buttery white upholstered provided ample seating.

Evan squealed. "Look, Mom, it has a slide on the back. Can I try it?"

Ricky grinned proudly and winked at the boy. "We'll give it a whirl when we stop to swim."

Sam cast them off with her cute southern inflection. "I filled the gas tank earlier this morning, so ya 'all are good to go. Have a great time, ya hear?" Ricky signaled from the captain's seat starting the engine as Sam untied mooring and waved.

They cruised at slow speed. Clearing low wake markers, Richard gave it more gas. The boat sped until it cruised on a smooth plane, not fast enough to blow their hats off but enough so chop didn't cause a rocky ride. The men pointed areas of interest while they toured the lake and told stories of good times enjoyed at locations they passed. The group laughed constantly at pranks and tall tales.

♥♥♥♥

Becky was unaware of his watchful eye as they enjoyed the beautiful day on the water. A vision with wind-blown tendrils fluttering haphazardly across her exquisite face gave her an endearing angelic appearance. He ached to touch her face or brush an errant curl away. Was her hair as silky as it looked?

Becky spoke to no one in particular. "What's the rest of the world doing while I'm being pampered on the lake? This is an incredible luxury. I think I died and woke in heaven."

Soon as the words came out, she must've regretted having misspoken. She glanced at Richard with guilt on her face. He smiled assuring her he hadn't taken offense.

Boating stirred breezy air, fresh and cool as they journeyed. Bright blue sky dotted lightly with fluffy clouds proved Becky's description of a heavenly day accurate.

Evan studied the clouds, keeping the adults in stitches. "That one looks like a dog. The other one is an airplane."

"Nah, that one's a bulldozer." JJ laughed joining the game.

Sea gulls flew over, occasionally landing on the surface submerging as they fished for dinner. Sadie gasped pointing. "Look, there's an eagle." She smiled at JJ who nodded. She grabbed her camera attempting to take its photo. "It's too fast for me. I took several shots of sky."

Ricky pointed toward the strip of land on the far bank. "Eagles nest in those treetops at Land Between The Lakes. We frequently see them, and bird lovers flocked here to get a glimpse."

Southward along the channel they admired scenery on the main lake. Ricky extended a hand to Evan. "You ever drive a boat?"

"No, sir, I've never been on a boat before." His eyes widened.

"Well, it is high time you do. Justin drove boats about your age. It's never too early to learn to boat safety." Taking Evan's hand he pulled the boy into his lap. He pointed to controls, explained how things operated, talked about equipment needed and required and why. He discussed courtesy and boating laws. He allowed the boy to steer and gauge movement of the craft in the current.

Becky swallowed hard, watching her son interact with Ricky seeming overcome, observing the three men showing her son extreme thoughtfulness and patience.

Evan soaked it up like an excited sponge, beaming, listening closely interested in everything Ricky said, and eager to learn and please.

After an hour they changed course and travelled north to a hidden inlet barely visible from the channel. An opening brought them into a round cove with towering rock walls painted with colorful graffiti.

"On one hand, I'm appalled people dared paint these boulders. On the other, I'm in awe of their beauty. Each design is more intricate and elaborate than the next. Some were names and dates, but many can only be described as art." Sadie clutched JJ's wrist sitting close beside her on the bench seat. Heat radiated from him through her hand and as their naked legs touched in shorts, they both wore. Their eyes met. Those deep pools like dark-roasted coffee took her breath away.

JJ's sweet smile showed pleasure. "Past partying crews made their marks here. It's a tradition."

Richard stopped the boat in a strategic spot near one bank. Justin grabbed a branch jutting from a shoreline tree as the boat drifted close. He tied the boat so the rocky cliff- shore rested against bumpers hanging from the boat's side, cushioning and protecting the pontoon.

Justin tossed his tee shirt on the seat and dove in. He swam to shore at another angle and tied a rope JJ tossed him to another tree mooring them along the majestic stone wall. Justin swam back to the boat and climbed the ladder.

Becky gaped at him with wide eyes breathing erratically, as Justin snatched a colorful towel and began blotting water streaming across his suntanned, muscular chest. His arms bulged with nicely defined muscles. Sadie stifled a giggle.

Becky likes what she sees.

"He's a hunk, isn't he?" Sadie whispered so only Becky heard.

Becky shook herself into the moment blinking and smiled pinkly. "Mmmm, yeah, he must work out." She blew out air.

"Party goers come here to cliff dive. You gals game?" Glistening beads clung to tiny dark curls across rolling belly muscles as Justin grinned, swabbing himself.

"Cliff diving? Cool." Evan's eyes begged. "Can we, Mom?"

"May we," Becky corrected, turning to Justin with horror on her face. Shock, excitement and fear played across her face. "I've never done anything so daring."

"Come on, ladies. Let's get to it. Evan, maybe after your Mom tries it, she'll consider letting you jump from a low rock." JJ tugged Sadie to her feet, obviously wanting her to join him in a dive. Justin took Becky's hands and did the same as she hesitantly allowed herself to stand.

Sadie giggled and grinned at JJ. Obviously, Justin barely resisted pulling Becky closer. She'd been right. Justin fancied her sister.

Justin wondered how Becky's bare belly would feel against his. She smelled sweet, sort of floral, and he longed to hold her against his chest and breathe in her scent. Her fragrance drove him crazy sitting near her on the boat ride. Partly why he'd dived into the water for a few seconds of distance. He suspected the delightful scent came from her shampoo, and it suited her. How could he maintain his cool with her unaware of her delightful seductiveness?

"I don't know about this." Becky returned to her seat. Justin didn't release her hands—*damn, soft*. It made him wonder about the rest of her.

"Come on, sis, let's give it a whirl." Sadie stepped out of her shorts and tossed her tank top on the seat. JJ sucked in air at the sight of her in a string bikini perfectly displaying Sadie's curves. Cups shaped to accentuate cleavage. She smiled shyly as he let out a whistle. *Yep,* his buddy Jack had it bad for Sadie—*not a bad thing.*

"Becky, don't be a stick-in-the-mud. You're not an old lady. Get off your tush." Sadie begged. "People do this every day. You're a great swimmer. Besides, we'll wear life jackets."

Sadie's eyes pleaded. Sadie tossed her a preserver. Becky winced, having a hard time resisting Sadie's plea. Justin laughed to himself, wagering Sadie got her way often as a kid.

"I guess so. It can't do any harm. I'll give it a try, but not too high. Okay?" Becky's eyes begged Justin, and his heart fell into his stomach. He could deny this woman nothing. She slipped into the jacket and buckled it, obviously stalling for time.

Becky's bright green one-piece suit had high legs, showing off a tiny waist and flat stomach. Justin nearly choked when she laid her sun glasses down. Green suddenly became his favorite color.

"Sure, but you're going to love it." He snatched her hand he'd been dying to hold. He and JJ helped the women climb safely about twenty feet above water level. They hung out there for a few minutes, allowing the gals to get their bearings and swallow their fears.

"What're you waiting for?" Justin grinned and jumped, hitting the water with a tall splash. He surfaced wiping water from his face. "Come on in. The water is amazing. Either put your arms straight above your heads in the air or along your sides when you jump. That way you won't slap them causing a splash burn. It stings."

Sadie jumped five feet to his side yelling, "Geronimo."

JJ followed jumping far enough away to Sadie's side. He came up with a sputter behind her and wrapped his arms around pulling her back against his chest. Her head leaned on his shoulder, and he gently kissed her neck. She shivered and wiggled at the spark his kiss clearly created. JJ smiled knowingly.

Justin's heart ached with jealousy regardless of his happiness for Sadie and JJ. Their budding relationship emphasized his complete aloneness—a new thing for Justin who had never experienced loneliness, even when he'd been alone in the past.

Becky stood nervously jittering alone on the cliff. Justin eyed her curiously. Her formidable, admirable will, clearly wrestling demon fear had no choice but to grin and jump. So she did.

Hitting the water hard a tall splash shot up. She emerged sputtering and laughing. "Wow, exhilarating and terrifying—what a thrill." Becky swiped water from her eyes. "I'm glad you talked me into this. I'd never have done it on my own."

Justin swam to her side. *Extraordinary, one*

of a kind.

"I knew you'd love it."

"Nothing ever gave me a shot of adrenaline like that; thanks, guys. It was fantastic." Sadie gave JJ a peck on the cheek.

Justin and Becky helped Evan, clad securely into a life jacket, and together the three climbed eight feet above water level to a flat rock. Sadie and JJ waited in the water a safe distance from the jump zone ready to help if needed.

Becky took one hand and Justin the other. Together they jumped. They released Evan's hands as they hit the surface so they wouldn't drag him deeper than his own weight would submerge him. They screamed when they jumped and created a beautiful elevated splash simultaneously hitting the lake.

The adults rose quickly. Each reached out to the boy so he wouldn't panic at being alone. Evan surfaced with a huge, priceless grin. "Thank you Mommy and Justin. It was sooooooo much fun."

They boarded the boat again. Richard handed them beach towels, and grateful swimmers wrapped themselves and dried off. Justin released the boat's mooring, and they set sail onto the main body of water. Justin passed bottles of water to everyone and opened a can of salted peanuts for a snack.

JJ snuggled Sadie close. She melted into his arms like she was a part of him and where she belonged. Her head leaned against his extended arm. They appeared relishing heat the other produced, each soaking it up like a sponge. Justin envied the heady feeling of being so comfortable in another's arms.

Richard drove the boat in a wide cove surrounded with sandy beaches on three sides. He guided the boat through shallow water to the shore. Justin jumped off the front onto land and secured the anchor.

"This is a great place for swimming and a picnic." Richard cut the engine.

Sadie and Becky pulled food from the cooler. They set the table for their meal. Sadie had packed a tub of fried chicken she prepared the day before. A bowl of potato salad, a bag of chips, raw carrots and celery sticks with ranch dressing, and a broccoli salad completed their feast. Sadie had prepared an icy jug of lemonade, so Becky loaded plastic cups with ice and poured, surprised at how hungry she'd grown.

"It must be this fresh country air. I can't remember enjoying a meal so much. Thank you, Sadie, for this feast. And thank you, Justin and Richard, for your hospitality. This is lovely." Becky patted her full belly.

"Yes, thank you. It was delicious." JJ fingered a tendril of Sadie's colorful hair. She leaned into him and kissed the tip of his nose.

Evan blew out a gush. "Yeah, this is great. Can we play on the beach? I want to see what I can find. Justin said I can use his metal detector, and he brought a tiny shovel and bucket for my treasures."

"Sure." Becky beamed as Justin took her hand and helped her off the boat.

♥♥♥♥

Becky tried unsuccessfully to ignore energy surging from Justin's touch. The man had an electrical field which shot through her whenever he neared. She longed for him in places she hadn't been touched in years. Heat his nearness generated appealed, and she longed to experience it.

A good thing? It hadn't been her experience in the past, but she wanted to find out.

Becky and Justin strolled along the beach, talked and tagged along behind Evan. The inquisitive boy checked out every shell, piece of driftwood, and odd thing nature washed ashore in search of *treasure.*

They laughed at his many questions. Justin patiently answered every inquiry patiently, taking time to explain about tides. Fascinated, Evan and probed for more. Justin acted impressed with the boy's inquisitive mind.

Justin instructed how to use the metal detector covering every aspect of its operation. Evan listened intently to different sounds it made while holding it above the sand. He stopped occasionally to dig until he found the bounty. Within an hour, he had accumulated two dimes, sixteen pennies, a quarter, and a nickel. He also located an old wedding band thinned by years of wear and its uneven, chipped surface roughened by the environment. Evan presented the ring beaming proudly.

"Look what I found you, Mommy."

"Wow, it's quite a find. I'll clean it and wear

it on a chain. It's too lovely to not be displayed."
She put it carefully into her shorts pocket so that she
wouldn't misplace it.

Sadie joined them on the beach. They sat in
the sand building a giant castle. Finally covered
with sand, they swam and washed off.

Justin and Becky took Evans hands. They
led him into deep water where he exclaimed
excitedly. His life jacket kept him bobbing about
alone, enjoying the floating sensation of the current.
Adults never far from him, didn't want him to get
scared or for current to pull him too far along the
shoreline.

Taking turns splashing each other, they
played like children in refreshing water. After
drifting far enough along the beach, they headed
back toward the boat.

Becky glanced around for Sadie. She and JJ
weren't on the beach or boat. Finally she spotted the
couple, shoulder deep in the water shaded by the
craft, floating locked in a romantic embrace
engrossed in a kiss.

Discerning Sadie wouldn't act that way
unless it had grown serious. Becky hoped Evan
hadn't noticed. She dreaded his probing questions
concerning Aunt Sadie's new flame.

By the time they reached the boat Sadie and
JJ climbed on deck. Sadie's sappy, dreamy gaze
proved her taken with JJ. Becky hoped him the
good man he appeared for her sister's sake. She
didn't want Sadie hurt, but seeing Sadie happy
brought Becky tremendous pleasure.

Remembering their passionate kiss, she

longed for the same from Justin. It was silly, but she couldn't deny longing to taste him, or yearning for a touch of his arms holding her tight.

I'm being foolish. Justin doesn't see me that way. He's being kind, thankful for my bringing Sadie to them. Stop fantasizing. I'm a grown-ass woman, not a dopy teenager.

Evan played in the water for a few more minutes laughing and splashing as he took turn after turn gliding into the water from the slide. Eventually exhausted and thirsty, they rinsed sand off and climbed aboard. Justin helped Becky up last.

Familiar electricity pulsed through her. Heat centered in her middle at his touch. Did she imagine it? Or did his hold on her waist linger longer than necessary?

❤❤❤❤

Justin turned away releasing Becky's waist. Soft, warm, satiny skin, she weighed nearly nothing. With his hands on her waist, he pictured himself a giant easily lifting her into his impatient arms. He burned to cuddle her naked against his flesh.

Taking a deep, cleansing breath, he closed his eyes and regained his calm.

Becky appeared to be a complex female. Justin's emerging longing for her grew stronger by the minute. She began dominating his thoughts continually growing on him becoming a part of him, an essential part. But she wasn't his woman.

He tried unbearably to curb his need for her,

and he didn't want to. Justin wanted Becky—badly. He needed a handle on his mental state, take it slow and not risk scaring her away.

Appreciative of the distraction, he lifted the weighty anchor onto the pontoon. He pushed them into the surf and jumped aboard. It gave him time to change his train of thought.

Easy boy, this is important—real. This woman is special. Be careful with her and don't scare her away.

Not just another conquest, his heart recognized Becky as his future, the essence of happiness, his chance to have it all. He would not shatter it before could develop on its own. He'd be a gentleman and curb his instincts. He'd woo the lovely creature hoping she'd grow to love him as well.

Love?

Yeah.

He sat on the deck floor observing the comfortably, casual group. The beautiful girls' wet hair curled deliciously around their faces as they laughed at a comical comment JJ made while toweling off. Evan smiled sipping a juice packet. Richard appeared satisfied and content expertly guiding the craft from the bay.

Justin was the luckiest guy in the world, here and now with these people living in the moment—more than he deserved, more than he realized he wanted. They were his chosen clan. His heart understood it before his brain followed suit. He'd forever treasure the memory of this day.

Evan moved making room between him and

his mom. "Sit by me, Justin."

Had he died and gone to heaven?

The space was tight, but he didn't mind. To fit in the cramped area Justin slid an arm around Evan and Becky. Eyeing her questioningly he tried adjusting his arms. She didn't appear concerned, only nodded. His arm across her back was right where it belonged.

They stopped in another bay with a rise of rocks beneath the middle. A hill crest had once been there before the land flooded creating the lake Richard explained. He expected they'd catch some beauties here in his favorite catfish hole.

Justin set the anchor and selected a rod. The pole, built to take a beating with a closed-bale reel, had been Justin's favorite. He had owned it since he was sixteen. The other men did the same.

Justin baited the hook with a night crawler and explained to Evan attaching a bright orange and yellow bobber on the twelve-pound- test line, explaining what he did the whole time. Evan listened intently.

Justin instructed how to operate the reel and how to cast. He knelt behind the boy wrapping his arms around him and showed him exact movements of a proper cast. He told him where to aim for the best chance at getting a bite. Evan did exactly as Justin explained. Evan executed a successful cast then grinned at his mom bringing tears to her eyes.

Becky smiled. "I'm so indebted to you and Richard for being patient and attentive."

Justin stifled the urge to throw his arms around her and kiss her. Instead, he helped Becky with another rod and reel so she could fish. JJ assisted Sadie with hers, and soon everyone had a line in the water.

Richard caught a couple of nice catfish about twenty inches long. He put them in the live well and deemed they would be supper. Justin caught one about twenty four inches long, hefty and strong. It took a few minutes to play the fish until finally it tired enough to net it.

Sadie caught a couple of small sunfish which they threw back, and a baby catfish. She and JJ had fun fishing off the back of the boat lost in conversation. The two of them were learning about each other the way new lovers did. They seemed compatible, held similar values, and shared many likes and dislikes.

Too busy netting fish to catch anything of his own, Justin ran constantly from one end of the vessel to the other helping someone by netting a fish. Each time he checked his own line, something had stolen his bait. He didn't care. This was more fun than he'd enjoyed in years.

Having the time of his life, Justin had forgotten how much enjoyable fishing and boating could be. Even more exhilarating with Becky—and her family, it seemed perfectly natural like it was supposed to be this way. Fondness for the inquisitive boy, not to mention his sexy mommy, brought joy Justin had never before experienced. Swamped, emotions rolled over him and left him full of hope and happiness.

Evan caught a bluegill. Richard deemed it large enough to eat, so Evan beamed with pleasure depositing it into the live well. He caught a yellow bass and threw it back. Finally he hooked a catfish. It took a super dive without warning heading straight to the bottom. Submerging the bobber, it tried to make a get-away with his bait. Evan did as instructed, jerked the pole upward and kept the rod high as he fought the weighty fish.

"Keep reeling, Evan." Richard hopped up excitedly. "Don't give him any slack.

The end of the pole flexed and bent allowing the fish to move about without breaking the strong line. The sturdy rod did its part and stood up to a beating. Evan struggled with the weight of the strong fish. Squaring his feet he braced as the strong catfish swam, fought, and dove one way and the other.

"Hold the pole here with your left hand. Keep the other on the handle." Justin demonstrated placing the butt end against the boy's stomach and pushed the handle against his belly for leverage.

"This will keep his pull from hurting your wrist. Play him, son. Let him run until he tires. When he stops pulling, reel. Don't crank while he is running though. It would twist the line on your pole." Justin had never been so anxious to land a fish before.

Evan did as instructed. Finally the fish tired enough to bring him close to the boat. When the creature viewed the craft it jumped out of the water and wiggled in air before splashing back into the deep. The crowd watching gasped loudly oohing and aweing. Evan reeled him closer.

"Wow, did 'ya see it?" He shouted.

"Backup, Evan, until he's close enough so I can net him. Keep your pole high." Justin approached the edge manned with the net as the boy walked backward. Justin reached with the mesh tool and lifted the huge fish onto the deck.

"Wow, he is a hog." Justin sighed appearing as spent as the flopping creature lying in nylon webbing.

"Man, I figured I'd never land him. He's enormous and so strong." Evan beamed with happiness. Justin helped the boy hold the sizable fish so Becky could take a photo with his trophy.

"Take one of me and Justin together, Mom. I want to hang it on the wall in my room. Without Justin's help I'd never have caught this monster." They posed together, Justin kneeling beside Evan holding the impressive fish in front of them.

"Now what do we do with him?" Evan glanced from Richard and Justin. "He's at least twenty three inches long. Can we let him go?"

"Sure, he is a good size to breed. Let's toss him back so he can make more catfish for us to catch. He's too big to eat, anyway. Smaller ones taste better." Richard glowed with pride in his new prodigy.

Evan tossed the fish overboard proudly observing him swim away.

"Time to go." Richard fired the engine.

Sadie smiled sweetly, snuggled beneath JJ's arm. "Yes, Ricky, you could use a rest. We've all had enough sun for the day."

"You're right. I'm beginning to tire. We have enough fish for a good meal." Everyone agreed, so Justin pulled anchor.

They chatted having a great time while cruising across the main channel into the bay toward the marina. The men loaded gear into the golf carts, and they left the fish in the boat for now, returning to the cabins.

Sadie helped Richard prepare for a nap.

Justin placed a hand gently on Becky's arm, unable to resist the innocent touch.

"Can Evan help me clean the fish?"

"I guess so, if he wants to." She glanced at her son who obviously thrilled at the idea. "Be careful around the knives." Her cocked brow warned. She flashed a brilliant smile on Justin. "You will watch out for him. Right?"

"Of course, we'll be very careful, but I'll let him help. He can learn knife safety." Justin winked at her so Evan didn't see, and when she smiled brilliantly back his heart received a double jolt.

"Okay, be careful."

Justin stuck a zip-lock bag in his back pocket and secured his filet knife on his hip. They took off in a golf cart.

❤❤❤❤

JJ took Sadie aside out on the deck, leaned against the rail and grasped her hands pulling her to stand between his legs. He kissed her gently and briefly running hands into her hair and holding her face so their eyes locked. "I had fun today, Babe. I don't want the day to end."

"Well, don't go. Stay for dinner. We're

having catfish." She gave him her most sparkling smile.

"I hoped you'd go to dinner with me. Your sister is here with her son; but honestly, Justin would appreciate alone time with them. He acts seriously into your sis. I promised my brothers I'd meet them at the theatre to hear Bobby. He's a steel worker by trade, but plays a mean lead guitar. The regular guy's wife went into labor this morning and may be having her baby by now. Anyway, he needed to be with her, so arranged for Bobby to sub for him when the time came. It is tonight. Please come. I'd invite Becky and Justin, but the little guy is plumb tuckered out, and there would be no one to stay with Richard."

"Wow, it sounds exciting for your family."

"It is a rare treat for Bobby to play with pros. I promised to be there so I have to go. I wish you'd join me. You'll have a swell time. It is country and bluegrass skillfully done, and they put on an entertaining show. Say you will."

She was being sucked into those smoldering pleading eyes without reservation. "It sounds great. You sure you're ready for me to meet your family? Tell me about them." Quivering in her middle region announced her nervousness. Things moved fast with JJ, but she couldn't bring herself to slow them down.

"It'd be an honor. Kelli's a dentist. She and Bobby have a one-year-old cutie-pie, Bobby Jr. He'll be home with a sitter. Mason and Sara will be there. He's an insurance adjuster, and she teaches high school. They have a ten-year-old son, Levi.

The kid's a hoot with a wacky sense of humor.
You're going to love him. He's into music like his
dad, so his mom insisted he learn piano. But he
wants to study guitar and banjo. She promised him
lessons once he masters piano. I doubt he'll be
there. They don't usually let him stay up late, and
the show ends at eleven."

"Wow, they sound like a cool bunch." Her
jitters began settling, but she continued feeling the
drumroll in her nervous belly.

"After the show we're going to the new
restaurant in Paducah for a late supper. It's called
the Avenue. Their burgers are the size of a dinner
plate, and it's supposed to be fabulous. We've been
anxious to try the place. You game?"

Sadie considered it a couple of minutes
while helping herself to kisses around his neck. She
delighted in driving him insane as his neck stretched
upward, eyes closes, and he moaned. He relished
the tender torture, and his hard response pressed
insistently against her belly. She should cool it
before someone noticed his bulge. Backing away
still holding his hands she devilishly chuckled.

"Let me check with Becky. If she's okay
with it and doesn't mind seeing to Richard's meds
tonight, I'd love to go." She winked glancing at his
waning erection and grinned wickedly. She spun
and skipped into the house leaving him humming,
trying to make it disappear before he caused a
scene.

Justin and Evan finished cleaning fish, and
Justin parked their cart beside the cabin. Evan took
the two steps onto the deck to JJ.

"Mr. JJ, you won't believe this. Justin cleaned the first fish. He let me hold the knife and showed me how to do it, so I cleaned the next one. It was awesome."

Becky and Sadie had stepped outside in time to hear the news. She sat with her glass of iced tea, and her face paled. "Tell me about it."

Evan leaned against the inside of her right leg. "Mom, it was so cool. I know how and could do it alone now. I listened to everything Mr. Justin said. I remember how to do it. When I got the feel of it, it was easy, easier than I thought. You'd be grossed out though. There is like blood and guts and stuff. But don't worry. If you catch a fish, I'll clean it for you, so you won't have to do the gross stuff. You can cook it. Okay?" The little guy had it figured out.

Becky laughed at her adorable son and ruffled the hair falling onto his forehead. "Sounds good to me, but you're young to be wielding a knife alone. Right?" Becky eyed Justin sternly and put her smile on for Evan.

"I guess so. Mr. Justin told me the same thing. But he said it would be okay if he held my hand and controlled the knife." Evan's enthusiasm vanished, and he appeared scared of being reprimanded.

"I see. It sounds okay with me too." Becky's words came out soft and easy, and she smiled at Justin with an expression asking forgiveness for her momentary lapse assuming the worst. Justin's brilliant grin shot Becky's way assuring, she hadn't offended him.

Justin took the filets into the house to wash and soak them in salty lemon water before dinner.

"There will only be the four for dinner, Justin. I'm going with JJ to meet his family and see his brother play at the Opry if it's okay with you. Will you and Richard be comfortable and do you mind entertaining Becky and Evan without me?"

Justin glanced at JJ and winked. "Of course, go. Have a good time. Becky and Evan are in good hands. We're going to grill catfish, eat my famous potato salad, Dad's favorite cole slaw and have a feast. I plan to make homemade hush puppies. Sure you all don't want to eat before you go?"

"We'd love to, but the show starts at seven. Once Sadie finishes getting ready, we're going to stop by my place for a quick shower and change, and be on our way. We don't want to be late for the performance. I want good seats, and time before the show starts to introduce Sadie to everyone."

"Grab a snack while Sadie gets dressed." Justin pointed to the tray of vegetables, salami, cheese, crackers and dip Becky placed on the picnic table. JJ helped himself.

Sadie walked off to prepare, promising to return in half an hour.

♥♥♥♥

JJ did a wolf whistle when she sauntered toward them from her cabin. Her black, low-cut tank top dress of silky fabric clung to her curves. The glint in JJ's eyes and the way he rubbed his fingers together hinted at his eagerness to touch it.

The bias-cut hem made one side fall above the knee and the other halfway between knee and ankle. Black and silver fringe caught light glittering from her sultry sway. High-heeled black ankle boots with shiny silver chains hanging around the cuffs emphasized her long, lean legs. One side of her hair was pinned high above her ear with a sparkly silver comb. The pink streak fell sexily blanketing her right cheek. Matching eye shadow looked sexy as hell.

Becky swallowed hard. Her little sis had grown into a full-blown woman, sensual and strikingly beautiful. Poor JJ had no idea what struck him. He acted ready to swallow his tongue any second and might turn blue soon if he didn't catch a breath.

"Wow. You look amazing." JJ gasped sounding a low growl.

"Aunt Sadie, you're beautiful." Evan gushed, throwing his arms around her hips, hugging her tight.

She mussed his hair, bent and kissed him on the cheek. "Thank you, little man." She turned to her sister. "So Becky, you know where Richard's meds are. Make sure he gets plenty of fluids and eats well before taking evening medications."

Becky nodded. "Sure, Sis. No worries."

"Thank you so much for allowing me to go tonight. I'm excited." Sadie dressed and acted cocky and confident, but tonight a tinge of nervousness showed.

"Nonsense, I'm in great hands with the three men in this house. Besides, I'm exhausted from all the running and swimming today. Fresh country air is draining. I'm happy to see you going out. You deserve a night out."

Sadie obviously adored JJ, and it filled Becky with joy. Becky would never begrudge her that. She fit well into this country life, making her mark on this community, and claiming her people— a good thing. Sadie deserved this. But a tiny part of Becky worried things would never be the same. Would it be a good? Or not?

"Go. Have a great time." Justin patted JJ's back. "Dad and I are tickled to have Becky and Evan to ourselves."

"Thanks, man." JJ drew him into a man-hug. "Have a great time too, pal." JJ winked as he whispered so the girls and Evan couldn't hear, but Becky caught the words. Justin grinned embarrassed at his friend and winked back. Was Justin anxious for alone time with her and Evan? JJ took Sadie's hand, and they strolled to his cruiser.

True to his word, Justin ensured they had a delightful evening. He and Becky taught Evan to play a dice and tile game while Richard rested. Once he woke, Justin made dinner while Becky and Evan kept up the game with Richard watching from the deck.

"Justin, are you sure you don't want help cooking? I don't mind at all, and Richard can play with Evan."

"Nope, you stay put. I don't want anyone learning the secrets to my special dishes. Relax and enjoy." He winked. Richard caught the interchange.

She blushed, returning his smile. "You're

spoiling me."

"You can return the favor making me dinner sometime soon."

"It's a great idea." A vision of Justin lounging in her over-sized lounge chair chatting with her while she cooked him a splendid meal in her beloved galley kitchen sent tingles of pleasure rippling along her back.

Their quiet, comfortable evening together was enormously pleasant. The more Becky spent time with Richard and Justin, the more she grew to enjoy them.

As she washed dishes while he dried Becky chortled. "I must admit, your dinner secret recipes deserve any fame they've earned. It tasted delicious."

Evan skipped in from chatting with Richard on the deck. "Mom, can we walk to the marina again for ice cream?"

Becky grinned at her precocious son, drying her hands and putting them on her hips. "Evan, how can you be hungry already? We only now finished cleaning up dinner. Besides, I don't want to leave Mr. Richard alone."

"I'll walk with him for a cone, if you'll hang out with Dad." Justin's eyes brightened as though anxious to go with the boy.

She brushed Evan's blonde mop with her hand. "Okay, but you be good and do as Justin says."

Squirreling one side of his face Evan shook his head. "Of course, Mom. I know how to behave."

"He does." Justin laughed putting an arm

around the boy's shoulders. "Let's hit it, pal."

They strolled along the graveled hill driveway toward the dock, chatting like two old friends. Becky joined Richard on the deck. "I hope the boy wasn't driving you nuts while we cleaned in there. She sat in the chair beside him.

He reached a frail hand and patted hers. "Not at all. I find Evan completely refreshing. It's a delight having him around. You too. We're happy having you both here."

Before long the two males came strutting up the driveway to the cabin. "Look, Mom." Evan boasted stepping onto the deck handing her a bag. We brought you and Mr. Richard some, too." Becky glanced into the bag surprised. "You boys are sweet. Jamocha Almond Fudge is my favorite." She blushed flattered Justin remembered. She'd ordered it the night before and told Sam of her passion for it in passing.

Not only did Justin radiate sex appeal and good looks. A fabulous cook, fun to be with, considerate and thoughtful, surely something must be wrong with the guy. What? She would enjoy him while she could.

After ice cream, Becky helped Richard take his meds and ready for bed. Justin watched from the deck while Evan caught lightning bugs with camp kids. Returning outside, Becky announced bedtime to Evan. Reluctantly he wandered over.

"Thank you, Mr. Richard and Mr. Justin, for the swell time today. Goodnight." The boy gave each of the men kisses then sauntered to their cabin. Filled with pride in her offspring, Becky followed.

Once ready she tucked her boy in bed with a kiss on the forehead.

Feeling antsy, she selected a magazine and wandered to her deck. Something felt undone, incomplete, and she couldn't put a finger on it. She curled into the cushioned swing thumbing through the book without interest.

"Mind if I hang out with you for a while?" Surprised at Justin's voice, she jumped in her seat Her heart skipped a beat at the sight of him.

"It would be great." She extended a hand, and he joined her on the swing. He handed her a bottle of beer. "Thanks." She took a long sip. "Mmmm, it hit the spot."

The sultry hot night grew darker as light fell behind the horizon. Stars started appearing and camp lights dotted the tree line here and there across the lake. Near darkness made it hard to distinguish landmarks and visible skyline in the moonlight. Quiet filled the air. No need to mar it with idle chatter. Justin and Becky sat silently for a while enjoying peaceful tranquility.

"Becky, I hope this doesn't upset you. But I have to share what I'm feeling. I'm touched by how sweet your polite little boy is. I'm falling in love your child. I can imagine how it would be with Evan for a son. I never gave kids much thought, but now I know. I'd love being a Dad, especially if the kid turned out as sweet as yours."

Her eyes glistened in darkness. "It's the nicest thing anyone ever said to me. Thank you. Yes, Evan makes life worth living." She backhanded tears trying not to let him see, but too late. Moonlight caught their glow before she realized they filled her eyes. He didn't mention it, but smiled understandingly.

"Want another?" Heat between them became tangible consuming the air. She reached for the empty bottles. Fingers brushed by accident. Electricity took her breath away. They froze, and their eyes locked.

She inhaled and sighed softly. Her eyes fell to his lips. Her bottom lip slipped in, and her teeth nipped it.

Warmth fluttered in her belly demandingly becoming increasingly anxious to discover more, yearning to hold his hands and feel them on her skin. She hungered to know his taste and experience his breath on her body. She wanted him at least once if nothing more came of it.

She hadn't had sex in years, hadn't given it much thought—until now. Something in her had awakened and Justin fired dormant senses to life. Could she allow herself a fling if the opportunity presented itself? She vowed to shuck her fears at least for now and take a chance. She'd consider it a growing experience.

Ebony sky splattered with brilliant starlight carried a gentle breeze scented of magnolia. Tree frogs chirped a love song. A screech owl howled in a distant forest, and the lake sparkled like sprinkled with diamonds—a magical night, a night of miracles.

Finally Becky's yes tore from his grasp and her glance fell to where their hands met. Each of them afraid to breathe, not daring ruin the moment, neither pulled away. Justin slipped his broad hand around her smaller one. He held her hand for a long time studying it carefully, gently caressing skin with his thumb. He flipped it over and tenderly traced fine palm lines with a fingertip. He bent to kiss the center.

All she managed were jagged breaths as her chest rose and fell heavily. His breath on her skin sent ripples along her spine and she shivered from the heat.

Spreading her hand across his face, he held it breathing in the smell of her, breathing deeply to enjoy her fragrance. His lips stroked soft and firm. His cheeks started growing light stubble, but flesh was smooth and firm. He sucked in first one finger and another, lightly, leisurely gliding his tongue across it, tasting her.

Her shoulders shook as tingles raced up and across her neck. In a daze, hypnotized by the man, she couldn't pull away if she wanted to. She didn't want to. Sensations in her fingertips shot goose bumps covering her body as she longed to prolong each caress. She dared not move for fear of ending the incredible electrifying stimulation she never wanted to end. Capable of nothing more than being motionless and experiencing a profound connection she tried her best to remember to breathe.

Justin kissed the inside of her arm. Casually traveling leaving a trail of kisses he found the inside of her elbow. She shuddered faintly as he kissed her there. He exchanged the hand laying it in her lap and reached for the other. She willingly allowed him, and he did the same.

Her ragged breath seemed to bring him pleasure. His face played a thrilled grin at her occasional sudden intake of air, relishing power to excite her and content in their closeness.

He seemed eager as he tasted her and she yearned for the same treatment on the rest of her body. For now she'd settle for the shivers he sent running up her spine. She wiggled slightly in her seat and moaned. He grinned happily.

Facing each other, Justin took her arms in his hands, and their eyes locked. Words unnecessary, their eyes said everything. He wanted her as badly as she yearned for him.

Justin held her face in his hands and quietly pulled her to him. He kissed her lips gently and let out a sigh. He tasted of mint and chocolate and smelled like thick woodland during an easy rain.

His hands explored her face, pushed a tress from her forehead, and burying a hand in her hair pulled her closer. The other hand on her back lifted her onto his lap. She leaned into his arms and against his firm chest.

Their sweet kiss, soft at first explored with wonderment. Becky's lips allowed entry. Justin accepted the invitation delving into her moist gateway. She savored his taste, and he breathed in her honeysuckle scented hair.

Becky must set the pace. He wouldn't dare scare her away, not now, not when she started coming to him. He'd considered her so far out of reach he became giddy with pleasure at her welcoming his attentions. He wanted to cherish her, and he wanted her to want him. She acted like she was beginning to.

Something precious had finally come his way. He was terrified of spoiling it.

His hands explored her back, gently kneading one direction then the other, stroking her shoulders beneath the tiny tank top. Her silky skin made him hunger to touch her everywhere first with his hand then with his lips.

Becky's kisses grew demanding, and she leaned into him moving in his lap and driving him mad with anticipation. She must've felt pressure from his cock rising to the occasion as she wiggled against his stiff response.

He longed to shuck clothes separating them and touch his begging rod against her bare skin. How wonderful it would be, her bare bottom on his lap this way?

For now he had this and would be satisfied with whatever Becky willing gave, amazed and thrilled she was with him in this way. He suspected more to her past than she'd yet shared, and the asshole she'd married had probably been part of it. *Take it slow.* Hopefully she'd come to him of her own will. He sensed she needed control.

Her hands buried in his hair as she held him to her suckling his ear. She gently nipped it with her teeth and swirling her tongue circled and delved into it. Her heaving breathing caused him to shudder, and she grinned at the response with a brow arched happily. She enjoyed power to affect him, and it thrilled him seeing it in her eye.

She tasted him, gently drawing his tongue into her mouth like a delicious banquet she meant to savor every delightful taste. He would forever remember this moment with the soft breeze gently rifting through her hair. Katydids sang a love song while Becky created a memory he'd cherish for a lifetime.

Driving him crazy with wanting her, she must see what she was doing to him. No mistaking his erection greeting her soft bottom as she wiggled slightly adjusting her seat. He found it encouraging she acted empowered by the state of his pants. It proved all he could do to keep from losing himself when she moved on top of him, and he snickered under his breath, never breaking the kiss.

"God, Becky, I want you so bad I could explode." His whisper in her ear sent her into shivers. He thrilled his hot breath caused her to quake in anticipation—it definitely wasn't fear.

"Want a blanket?" His voice sounded rough and low.

"Heavens no, it is warm tonight and you're making me hot all over." Realizing where they were, she stiffened, glanced around, thinking they had better stop. She stood then, still holding his hands, straightened her clothes and attempted to fix her tasseled curls.

"We can't do this, not here. I'm sharing a bedroom with my son. We can't possibly sleep together in there." She nodded toward the sliding doors.

"It's okay. I want you. You know it, right?"

He barely recognized his voice but the ache in his pants was definitely his.

The porch light off on the dark night allowed them to watch the stars better. With a sensual sideways grin, Becky slid his hand beneath her tank top, uncovering her breast and placed it atop the soft, hot mound of tender flesh.

She whispered, "I want you too, but we can't make love in the cabin with Evan in my bedroom." He tweaked her nipple, and it became a hard pebble between his fingers. He longed to suck it into his mouth and taste her tit.

"It is okay. Let me touch you for now."

Justin played with her nipple between his finger and thumb. He cupped her breast with his hand and moaned hungrily. He slipped her top up, and his mouth covered the erect tip. Gently he sucked and flicked it with his tongue. She tasted sweet, like a flower must taste to a butterfly. He sucked harder and moaned at how the flavor filled his being.

She closed her eyes, and her head fell backward exhaling a soft sigh. Justin's other hand reach around cupping her buttocks, pulling her toward him. Still holding her breast, he began deliberately kissing a trail across her belly to her waist. Her knees buckled, and she leaned into him.

"I never wanted a man so badly in my life. I'm sorry; Justin, but we can't do anything about it now."

"It is okay. We're taking this slowly, anyway. I want you, Becky, but tonight let's not mess this up with a quick roll in the hay. Let's play a little and get acquainted. Let me touch you. Please?" If she'd refused him, it would likely kill him, but it was up to her.

She showed no hesitance on her part as she leaned toward him and pushed her other breast from her bra. He pulled her nipple into his mouth greedily and sucked like a starving man. Both hands explored the shape of her firm, heart-shaped ass. *Geez, she feels good.* Her willingness provided a huge turn on.

"So perfect, so sweet," he whispered without letting go.

He administered to one breast then the other reveling in their taunt, eager tips. Justin pulled her gently toward the swing and sat her on his lap. He covered them with a blanket lying beside them. He kissed her deeply, and her arms circled his neck holding him as though her life depended on it.

He slid the zipper of her shorts open and his hand delved inside. No resistance, her back arched spreading her legs more. The tiniest bit of lace greeted him. Lifting it his fingers caressed slight curls, and he moaned.

Ready for him, she was wet and slick. He longed to give her satisfaction. He cupped her mound tight. She pushed into his palm giving him better access. Justin gently kneaded the area giving her clit friction it craved, as she rocked against his hand.

Never releasing their passionate kisses, he separated her gently with his fingers, flicking her colitis. She wiggled against his hand, and a single finger slipped inside. He nearly came himself—she was so hot and damp. She wanted him. Her experience became the important thing in his world for the moment. He'd never been this euphoric in his life.

He wanted to bury himself deep inside her and experience her tightly gripping him with her sweet snatch. The scent of her juices heady in the air surrounded him, all he could smell, and all he wanted. Needing their taste, he brought a finger to his nose and sniffed. Wickedly smiling he licked. "Sweet." Ready, her body begged for release. His hand returned where it did her the most good.

God. I want this woman.

He had never wanted anyone more. Ready for her too, he did everything he could to keep from coming himself. He couldn't have her right now, but he would give her what she needed. He would give her pleasure. He needed to see her come— needed her to come for him.

Expertly working fingers in and out he massaged. Becky rocked bolder, pressing into him, and he matched her rhythm stronger and fiercer. Her eyes rolled upward and her breath caught as she began panting wildly suppressing a scream. She stiffened then quivered wildly as she came with abandon.

Her juices filled his hand as her body fell limp against him. Her head dropped to his shoulder—a poignant conquest, without protest or regret—a perfect climax.

They sat for a while, enjoying the closeness. Justin thought he had died and gone to heaven. Her orgasm fulfilled his need. If he died now, he'd die a happy man.

Finally in a meek voice whispered, "Thank you; it was incredible." The intimacy brought tears to her eyes. He kissed them away.

"My pleasure. I should thank you." He smiled and tilted her face with his finger so he could kiss her lips.

"Um, you taste good, salty." He grinned.

Reluctant to release her, he held her petite frame close enveloped against his body. His legs crossed hers, and he marveled at how well she fit in his arms.

"This is how it is supposed to be, a perfect fit." She giggled.

♥♥♥♥

She wouldn't deny herself being with this man who proved to be a blessing she couldn't reject. Fulfilled and comforted she sat with his arms around her blissfully wrapped in the blanket listening to his breathing.

"You sure have a monstrous piece of sky." Becky admired the sparkling star scape above.

"Yeah, I'd forgotten how close I was to heaven living here. I never realized how much I missed it." Justin chuckled. "This coming home is an eye opening experience in many ways."

"What will you do later? Go back to your life in Tennessee?" Becky gazed into his beautiful, deep green eyes, the color of a fine emerald.

"Not sure. It feels like another world now. I'm not sure I fit into it any longer. I'm not sure I want to."

"Don't you miss the excitement, nightlife, and culture? What about your friends and job? Don't you miss them?"

It seemed a waste to send this spectacular man back to strangers when she longed to keep him to herself—a fantasy. This was his life.

"I have acquaintances, friends and enjoyed the bustle of the city when there, eager and happy. But that was far away, insignificant and unimportant now. I did the job. I proved myself. I was successful and made plenty money. I had power and created a name for myself. For what, I wonder. I don't know if I want the same things now. It feels like a part of my life I put to bed. Maybe it will be my future, maybe not. I'm not sure. Either way, it is okay. I'll figure it out when I need to. I don't need to now."

"I understand." She kissed him gently and laid her head back on his shoulder. "Don't worry. Live in the moment. Enjoy each day, the way you have been."

He hugged her tight and winked. "I sure have enjoyed this day."

"Mmmm." She snuggled into his arms.

They sat that way until they heard JJ's cruiser quietly roll into the parking spot next to the cabin. They straightened up and sat farther apart on the swing. Becky pushed the blanket between them.

JJ and Sadie walked onto the deck. "Are you waiting for me, big sis?" Sadie laughed, hands on hips.

Becky grinned. "Not at all, simply enjoying

the beautiful night sky."

"Sure thing." Sadie chuckled with a knowing expression.

Justin stood. "Goodnight." He shook JJ's hand and gave Becky a friendly, quick hug.

"See you in the morning." Justin strolled to his cabin.

Becky hugged Sadie. "Good night, Sadie. Goodnight, JJ."

"Night, sis." Sadie grinned as though reading Becky's mind.

"Night, Becky." JJ's deep baritone echoed as she gave them privacy of the porch.

CHAPTER 14

Becky and Evan arrived at the main cabin the next morning for breakfast. Sadie and been up for a while having helped Richard with morning meds, a shower and dressing. "Wow, what a spread. Look, Mom, breakfast is ready. Smell the waffles, bacon, and scrambled eggs?" Evan chattered excitedly taking his seat.

"Yes, Sadie puts out a fine breakfast. You need this fruit." Becky spooned pineapple and strawberries onto his plate while Sadie poured her a cup of coffee. "Thanks, Sis. This looks luscious."

"Sadie's spoiling us. She cooks like this every morning." Justin grinned from the seat between Richard and Evan where Becky had a perfect view of his handsome face. The more she saw of him, the more she wanted to.

They ate heartedly and chatted about the day before laughing at one thing or another. They got along well, like they'd known each other a lifetime.

"I love living here participating in this little family. Living with Becky and Evan was great, but somehow this feels homier, such a comforting family atmosphere. I haven't felt this way since Mom and Dad were around. I'd forgotten how good it felt being part of a big family." Sadie gazed thoughtfully around the table.

"Speaking of which, how did it go last evening meeting JJ's family?" Becky propped her chin on her hands studying her sister's reaction to the question.

"They were wonderful, kind and welcoming. We talked like we'd known each other forever. I really liked them all." Sadie had grown not only independent, but confident and self-assured as well. Little sis blossomed into a well-seasoned woman.

"Dad and I have lots of friends and full social calendars. After Mom passed, our clan dwindled to the two of us. This family atmosphere is a blessing, and we're obliged to have you ladies and Evan as part of our little tribe. It's a luxury having women in the house, and Evan is a special treat." Justin smiled around the table. As his eyes locked on Becky, they communicated a private message only she heard.

Richard beamed from across the table. "Becky, your son has totally stolen our hearts." The glint in his eyes proved his words. He and Justin succumbed to Evan's spell.

The boy focused on dabbing pancakes in a deep puddle of syrup, not listening to the adults. Finally he glanced up. "Mr. Richard, I think you'd make a great grandpa. Mine lives in heaven now, with my daddy. You think maybe you could be my new grandpa?" His eyes held seriously intent on the older man's face.

Becky's heart skipped a beat. She'd hoped Evan didn't miss what he'd never known, but here he sat telling a man he'd begun to bond with something he'd never mentioned before. He missed having a dad and grandpa around. Holding back due to fear had she missed opportunities and selfishly deprived Evan of the family he apparently craved?

"I'd be delighted, Evan. I'd love having you as my grandson." He clasped the boy's hand and held it acting as though he might cry with obvious joy. Becky glanced from one to another. Locking on Justin, he sensed her gaze. His elated eyes brought a tear to hers. He appeared wanting to snatch Evan up, hug and swing him around jubilantly.

The mood broke, and the group finished breakfast. Justin and Richard sipped a last cup of coffee on the deck while the women cleaned the kitchen up. Finally alone, Becky and Sadie anxiously talked.

"So it went well last night?" Becky sought further confirmation. She'd lost her little sister to another life, an adult independence Sadie deserved. It appeared right and good, but Becky needed certainty Sadie was on the right track. In her blood to watch out for Sadie, her goal had been helping Sadie avoid pitfalls she'd been buried in.

"It did. JJ and his brothers get along well. They cut up and tease, but fondly like it's a game they play. Their women are kind and happy. I can tell they adore each other and their children. JJ dotes on the younger ones and wants kids of his own someday." Sadie stuffed the last leftover into the refrigerator.

"I'm sure they liked you as well. You're easy to love." Becky adored Sadie and as much as she wanted Sadie to have a full, normal life, things in their household would never be the same, and she'd miss it terribly.

Sadie glowed as she placed her hands on Becky's shoulders. "They seemed to. Now, what happened with you and Justin? You've acted strangely since you met him. Last night when I got home you acted different. Do tell, sis."

The situation with Justin seemed volatile and unsettled. *How much to share?*

"He came to me after we put Richard and Evan to bed. We star gazed and talked. We've hit it off. I like him—a lot, more than anyone I've ever met. I don't know where this will lead, but I'm not opposed to finding out."

Sadie grinned cheekily and snaked an arm around her shorter shoulders, snuggling Becky to her side as she walked her toward the doors. "I knew it. You're sweet on him. And he's goo goo for you. Any fool can see it."

She glanced into her taller sister's face. "Really, it's obvious?"

As they strode toward where the men waited Sadie nodded brazenly. "Yep, he's a goner, sis. Reel him in and net him." She chortled.

Everyone piled into Sadie and Justin's cars and headed to church. Justin dropped Richard at the door so he wouldn't need to walk any more than necessary. Sadie did the same for Becky, so she took the church steps with Richard.

Friends and neighbors eagerly greeted

Richard wishing him well and welcoming him home. Becky helped him to a pew, and Evan sat beside Richard leaving a space on Sadie's left. Richard held the boy's hand in his lap. Justin strolled in with Sadie and took his place at his Dad's right side. Becky settled beside Justin.

JJ rushed in as the service started wearing his uniform. He quietly seated himself next to Sadie where she had saved him a space. He gave her a peck on the cheek and held her hand in his lap. He whispered to the others, "I'm on duty. I hope I don't get a call until the service is over."

Sadie seemed to have difficulty concentrating during the service. Her thigh rested against JJ's, and she appeared more focused on it than the sermon. JJ eyed her from the side looking mesmerized.

Becky tried to engage with the sermon, but the aura coming from Justin distracted her best intentions. His scent mesmerized her, and she wondered what cologne he wore. It fit him perfectly. She yearned to lean against him and have his arm wrap around her shoulders pulling her close so she could absorb heat wafting from his hot body.

Sharing a hymnbook, she struggled to center on the song they sang. Softness of his fingers meeting hers beneath the book cover enticed her, driving her wild with desire recalling them expertly playing a tune of ecstasy on her body the night before. She longed to bring his hand to her lips and taste the digits of pleasure.

Justin's foot met hers beneath the pew and swept around her foot as though cradling it.

Peripheral vision showed his silent smile accompanying the childish gesture as they played *footsie* below. She didn't care, needing to touch him in some manner. They weren't causing a scene, and this turned out better than other scenarios she came up with. She glanced, smiling then returned face forward, but didn't withdraw her foot. Instead she leaned it into his feeling at peace.

After the service JJ said goodbye and gave Sadie another swift, sweet kiss on the lips then headed to work. "I'll swing by later this evening after my shift, Babe."

Walking toward the exit Becky followed Richard with Justin behind her. A pretty woman in a casual dress suit stopped them, placing her hand on Justin's forearm. "Justin Martin, I'll be dad burned. I haven't seen you in a coon's age. I heard you came back in town. How've you been? We should get together sometime soon."

Justin acted cordial but not flirty. He slipped his arm around Becky's waist tugging her toward him. "Hi, Mary Jane. Yes, I'm staying with Dad. I'm fine. Thanks for asking. This is my dear friend Becky Simms. Becky, Mary Jane Withers—it is still Withers. Right?" The emphasis on the word dear sounded strong and gave Becky's green-eyed-monster a pleasant twinge.

Mary Jane smiled adoringly showing off straight white molars. "Sure thing, Justin, I'm single. I hear you are, also. There aren't many fellas around these parts who stack up to you. I hope you're home to stay. Let's get together soon and talk over old times."

"I'm not sure of my future plans. My focus is on Dad and his health these days. I'm pretty tied up with him for now. See you around." The nudge his hand gave Becky's back encouraging her forward out of range of Ms. Wither's sphere gave Becky a special kind of thrill.

Justin went for his car. So did Sadie taking Evan with her. Becky helped Richard maneuver the short distance to the front of the church. Waiting for their rides, friends and neighbors stopped constantly assuring Richard of their prayers and happiness seeing him. A few offered help if needed. He introduced Becky to those who stopped to chat.

It warmed Becky's heart. "Wow, Richard, you're well loved. I'll never remember all the names."

Richard winked mischievously. "They're curious and jealous, wondering how I scored such a looker on my arm." He patted her hand laced around his elbow.

"You're a charmer, Richard." She glanced toward the parking lot where Justin arrived at his destination. "Your son is a woman magnet. I thought he'd never make it to the car. If one woman stopped to flirt with him, a dozen did."

Richard chuckled deep. "Yeah, they're not exactly shy either. Did you see the last gal shove her contact information in his hand? Wonder how many date invitations he received."

Becky tried not to allow her jealousy to escape though it struggled for air. Justin hadn't committed to her. Giving her the best orgasm yet experienced, hadn't pledged undying love and devotion.

Certainly not a monk, the charming free-agent had moves and oozed sex appeal. No doubt Justin's popularity provided his share of conquests.

Why was she so desperate, thinking of him with another woman? *Get over it. Damn—hard to do.*

They piled into the two cars and returned to the resort. Wiped out, Richard took a nap with Sadie's help. Justin and Becky served a lunch of chicken salad sandwiches, thick slices of fresh tomatoes, and a bowl of pasta salad on the deck table. A cool afternoon breeze rustled trees. Birds happily chirped helping themselves to seeds in the many bird feeders around camp while they discussed how they would spend the afternoon.

"We should stay here. Between yesterday and church today, Richard has had quite a bit of exercise. He could use a calm day at home. I'm concerned he might be overdoing it." Sadie sounded extraordinarily wise and in charge.

Becky filled with pride. Sadie was coming into her own skin.

Feeling guilty she and Evan were the motive for Richard's overdoing it she sought a way to provide relief. "I agree. There's a swimming pool by the playground. Evan would enjoy a dip with the camp kids. Let's walk there after lunch and take advantage of those inviting lounge chairs while he swims."

Justin smiled with something appearing to be gratitude. "It sounds great."

♥♥♥♥

He cleaned the lunch table and put the leftovers away, giving the women opportunity to change into their suits. Richard dozed soundly, so Justin placed Richard's cell phone with a note next to the bed reading, "Call my cell when you wake. We're at the pool." He changed into his trunks.

Richard exited the cabin with a beach towel slung across his shoulder. The ladies left Sadie's cabin following the animated boy. Evan wore a red inner tube around his waist and floaters wrapped around his arms, sporting goggles atop his head like a headband.

Sadie's black-and-white striped suit had a shocking V plunging in front exposing a tanned flat belly, but covered her pert breasts amply. She carried a pink beach towel, a magazine and wore enormous, round, pink sunglasses.

Becky's red one-piece turtle neck halter front covered her chest completely. Simplicity and modesty of her suit showed off rounded curves and an ample bosom. He recalled sweetness of their honey taste and ached to touch her testing firmness of those full mounds.

Maybe later.

He swallowed hard when she went to check on her son. Becky's straight back was bared completely where it indented pleasingly to an impish waist. Plunging fabric began at mid hip level wrapping her round bottom adoringly, making his hands itch to do the same. Her curls covered the tie at her neck. Visualizing her perky breasts exposed when he flicked the neck catch open with his teeth sent shivers through him and a twinge in his pants. From the back it appeared Becky wore a bikini bottom with no top. Her curves made the garment anything but conservative, especially from the back. Becky was the sexiest sight he'd ever seen. He ached to make love to her and yearned to bring her to climax again.

He'd agonized about their petting session for hours instead of sleeping, fearing his not being able to keep his hands off Becky might have sent things in the wrong direction. But their playing around hadn't hindered their budding relationship. If anything, Becky acted easier around him than ever, so it had pushed them forward on their path.

It was a matter of time. She acted willing, and he was certainly anxious.

"You ladies are lovely." He feared saying more. He didn't want to sound like a blubbering fool spouting accolades about how stunning Becky was in the sultry swatch of spandex. It led to visions of him peeling it slowly from her body.

Nope, it wouldn't do.

To distract his bodily urges, he bantered with Evan.

After a while Justin took a golf cart to the marina to check with Sam. Driving the steep grade toward the lake a boy dashed in front of him. Justin hit the brakes only to find there were none. Swerving to the right he avoided hitting the child. Maneuvering quickly avoiding crashing into a tree he finally tackled the incline turning the vehicle sideways and slamming against a concrete barrier.

Justin jumped out and examined the cart. The break line dangled, but the end didn't appear frayed. Again, someone had deliberately sabotaged equipment. Steam must be coming from his ears, his insides fumed so.

Sam glanced as he entered the store empty of patrons at the moment. "What the hay, Justin? Someone steal your bait?"

Her joke received a snicker from him and heat seeped from his system. "Damn it, Sam. Someone cut the brake line on Dad's cart again. Garrett fixed it last week. This is a deliberate act of vandalism. I want him to check every cart in service and make sure nothing else is wrong. Ask him to check those of our guests if they will comply. And I want security cameras on this place twenty-four-seven. So call someone and make it happen as soon as possible. We must nix this in the bud before someone is seriously hurt. First Sadie and now me, both times, Dad's cart—it scares me."

"I'll have Garrett take care of the carts right away. I'll get in touch with a security company on Monday and schedule a review soon as they can get to us. You okay, Justin?"

"Yep, I'm fine, just pissed off. Dad's cart is dented, and the front tire destroyed—nothing that can't be repaired. I'm lucky I didn't hit the child who stepped in front of me. Or I could've driven into the lake. It would've been the end of the vehicle."

"No wonder you were a basket case when you came in here."

"Thank God I didn't bring Evan along. He

could've been driving. I considered bringing him with me, but he's swimming with the other children."

He went over the questions he'd come to the marina to discuss with Sam then walked uphill to join the others. Evan had made several new friends. They competed in an exciting game of dive for the sinking coin as Justin tossed quarters in the water.

"He's a good swimmer." Justin laughed, speaking quietly with Becky while Sadie dozed in the shade of an umbrella with a magazine draped across her belly.

She smiled proudly. "Yes, I'm surprised how strong his swimming skills have gotten. He's opening up with these children. Many of his childish fears have dropped away recently before my very eyes. He is concentrating on having a good time." They laughed as Evan jumped off the side slipping under water without a nose guard. "This is really good for my son. My baby is growing up." Pride and regret both played equally in Becky's eyes.

Justin nodded. "They do it, I've heard."

Sadie came alive and sat stretching. "Wow, an awesome nap." She glanced at her phone checking the time. "Richard should be getting up soon. I'll head back to the cabin."

The sun moved toward the west. "We'll go with you. It's time to get the water logged child out of the water." Toward the water she gaily called, "Evan, it's time to go in. It's dinner time."

"Aw, Mom . . ." He wandered sadly toward the ladder where she met him and wrapped his short frame in a bright towel. A couple of the other mothers took the opportunity to gather their flock. Disappointment waned seeing his pals corralled for dinner as well.

"I'm starved. Let's get the feed bag on, pal." Justin put an arm around his short friend's shoulders and led him along the driveway to the cabin he shared with Sadie. The women followed the guys chattering about what a great time they'd had

♥♥♥♥

Becky and Evan planned to head home before long. Sadness settled in the pit of her stomach at the thought. Becky sighed. "This place is gorgeous. It's hard to leave." She told herself it's what it was. The beautiful man proved to be what she dreaded leaving.

Evan's sad face broke her heart and his eyes begged. "Mom, do we have to leave? I love it here. Can't we move and live in a house the way Aunt Sadie does? They have plenty of them."

Becky ruffled his hair and cupped his chin in a hand. "It is a fun place to be. Justin must've adored growing up here. I love it too, but sadly, Evan, Mommy has to work in the city. It is why we live there. We must go home." She swatted his behind gently. "We have to hit the road after dinner and I want no argument. Okay?"

"I guess. Couldn't you work here? Don't they have a hospital?" He sulked.

"Yes, they have a hospital in town. But Honey, I don't have a job there."

Becky took extra care dressing nice for Justin—and Richard, of course. Her pink silky tank top and white short shorts with matching pink flip flops showed off her new tan. She dragged a quick brush through her messy hair, but her curls had a life of their own after a day in and out of water. It would have to do. She didn't have time to wash, dry and curl her locks to tame them. She dabbed on mascara and lip gloss then joined Evan for a stroll to the main cabin.

Sadie brought out a plate of taco toppings on a tray. She placed them on the picnic table covered with a Mexican blanket. Her floral sundress with string ties in bows showed off her shoulders and the cinched waist displayed her tiny waist emphasizing her perky bosom. The full skirt floated around her when she walked, and purple sandals showed off a matching pedicure.

"Looking good, Sis." Becky winked.

"Got to, my man is coming over." Sadie's confession came without guilt or guile—simply stating the facts. How quickly JJ had gone from Richard's friend, to Sadie's male interest, to *her man*. Time flew when you were having fun.

Hell, time flies anyway. You might as well be having fun.

"So JJ is *your man* now, hum?" Becky wickedly teased.

Sadie coyly twisted and hugged herself, smirking. "He might be. At least, he's *my man* for now."

"He is definitely a great guy. Maybe he's a keeper." Becky hoped so, for Sadie's sake. Sadie fell hard for the guy.

"Maybe. Time will tell. For now, I'm enjoying the ride. What a sweet ride it is?" She beamed and raced inside for the rest of the food. They ate on the deck to take advantage of the last of the sun's rays.

Justin strolled out with a cold beer in hand. "Want one, Becky?"

"Thanks, but no, I have to drive home soon. Maybe some iced tea." He poured her an icy glass at the table.

"I'll have one, Mr. Justin. I'm not driving." Evan plopped at his seat with a wicked grin on his cupid face.

Richard laughed and approached the boy. He put a hand Evan's shoulder. "Maybe in a few years—want juice for now?"

Evan made a sour expression, and they laughed. "It will work."

They ate and chatted happily. When done Becky helped put the food away. She offered to help wash dishes, but Justin insisted he wanted to do them later. Sadie placed them in a soapy water soak.

Justin put his hands on Becky's shoulders facing her. "It'll give me something to do while I try to not miss you." His lower lip came out in an over-exaggerated pout.

Her finger tenderly stroked his sulking lips. "I'm going to miss you." Her voice sounded wistful.

Justin grinned wickedly. His brows wagged. "You're leaving me with fortifying memories. They'll have to last until I see you again."

"Well, we better head out." A gush of air and a shoulder shrug then she turned away.

"I will fetch your bags from the cabin and put them in your trunk. Say goodbye to Dad." He spun and left.

"Thanks, Justin. It is thoughtful." He considered her needs first, one of her favorite among his many charms.

Becky hugged Richard who rested with his feet propped in a chair at the table. "Thank you, Richard, for a positively splendid weekend. This vacation has been a luxury we'll treasure."

"Yes, thank you, Mr. Richard." Evan lingered in Richard's hug with his cheek relaxing on Richard's shoulder like he hated to peel away from the older man's arms. Richard gently patted his back. As he stood, Richard pulled the boy onto his knee. "I have an idea. I hope you like it. You asked me about being your grandpa. Maybe we can kind of adopt each other—not a legal adoption, but an adoption of the heart. It would give me so much pleasure if you would do it for me." Richard's fist patted his chest.

Evan's eyes grew wide eyeing his mom questioningly. Tightness in her throat threatened to choke her, struggling to withhold tears.

"It would be great. So if you're my grandpa, does it mean I get to spend more time with you?"

Richard's protective arm surrounded his tiny frame. "It does. In fact, it becomes your obligation to visit whenever humanly possible. You're welcome anytime without invitation, as family. Bring your mom. She's family, too. Okay?"

"Yes, sir, Mr. Richard." Evan threw his arms once again around Richard's neck hugging him in a death grip. "That's another thing. If you're my grandpa, could I call you that from now on?" The tot cocked his head questioningly.

"Absolutely. That would be grand." Richard's eyes welled full of moisture and he sniffed.

"Thank you, Grandpa." Evan hugged Richard so tight Becky feared for his safety, but the old gent must've been sturdier than he appeared. He appeared to thrive on Evan's enthusiasm.

"Come on young man. We need to hit the road. Thank you for your hospitality, Richard." She shook his hand surprised at the vigor in his shake.

"It's me who should be thanking you, Becky. Please return soon. How about next weekend?"

Zealous eyes showed he meant it. He had little time remaining on earth, and Evan gave him great pleasure. She couldn't deny his request. "Okay, we can manage. You sure we aren't any trouble? We don't want to impose."

"You bring sunshine into this old house. It has been a treat having you and Evan here. Haven't you witnessed the happiness you brought us? Justin beams when he talks with Evan. I enjoy watching him play. I love talking with him. You're both a joy to have around. Please come back."

"Okay. It is a date. We'll be here about five on Friday." Becky's insides flip-flopped at the prospect of something marvelous to look forward to.

Sadie heard as she exited the cabin and clapped hands favorably then bent to kiss Evan goodbye one last time. She whispered in his ear. "You're coming back next weekend to see Auntie Sadie." They shared a mutual grin and high five slap. She helped him into his booster seat and fastened the belt.

"I can't wait. Maybe I will catch a bigger fish."

"If you do, it might take all of us to pull it onboard." Sadie laughed closing the door. She strolled around the car for a last hug from Becky. "I'm so glad you're coming back next weekend." She released her sister.

In an impish voice Becky admitted, "me too."

Justin locked the trunk and strode around. He and Becky locked gazes, and Sadie stepped away. "I can't wait to see you and Evan again." He smiled broadly and Becky longed to fall into his arms and kiss those gorgeous lips showing off his pearly whites.

"Me too."

Justin gave her a friendly hug way too brief to suit either of them. He bent and waved goodbye to Evan sitting in the back seat. "See you next time, Evan."

"See you." Evan waved with a toothy grin.

Becky climbed reluctantly into the car and started the engine. Justin's hand rested on the open window. She covered it with hers and his thumb gripped hers momentarily before they pulled apart. She put the vehicle in gear and pulled out of the drive.

The rearview mirror showed Sadie and Justin waving, watching them leave the resort.

♥♥♥♥

They walked toward the deck where Richard waited. "She likes you, Justin." Sadie quietly observed her employer and friend.

"I hope so. I like her, too." Justin slipped his arm around Sadie's shoulders congenially, and they walked to the deck.

CHAPTER 15

Justin called Sadie each evening after Evan's bedtime. Their ritual became chatting for at least an hour nightly. Afterward Becky smiled to herself, her hand touching the empty pillow at her side. She was no longer alone.

Their talks explored the each other's depths, learning, giving and taking joyously without reserve, eager. They talked about important topics, mutual values and morals. They shared happenings from their days and found it easy confiding.

Both suffered broken hearts and were familiar with tragedy. Justin lost his mother. Becky's parents died too soon. And there was Evan's father.

Becky told of her vindictive husband. Torment and abuse inflicted on her sickened Justin. The melodramatic scene described forced bitter bile to rise from his stomach. Anger flared, and he shook with emotion. Had the man been alive, Justin would have sent him to hell for what he had put her through. He swore Becky would never fear for her safety again.

"I admire and respect your struggle as a single parent. It couldn't have been easy, especially without your parents. It's admirable how you refused to tolerate abuse. The ass may've inflicted pain on you, but he never broke your spirit. You're the strong, courageous and the most incredible person I know. With fortitude you challenged the system and refused to let yourself and Sadie become pawns of the system, fought back and claimed victory. Your sheer determination prevailed. Not many women have such confidence and strength." He became more in awe of her the more they talked.

"It's sweet of you, Justin. I simply did what I had to do. Sadie's family. One doesn't abandon family." Becky sounded adamant, she had no choice.

"You could've grown bitter or retreated within yourself. It isn't your style. Instead you refused to allow haunting memories to cloud your life. You're mature and discerning without being skittish, cautious without being suspicious and untrusting. It is inspiring."

"You're making me blush." She sounded shy. He pictured her face growing pink then filtering along her neck toward those delightful breasts she longed to kiss.

"You did a good job raising Sadie. She is quirky, which is an endearing part of her charm, and a wonderful woman herself—because of you. You did all of it while building a new life, escaping an abusive marriage, and giving birth becoming a single parent. I doubted I could've been so resilient."

"You're a brilliant lawyer, successful and smart. You're an amazing, loving son, and a good friend. Don't belittle yourself to me, Justin. You're a force to be reckoned with." Praise and pride in her voice filled his chest to bursting.

"Becky, I adore you. You're remarkable, one of a kind, a breath of fresh air. The more I learned about you, the deeper I fall under your spell."

It became more and more clear. He wanted a life with her, but she wasn't ready for him to profess undying love yet. Exhilarated at the idea he pondered how to bring her on board. His intentions were true, and she seemed to more than like him. In fact, he delighted in the turn of events, but he needed to make her love him.

He didn't want to screw this up. His heart told him he'd never have a chance like this again. He'd need to take it slow and not pressure her. Let her set the boundaries. His behavior would not compromise who she was, and he would be the man she needed.

He'd show her the love ebbing from his heart. Pure and simple, his instincts would guide him. Squaring his shoulders with resolve, he'd declare his feelings a little at a time seducing her with charm, romancing and revealing gradually endearing devotion at the right time.

Anticipation of holding Becky in his arms again quickened his pulse and erected life where in a useless location in his jeans, without Becky around. The idea of her sent him on a sultry bender.

Life had a will of its own. Incredible and improbable, things started turning out different from planned. What did they say about best laid plans? Strange but real—his new reality—a love-saddened fool doing his damnedest to woo a broken maiden and consumed by it.

Love flowed from his inner being and shocked his system. He hadn't pursued it, or considered it could happen. He hadn't believed in true love, let alone wanted it for himself.

But it existed. Damn straight.

Breathing fresh air for the first time, he couldn't get enough of Becky. Love for her filled him, completed him—a new and superb sensation he reveled in.

♥♥♥♥

Becky and Sadie enjoyed their afternoon talks when Becky came home from work while Evan colored or did crafts at his kitchen countertop desk. "You've lowered your defenses with Justin, Sis. I'm proud of you for taking a chance. He's a great guy and really into you."

"He's easy to talk to, non-judgmental, understanding and supportive. I'm confident talking with him about anything. He makes me feel strong and safe. It's new to me." Becky pulled macaroni from the cupboard and opened the refrigerator searching for cheese and milk, so she could prepare Evan's favorite meal, macaroni and cheese.

"Understandably, you've not had the best of experiences with men and had only yourself to depend on since Mom and Dad have been gone. You've literally lived for me and Evan, and we needed you. Letting your barricade down and allowing someone to care for you is a new experience."

"And so far it's wonderful. I'm young, free, desirable and powerful with him. Knowing I'll talk with him later each evening helps me derive more enjoyment from each day. I'm light and happy, like the sun is suddenly shinning in my world and I can accomplish anything." She kept her voice low so her son wouldn't hear.

"Becky, you know I think you're invincible."

Becky snickered. "I'm not sure how I garnered the impression. I've been stumbling around, trying to tread in a forward direction and barely kept things moving around here."

"It's the point. You did keep things moving forward, and you did it better than you realize. You've carried a tremendous burden alone, and you've done it well."

"A heavy load lifted from my shoulders, and I'm experiencing lightness of heart I haven't known since childhood." Aware of her falling in love with Justin, it determined to be beyond Becky's control. "I certainly hadn't been seeking this, and I don't know where it'll lead, but I'm not going to pull back. I'm willing to see where this thing between Justin and I lead." She pictured herself watching Justin sleep on the empty pillow at her side. "The idea of not being alone forever is comforting and thrilling at the same time."

"Funny, when you least expect it, when you aren't in the market for it, don't realize you're open to it, love sneaks into your heart. It's how it is with JJ and me. I'm falling for that big lunk, and I'm all in." Confidence and joy in Sadie's voice brought a tear to Becky's eye. Her little sis morphed into a grown woman in love.

"I've sheltered my feelings for years, avoided problematic relationships, and kept men at bay. Justin Martin waltzes into my life and steals my heart. It's beyond control. And, Sadie, I don't want to control it. I want it to happen naturally, the way it should. And I want to enjoy it."

"As you should, Becky. Love is to be cherished. If it's the lasting kind, you'll soon know. Whatever it is, live in the moment and get the most from it."

"Sage advice—when did my little Sadie become so wise?"

Sadie chuckled. "Be smart and take it."

"I'll give myself this experience—for better or worse."

"Good to know. You're worthy of love and deserve happiness. Enjoy it."

"I will, Sadie. I've decided to relax and go with the flow, to see where this leads. Perhaps it would end in heart break, perhaps not. I won't worry. I'll simply go with it and enjoy the ride."

CHAPTER 16

On Tuesday after a day of resting from their weekend on the go with their company, the two men set out on Richard's bass boat intent on getting the rest of Richard's story out in the open. "I won't rest well, until you know the whole truth about me."

Justin wasn't sure he needed more. What he'd learned had made him sick, considering the horrors his dad experienced as a child. Thank God Richard had gotten away and made a good life for himself.

Finally moored and baited, they sat ready to talk. "Where did we leave off last week?"

"You escaped the abusive farmers who brewed illegal liquor for the mob."

"Oh, yeah, I hitched a ride from the little town, not knowing where to go. The guy worked at a restaurant on Monmouth Street in Newport and dropped me on a street corner. He told me if I came to the back door, he'd sneak food out for me. He took pity on me, a scared and hungry child. I walked into the alley. He brought me a dinner plate. It tasted good, and I was indebted. It had been a couple days since I'd eaten. I gobbled the plate of meatloaf, mashed potatoes and green beans then placed the empty on the door stoop for him to fetch later. I lived in alleys for a while, scrounging dumpsters and garbage cans, sleeping in boxes or crates I found. The dirty life didn't stink any worse than the pig farm. Sifting through trash behind a hotel, a slick-looking gent sauntered out, lit a cigarette and leaned on the door jam.

"Hey kid, what're you doing?" I figured he was pissed I dug in his dumpster, but he didn't act angry.

"Nothing," I uttered. "Seeing what good stuff got thrown out."

"Why would you do it?" He scrutinized me curiously.

"They sometimes toss blankets, pillows, or clothing—you know—useful stuff. Some pretty decent food in this bin. You'd be surprised what good grub gets tossed out."

"Doubt it," he snickered. "So you're hungry, are you?" I nodded. He signaled to wait a minute. He returned with a tray loaded with food and pushed a chair next to the door lighting another smoke. He gestured for me to eat. It tasted great still hot with me starving. Roast beef with gravy, mashed potatoes, corn, green beans, a hot buttery roll, and a glass bottle of milk, with a piece of the best chocolate pie I ever ate." Richard rubbed his chin.

"To this day when I eat chocolate pie, I remember my gratitude. I didn't waste time talking, but scarfed it before he changed his mind. I handed the tray and told him, "Thank you, Mister. It was a right fine meal." I started to walk the alley when he called. "Where are you going, kid? Where do you live?" "Nowhere, here and there, wherever I find shelter," I told him."

"So you're homeless, right?" he asked. "Guess so," I told him. "You in trouble with the law?" he asked. "Don't believe I am, Sir, unless my no account foster father sicked 'em on me for defending myself. A run-away, 'umm?" "Yeah Mister, and I ain't a goin' back. So don't get no ideas 'bout trying to make me. I'm a free man, seventeen and nearly a legal adult. I won't be used for a slave any more, or someone's punching bag."

"Oh, so that is how it was, mmmm?" He rubbed his chin and squished his cigarette butt with his foot. "You can defend yourself?" he asked. I nodded. "Good, it's a fine thing for a young man to do. I enjoy a fella who doesn't take crap off anyone. Son, how would you feel about a job? I could use a good man. You up for it?" Boy was I ever? He took me in, cleaned me up and bought me clothes. He helped me find a cheap room to rent and taught me his business. He was a middle manager for the Mob, a mobster, a gangster. He worked for the Syndicate that ran illegal activity in the area at the time. They basically controlled in one way or another successful clubs, restaurants and hotels, and connected to those in New York, Chicago, Miami and Las Vegas. They were powerful and didn't take *no* for an answer. If a business owner of an establishment they wanted didn't cooperate or sell, something bad happened to them. If they cooperated

it became profitable, and the mob left them alone—
a matter of survival. One way or the other, they got
what they wanted. Newport rocked as a happening
place with clubbing, strippers, illegal gambling,
prostitutes, big name entertainment and great places
to stay and play. Celebrities frequented town. Some
came to entertain. Others came for a great time.
Anything you wanted, the mob happily provided at
a price. Cops turned a blind eye. It rained money for
one and all. The mob got away with whatever they
wanted to do. As a rookie, I made daily runs to
gaming clubs, bookies, numbers runners and
prostitution houses. They bagged their funds, and I
took the dough to a club called Glenn Schmitt's,
where I delivered it to be accounted for, hazardous
work, but no one dared mess with me. If they did,
the Syndicate jumped on their back before they
spent a penny. I didn't carry a gun, but I had the old
chain hooked on my belt, and I carried an ice pick.
It became well known before long. I didn't take shit
off of anyone and would defend myself. I wasn't
shy about stabbing someone if they came after me.
The guys nicknamed me Ice Pick. It started as a
joke teasing me, and it stuck. They figured it would
prevent some brute from trying to overpower me. In
the business, it paid to be feared. I did pickups for a
couple of years. The boss promoted me to a bouncer
at a nightclub called The Pink Palace. A happening
place employed strippers, prostitutes, and illegal
booze. You could gamble in the basement casino
day or night. Many area clubs had *private parties*
after legal closing time. They made it appear closed.
In reality they stayed open whenever they wanted."

Justin sat with elbows on knees listening in a daze. It sounded like a cheap television program on an off channel—not like real life—his dad's life. His eyes trained on the water, fearing they'd burst into tears if he caught sight of Richard.

"One of the guys disappeared, but no one had the nerve to ask what happened to him. He was gone, probably dead, anchored and tossed in the river; or buried in a new construction foundation somewhere. It was usually how people exited the business. You knew too much, so you couldn't walk out or quit. Moving up in the organization, proud to be trusted more and more, Aware it was illegal, it didn't bother me. I told myself I wasn't doing anything wrong. We provided what people wanted and willingly paid for. I hadn't witnessed much violence, so it became easy to pretend it didn't happen. Cops looked the other way. The town thrived, so it didn't seem awfully wrong . . . for a while."

Richard rubbed a hand on his face wiping sweat from it. This confession was taking its toll, which worried Justin. But he didn't interrupt.

"Until the shit hit the fan—I hung out at the club bar chatting up the one of the dancers. The boss came out of his office in a huff with a trusted man at his side called Rocco. His real name was Raymond Bonetti. The boss told Rocco to take me as his driver to do a job. Get our asses back there quick; but not to return until it was done. I had a premonition as we scrambled into one of the bosses black cars, but tried ignoring it. Rocco tossed me the keys. I had no choice. Whatever was happening would occur with or without me. I couldn't bow out of the deal without putting myself in jeopardy. So I drove keeping the speed limit. Rocco sat behind me in the back seat and directed me a few blocks along York Street and told me to park with the headlights off. I shook something awful, figuring he'd put a bullet in my head and wondering why I deserved it. The shot didn't come, and I noticed Rocco watching an antique store across the street. Scared to death, my gut wrenched, and feeling queasy I suppressed a gag. The street was deserted at the late hour with few cars on the road. Lights shut off in the shop, and Rocco told me to keep the engine running until someone came out then pull onto the street without headlights and drive slow. I did as told and heard him roll the back window down."

Justin straightened in his seat taking a deep breath gazing across the water, knowing what came next. This story was what legends were made of, too horrifying to be true.

People you know and love don't live through things like this. Or do they? How could this be? Justin leaned in his seat bracing for the rest.

"A man exited the shop and locked the door then walked the street. We pulled alongside him. The gun shot off behind my head. My ears ached, deafened from the shot leaving a ringing in my head. Red fluid exploded from his chest. Shock showed in the guy's expression. In slow motion, his knees buckled, and he landed on them onto the sidewalk, poised that way for a second. It registered on his face before his expression fell blank. He pitched forward. Lifeless, he lay silently face against concrete, having never made a sound. Rocco shoved my shoulder and told me to drive slowly the next block. At a stop light a couple blocks away, he told me to flip the headlights back on. We turned right on Tenth. A few cars drove along the street heading the other direction toward clubbing action. We took a bridge across the Licking River into Covington and stopped midway. His door opened. He stepped to the rail and tossed the weapon into the deep. The waterway must be plumb full of steel. We returned to the alley using a back entrance to the club. The boss came out of his office and eyed Rocco questioningly. Rocco nodded. The boss put his arms around the two of us and told us to get drunk because we were off duty the rest of the night. Drinks and girls were on the house for us. I never needed a drink so bad. Eventually cops arrived to question everyone and asking about the shooting. By then Rocco lounged shit-faced in a booth with two prostitutes. One had his tongue in her mouth and his hand up her skirt. The other was giving him a blow job. I sat at the bar drunk on tequila shots. A bouncer told the fuzz none of the bosses' men had left the nightclub all evening. They didn't question me or acknowledge Rocco having sex in the booth. They left. I stumbled into the men's room and tossed my guts wishing I was dead. Someone must've driven me home to sleep it off. I woke sprawled on my bed the next morning wearing my clothes with a note taped to my chest telling me to take the day off. I had the worst hangover of my life. I showered and forced myself to drink instant coffee made on a hot plate."

Richard took a deep breath, sighed and closed his eyes a few minutes. Justin didn't bother him, leaving him to his thoughts, giving him time to regain strength to finish the story.

"I decided to get out but didn't want to end up in a river or concrete grave. I had to run for it. If I left right away, they wouldn't miss me until late the next day. They might not begin searching for a couple days. I ripped out the floor board beneath my bed where I hid my cigar box stash, tossed stuff into a pillow case and left. With only a few possessions, I hoped no one in the building realized I took off. I jumped into my pride and joy, a 1957 Chevy. She was a beauty with gleaming aqua and white paint, shiny chrome, white leather interior, and my only splurge. I drove to Tampa and settled into a motel. I loved Florida, but only stayed a week. Florida was another gold mine run by the Mob, so not safe. I was crazy for the car, but she could easily be traced. So I sold her for cash at a lot in the panhandle. I bought a ragged, inconspicuous Volvo which I never titled into my name. So it couldn't be traced to me. Driving west along the coast I stopped in New Orleans. What a fun town. I enjoyed it for a couple of days as a tourist. It was similar to Newport but way raunchier if it's possible. With the crime, it seemed a good place for Mob influence. So afraid to linger long I headed west through Texas, stopping to eat and sleep when I needed to. I considered Vegas, but it felt too risky. Casinos run by the Mob, meant they'd catch me there. I ventured north through Denver, but kept driving. Wyoming is a beautiful state, but I couldn't take cold northwest winters; so I meandered east. Detroit and Chicago were definitely out, being headquarters of the Syndicate. Kansas or Iowa lay too flat and too much farm land with no jobs except working fields or ship yards loading cattle, a lost soul seeking redemption."

He paused and finished his beer, with a long sigh.

"At a St. Louis motel sitting on a picnic table in front of my room sipping a beer, a couple of trucks pulled in. Some guys unloading gear spoke to me. They acted like a friendly bunch, laughing and joking. They brought out a cooler and joined me for a few beers. I enjoyed having people to talk with. Their fishing trip to Kentucky sounded fun. The next day they acted bummed out. One guy had a family emergency and headed home leaving his fishing buddy without a partner. They tried to decide what to do, but didn't want to cancel their trip. The odd fellow asked what I had planned for the next week. Of course I had no plans. They invited me to join them. I needed a good time at this point, so I tagged along. We had a blast and ate fish every day for lunch and dinner. When time came for them to leave, I didn't have anywhere to go. I rented a unit by the month. The owner had an old trailer he'd been working on. I helped him finish refurbishing it. I rented it figuring to hang out a while. That fishing camp is this resort, the home you grew up in. I spent time with the owner working on docks and the marina. The great old guy taught me useful things and how to manage the place. I learned maintenance, marketing, book keeping, customer service, ordering stock, boating, and fishing. Eventually we worked out a deal—my work for rent. He wanted a son and treated me like his. He loved his daughter, but it wasn't the same. When he retired and moved to Grand Rapids to live with her, he asked me to buy the place. I had cash left, and he held the mortgage on the place charging no interest; so I managed to purchase it from him. He became a friend and mentor, like the dad I never had. Sadly, his daughter called a year later. He'd passed. He willed the place to me free and clear. I tried to pay her the outstanding debt; but stubborn like him, she insisted I take it. She had no need for the resort or the cash. It's how I came to own this fishing camp. A couple years later I met your Mama. She slammed me a good one, like a dam burst in my heart. One look and she owned me. Life became suddenly worth living. I found the anchor I'd searched for. She was it for me—my foundation, my savior, and the love I'll never get over."

Justin stole a glance his dad, happy seeing a smile on his down-turned face. Richard chuckled and wiped a grey strand stuck to his sweating forehead. Justin adjusted his ball cap fidgeting nervously, noting Richard's dreamy expression. Justin remembered the smile—the one Richard wore when he'd viewed Mom without her knowing it, filled with undying love.

"I worked on the pier replacing rotten deck boards when Rose, your grandma, parked beside cabin one to clean. I could tell someone occupied her passenger seat. It's when I got a load of your Mamma for the first time. She was a sight to behold." Richard chuckled loudly.

"I could hardly breathe when she stepped from the old truck. Long, tanned legs in short, cutoff jeans took my breath away. I lost it when she bent over the bed retrieving a basket of cleaning supplies. I hadn't realized a woman's butt could be shaped so beautifully—a perfect upside-down heart. She sure stole mine that day, and I wanted to get close to her. Mesmerized, I stared soaking her in and memorizing every detail. A white, button shirt tied in a bow exposed her slim waist and midriff. God Almighty, she was stunning. Sunlight radiated from her black ponytail swinging from side-to-side when she walked. I wanted to pull the elastic and tangle my fingers in her glossy hair. When they finished the last cottage, I loaded my tools in the golf cart and drove there. I was lucky. They walked out when I reached Rose's vehicle. Rose smiled and introduced her daughter. Your mom came home from college, having graduated from Northern Kentucky University. I helped her load the bulky cleaning supplies into the truck bed and spoke awkwardly. "Sure was nice of you to help Rose out." She explained Rose wanted to finish early and take her to town to do errands. I asked if she was busy that evening, and she grinned all flirty asking why I wanted to know. I told her I'd be pleased if she'd let me take her to dinner. She laughed and said to pick her up at seven. That was it for me. I spent the rest of the summer sweet-talking her and basking her glow. I was one lucky son of a gun, getting her attention. I'd fallen head-over-heels for-lifetime-deep in love. I couldn't breathe if she wasn't in my world or face a day without seeing or talking with her. My life depended on it. Even more surprising, she felt the same. It presented a wonderful, yet terrifying situation. I had no idea this would happen and didn't know what to do. I couldn't make a commitment and had to be honest with her. Scared to death of telling her about my past, sure I'd lose her knowing it would've been kinder to let her go. I tried pushing her away, but she refused. I explained I wasn't good enough, but she wasn't having it. Finally, I told her the whole disgusting story, trusting she'd keep it to herself. I explained how wrong I was for her and I wasn't nearly good enough. She listened then told me a thing or two. No way did I get off easy. I couldn't make her love me then toss her aside, even for her own good. She demanded I be the stand-up fellow she believed me to be and insisted I marry her. She wouldn't take no for an answer. Grabbing me by the hand we headed to town and bought her a ring. I tried talking her out of the ridiculous idea; but your mamma when her mind's made up rolled like a bull dozer. You'd better go along with the program or get out of the way, because she took no prisoners." He laughed glancing at Justin, who silently nodded and smiled.

"She sure was a dynamo. The woman was unstoppable and amazing. No other way to describe her. She got what she wanted—always did. I could never say *no* to anything she asked." Justin smiled with his mouth closed, knowing well how his mom had been when she wanted something.

"If she was so set on being my bride, I had

no choice but to become the man she deserved. I'd
change my ways for good and be an up-standing
fella who would love her until the day I die. She
deserved no less. A month later here at the lake I
married the most beautiful bride ever wore a
wedding gown. She brought tears to my eyes. The
lump in my throat grew so huge I could hardly
speak my vows. The love never lessened. We led a
good life, enjoyed every moment, and never in my
wildest dreams did I see it coming. I didn't know
this world existed, or people lived this way. It was
foreign. I assumed everyplace and everybody lived
like where I came from. I'm thankful to your mama
for changing my life and introducing me to a realm
where basic goodness exists. Everyone possesses
flaws and problems. Folks make mistakes. But in
general they're decent at the core. She saw it in me,
showed me how to appreciate it in others, and made
me a worthy man. I owe her everything and will
never stop loving her. It was another thing she
taught me—how to love, be happy and thrive. She
showed me I could start fresh and live a life to be
proud of. I strived to give her the life she deserved."
He paused taking a fortifying breath. "I was
honored hearing your mom happily call me her
man. Justin I'm tired of running and hiding."
Richard bent resting head in hands gulping air,
trying to maintain a calm demeanor. He studied
Justin as though gauging his thoughts.

Justin's blankly stared toward the water
without seeing. His skill at hiding emotions and
beliefs struggled as he focused. Inside he quivered
erratically with each nerve on edge. Everything in

him wanted to release a flood of tears threatening to overtake him. But his father bore enough stress.

"We figured a day would come when I needed to tell you. I dreaded it, hating causing you distress and losing your love and respect. I owe you the truth. Getting this in the open lifts a hefty burden from my shoulders, but I'm sorry it causes you anguish. It's not my intent transferring the weight to you. Through the years I've debated over and over, reluctant to share, but it's time. I put it off long enough. Hurting you is the last thing I want, but there's no way around it. You deserve to learn about my sordid past, about the man I am. This will change things between us. I won't blame you if you despise me. I'm despicable. I haven't earned the right to ask forgiveness, so I won't. But, Son, I'm sincerely sorry. I regret more things than you can imagine. I'm not afraid to die. I'll be with your mom, so it's okay. I led a decent life with her and you. I've many things to be obliged for. I've been happy, more so than I rated. My worst remorse is leaving you alone. I'd hoped you'd find someone the way I did your mom—a strong, genuine love; and you'd settle down with a family before I go. But we can't pick our time. So here I am, dying; and you'll be alone in the world with no one to love, and no one loving you." Richard sat erect, stretched, and clapped his hands together as though clearing his head.

Justin gazed at clouds struggling to take it in. Neither of them spoke for a long time. Justin tried grasping revelations rocking their existence, in shock and numb conflicting emotions surged at lightning speed, and his head ached. His heart pounded wildly trying to escape his chest. An invisible band around his throat choked, and he feared speaking.

Richard expected nothing from him. Was he capable of giving anything of value?

After a while Richard reeled his line in. Justin followed suit. They had ceased fishing a long time before, so their bare hooks had long since had the bait stolen by fish. Richard reached for the ignition key, starting the vessel.

Justin put his hand on his Dad's stopping him. "Wait, Dad, we aren't done." He sat back staring at Richard's face. Richard waited patiently. "You owe me no apology. I appreciate you telling me this. It's a shocker, no doubt. It hasn't soaked in yet." He wiped a tear with the back of his hand. "You've been a wonderful father and a loving husband. You're strong, thoughtful, generous, and a good friend to your buddies. You're an upstanding citizen, well respected in the community for good reason. You earned it." Justin took his hands, rubbing them fondly. "I love you, respect you and am appreciative for the way you raised me. You taught me how to be a virtuous man. You've been patient, devoted, loving, and a worthy role model. So don't apologize. You've done nothing requiring my forgiveness."

"But, Son, my past is horribly ugly. I'm ashamed of the foul life I led, the dreadful things I did."

"I understand it. I'm not the one needing to forgive you. You must forgive yourself. You were a victim of a wicked circumstance, a boy trying to survive amidst violence. You lived in a corrupt environment with no way out. You knew no different and did what was required to survive. Thank goodness you escaped and got a new start."

"Thank you, Son." Tears streaked across Richard's tanned cheeks. He brushed a hair from Justin's face. "I'm sorry to leave you this way."

"I regret it too." Justin sat upright. "At least we have this."

"Yes, time is precious. It means the world you've stayed with me. Will you go now?"

Justin pulled the older man into a tight hug. Closing their eyes relishing the moment, they patted each other's back. Justin tried to absorb the essence of the man he loved with all his heart soaking in warmth from Richard's frail body.

"Dad, I can't contemplate being anywhere else. I love you and want you to understand it." Justin pulled the anchor. "We better head home before Sadie sends the Water Patrol searching for us. She probably has supper ready. She sure is a great cook, our little Sadie." Justin sat casually beside Richard.

"Yep, she sure is." Richard started the engine. "I had hoped romance might spark between the two of you. Sadie's a looker and a wild, untamed thing. Joy follows wherever she goes. I thoroughly enjoy her company." He laughed slapping his leg.

"She's a wacky little gem, and I appreciate her strange sense of humor. Her wardrobe is certainly original but suits her. I never saw anyone wear black leather shorts before." Justin laughed, and Richard joined him laughing along. "I believe the thing between Sadie and JJ is serious. Don't you?"

Sadie showed up in leather shorts and matching vest going for a tough, biker-chick look. Somehow it came off quirky and cute.

"Yep, JJ is one lucky son-of-a-gun." Richard appeared reserved but not unhappy.

"She's dedicated to you. She's a brilliant nurse and makes our lives easier in many ways."

"Our Sadie understands the importance of this time together. She's young but wise beyond her years. She's determined for you and I to have the best quality existence possible during what little time we have together." Richard grinned. "And I love it when she calls me Ricky."

"Yeah, she's a character. But, Dad, Sadie isn't for me. She's the little sister I never had but wanted. I have no inclination toward romance no matter how eccentric, wacky and adorable she is. With everything she does for us, I'm happy we hired her."

Richard pulled the boat into its slip and laid his forehead on the steering wheel taking couple deep breaths. Justin tied it to its moorings then hopped aboard. Richard struggled to stand, and his face paled, so Justin helped him to a bench on the dock. He closed his eyes trembling.

Was this it?

"We've had all we can stand today." Richard's voice quivered.

Justin studied him afraid to push. He gave

him a bottle of cold water, and Richard sipped. "Sure, Dad, rest. We'll be home in a jiffy. You need a good meal."

Sam had seen them approach and fetched their golf cart. She parked it beside the bench where Richard rested. "Richard okay?" Her quiet voice sounded alarmed.

"He's exhausted. We stayed out too long." Justin woke his sleeping father and helped him into the vehicle. "Thanks for bringing this."

"No worries. Take care of Richard." She gave him a peck on the cheek, and Richard winked sweetly. "You guys go home. I'll stow your gear." Sam stepped onto the boat not waiting for a reply.

"Thanks. See if the guys in the cleaning house want our catfish in the live well. If not, please turn them back. We aren't up to cleaning fish."

"I'm sure they will." Sam waved them off.

They sped toward the cottage. Sadie's sprinted toward them as they approached. Her expression revealed understanding, and Richard slumped pale and listless.

"How you doing, Ricky?" With a cheerful smile she assisted him from the vehicle bringing a grin from the man. He gently patted her cheek, leaning with her arm around his waist and his circling her shoulder. Justin rounded their ride and scooped Richard into his arms. Richard drooped against him without resistance.

"He's tired. We overdid it. Let's put him to bed and you can check on him." Sadie ran ahead opening doors and flipping covers back. Justin laid him on the bed.

Sadie touched his forehead. "No fever." She stuck a thermometer in his mouth, checked his pulse and blood pressure. "Your breathing is erratic, Ricky. Your pulse is slow and temp is fine. How're you?" She grinned flirtingly wagging her brows.

"In love, Sadie, my dear." His cheerful grin brought a chuckle from the younger two.

Justin left Sadie to make his dad comfortable. He had thinking to do. He needed to find a way to help his dad leave this world without regrets. Flipping his computer open he located his private investigator friend's contact information and shot off a note to him. An immediate response hinted he'd get right on it. Justin didn't reveal his personal need for the data, so the PI would assume it pertained to a law case.

CHAPTER 17

On Friday Becky and Evan arrived at the resort at five thirty. Justin spent the day in town in court, so they joined Sadie and Richard for a chance to catch up on the latest before Justin arrived home. When Justin's car pulled next to the cabin Evan shot to his feet and sped to meet him.

"Justin, I couldn't wait to come see you again." The antsy boy jumped around excitedly.

Justin's heart filled so tight he feared it would burst. He'd forgotten how incredible the young boy's admirations made him feel. He bent to the child's level and opened his arms for a hug. Evan lunged into them. He swept him into the air and spun him around, landing safely back on his feet.

"I missed you too Evan. I've looked forward to your visit." Evan's tiny warm hand in his warmed Justin's heart as he led him to the deck. He wanted to never let it go.

"Hi Justin, I'm glad to see you again. Thanks again for having us." Becky acted relaxed and at home sipping iced tea with Dad and Sadie on the deck, a vision he'd hold precious in his memory for the remainder of his days.

"My pleasure." He felt the glint in his eye as he neared, and she stood. He drew her into a quick, friendly hug. They acted awkward with each other in the presence of their families, having shared so much in private on the phone. If alone, he'd have swept her into a passionate lover's kiss and dragged her to the nearest bed. Yet being newly together was intimidating.

The five of them spent a pleasant evening together. Becky, Sadie and Justin prepared a delicious meal. Evan and Richard played checkers on the deck.

JJ arrived as the burgers came off the grill. He and Sadie had been seeing each other as much as their respective work schedules allowed, during the past week. So they acted casual and comfortable together. He kissed her when he arrived in an appropriate manner for mixed company, only hinting at an intimate relationship.

"I've made exciting plans for tomorrow. Dad's buddies are joining him for a day of cards and televised sports. Sadie made reservations at the park for horseback riding for the rest of us. We're picking up lunch for our saddle bags at a local restaurant that I've grown fond of, and we'll have a trail picnic."

"Wow, it sounds exciting." Becky grinned happily anticipation glowing in her eyes. "Sadie and I last rode horses as children on vacation with our parents. I'm no horsewoman, by any means. Evan has never ridden. Sure it's safe?"

Justin patted her hand reassuringly. "I've arranged for well-trained, tame saddle-bred rides."

JJ grinned and his dimples showed along with the cute cleft in his chin. "The horses will be safe to ride. They're mostly old, seasoned geldings who could walk the trails with their eyes closed. The trails are easy without steep hills to maneuver. You'll do fine."

Saturday morning Sadie prepared ham, eggs, biscuits and hash brown potatoes for breakfast. JJ Arrived in time to eat with them. "Thanks for having me. I wouldn't miss a meal like this and this great company for the world."

"Our door is open to you, JJ." Richard smiled happily across the table full of friends and family—his new, larger extended family. His eyes lingered on the tot at his side gulping a last bite of cheesy hash browns. They grew moist with an obvious love for the child.

Richard's friends showed up around eleven. They watched a game on television and soon became engrossed in sports talk.

The others loaded Sadie's car with saddle bags, ice and drinks then set out. They picked food up on the way and drove to the stables. Ranch hands had tacked the horses when they arrived. Justin loaded saddle bags on his steed.

Evan nuzzled a short roan pony. "Look, Mom, I love this one. His name is Smokey. The man told me I can ride him." Smokey acted content, letting the boy rub and dote to his heart's desire. When he paused from petting, Smokey put his nose beneath his arm and nudged him to continue. Evan scratched behind his ears, and the pony was in heaven.

A groom patted the pony's head, glancing to Becky. "Smokey knows her job. She'll take good care of Evan."

"Thank you," she smiled feeling somewhat reassured.

Justin tightened Evan's saddle one last time. He hoisted the boy onto the saddle. "Her you go, Evan. How does she feel?" He handed him the reigns.

"Awesome, Mr. Justin, I'm a real cowboy now." He gave Justin a toothy grin.

"Okay, cowboy, sit quietly until we're loaded up." Justin delved into great detail with the boy explaining how to ride safely. Sadie and Becky listened intently, eager to learn as well, anxious to have fun, and be safe on the woodland trails.

Justin checked Becky's saddle. He held her reigns while she lifted herself into the saddle.

"It is a good girl Cheyenne." Becky quietly cooed and rubbed the palomino's blonde mane.

JJ did the same for Sadie. He helped her onto the buckskin. "Your horse is named Crockett."

"Hello, Crockett. I'm sure we'll get along fine." Sadie's chipper voice received a head turn from the splendid animal.

Once the girls came aboard, the men climbed into their saddles. JJ rode a paint named Cody. Justin rode a black horse named Comet. JJ led the pack followed by Sadie, then Evan, Becky and finally Justin. The girls and Evan sat safely cocooned between the men so they could watch out for them. They chatted happily while they rode, enjoying themselves.

Birds sang in treetops on the breathtaking day, and the sun shone brightly with promise. A slight breeze fluttered branches carrying the scent of pine boughs, freshly cut grass, the wilderness and horse sweat.

Becky sighed. "This is an ideal day for a ride through the forest. A great idea, Justin." She smiled his direction, and he tipped his cowboy hat with a grin.

Well-kept, wide trails freshly cut had been well-marked. They easily ambled along two astride in many places. Low hills provided variety as they strode across one then another, but none steep enough for tough challenge. They trampled through an occasional mud puddle, and the horses skirted the edge of the trail avoiding thicker holes of slop. They guided them sternly to avoiding brushing through cedar boughs. Thick trees surrounded them and a scent of mossy undergrowth mixed with pine lingered thick in the air. Thick woods occasionally opened into grassy fields.

After a couple of hours they tired and took a break. JJ chose a clearing in the woods where downed logs served as benches. The men with Evan's help tied the animals to branches and fed them water from canteens tied to the saddles. Evan followed asking question after question, which they answered patiently.

"Evan, you'll drive them mad with all the questions," Becky warned.

"Nonsense, evidently the boy enjoys riding

and is eager to learn," JJ patted his young friend on the back. Evan beamed proudly.

Once the horses had been cared for, they enjoyed their lunch of turkey, bacon and jalapeno mayo on whole wheat toast. Each sandwich came with a pickle and a bag of chips, and for desert fresh apple turnovers with a light glazed top.

"I understand now why you like the café. This meal is scrumptious." Becky wiped her mouth having finished.

"Glad you like it. I eat there sometimes when I go to town for court."

"I didn't think I'd be so hungry after the enormous breakfast." Sadie blushed at JJ.

"It's the fresh air and exercise." He slipped an arm around her shoulders and gave Sadie a quick hug.

They stowed the garbage from lunch into an empty saddle bag, climbed aboard and followed the horses' lead. A few minutes passed before Evan's horse cleared the area. As Crockett followed him, the seasoned animal began misbehaving, backing up, snorting, blowing and dancing sideways. Crockett crow hopped threatening to rare and spin around. It would've resulted in bumping into those following him. Becky clutched the reigns tightly so he couldn't rare, but terror in her eyes must've been evident. Less than confident she could control the fearful creature, she struggled to stay aboard and keep him from ramming the others. Apparently Crockett wanted to buck and run.

Justin spotted the problem. Evidently to the right of the trail, aggravated by Smokey and Evan riding through the clearing, a copperhead coiled ready to strike when Becky and Crockett came along. Crockett scented and spotted him in time to back away but the snake lay within striking distance. No telling how long Becky could control the petrified animal.

Justin jumped from his horse reacting immediately having assessed the situation. He had no choice but to protect Becky, Crockett and the rest of the group. This demon meant business. Justin pulled the Ruger pistol he wore riding in the wilderness.

Everything quieted as the group registered shock. They halted and backed away avoiding Becky's scared animal. They were too far away to be of help and barely able to witness what transpired. The scene unfolded in horror. The life and death struggle played out before their eyes.

Becky glimpsed the coiled viper, comprehended what provoked Crockett, and the peril they faced. Her blood-curling scream filled the air.

At the same time Justin aimed and fired at the treacherous serpent as it struck, hitting his target. The poisonous beast's head shot forward then fell, its body going limp. Another foot and it would've made contact with Becky's ankle. Blood drained from Justin's face.

The silent group sat wide-mouthed. Evan spoke first, and his eyes opened wide. "Holy cow, mom, are you all right?"

Becky shook herself to keep from crying. "Yes, Evan, I'm fine thanks to Justin's quick thinking." She wiped a tear away with her hand and attempted a smile to comfort her son. It came off more like a grimace, however. She breathed gusts inhaling heartily while her chest heaved and burned. She blinked trying to still tears forcing their way toward her eyes.

Justin dismounted and walked to her. He lifted his hands to her waist and pulled her from her seat. Taking her in his arms, he wrapped her tightly, and she melted into his love. He kissed the top of her head. She buried her face in his chest and let loose. Tears of relief erupted while she made loud sobbing sounds, and he stroked the back of her head.

Finally she gazed into his adoring eyes. He bent to meet her invitation. Passionately he kissed her, communicating his terror and relief at the danger had horrified them. Their contact pulsed strong and full of pent up emotion. Becky's breathing grew steady as she accepted safety and comfort while she calmed in his arms.

Finally Sadie snickered. "So are you two going to be at it all night? Or can we get back on the trail?"

"Gosh, Mom, you trying to eat him or something? Let's go." Evan giggled and spun Smokey around following JJ and Sadie's horses, leaving Becky and Justin to saddle up and follow.

Justin whispered, "Guess we had better join them. We'll come back to this later. Okay?"

She nodded, and he hoisted her back into the saddle. The rest of their ride rolled by uneventfully. At the stables, they dismounted, helped water and feed the horses, then brushed them.

Evan kissed Smokey, patting his neck. "I hope I ride you again someday, Smokey. Thanks for the great trip." The horse nodded as though in agreement. Everyone laughed.

At the resort Evan went to play with camp children. Sadie and Becky changed from their nasty clothing stinking of horse sweat.

"Some kiss you and Justin shared." Sadie eyed her curiously.

"Yes, it sure was. I can't believe how quick he responded to the snake. I'm lucky to be alive."

"You're about to get luckier." Sadie laughed. "Tell me you'll sleep with the incredible man. Please?" Sadie spelled each letter and wrapped her arms around her sister.

"We'll see."

Downright giddy at the prospect, Becky could hardly wait for the chance to make love to Justin. She didn't need to tell Sadie.

Being near him her body surged with pleasure. She wasn't about to deny what it craved.

But they needed an appropriate location, time, and discretion so she could protect her son. They couldn't possibly do this weekend, but it was worth waiting for.

CHAPTER 18

As dusk blessed the evening sky she and Justin sat by the water on a picnic table watching Evan catch lightning bugs with the camp kids. They held hands and occasionally stared at each other. The water glistened as it rippled in the slight breeze floating on the evening air. The sun sank as they talked about their past.

Becky was blissful and more at peace than she since her childhood. Being with Justin was good for her soul.

Justin told her about his college days, his job and life in Nashville. "Why aren't you married or at least with a steady woman?"

"I didn't want it. I've had women in my life, of course; but never someone I loved. I got engaged once, but broke it off."

Becky laughed. "I'm sorry. You never met the right woman."

He brought her hand to his lips. "I must agree, and there's nothing to be sorry for. It wasn't right for me, so I ended it—no big deal."

"It sounds like a big deal." She brushed a stray hair from his forehead and her finger tenderly traced his hairline. She longed to slip her fingers into his thick make and pull him to her for a passionate kiss.

"At a young age I realized marriage and forever love don't exist. After losing Mom, I couldn't bear being hurt again. Dad suffered worse. I decided I'd never fall in love."

An interesting turn of events. "Is that so?" She eyed him critically.

"Now I'm starting to believe I may've taken the chicken's way out. Shielding my heart from complex relationships, even with my fiancé, I held back, and cheated myself from infinite possibilities."

"We don't have the power to make the decision. With the right person love is unavoidable. It happens. You don't have a choice. Anyway, it is what I believe."

"You might be right. Was it that way with you and your husband—before he became a raging maniac?" Those deep green caverns of light beckoned her to enlighten him.

"Not at all—youngsters, we dated all through school. We knew each other well and were comfortable together. Everyone expected we'd marry. And we did. Things were fine until he started going downhill. Something inside him snapped, and he became a stranger. But I never had passion or experienced any sort of irresistible pull with him." *Not like with you.*

Conversation was unnecessary between them with no awkward gaps, simply enjoying the view and the person sitting quietly beside.

"Uninhibited laughter of children is a glorious sound." Justin nodded toward the kids playing joyfully.

"Yes, it keeps you present in the moment. It's magical. So giving up on marriage, you ruled out becoming a father. See what you're missing out on?" She couldn't fathom life without Evan.

"I never gave kids much weight until Evan came around. He'd quite a young man. You're lucky to have him."

"I am." Gratification at hearing him praise her son made her realize his opinions mattered, more than they should so soon.

"What about you? Why haven't you remarried? Why isn't there a special man in your life?" His face showed concern she might bring one up.

"I developed a debilitating distrust of men in general. I dated, but not for a long time. It wasn't worth the effort to be honest—a waste of time. I don't have the energy to devote to dating. I never trusted any man enough to let one close. Besides, there's Evan to worry about. He's the special man in my life. He and Sadie need me. It wouldn't be fair to parade a string of guys through Evan's life."

"Sadie has grown into an independent woman."

"Yes, and I'm glad. But Evan's still a boy. There's much he doesn't understand."

Becky opened up to Justin concerning her abusive marriage. She discussed the torment both mental and physical. "I've got control issues. I've struggled to make a life for us and done it controlling every aspect. I'm afraid to let go of control."

"Sadie is self-sufficient. You did a good job with her, and should be proud. Evan of course, is still young and vulnerable. I understand protecting your son. But I'm confused about one thing. Your husband sounds like a son of a bitch. Why is Evan so proud of him? He bragged about his daddy the football star who everyone."

"People loved Brent. He was fun to be around. A high school football star, he played in college until injured. He changed him. He considered himself a failure. He drank heavily. I heard he cheated on me. It doesn't matter. He lost his job because of the drinking, laid around the house all day in sweats drinking. Something broke inside, and he gave up. He started verbally abusing me. He blamed me for everything bad ever happened to him." She wiped a tear from her eyes. After all the years, it still hurt.

"I couldn't get through to Brent. Each time I tried talking with him he grew madder. He started knocking me around and used sex to hurt me. One night he beat me badly. I had enough. When he passed out, I grabbed my purse taking the clothes on my back. I drove away in my car, which I paid for, and never looked back."

"I see." Justin put his arm around her shoulders. She laid her head against his.

"You never told Evan about his Dad's mean side?" Justin didn't accuse, only asked.

"No and I never will. It serves no purpose. Brent doesn't realize he exists. I doubt he'd care. Evan isn't aware of the divorce. Far as he's concerned, his dad died when he was a baby. Revealing the truth would hurt Evan. Brent has injured us enough. I won't allow his memory to upset my son. It's best he has fond memories." She stiffened in his arms and their eyes met.

"It's kind and wise of you. Your secret is safe with me." She relaxed into his embrace. "Tell me about you and Sadie."

"I'm exceedingly proud of Sadie. She has grown into an amazing woman. You're right about her. She is mature and self-sufficient. I've depended on her too much. She deserves a life of her own. Time she had freedom. This move has been good for her. She's blossoming more every day." Becky sat erect to face him. "Sadie was a teenager when our parents died. A single mom starting a new life I struggled, balancing baby-sitters and a full hospital work schedule."

"You've done well. What happened to your parents?"

"They took a vacation with another couple. Their rented plane crashed in the Colorado mountains. It was a shock. Sadie and I adored them. They were incredible parents, there for me with love and support when I left Brent, and anxious to become grandparents."

"They willed the house to me and Sadie. I moved out of the apartment and into it to be with

Sadie when the court awarded me her guardian. I helped her finish high school and college. She helped me raise Evan. We're a team and love each other very much. I couldn't have survived without Sadie." She beamed with pride.

"Your bond and shared love is unmistakable."

They returned to the house at dusk, time for Evan to hit the sack. He kissed everyone goodnight. Becky helped him ready for bed and tucked him in with a kiss.

"I love it here, Mom. Mr. Justin and Grandpa Richard are super. Mr. Justin is so nice and likes me. Doesn't he?" Evan acted hopeful.

"I'm sure of it. They both like you. And you bring them a boatload of happiness." She kissed his forehead and tucked the covers snuggly around him.

"I wish we could stay forever." Evan smiled and closed his eyes, having no idea how complex a wish he had, or how much his mom wanted the same thing. Evan had the right idea. Becky liked Justin more than she'd known possible, and would adore living in this peaceful place.

Too much, too soon.

"Sleep tight. We'll visit Justin and Richard whenever we can." Silently she closed the door.

The grownups spent the evening playing Euchre in the living room of Sadie's cottage so they could be close to the sleeping boy. The next morning they breakfasted together as usual.

They piled into cars and drove to a bluegrass festival along the lane at another resort. Armed with lawn chairs and a cooler, they sat close the stage.

Justin held Becky's hand while they listened to professional music, and everyone enjoyed the entertainment.

Evan spent the day romping around the camp with other children, having made a few friends during his visit. Many vacationed at Richard's resort having come for the festival.

"This is delicious Kentucky burgoo and cornbread." Becky took the last bite of the steamy stew.

"They cater it here from the restaurant in town where I bought our horseback picnic lunches."

"The hot metts loaded with sauerkraut and mustard are wonderful, too." Sadie wiped a dab of mustard from JJ's cheek with a napkin.

"I couldn't resist trying those ghoetta burgers. They tasted delightful on steamy sesame seed buns with lettuce and mayonnaise." Becky handed Evan her last bite of the delectable sandwich.

"I agree. I've never tried ghoetta on a sandwich. I've only fried it and had it for breakfast with eggs. This is a surprising treat." Sadie laughed at JJ who sped off to buy another sandwich, still hungry.

As they packed everything into the carts for the trip home Becky leaned against Justin's side. "We had a lovely time. This is a fabulous idea. Thank you."

He bent and kissed her on the lips. The soft, sweet brush left her wishing for more. It was all they could have now, and it was wonderful too.

Had she died and woken in another realm where life came easy, love was possible, and everything was perfect? She dreaded leaving the foreign world for home. Life had been anything but easy or perfect, but she had a couple of wonderful people in her life making it worthwhile.

Pulling away from these people would be difficult. Becky was at ease with them. They made her comfortable, right at home and she was growing to love them like family. She hadn't realized how much she missed having a large family—time to return to the real world.

"Will you return next week?" Richard hugged Becky goodbye.

"Evan has a scouting trip next weekend with his troop. He'll be camping with his scout buddies."

"You can come by yourself." Richard's green eyes were milkier but sported the sparkle his son's had. With hesitation y she resisted their pleading.

Sadie clutched her arm anxiously. "It would be great, Becky. Can you?"

Eager faces and encouragement in Justin's enticing eyes caused her to surrender.

"I could drive there after putting him on the bus at four and be here around five. Is it okay with you? Sure you don't mind me coming without my charming son?" She tweaked Richard's cheek teasingly.

"The boy is a definite plus, but we love you too, Becky. We'd love having you around." Richard kissed her cheek.

Sadie helped Evan into his booster seat and locked the seatbelt. She gave him a quick peck and mussed his hair. "Don't burn the woods down next weekend. Okay?"

"Aw, Aunt Sadie, they won't trust us to tend a fire alone. We'll be careful."

With another peck on the tip of his nose, she grinned. "Well, have a blast, man." They high-five slapped, and she shut the car door. Sadie gave Becky one last wave and trotted to the deck where Richard waited.

Justin walked to the car and loaded Becky's bags while she gave Sadie one last hug and kiss. "See you Friday, Sadie. I love you."

"Sure thing, Becky. We'll talk tomorrow." Sadie headed toward the door. "Ricky, I'll grab your evening meds."

Becky strolled to where Justin waited by her open car door. She eased closer toward him so they were nose-to-nose and his head tilted toward her. "I'm excited about you returning next weekend. It makes your leaving bearable. I'll miss you something awful. As much as I love the little man, it will be nice having you to ourselves for a change." His voice low and gravely, filled with pent up emotion, only for her ears. "I hate your leaving. We've only begun to understand each other. I want to spend time with you. I've never been so desperate to be with anyone before." Taking her hands in his, he brought them to his lips and kissed, making it hard for her to draw breath.

"Call me?"

"Of course, if I can't hold you in my arms and touch you, at least I can hear your sweet voice on the phone. We'll talk every evening, like last week." His longing eyes mirrored her desperation.

"It would be great." She tried not sounding choked up and wasn't sure she succeeded.

His hand tenderly cradled her head, and he pulled her to him. The other slid around touching her back above the waist. A shock raced through her at the contact, and she savored heat he transmitted. Pulling her lips to his they kissed, and her world ceased rotating for those seconds.

Agonizingly parting he whispered, "Something to remember me."

She smiled and climbed in straining to suppress tears. She waved and drove out of the resort with a sniff.

"You okay, Mom?" Evan's cupid voice sounded alarmed.

"Sure, honey. Mommy has something in her eye. I'm fine."

Justin called Becky nightly after she put Evan to bed. Lounging in bed they talked for hours each evening, gradually becoming more aware each other. They discussed their childhoods. Justin told hilarious stories of harrowing escapes during his and JJ's youths.

They both had enjoyed healthy, fun experiences growing up in wholesome environments—though Justin had recently learned his past held a frightening, disgusting secret concerning his father. He worried how to handle it, but didn't discuss it with Becky. She had no need to learn the appalling truth about Richard's past.

Becky revealed her terror when her man turned on her, and abuse shattered her life. No wonder she sought control in personal relationships and had avoided involvements as a self-defense mechanism.

Thankfully, she wasn't instinctively fearful of Justin. He wasn't sure why. He couldn't wait to see where their budding romance led.

"I never discussed my fear of loss with anyone until you, Becky. And lately Dad and I chatted about it. We're getting into deep discussions these days. No time to waste."

Completely unlike himself, Justin shared something as intimate with another soul. He never met a woman worth the risk—until Becky. He viewed things differently. Richard's illness forced him to rethink life re-evaluating what he wanted. He had begun lowering his defenses.

"Business success and excitement was fine, but I've started realizing I want more from life." He wanted someone to share it with, someone who understood him and cared. He wanted someone to love. He wanted Becky.

"It sounds like you've experienced it and it's lost its luster. Maybe you're ready for something different. I love my work and genuinely care for my patients." Her soft voice over the phone made him wish she cuddled in his arms.

"It shows in the way you cared for Dad and me. You're the best nurse I've ever met."

"Sadie isn't too shabby." Becky teased.

"No, Sadie is amazing. She's a godsend. Thanks so much for letting her stay with us this summer. She's made a world of difference in our lives, and Dad loves her to distraction."

"She's pretty darned lovable."

"She is, but so is her sister." Silence on the line scared Justin. Had he gone too far?

Justin told her hilarious stories about his work. "I'm enjoying Ben's practice more than I ever did corporate law. It's so personal, gratifying and meaningful. I'm bettering lives of people I help. They're glad for my service. I'm a friend helping friends. It's a humbling experience."

"Maybe you're better suited to small town practice."

"Maybe it's something to consider." He'd been considering all manner of strange notions lately, and his world had flipped topsy-turvy.

Becky and Justin bared their souls delving into their worst fears. She finally leveled with him. "Evan's dad isn't really dead. Brent Simms is his father. I was unaware I was pregnant when he nearly killed me and I ran away. He never saw me during the divorce. I didn't want him in Evan's life because he would only hurt the child in more ways than I can fathom. He doesn't deserve Evan. I'll never give him the power to hurt my son—not like he hurt me. It is best Evan continue thinking his dad a decent guy, and we were blissfully happy when he died. At least, he can look up to him—and Brent can't hurt him."

"Wow, it's one hell of a revelation. Sadie knows?"

"Of course, but the devil himself couldn't drag it out of her. She loves Evan as much as I."

"Becky, I understand why you kept it all these years. I'm sure it's been a burden. Thanks for sharing. What happens if Brent finds out?"

"I'd kill him before I let him near my baby." Vehemence in her voice frightened Justin. It hurt him hearing about her pain and knowing she carried such a terrifying load on her slim shoulders. They laughed and joked, enjoying each other's company more every day. Each night they grew closer and closer.

Justin burned to make love to Becky. Recalling her reaction on the swing the way she writhed in his arms. The scent of her, the honeysuckle aroma of her hair, the way her tongue tasted and how silky his mouth was against her tongue. He relished the sparkle in her eyes when she gave in to her orgasm. The sound of her gasp as she climaxed for him still echoed in his mind.

He had smelled her on his hand afterward and hadn't washed it before retiring so he had fallen asleep sniffing her scent. Memories drove him mad with anticipation, and he could hardly sleep for dreaming of her.

By Wednesday night Justin signed off with a signature blessing. "This is me kissing you goodnight, sweet Becky. I can't wait to see you on Friday." Feeling silly like a fool schoolboy, he couldn't resist. He made a kissing sound which she repeated. They hung up wistfully retiring.

♥♥♥♥

Becky grew deeper and deeper in love. She talked each evening with Sadie as well. "Justin is amazing. He treats me like I'm precious. It's easy opening up to him. We talk about things I haven't discussed with anyone before. For the first time since childhood I feel secure because of him, and it is comforting knowing he cares."

"I feel that way about JJ, too. He's such a gentleman. He treats me like a treasure he cherishes. I love being with him and ache for him when he leaves."

"We've got it bad, Sadie. I hope we survive this summer."

"Me too, but what a way to go." Sadie wickedly giggled.

"You know, I married Brent, but it's different with you. I guess I loved him at first—in a way. Now I'm questioning whether I ever loved him at all. Maybe we were just comfortable together and took the easy way out marrying each other."

"Whatever it was, you're better off without the deadbeat." Sadie gave Brent no slack and loathed him for the way he'd treated Becky. "The jerk-off couldn't have been any good in the sack."

"Honestly, I tolerated it. It made him happy. I never felt sexy or wanted sex with Brent. I wanted to please him. It wasn't unpleasant during the good years, but it wasn't earth shattering either. When he became cruel and abusive, sex became torture. Sometimes I used sex to calm him, to help him fall asleep so he wouldn't hit me."

"The pig. He's despicable." Sadie spat the words. They turned teasing. "You have the hots for Justin. Does he make you feel sexy?"

"Justin is different. I feel good about myself with him. He's proud of me—not threatened by me. When our eyes lock my pulse shoots into overdrive." He made her hot with desire, beyond her control igniting a smoldering fire threatening to burst into flames at his touch. The prospect of being with him energized Becky.

"I find myself day-dreaming about him imagining how it would be between us." His skin against hers, his lips on her lips, she wanted to touch him, to taste him, and to make him wild with desire. She longed to experience him inside her, to hold him naked against her bare skin, and experience his surrender coming inside her.

How would she act? Maybe call out his name? She shivered reflexively at the image in her mind of her lying beneath his heated body covering hers, skin-on-skin. She wanted to please Justin in every way, and he confessed on the phone he felt the same.

"I can hardly wait to see him on Friday." Becky was determined to make love to Justin this coming weekend.

"Becky, the man's a basket case, talking about you all the time. He can't wait to see you too." Sadie sounded as though she approved.

No week ever lasted so long before.

CHAPTER 19

Justin had court on Friday and should arrive home by six. Sadie and Richard would be home when Becky arrived. Richard started weakening and spending much of his time in a wheel chair these days to conserve his energy for better things. But they still tried to keep things as normal as possible.

Richard and Justin went out on the lake fishing on Tuesday. They took the golf cart to Richard's private bass boat Justin had loaded with their gear. Richard pulled the boat out of the slip and started cruising through the no wake zone. His face showed concern.

"Something isn't right." They listened to the boat sounds.

"The bilge pump is working overtime."

"That's it. It should be moving along easier but is struggling and feels heavier than normal. She's taking on water."

As they reached the end of the no wake zone, he put the boat into a higher gear attempting to bring it onto a plane so it would ride smoothly. The motor continued struggle to achieve appropriate speed. They exchanged worried looks, and Richard spun the boat around toward the dock. Instead of mooring in his normal slip, he guided it carefully onto the boat lift in its special slot and shut the ignition off.

"Unload while he called the mechanic." Richard pulled out his cell and made the call. "We fish off the dock today." After the call, settled into deck chairs in a shady spot on the marina deck, they baited hooks and cast lines. "Bob will check on the boat soon as he finishes a job at Bear Foot Landing."

"Glad to hear it. I noticed a gas film following us on the water as we cruised in. There must be a fuel leak."

"Yeah, and the craft is obviously taking in water."

They fished for a while. Bob arrived with his tool kit. He set to work. By the time he finished the exam and reported, Richard and Justin had caught two catfish, a seven pound bass and half dozen crappies.

"You had a successful afternoon after all." Bob leaned on the support brace.

"Yep, not bad. How is our beauty?" Richard eyed his friend.

"A leaking hose to the live well cause her suck water."

"It doesn't sound too bad. You can fix it. What about the fuel?"

"I sealed the hose and put a new line in. It wasn't such a big deal. Had it been merely that, I'd consider it simple wear and tear, though it didn't appear to be. The fuel tank leak is another story, definitely not wear and tear, but a deliberate puncture."

"We took it out last week but didn't hit anything to puncture it."

"Yeah, it wasn't an accident. Someone punched a hole in the line with what appears to have been the tip of a knife. It is a clean stab mark." Bob cleaned his wrench with a hanky shaking his head.

Richard acted pensive. "Our vandal is at work. I'll report it to JJ."

"It's unusual for you to have vandals. I don't ever recall it happening before." Justin cocked his head pondering.

"You're right. Sam contacted the security company. They dropped off a couple brochures. We should select a plan and let them install cameras."

Bob prepared to leave. "I'll bring a new tank tomorrow and replace the damaged one." After Bob left, they chatted while Justin cleaned the fish.

"It is a good thing you know your boat well and spotted the problem before we cruise too far from the marina."

"Yeah, if made it onto the main lake before noticing the issue, the boat would've sunk, and we might've drowned."

Justin cringed, thinking of what little time he had left with his dad being stolen by a reckless vandal. It irked him someone dare mess with Richard's personal equipment. Third strike, something was fishy in the camp, and it didn't come from the water.

He walked toward the marine store where

Garrett changed burnt out lights. After initial greetings and catch up chatter, Justin got to the point. "I want to review security footage to see if anything turns up to aid the JJ's investigation. Would you inspect our guests' boats and rental fleet? Make sure there's no further damage. Also, please drain Dad's fuel tank of remaining gas, so Bob can replace it tomorrow."

"Sure enough, Justin. I'll get right on it. Sorry about your trouble."

"No worries. We'll get to the bottom of it."

By the time he returned to Richard, he'd had a heart to heart with JJ about vandalism. There had been no surge in problems brought to JJ's attention, but he promised to check out resort guests in case one of them could be the culprit.

"It won't help. Our cabins turned over twice since this started a couple weeks ago. New renters arrive weekly. Between Sadie's escapade, yours, now this, each incident occurred with a separate group of customers staying here. It's more likely a local thing. JJ's checking with nearby resorts making sure they aren't having problems they haven't yet reported."

"Good. We need kick this thing in the bud before it gets worse or someone's seriously injured." The idea sent shivers through Justin's spine.

The week flew by smoothly with no

incidences found. No evidence showed up on video. Richard and Justin chose a new security system, which would soon be installed when the company could work them into their schedule.

Thursday Justin finally received the private investigators report with information on the shooting incident from Richard's past. Omitting Richard's name from the request and not explaining why he sought the information raised no flags with the professional. Confidentiality the PI's stock in trade, he didn't press Justin with questions, only gathered enough facts to do his job—the rest none of his concern.

The victim's widow partnered with the mob on her clubs, unlike her deceased husband. She inherited his share of a couple co-owned clubs. It sounds like she either became coerced by his murder, involved in it, or wanted to improve profit margin.

Her partnerships proved profitable, accumulating a substantial nest egg. She later sold the clubs, netting a sizeable sum of money soon before the FBI targeted mob activity in five major cities during the mid-seventies when Newport ceased to be a gambling and prostitution mecca.

Her other business ventures proved not so fortunate, like her prostitution ring operated out of a motel. A call girl took a personal check from a local politician, and it proved to be her downfall when the press heard wind of it. It collapsed from there like a sandcastle in the surf. The FBI stepped in and the widow served a ten year prison sentence for pandering, released six years later for good behavior.

Sadie retired to her cabin after dinner. The men half-watched a baseball game on television when Justin handed his dad the report. "Dad, I made inquiries thinking you'd like to learn how things went down after you left northern Kentucky."

Staring at the report Richard let out a huge sigh. "I feared you'd do something like this. I best face the demon. I was always afraid to check into it, for fear of stirring up something I couldn't finish." They sat quietly as Richard perused the paperwork. He smiled and patted Justin's hand. "Thanks, son, this gives me peace of mind, though I'd never have had the guts to seek this data out. I've worried all these years about the family of the man who died the fateful night. I was responsible though I didn't pull the trigger. I participated, though I didn't know they planned the shooting. I had no idea who he was. The guy had a wife and daughter. I never knew. Guilt weighed oppressively all these years. It is awful. I didn't step up to testify. They'd have killed me too, so I'd never have made it to trial. It doesn't matter. I should've done more. A coward of the worst kind, I fled for my life."

"The murder remains an unsolved cold case, a mystery all these years. The mob stood behind the shooting, but couldn't prove it. With the police under their thumbs, you're probably right. You'd have ended up in the river with the murder weapon or in a building foundation surrounded with concrete. The trigger man never being identified in the mob-style killing and no evidence linking them to the crime, there's no way to prosecute."

"My boss in the mob and the shooter got away clean after delivering the message to play their game or die." Richard swiped his hands from chin to hairline with a gusty sigh.

"Most business owners complied after the man was gunned down. They got what they wanted from one slaying. Those who did grew wealthy playing the Devil's game, including the man's widow." Justin grasped his dad's frail, cool hand. It had grown slick and thin-skinned lately, bruising easily reminding them of how short his existence would be.

"The shooter's nickname is Rocco Bonetti. I have no idea what Rocco's given name was. Newport heavily populated Italian families, is home to hundreds of Bonettis." He eyed his son questioningly.

"Dad, without a first name we have no way of tracing the man and learning what became of him. He could be still around living a legitimate life. Or he could've died along the way, either during the mobster heyday or afterward naturally. The man you named as your boss, however, was arrested and convicted. He spent years in a federal prison and died there of a liver disease."

"I'm not sure I wanted to know what became of Rocco. I'm not worried about me, but digging into this too deep could stir trouble for you after I'm out of the picture. If he's still out there, it's in our best interest to stay far away from Rocco, the mob and Newport. Lives of people I care about could depend on it. Some things are better left alone—this being one of those." Richard patted

Justin's hand. Justin nodded, though it soured his stomach knowing a murder might have gotten off easily.

CHAPTER 20

Friday morning Sadie went straight to Richard's room as usual. He slumped, sitting on the edge of the bed, tiring more and more each day. His poor heart struggled to keep him alive. Her heart filled with sadness for him and Justin.

"How you doing this fine day, Ricky?" She grinned happily, faking it, and handed him his robe.

"Been better. You sound very chipper, my love."

"Of course, it is a beautiful day, and I get to spend it with a handsome man." She kissed his cheek and helped him to the bathroom for a shower. She took a seat on the porcelain throne.

"Is JJ joining us?" He called from beneath water spray.

"I meant you, silly." Sadie forced a laugh.

Stepping from the shower, she wrapped his frail body with a huge towel. He wagged his brows wickedly, making fun of her.

"I will be right here if you need me." She stepped out of the bathroom into the bedroom giving him room to towel off. Soon he opened the door wearing his robe and handed her his pajamas, which she tossed into the hamper.

"Ricky, do you know anyone called Ricky the Rock or Ice Pick?"

Stunned he glared. His expression lost emotion going blank. "Those are weird names. Why do you ask?" She handed him a shirt which he slipped on dropping the top of the robe.

"It's weird. Last evening when I walked to my cabin a guy stepped from the shadows. It appeared he walked through the woods from the next camp. He startled me but didn't approach, only asked if I knew his friend; and he gave me those names."

"What did you tell him?" An edge to Ricky's voice caused nerves to itch on the back of her neck.

"I haven't met anyone by those names. I explained you and Justin own the resort, so you might know the guy. You're friends with everyone around. I gave him your name, but it didn't appear familiar to him."

"What else?" Ricky tilted his head with a serious expression.

"He'd stop over sometime for a visit to ask you."

"What did this guy look like?" Richard sounded worried as he zipped his trousers.

"I didn't get a clear glimpse at him in the dark, and he stayed in the shadows. Tall, maybe six-two or better, probably around your age or older with grey hair visible in the moonlight with dark streaks shooting through it; he had a mustache and chewed something while talking, maybe a toothpick the way ex-smokers chew things to distract from the urge for a cigarette. He appeared thick around the middle the way older men sometimes get, but no huge belly, only a paunch."

"He doesn't sound familiar." Richard slipped socks on and reached for his shoes. "Before you fix breakfast, could you reach something from the top shelf of my closet?"

"Sure." Sadie retrieved the folding step stool from the kitchen then climbed up. "What do you need, Ricky?"

"A shoe box in the back, can you hand it down?"

She reached back, moving stored hats and scarves until locating the carton. "Here are your shoes, Ricky. Holler if you need me." She cheerfully placed the weighty box on the bed next to Ricky, folded the ladder and shut the door.

Sadie and Ricky played Scrabble. Justin laughed at their arguments, handing Sadie a dictionary. "You two are hilarious with your strange spelling skills. You're both making up words. Use this."

Justin went to court early afternoon, and Richard took a nap. Sadie prepared a casserole and salad for dinner. She put them in the refrigerator for later. She relaxed with a book on the deck until Ricky woke. Late afternoon after his nap Ricky and Sadie enjoyed a game of gin rummy on the deck.

Laughing at a story Ricky told, they stopped to observe a strange vehicle speed into the resort. It drove too fast for the gravel driveway where guests and children mingled, and well over posted limits. A dust trail erupted behind as the sports car raced down the lane speeding past their cabin to the marina parking lot.

Richard whistled quietly when a long, lanky female emerged from the car. Sadie laughed. "The old boy still has spit and vinegar in him."

"Damn straight. I'm not dead yet." He eyed the leggy blonde.

The stranger stood out at a resort, definitely not dressed for a weekend at the lake. Long, golden tresses reflected the sun's rays as she swung them across her a shoulder to rest mid-way across her straight back. Dark sunglasses shaded her eyes, and she wore a white suit that fit her size two physique perfectly, probably designer and likely costing more than Sadie made in a month. The rock would do a job on her spike heels crunching in gravel as she walked, emphasizing how poorly she fit in the scene.

"The gravel is going to ruin her Jimmy Choo. It's right about a four inch heel."

"What is a Jimmy Choo?" In awe he asked without taking his eyes off the stunning woman.

"Those gorgeous white heels she is wearing. I see red soles from here."

The striking gal picked her way along the planked dock trying not to let her heels stick between decking. Finally she disappeared into the marina store. Returning minutes later she picked her way back to her auto and sped back along the driveway.

"Let's go in. It's time for your afternoon

meds and a snack." Sadie helped Ricky into the cabin.

"Wonder who the woman was?" Richard shook his head. "She sure is a looker, from what I saw."

"Who knows? Maybe she got lost and stopped to ask for directions."

❤❤❤❤

A strange woman in a red sports car sat partially blocking the entrance to the resort when Becky arrived. She searched on her phone.

"You okay?" Becky asked, having stopped beside the stranger's ride.

"Oh, yeah, I'm fine. I need directions to the courthouse. The gal at the marine store told me Justin's there." She drawled sweetly, clearly perusing Becky as though weighing her importance.

"No problem. Take this road for a couple miles and turn left on route seven. It takes you into town and you can't miss the courthouse, front and center." Becky spoke as the strange gal took notes on her phone.

"Thank you, it's very helpful. You are?" Her proprietary tone didn't set well with Becky as the woman studied her across the top of her sunglasses.

"I am Becky Simms. And you?"

"Oh, so you're related to the nurse. I suppose you came to see her." The woman got under Becky's skin.

"I'm Sadie's sister, if it's any of your business. I'm here to visit her, Richard and Justin.

Why do you ask?"

"Clearly you are out of the loop. Justin probably forgot to tell you I'd be here." The blonde bombshell retorted rudely with a cold, indignant glare. "I'm Yancy Bridges, Justin's fiancé. We're spending the weekend finalizing wedding plans. I'm off to town now to meet him for dinner and an evening out. My Justin is such a party animal." The southern belle smile riled Becky as the woman stood her ground, daring Becky to contradict her. "Would you mind telling Richard not to wait up? We'll likely spend the night in town somewhere. We need privacy and will sleep in tomorrow. Perhaps we'll see you sometime, if you're still here." She paused to allow her words to sink in.

"Have a nice visit with your sister." Yancy revved car and sped away, leaving a trail of dust in her wake.

Becky sat stunned, mouth open, not knowing what to say or do. Tears sprang from nowhere. She wiped them with her sleeve. Any rational person could see it plainly. Yancy made things perfectly clear. Becky had tried to intrude on her territory. She needed to get away.

Gravel crunched as her car hastened turning around. The prospect of running into Justin soured her stomach compelling her to flee for safety only distance provided. She sped from the resort as Sadie's image appeared in her rearview mirror.

Furiously sobbing tears blurred vision making the trip hazardous. She sniffled and wiped her eyes trying to see. Truth flashed before her causing unbearable pain consumed with grief and self-loathing having allowed this to happen. Knowing better, she relaxed her guard and allowed Justin in. Justin implied he was free and falling for Becky.

A sham.

He'd played Becky for a fool and she fell for it hook, line and sinker—funny they'd enjoyed fishing together, or at least she had. The no-account player was cruising for a summer fling while his wealthy fiancé orchestrated their wedding in Nashville.

Why had she trusted a man? She knew better. Truth and honor weren't the nature of the beast. Justin was like all the rest and a fantastic actor.

An imbecilic fool, she fell into his mantrap.

CHAPTER 21

Briefcase in hand, Justin chatted with his client while leaving the courthouse. Happy at the prospect of a fun weekend with Becky he hadn't a care in the world. He shook hands in the atrium. "Thank you, Mr. Bader, for your business."

"It is I who should thank you, Mr. Martin. You helped me close probate on Uncle Mo's estate in record time. Being executor wasn't as grueling as I suspected, with you on my side." The older man drew Justin into a hug.

"Take care of yourself. You hear? Don't be a stranger. Dad would love you to drop by sometime."

"Thanks Justin. You made my life easier. I sure appreciate it Son. Tell your daddy *Hey* for me. I'll stop to see him soon." Mr. Bader walked out the door.

Justin approached a bench checking voice mail to see if he needed to do anything before heading home. He hoped to avoid a stop by the office, anxious to rush home to Becky. It seemed like ages since he saw her. Nightly calls made him miss her more.

A tall blonde smiled from across the room. An audacious spectacle, she appeared totally out of place in the ancient, rural courthouse, casual being the key word.

Yancy threw her arms up and strode quickly as her oversized pumps allowed toward Justin. She drew him into a passionate embrace. Surprise, an understatement, Justin was floored.

"Baby, I missed you so much." Yancy gushed taking his shocked face into her hands and smothering his lips. Friends and neighbors stared at the spectacle, either grinning or shaking their heads and laughing.

"It's been too long. I missed my man." Her cooing invaded his space.

Finally getting a grip, he lightly peeled her off him. "What on earth?" He used a demanding voice hoping it would be effective, but it fell short.

"I came to see the love of my life. Naughty boy, you haven't returned my calls, so I came to you. We've so much to do to prepare for our wedding. Plans must be made if we want a fabulous venue; and of course, we do." Her most persuasive smile laid the charm on thick, and her twang played the *southern belle* card.

"What the hell are you talking about? We're not getting married, not now and not ever. I told you we're through." He emphasized those three words. "You shouldn't be here."

He trod toward the door. Close on his heels, Yancy followed rushing to keep pace with his lengthy stride. Clicking of heels behind him riled more than he liked.

"Justin you didn't mean it. You were under terrible stress concerned about your daddy. I've decided to forgive you and overlook it, due to your suffering."

"It's time you came on back home to Nashville, and we get on with our lives." She shadowed him to his car. He opened the door and stared at her.

She leaned into him seductively clutching his jacket lapels. Pity replaced anger and astonishment. He gently pushed her away before she could land another kiss. He hated hurting Yancy more than necessary, but she must understand and go away. Her display forced him to be blunt.

"Yancy, I don't love you. You're a spectacular woman, and I like you. You deserve to be loved and cherished. I have no intentions of marrying you. I made myself clear. I'm sorry you didn't like it, I understand, and it hurts you. Believe me. We're done. Go home to Nashville and get on with your life. Find a man who appreciates the incredible woman you are."

"But, Daddy—"

"It's your problem. You let Landen rule your life. I don't give a damned what your daddy said. You shouldn't either. Don't live your life to please him. You're a remarkable woman. You warrant better than a loveless marriage of convenience. You deserve someone who appreciates you for who and what you are, a man who loves you for yourself, someone better than me. Go home. Find real love. Landon will learn to live with it." Turning his back on the speechless female, he unlocked the door and climbed into his car.

She slid a disapproving finger across the fender leaving a clean streak then eyed her dirty fingertip with her face screwed up. "Yuck, Justin, you've never let your Jag get so dusty. It must be the nasty gravel lane."

Ignoring disapproval he shook his head aimlessly. "I'm sorry, Yancy."

Rejection alien to Yancy who got anything and everything she ever wanted. Stunned, she pouted like a child who had been slapped.

Justin ached witnessing the unavoidable pain he caused. "I treasure good times and fun we shared, but it's not what futures are built on. It isn't enough."

"Justin, you're wrong. We can have a great life."

"It's the saddest thing I ever heard. Yancy, you rate better, and so do I. I sought wealth and power, but no longer. I want love. I wish you the best, Yancy." He rolled the window up, pulled away and headed home to Becky. Yancy stared as he drove away.

♥♥♥♥

Surprisingly Becky's car wasn't in the lot. Sadie and Richard viewed a game show in the living room.

"Hi, Dad, Sadie, what's up? Becky should be here by now. Is she running late? When will she arrive?" He flopped in an easy chair, and propped his feet on the ottoman, exhausted but anxious to see Becky.

"I'm not sure. I may've seen her car earlier." Sadie sounded worried. "She didn't come in. Maybe it wasn't her. The car stopped at the end of the lane pulling out of the resort around the time I expected Becky."

"Why would she leave? Have you tried calling?"

"Oh yeah, I called her cell a couple times. She doesn't answer. Maybe she's in a dead zone. I rang the house too and left a voice message. She hasn't returned my calls." Concern tremored Sadie's voice.

"Maybe you should try her again. Son, you should've seen the visitor who stopped by here today. The gal was a looker—a tall blonde dressed like a queen." Richard snorted.

"Soon after the woman stopped at the store, then sped out of here, I noticed a car like Becky's." Sadie's eyes grew suspicious.

"Oh man, don't tell me." Justin sat at attention. "Yancy came by the courthouse this afternoon. I suspect she stopped at the marina. She wore a white suit."

"So did this gal—must've been your Yancy." Richard gave him a disapproving glare.

"She's not my Yancy—not anymore." Guilt choked him, but he needed his voice. "I cleared things with her today—for good. Geez, I hope she didn't cause trouble with Becky. I wonder what she said." He winced.

Richard grimaced. "Your delusional ex might've been jealous. After all, you haven't talked with her for a while. If she had any clue of something between you and Becky, would she be vindictive?"

"Oh wow, Dad, I'm afraid she might. She ambushed me at the courthouse. I didn't know what hit me." Dread swarmed him like a humid breeze. "I told her we were through a while back. It didn't sink in. She decided to come here, and we'd pick up where we left off. She wanted me to return to Nashville and pretend I'd never mentioned breaking up."

"How did you handle it?" Richard glared with an, *I told you so* brow cocked cynically.

"After the shock, I explained I don't love her. I have no intention of marrying her and am not sure I'll return to Nashville. That life was eons ago, another world, and I don't fit there any longer. I no longer want the same things." He blinked clearing cobwebs. "I sent Yancy home. She should be halfway there by now."

"I'm glad it's settled." Stress lines on Richard's face dissipated. "Now you need to find Becky."

Panic set in. "Good grief, if Yancy and Becky met, I bet Yancy gave her a piece of her territorial mind. God knows what she told Becky."

He pulled out his cell and dialed Becky's home number leaving a message when he heard her machine. He tried her cell. Her message system was full and not taking messages. He tried it again, getting the same thing.

She's avoiding calls.

"Oh man, I'd better find her. There's no telling what nonsense Yancy put in her head." He snatched his keys and bolted out shouting as he slid the patio door shut. "Don't wait on me for dinner. I have no idea when or if I will be home tonight. I have to fix this." He jumped into his Jag and raced out of the resort.

Justin tried Becky's phone again while driving but each time received a recorded message. Increasingly worried, he dialed his dad again. Neither Richard nor Sadie had yet heard from Becky by the time he stopped for gas. While pulled over, he rang Yancy.

"Yancy here." Her chipper voice sang of an obvious full recovery.

"Yancy, this is Justin."

"How sweet of you to check and make sure I didn't drive off a cliff. It's quite an ego you have, Justin. Listen, buster, I will get along fine without you. Actually, I'm perfect. An overbearing weight has been lifted." She had a right to be sarcastic.

"I'm glad you're well and wish you the best." He meant it. Yancy wasn't at fault for their failed love affair.

"What do you want?" Her normal demanding disposition returned. At least she bounced back quickly, a good thing.

"By any chance did you meet a woman today at the resort?" His breath stalled, willing her to say no.

"Well sure. I met a lovely woman, Sam at the marina."

"Yes, Sam is a sweetheart. She and her husband work for Dad. Anyone else?" A long sigh eased out.

"A mini-brunette in a nondescript grey sedan gave me directions." Her voice loaded with contempt. "The nurse's sister called you and your dad *friends*. You sound worried, darling. Is there a problem?" The way she spoke laying on the southern belle charm emphasized she understood exactly what he meant.

"What did you tell her?" He moaned, wiping sweat from his brow.

"Is she your new squeeze, Justin baby? I can't believe you threw me over for a drab little mouse." She cooed menacingly.

"Get off it, Yancy. I didn't throw you over for a woman. I broke up with you before I knew her. Becky is more than a friend. She doesn't deserve to be hurt. What did you tell her?" She wasn't used to anyone using such a rough, demanding tone with her. He'd never spoken to Yancy that way, not to any woman. Remorse came with his words, but he needed her to level with him.

"Gotten over me so quickly, hum?"

"There is nothing to get over. We weren't meant to be together. I figured I could spend the rest of my life with you though I never loved you. Love was a bunk, a concocted excuse used for sticking with marriage when passion died. Now I know better. I've changed in the past month and see things differently. I didn't leave you for Becky. I broke up with you then fell in love with her. It's a real, forever love."

"Is that right?" Her cynical voice made hair on his neck stand erect.

"Yes, and I hope you find it too. Now tell me what you said to Becky."

"All right. I told her, you and I were making wedding plans enjoying a lover's weekend together, would be out late and would sleep in. I had no idea the little twerp was important to you. I assumed she was a distracting dalliance, a minor indiscretion. I was willing to forgive you due to stress."

"It's big of you, Yancy. Your territorial jealousy may've destroyed the most beautiful, worthwhile, important thing in the world to me."

Desperation in his voice must've bored through her thick ego. Her voice sounded remorseful and frank, shocking Justin. "I wonder if anyone will ever care as much for me. I'm truly sorry, Justin. I had no idea you'd become serious about this woman. I hope I didn't ruin your chance with her. Please forgive me."

Maybe he'd gotten through to Yancy— finally. She wasn't a bad person. Self-centered and spoiled—yes, but she sounded concerned and regretful.

"Thanks for the honesty. I need to make her understand. If she cares, she'll listen." At least he managed sounding confident.

"Thank you, Justin. I hope it works out for you. You've been nothing but honest with me. Not many people are. Bye, love." Yancy clicked off.

CHAPTER 22

In her sanctuary Becky lay on her bed engulfed in tears refusing to stop. Humiliated, she couldn't remain at the lake, a party to Justin's unforgivable deceit. A summer fling with her might not mean much in his world, but it devastated her.

Suspicion flourished in her mind. Defensively she protested, not wanting to admit she'd allowed herself to be used cheaply. Evidence was there all the time, and she ignored it. Like a fool, she never inquired about his love life.

She assumed when he kissed her, he was free to do so. Her perception dead wrong, she had no idea he wanted a brief fling, something to take his mind off Richard's illness. *Unfair.*

Her lack of resolve brought dreadful consequences. Her fault and she had no one to blame. She shouldn't have needed to interrogate him. *He should've been honest.*

Like a sap she'd allowed Justin's boyish charm to breach her defenses. So unlike herself, she had been impulsive, luxuriating in the blissful sensation of falling in love. Now she paid the price.

313

Betrayed by her heart, evidence proved she genuinely cared for the cad. She allowed him to deceive her thinking he cared. Her drastic error in judgment oblivious to his scheme had deemed him honorable. In denial, she welcomed the interlude with open arms, and he had his fun.

What a fool? She didn't know him at all. They remained virtual strangers.

Consumed with hopelessness, she cried until emotionally and physically drained and tears came no more. No stranger to abuse, having grieved tremendous loss, but somehow this hurt worse. Intense sorrow was excruciating.

She didn't need a man. Usually she heeded intuition and kept a distance. It worked before. Instinct failed this time. No warning signals to be ignored—none came. Her dulled sensitivity gave no hunch Justin played an imposter and loving him had destroyed her.

How would she go on having loved Justin and lost him? But that wasn't true either. She never had him. *He belongs to another*.

Irrelevant. She needed to focus on Evan and forget her needs. A deep fortifying breath didn't dull the painful experience, but past taught her intensity would gradually diminish with time.

She needed to shake memories she couldn't afford. Dwelling on their love making would increase pain.

Damn.

She'd miss his kisses and warm embrace.

CHAPTER 23

Becky's car parked in her driveway. He bolted a few steps to a porch and banged on the door. *No answer.* He rang the bell, and it chimed inside. *No answer.* He rang again to no avail then paced around before banging again.

"Becky, I know you're home. I must talk with you. Let me in, please."

She lay in her bed gripping a blanket, struggling to block his pleading voice. She wasn't good at confrontation and didn't want to speak with him.

The damned pounding continued. "I'm not leaving." His defiant voice shouted.

Neighbors would notice. She needed to send him home. It wouldn't be easy facing him, and she trembled at impending conflict.

Foddering the neighborhood gossip grapevine, Justin paced wildly. The guy next door watering his lawn stared. The lady across the street carrying in groceries leaned on her trunk watching with arms crossed.

Justin shrugged then yelled, "Becky, I'll

continue making a scene until you let me in. Open the door. I'm not going until I talk with you. Let me in before someone calls the police."

Time to face the piper and make him leave. Get it over with.

Reluctantly opening the door, she stepped aside allowing entrance with palpable tension firing the air. Angry and shaken, she put distance between them fleeing across the room to escape nearness.

♥♥♥♥

Realization struck a blow. She feared him.

No wonder with her past. He deeply regretted his frustration caused this reaction.

Tempted to grab and hold her close, he fought the instinct. Instead of reassuring her it would have the opposite effect. He forced his barely controlled temper to calm and bury itself.

With a clipped voice she glared. "What do you want?"

"I expected you at the lake."

"I got busy and forgot to call Sadie to say I wasn't coming. It slipped my mind. It was unnecessary for you to drive all this way." Her weak smile and ineffective lie evidenced her struggle to maintain dignity. She kept moving putting increasing space between them.

He pictured them comfortably lounging on the couch in the comfy room, or propping feet on the wicker trunk serving as a coffee table, watching television.

"I 'ah needed to see you. I worried when you weren't at the resort. I need to make sure you are okay." Eyeing her suspiciously, swollen, red eyes and disarrayed curls showed she'd been crying. Responsibility for her tears ripped a gash in his gut and he grew weak.

"I'm sorry. You drove all this way for nothing. I stayed home. I should've called to explain." She sniffed and blew her nose on a tissue.

"We were concerned. Dad, Sadie and I have been trying to reach you by phone. Our calls went straight to voicemail." He stepped toward the center of the room.

Instinctively she retreated further. Nearness frightened her. "I apologize. I was busy with projects, and time got away from me. I didn't realize my cell died."

Justin wasn't buying the lie for a second. Her appearance said it all. "I'm glad you're okay."

Contempt flared across her face; but her words refused to acknowledge it. Lying came easier when you didn't have to face a person. She must be regretting not taking his call.

Obviously extremely upset, she attempted avoiding eye contact, staring into the backyard. He pictured her tending the vegetable garden while Evan swung on the swing set.

"I'm hoping to persuade you to reconsider. Come to the lake with me." He tried pleading with his eyes, but she avoided him.

Justin anticipated her being hurt and angry. He hadn't considered she'd try to hide or ignore it, pretending they'd meant nothing to each other.

Why doesn't she scream and yell?

How could she send him packing without telling him off? She acted resolved to avoid inevitable conflict.

A*voidance due to abusive history?*

His heart did a nosedive, and every ounce of fortitude he'd mustered dissipated. *Revelation*—he lived in that category now—with her ex-husband— a potential abuser. *Damn.*

Attempting to appear gracious she assumed a light hearted approach. The act came across as anything but carefree as she struggled to pretend she was.

She retreated to the kitchen, leaned on the counter with feet riveted to the floor, and arms crossed tried to mask what appeared to be contempt. With unwavering resolve she shook her head with an exaggerated refusal.

"No thank you, Justin. You wasted your time." She turned her back, busily wiping the counter. "I have too much to do."

He didn't respond, only waited. Finally with determination, "Go now." She tried to sound firm and demanding. Instead it came across pleading.

"We need to talk. I want you to understand." Justin ventured closer intrigued by her attempts to dissuade him. She must care or she wouldn't appear so upset. He refused to be distracted by her obvious need for detachment.

Taking a seat at the bar across from where she worked aimlessly rearranging countertop items, he hoped to send a signal. He wasn't leaving unheard. He must explain. He had allowed this to occur ignoring Yancy's delusions and responsible for hurting Becky; but determined to rectify her misperception.

She may never forgive him, but she'd hear the truth. He owed Becky complete honesty.

At best he'd declare undying love for her. He wasn't sure how she'd take it. So he must play it slow. At worst, they'd clear the air, and she'd tell him to hit the bricks anyway—*her choice*.

Even with smeared mascara and swollen eyes Becky was tantalizingly lovable. He longed to cuddle her in his arms and shield her from lurid visions running through her mind about him. He deserved her scorn. He sought any sign of encouragement, but found none.

"There's nothing to talk about." Anger flashed across her face, yet she denied its existence. Apparently she had determined to hide her emotions.

"First, I need you to know, I'd never physically harm you. You've no need to fear me."

"I . . . I'm not afraid." Her quivering voice begged to differ.

"Becky, don't pretend. You came to the lake . . . and met Yancy. She told me what she said to you. It's a lie."

"Yes Jason, I met your lovely fiancé. I'm pleased for you. How thoughtful of her to surprise you with a romantic weekend, though it cramped your style a tad. Go home to her." Her voice fell flat, devoid of sensation and barely audible. Her normal even-tempered personality distorted by the only sign of sentiment—her tell-tale blush as she gazed out the window. *Beautiful*—all he could do to not reach and touch a corkscrew curl falling across her forehead.

Integrity blemished. Justin expected an interrogation, accusations and anger. Instead he faced a precious woman's generous efforts to mask pain and anger. This foreign scenario where something inside snapped proved he'd destroyed his chances with Becky.

He groaned loudly, and laid his head across his arms on the bar. Pounding his fist on the surface a tea cup sitting beside it bounced and clanged.

Becky jumped and gasped holding her hands still clutching the dish rag against her chest. Her eyes widened and she paled as though blood drained from her face.

Damn it, he'd done it again.

When he didn't stand allowing his controlled fury to take over, she took a deep breath then blew it out her mouth. Her shoulders rose and fell. She shook them and blinked.

"Becky, I'm so sorry. I didn't mean to startle you."

Garish images playing in her head made her furious, but she kept her anger at bay. She couldn't risk allowing him to see it.

She had no intention of sharing her bruised ego. She'd tried hiding pain lurking beneath the surface threatening to devour her. Refusing to linger too close to the flame, she'd escaped to the kitchen.

How dare he blame me for worrying him?
He lied to me. Some gall.

She struggled to defy conflicting emotions
flaring. Fury and resentment at his invasion of her
safe haven, her home when broken hearted she
sought privacy to lick her wounds. She abhorred
these intrusions.

On the other hand, she wanted his arms
around her. But recognizing it for a lapse in
judgement she'd eventually get over.

Reality of Justin in her home made it worse.
She dared not allow him to learn his power over
her. She'd tried convincing him to leave before she
succumbed to the scoundrel's attraction. But Justin
proved to be a skilled, well-seasoned player
pretending sincerity.

Realization struck a hearty blow—had she
known no better, she would've raced into his
unworthy arms. Horrified at her involuntarily draw
to him, she resented recklessly falling in love with
Justin. He did not deserve it.

"We planned a weekend together, a few
laughs and a good time. It changed to a romantic
interlude with your fiancé. I'm getting on with my
life. It's simple. There's no need to press the matter
further. Go." She faced him and leaned against the
counter, arms crossed. *Matter settled.*

"Be reasonable, Becky. Give me five
minutes and a chance to explain. Afterward if you
want me to leave, I will. Hear me out." His words
sounded soft and without anger.

He stared intently, as though trying to read
her thoughts. His hand lifted toward her as though

to touch her. She backed away until her butt rested against the range. His hand shot back to the other, and they clung together on the counter.

"Reflecting on our time together and the incredible meaning I've found in it, you're being exceedingly decent with me. I want to acknowledge it, and thank you."

"It's nothing. I'm bowing out of an illicit affair, allowing you freedom to continue your relationship with Yancy unscathed. She's your life. I should've realized I only substituted as a temporary dalliance."

"Becky, your generosity is both endearing and demeaning. I hate it. You deserve more than you've been dealt."

Forcefully he talked without standing, like he feared she'd bolt—which she might. "I must clear the air. I won't allow Yancy's outrageous accusations to control fate of our relationship. You're too important. You're the best thing ever happened to me, and I won't give you up without a fight."

"There's nothing to fight about. Everything is fine. We had fun. It's over. End of story." Words barely audible, she hardly recognized her voice.

"I make no excuses. This is my fault. I failed you. I failed both of us. I don't deserve forgiveness. There's no one to blame but myself. We're paying a high price for my procrastination. I won't attempt to justify my actions, but I owe you an apology. Thank you for the gift of hearing me out. I'm sorry I've hurt you."

He emphasized his seriousness, but she

didn't trust her instincts with Justin. "I took greater care dealing with Yancy and her feelings. For that I'm sorry. Distracted by Dad's illness and shocking revelations of his past, I neglected to handle the situation with her. She harbored hope of reconciliation, yet I allowed it to linger, putting off the unavoidable. I should've known better, understanding how unpredictable she is. I should've made her accept the end of our relationship before starting anything with you. I tried to keep her dignity intact and hoped she'd see the light and dump me or realize I was right for her. Delaying confrontation has injured you and ruined what we had together."

"We had nothing but a good time between us, Justin. No worries." Her shaky voice sounded weaker than she meant it to.

He may be penetrating her armor, but she didn't want him to know. She leaned against the stove with arms braced and feet apart in warrior princess stance.

"Don't say it. It's not true. I should've protected our blossoming love. I've shamefully wounded you beyond repair, and any chance I had to win you over has been destroyed. Purity of what we shared and emotions surfacing between us are what futures are built on. You're way too good for me, and I don't deserve you."

She eyed him directly for the first time. "No, you don't. And there was nothing real between us. You're a player, a user. You omitted facts and deceived me."

Hell.

He could hardly stop himself from rushing to pull her against him. He loved her more than he realized, and his world seemed an empty cavern without her in it. He wanted and needed her in his life and had to try winning her back—even if he failed.

"I didn't lie. It doesn't matter, but Yancy fabricated the story she told you. What matters is I put you in a compromising position allowing her to do it, and how badly it damaged our chances to be together." Desperately he quietly studied her reaction.

"You're the most irritating man in the world." For the first time, Becky raised her voice and balled fists at her sides.

It shocked him but gave him hope. If she'd let the anger out, it might heal. "You're right. Your accusations and suspicions are accurate. In the past I wanted superficial relationships and good times. I intended to marry Yancy. I liked her, but I never loved her. She was fun, exciting and beautiful—a win-win situation. I received unlimited opportunity, power and access to wealth. She married someone to manage her life and take care of her every need. All she and I wanted at the time, so we settled for it. I met you. You healed something I didn't realize had broken inside me. Your sweet-tempered kindness, tenderness and encouraging patience made me realize more important things than money and power exist in life. I chose happiness—before I realized you stood at the center of it for me. I broke up with Yancy before you and I became close, but she didn't want it to end. My ignoring her is why we're here at odd ends today. I can't tell you how sorry I am for allowing this to happen."

"So you've hurt Yancy as well as me." Her glare included one cocked brow as she eyed him along her nose with her chin high, shoulders squared and feet apart.

"She wanted marriage, but didn't love me any more than I did her. We both settled for less than we deserved. I hope she finds someone who appreciates her for the woman she is, but it's up to her. She's better off without me—for sure. When Dad became sick striving for the best last days he can manage, it made me reconsider my life and what I want. Life is too short to settle."

"So you didn't break up with Yancy because of me?" Her head angled sideways pointedly glaring defying him to lie.

"You were there, and so sweet and good to us, but no. Realizing how precious time is caused me to break it off with her. She proved how little she really cared, and I realized I'd be miserable tied to her for eternity."

"I'm glad something positive came from Richard's problems." Her face softened a bit, and she unclasped her arms, leaning against the cabinet on her hands.

"You and the kindness you showed us changed everything. You made me see I could love, and I wanted to. I'll forever be indebted to you." He reached his hands toward her across the countertop.

She stood her ground, ignoring the gesture.

"I planned no romantic rendezvous this weekend with Yancy. She came to the resort with intention of reeling me back in onboard with her plans, ignoring our breakup. She wanted me to return to Nashville and get married."

"Did she know about me—about us?" Sadness or regret, something sympathetic played on her words. He wasn't sure what.

"No, but she's perceptive and extremely bright. When she learned who you were, she must've suspected something between us. She's territorial. She intentionally misled you, implying she and I were betrothed."

Her demeanor changed slightly quietly scrutinizing with an unreadable expression.

"My reluctance to hurt Yancy, letting her down easy backfired. Yancy is spoiled and always gets her way. She had the idea she'd waltz in, and we'd pick up where we left off. She was wrong. I'm embarrassed. I allowed this fiasco to happen. Understanding Yancy, I should've anticipated her reaction. It's my fault. I should've known her irrational refusal to let me go would bite me in the ass. Now it's upset everyone involved."

Anger began to dissipate. Realization of facts began to sink in. Evidence stood in front of her as she appeared to mull over his words. "My suspicions about your character were evidently wrong. I believe what you've told me"

His stomach fluttered and soured.

"I'm guilty of misjudging you. You're the injured party here, not me. I did to you what Yancy did to me. You used poor judgment with her, but didn't deceive me or her. You've done nothing to warrant my failure to trust you. I've been unreasonable, and I'm sorry. I ran like a scared rabbit. I should've sought you out and demanded an explanation. You could've cleared the misunderstanding, but I didn't give you the benefit of the doubt or a chance to explain."

"I suspect your history tainted your attitude and actions. Your inclination toward suspicion and lack of trust reared its head confronting her lies. It's understandable. You've no need to apologize." His hands splayed in front of him, looking empty without hers in them.

She closed her eyes and shook her head toward the floor. "I suppose you're right. My reservations dissipated through the years. Though dormant, my qualms come second-nature to me. I acted out of character with you, letting my guard down. It's not me."

"You earned the right to hesitate from experience. At least you recognize it for what it is." Hopefully he understood where she came from.

"I assumed I'd grown stronger and gotten past it, but apparently it's not the case. Yancy's insinuations sparked it to life like a blaze of fire. I allowed it to come between something which could've been beautiful with you. I misjudged you. Is there any way you could forgive me?"

Softening of her demeanor gave him courage. "There's nothing to forgive, and if there were, you've earned it. I'm the one who's sorry, and I don't deserve forgiveness."

"Everyone deserves forgiveness—almost."

Brent?

"I want more than the type marriage Yancy and I would've had. I want devotion, passion and a true, last-a-lifetime love—now I'm certain it exists. I found it with you, Becky. You inspire me to be a better man and healed me like balm on my wounds. You unleashed my heart and opened me to a possibility of true love. With you protective walls I built disintegrated. You taught me to allow myself to receive, and gave me something I didn't fathom I needed or wanted, something I never thought possible. I deserve love. Maybe you won't love me, but it doesn't prevent me loving you. You're worth the risk. Becky, I love you with all my heart."

She blinked several times fidgeting and glancing about with a sigh. Like in a daze, she stared into floor space between them then met his pleading eyes.

♥♥♥♥

Truth in his eyes showed pain and fear. She leaned toward the bar then took his hands in hers. Silently their eyes led the conversation as they stood that way for several minutes while she summoned courage.

"I love you Justin." Her meek voice filled the room, and the air became scarce.

He rushed to her side. Taking her face in his hands he softly kissed her forehead. He kissed her nose and eyes. She tilted toward him accepting his soft lips. Slowly, tentatively, they spoke a language of love. Tenderly savoring the taste of each other, the essence of what promised to follow. Justin pulled her close, sheltering her in his arms. Neither of them wanted to break the spell.

Becky leaned into him slipping arms around his neck. She relished the silky touch as her fingers slid through his thick mane.

Their kiss deepened. Each demanded more of what they needed. Their bodies responded in kind. When heated grazes were no longer enough, Justin scooped her into his arms. He carried her to the bedroom and laid her on the mattress where she recently mourned the loss of their love. The bed would enjoy a welcome rebirth.

Untamed and fathomless, they meant to explore their adorations massive depth, so simple, yet so complicated. Impatiently undressing each other with urgency, surrendering they committed to the interlude they craved.

Her pulse quickened. A delightful rush of heat shot through her when pulled against his masculine frame. His responsive need pressed rigid against her belly. Searing passion took a magical dive heading south when the kiss deepened, meeting enthusiastic abandon.

Finally willing to give her all, to surrender to what she wanted, she leered seductively with an eyebrow raised and licked her lips unashamed. Justin grinned. With scandalous flirtation out of character, she came to him unafraid and uninhibited casting an enchanted spell and belying her shy, innocent demeanor.

Anything but naïve, she wanted him

heatedly. Clearly a smoldering fire within her had long been denied. Now awakened sensuality intoxicated him and endeared her to him. Their worlds would forever change this day, and neither would be whole again without the other.

Their tender embrace teased, explored and surrendered. They clung together, an exquisite pleasure long denied. Becky's breathing labored. Flaming blood surged through her anxious body, engulfed in awakening her dormant carnal instinct. Tantalizingly unpredictable, she inspired illicit responses engaging romance in his heart.

Welcomed kisses scorched her skin, invigorating her soul. His rigid member concealed by denim intrigued her. Flushing she clutched it with her hand. His delicious mouth sighed deeply leaning against her grip. A spiritual moan escaped her mouth. Justin's eyes trained on her moist lips studying her reaction as she licked them then drew the lower into her mouth.

They undressed in a frenzy born of hunger. Neither would be denied. Wistfully she observed while he slipped out of his jeans and underwear intent on his solid and muscular body. He grinned as though amused at the scrutiny of her focus.

"Like?"

"Mmmm." She muttered nodding with a wicked smile. "Everything." Enthusiastically she stripped to a slim slip of white lace panty and matching bra. She reached for him.

Tauntingly she caressed his exposed member, at first tentatively, then more demandingly. Wickedly she gripped him tight moving up and down the firm shaft sending a thrilling sensation shocking his senses causing him to moan helplessly. Exposed swelling manhood thrilled her with wanton need to envelope him in her body. She teased first with her hands then knelt before him, taking him with her mouth giving the perfect gift bestowed on him. He gently held her head to him tenderly caressing her hair.

When he could stand it no more, he pulled her to her feet, slipped her bra off exposing pert breasts then unbuckled it. The lace fell away as he took first one firm nipple in his mouth, then the other. As he kissed and suckled her nipple, he coaxed her panties to the floor.

He explored her body with taunting reverence, his focus intent. Tasting her essence, his only intention became assuring her complete satisfaction and savoring every moment. Instinctively she clenched his powerful shoulders, teasing his chest with her breast. Memorizing her completely, first a touch and then a kiss covered each wondrous area. Attentively he worshiped her body and soul. As he touched and tasted her, he reached more than skin. He penetrated her whole being with his love.

She surrendered to euphoric, exquisite sensations overwhelming her and clung to him without protest, a purely sensual being. She surrendered completely, unaccustomed to the fever which held her.

Anything but naïve, having been married without passion, she proved exceedingly capable of it. Justin, the source, would remain a zealous love.

She willed it to be so as euphoria engulfed them; and he surrendered to her completely.

Modesty put aside, she opened to his intimate exploration lying before him on the bed relishing his gaze and probing. Nothing concealed, she surrendered to his survey of her naked body with sheer delight.

His touch traced skin trailing extraordinary tingles. She shivered. First a hand, then tongue ignited a spark. An electrifying surge sizzled through her being, leaving her breathless. As he licked she lost composure. Sliding a finger inside induced sensations she had longed to share. Calling out his name, delicious heat swiftly filled her being, scalding her soul. She gave herself to the intense release, panting and quivering, her body stiffened as she came. Euphoric release left her willingly dazed and not wanting it to end.

Poised above her he plunged into her wetness, penetrating her soul. Fullness of their love heated by need and desire, both unaccustomed to such exquisite torture joined in an exhilarating dance so intense time stood still. She matched his urgency, ravenous, unable to get enough of each other. They struggled for air. Fever took over. Surging need to be satisfied engulfed as they rocked together in a magical, fierce abandon.

The ultimate climax came feverishly as untamed desires peaked. They came together with an epic explosion of senses and simultaneous spasm of exhausting joy and exquisite torture.

CHAPTER 24

Love making exhilarated Justin and satisfied, willingly incapable of forgetting this woman. He belonged to her completely, and she to him. They lay spent tenderly clinging together, unaccustomed to such raw emotions. Unable to resist or deny them, they lay satisfied in each other's arms enjoying a timeless moment.

"You're a captivating sight, lying here with your *Just Been Fucked Look*." Justin grinned wickedly kissing the tip of her nose. "You need to wear it more often from now on."

"You need to see to it, Mr." She smiled and kissed his chest. Her breath sent a ripple arching through him sparking his senses.

Justin spent the night. For a while when too exhausted to do more, he watched her sleep against his shoulder, a picture of serenity. Her hair tousled and her mouth partially opened. He pushed a tendril behind her ear and kissed the top of her head. The moon shined through the window magically illuminating the room. Beams targeted her silky hair where falling across his chest branding his heart as her own. Enchanting with moonlight sparkling in her tresses, snuggling tightly together, he drifted off to the sounded sleep ever.

Their struggle over, they finally found a home in each other's arms.

The sun rose bringing the bedroom to life. Becky smiled harmoniously at the man in her bed. She traced a tender trail of kisses across his face bringing him awake.

"Good morning my love." He moaned trying to shield her from his morning breath.

"Good morning. You hungry? We didn't eat dinner last night. You must be famished."

"I had no idea how hungry I was." He rolled on top of her, and she spread herself to welcome him home once again.

♥♥♥♥

Sometime later they rose from the bed, both completely sated. Becky strode toward the bathroom with a brazen lack of shame knowing his eyes never strayed from her naked body while he reclined on pillows giving her power she relished. It was all she could do to suppress a girlish giggle. Her spirit, now released from bondage reveled in freedom. No fear. She'd no longer deny herself what she wanted, what she needed.

"You're perfection." He surveyed her bare bottom. "I've never been so fulfilled and carefree. I'm truly happy for the first time in my adult life."

Joining her in the shower, they made love once more with her back braced against the steamy wall and legs around his waist, exciting, titillating, liberating and fun. Afterward they toweled each other dry with soft towels and finally dressed.

They cooked breakfast together and spent the rest of the day relaxing, watching a movie and a Reds game on television rooting for their team. They laughed and teased like they'd been together for eons.

Another glorious night spent in each other's arms and another peaceful morning together on Sunday. Finally Justin drove home. Hating to see the day end, Justin promised to call her that evening, and they agreed to talk frequently throughout the coming week. Becky planned to come and bring Evan to the lake on Friday.

"Wild horses couldn't keep us away."

"How will I sleep alone, now I've spent the night with you? I'll be desperately lonely without you. Becky, I love you so much it hurts."

She put her fingers to his lips. "We've enough hurt to last a lifetime. No pain from here on out, only happiness. Agreed?"

"Agreed." He smothered her with kisses that needed to last five days. "Love you."

"Love you too." She closed his car door, and he pulled away. She waved until he drove out of sight. She drove to pick up her son up.

She'd been right when sending Sadie to live with Richard and Justin. Their lives would never be the same.

CHAPTER 25

Sadie giggled into the phone. "So, what happened during the weekend? Justin's acting like a crowing rooster. The boy's spitting testosterone with every breath."

Becky laughed at the vision her creative sister's words spurred. "I was an ass. I showed up Friday as planned, but ran into Justin's ex. She told me they planned a lover's weekend finalizing wedding arrangements. I panicked and high-tailed it home to lick my wounds. I was hurt because in my mind we had started something important between us."

"What happened when he showed up at the door? He never explained anything to me and far as I can tell to Ricky either."

"I jumped to conclusions without giving him a chance to explain. Yancy misconstrued things to confuse me and chase me away in case I became competition for her man. Turns out Justin isn't her man. He broke up with her when Richard first became ill before he and I started spending time together."

"Is it what you kids call it these days—spending time together? I figured you and Big J hit the sheets for sweaty bumping uglys. Tell me you didn't waste the weekend without getting a piece of that hunk of man."

"Sadie, you talk like a sailor too long at sea. But yeah, of course." She hesitated to elaborate.

"And . . . how was it? Did the stars come out? Did the earth fall away leaving only the two of you in it?"

A suppressed giggle turned into a full-blown laugh fest. "All right already. Yes, we made love, and it was amazing—everything it is supposed to be. I'm in too deep to walk away, Sadie. I'm in love with Justin, ready or not." It was liberating voicing it.

"It's about damned time, Sis. Justin is a catch. He's a hunk, a gentleman, and all around wonderful guy. I could tell he was into you the day you introduced me to him and Ricky. There was a special glow in those steamy eyes of his whenever he glanced your way. It's done nothing but grow stronger since. The two of you were meant for each other."

"I never figured to care for anyone again. It's scary and wonderful at the same time. But I'm not going to play the scared rabbit any longer. I'm going to let this play out and enjoy the ride."

"Good for you. You've been growing stronger and more resilient all along. I was so proud of you when you took a self-defense class. It was a step in the right direction."

"Oh, it was nothing. The hospital

recommended we do it because many times we have to walk to our cars alone in the dark of night. There isn't always a guard available to escort us. I panicked the night Brent approached me and totally forgot everything I learned. Thank goodness Justin was in the lot that night and intercepted us before he could drag me to his vehicle."

"Yeah, it had to be scary. The shit head took you by surprise. You won't let him get the better of you ever again. Hopefully he's seen the light and moved on, forgetting you."

"I hope so. I'd kill him before letting him hurt Evan."

"Yep, me too, Sis. Well, I best get off here. The men are on their way back to the cabin now. They've been fishing off the pier."

"See you this weekend, Sadie. I love you."

"Love you too, Becky."

♥♥♥♥

The week dragged by. Becky found it difficult to focus on work no matter how devoted to her patients. She never missed a beat.

Evan eyed her curiously. "What's going on with you, Mom?"

"Why? What do you mean?" Her brow furrowed as she glanced over her shoulder while stirring their soup on the burner for dinner.

"I don't know. You're different . . . happier. You bop around sing along with the radio or humming to yourself. You laugh at my dumb jokes."

She leaned across the counter and tweaked his pert nose. "Can't a gal be happy spending time with her favorite little man?" She stroked his chin and smiled into his eyes, definitely happier. Not surprisingly her sensitive youngster could tell.

"Has this something to do with Justin?" He returned to his coloring, but she noticed his keen interested in her answer.

"What do you mean?"

"I dunno." He shrugged without meeting her eyes.

"I am happy." She sat a bowl of steaming soup in front of him, hoping to distract. "Eat your soup. You can play your video game."

"Why?" he wanted to know. "Why're you suddenly so happy?"

"What do you mean why?"

"What's making you so happy?" Disturbingly perceptive, Evan asked innocently.

"I'm glad you're home safe and had a good time. I can't wait to see you at the lake this weekend."

"Me too, I miss Justin, Aunt Sadie and Grandpa Richard. I can't wait to see them and tell them about camp."

Happier, Becky smiled to herself.

"You've stayed busy this week, but you manage to spend your time with Ricky." Sadie chatted over morning coffee with Justin while Ricky showered.

"Yep, between Ben's law cases and resort bookkeeping I've been running at a fast pace all week."

"It's good you're busy. Ricky needs more rest now and tires more easily."

"It's frustrating watching him slide downhill and not being able to do anything about it. I worry constantly how much time we have left."

"He is starting a steady decline, as the doctor predicted. It's good you're sticking close to him. Take advantage of every second with him. You'll never get this time back." She put a hand on Justin's soothing. "You miss Becky, don't you?"

"Terribly, does it show? She consumes my thoughts day and night." His blush and honesty endeared him to her. No wonder Becky was nuts about the man. "I call evenings after Evan's bedtime so we can talk, but it's never enough. Becky's an amazing woman."

"She is." Sadie didn't need to explain, aware of their nightly phone sessions. Becky shared everything with Sadie. She'd confided, she and Justin had professed their love. Both surprised how strong their attraction already was. Neither considered themselves deserving. "What you and Becky have is a rare blessing, and you're lucky to find something so precious."

"I've never been in love." Justin's voice quaked as he spoke, nervous about sharing.

"Me either. I might be heading in the same direction with JJ. He told me he loves me." She studied his reaction.

"JJ is a fine man. You and he make a good

pair." He acted sincere. "Becky married before and must've loved her husband." He didn't sound jealous, only stating a fact, like he might be wondering how he measured up.

"Don't worry about Brent. You have more to offer than the asshole ever had. I assume she loved him at first, or maybe a kinship born of familiarity. They knew each other their whole lives. It seemed natural they'd marry like everyone expected. The easy thing to do, you know—comfortable. When she talks about it, she doesn't talk like a woman in love. They were very young. After her horrible experience with him, it's a wonder she let any man near her."

"No excitement, passion or mystery fired their relationship—no desperate need or hunger. When Brent lost faith in his self, he became a monster and a stranger." Fire lit his eyes like burning anger and as he spoke his hands fisted and jerked like he wanted to punch someone—probably Brent.

"The turd bag deserved everything he got." As much as Sadie would like to witness Brent getting the crap beat out of him, she hoped he and Justin never met. No good would come of it.

"The idea of someone being mean to Becky makes me physically ill. I'll never allow anyone to hurt her ever again. She is sweet and wonderful. I can't fathom anyone wanting to, but realize reality of the abuse she suffered. I will spend my life making it up to her if she'll allow me to. All I want is to make her happy and to be with her."

"Have you told Ricky how you feel?" Sadie

chortled surprised at Justin's openness.

He sheepishly shrugged. "Not yet, but I will. He knows I spent the weekend with her. We've not had an actual discussion about it."

"Ricky will be thrilled. He adores Becky and Evan, and he wants you to be happy." Justin was a good man, and Sadie had faith he'd be a good man for her sister. Becky confided her giddiness loving him, and her anxiousness for the weekend so they could be together—a good thing. "I'm happy for you both. Enjoy it. Love is a precious gift."

CHAPTER 26

Justin rushed from the cabin and waved as Becky parked beside his car. "Evan, welcome back." He grinned from ear to ear helping the youngster out of the vehicle.

"Hey, Mr. Justin, thanks for letting us come again. I can't wait to tell you and Grandpa Richard about my scout trip." The boy slapped Justin's raised hand in a high-five.

Taking Becky in his arms Justin kissed her on the mouth while Evan grinned with satisfaction. No surprise here.

"I missed you," Justin whispered huskily. "I hate to rush off. I have an errand in town. Can Evan go with me? We'll pick up dessert at the bakery." He winked at Evan who smiled his approval.

"I missed you too. I guess it'd be alright. Hurry back, though."

"Evan, you be good and do as Justin says. You hear?"

Evan grinned and screwed his mouth as to show he understood the routine. "I'm always good Mom." He groaned and jumped into Justin's sports car. Justin joined him and they sped away.

Evan examined Justin inquiringly. "So, what's with you and Mom?"

"What do you mean?" Justin grinned.

"You kissed her, which explains the dopey grin she wears all the time. She sings and everything. Your Mom's boyfriend now?" He studied Justin's face.

"She does? Um, how would you feel about me being her boyfriend?" He gaged the boy's reaction.

"It's cool, I guess. Mom never had a boyfriend before." Evan pensively wrinkled his freckled nose.

"I'm sure she has. After all, your Mom's a beauty and a girl long before you were born. Your dad became her boyfriend before they married."

"Yeah, I guess." Justin imagined wheels turning as Evan mulled it over. "Yuck, a guy doesn't need to think about his mom being a girl; but you're cool, Justin. I like you a lot. And Mom does too."

"I like her too. I want to be your mom's boyfriend, if it's alright with her." He smiled at Evan's satisfied expression.

"Good." They rode quietly for a while. Evan broke the silence. "Can you help me with batting practice after supper?"

"Sure thing, buddy, I'd love too. Thanks for asking."

"Thanks, Mom tries. She isn't good at it."

Justin gave him a conspiratorial nod, laughing inside. "It'll be our little secret. We don't need to hurt her feelings."

Evan grinned appearing satisfied.

♥♥♥♥

Becky visited with Sadie and Richard after a round of hugs at the cabin. "What's Justin's hurry?"

"No idea." Sadie pulled her toward the couch.

Richard glanced her way from his wheelchair. "Something about signing important papers needing mailed immediately. It must be important for him to leave soon as you arrived. He has been on pins and needles dying for you to arrive. The boy missed you, Becky. I think you've won my boy's heart."

She laughed happy Richard wasn't surprised or concerned about her romance with his son. "I missed you too." She kissed Richard's cheek.

Sadie, the epitome of a competent homemaker listened intently from the kitchen. "Supper's under control. Settle in while I finish here. Justin and Evan should be back by the time the roast is ready."

"Thanks, Sadie." She could hardly wait to be alone with Justin for a passionate kiss, unlike the two short appetizer shared earlier. She stowed their bag, applied a hint of eye shadow, blush and fresh lipstick. Fluffing her unruly curls, she added a layer of hair spray then coaxed them into a semblance of order. Lastly she spritzed her favorite scent between her breasts and smiled at her reflection.

Sufficiently ready to meet her lover, she headed to join Richard and Sadie. A shiver sensation zipped through her spine. She shrugged the aura of doom off.

Everything is fine. This will be a fun weekend.

The camp appeared deserted except for a few cars and boat trailers. Guests were either out on the water or indoors for dinner. She pulled the door shut and stepped off the deck.

She jumped, startled. An unexpected sound came from behind. The crucial observation came too late. Alarmed, she attempted to put distance between herself and the peculiar stranger.

He approached rapidly reacting to her alarm. He moved astonishingly for such a massive man.

No match for the huge guy, jerked swiftly backward by a burley arm around her neck her back braced against a bulbous hard belly. Her head forced against a muscular chest clad in sweaty polyester. A rude, hairy paw gripped her mouth roughly, and she gasped. Fear seized her. The rough villain dragged her fiercely toward the main cabin. She struggled for footing and air.

Desperately she challenged his grip. Cold steel of a blade against her skin rendered her immovable. His hand constricted around her arm tight enough to leave handprint-shaped bruise, and she winced.

"Quiet, little lady." The stranger's ominous whisper splattered her face with spit.

Dread gripped her. The man presented a threat, and his fierce glare meant to intimidate. Piercing, black eyes bored through her as he insinuated himself into her personal space. Hot, putrid breath assaulted her with overbearing garlic and onion fumes.

Becky winced. Her throat constricted. She fought back a gag.

Heartless eyes warned the intruder couldn't be reasoned with. "We're going to visit your friends. Be silent. Stay calm. No one will be hurt." The whispered warning, unlike his motive.

Unable to speak with a hand clasped firmly across her mouth, she struggled, fighting panic understanding he meant business—what business? Much taller, he roughly dragged her forward fighting to keep pace, terrified of what lay ahead. Inflection in his harsh tone warned he'd easily, without remorse use violence to obtain what he wanted—whatever it might be. Her struggles had little effect and protests, only a minor irritation for the towering, hulky man.

Determined to disappear inside before spotted, he mercilessly lifted her, maneuvering them forward. Oozing sweat threatened her senses as his breath grew ragged from haste, obviously overweight and out of shape. He shoved her onto the deck. "Open it."

She slid the door open, and they stepped into Richard's cabin, or the man did. Becky stumbled forward catching herself before tumbling to the floor.

Unaware of the drama being played outside, Richard watched television in his wheelchair with a blanket covering his lap. He startled, seeing Becky wasn't alone.

"What the—" He sounded indignant.

"Hi, Ice Pick, long time no see." The intruder's words seethed hatred.

He pushed Becky forward, and she fell against the bar. He slammed the door behind him and drew the drapes.

Sadie bent checking the oven. Seeing the stranger pointing a gun at her sister, a scream emitted as reality set in. She cut her panicked yelp short as he waved the weapon menacingly.

"Shut the hell up, woman, or you'll be sorry." The intruder spat, jerking Becky's arm roughly.

She and Sadie clung together desperately quivering. Noticing the knife Sadie had been using, Becky silently slipped it into her shorts pocket unseen while the invader glared at Ricky. Terror gripped Becky comprehending how unpredictable he acted, surely capable of violence.

"Hello, Rocco." Richard spoke calmly as though greeting an expected guest for dinner. "I wondered when you would pay me a visit."

Richard drew a calming breath as he assessed the threat, surveying the area with a keen eye. Becky concealed a weapon—a smart gal. He had an ally. Her swift action and calm demeanor would help in this volatile situation. Sadie acted as scared as Becky. She'd be quick to react as well, once she got it together. The women normally worked under incredible stress dealing with heart patients and surgery.

Rocco remained a vindictive asshole. His twisted character and hostile ability to remain detached about murder posed an imminent danger.

Richard must keep the situation from escalating. He had to slow things down for them to survive.

"Who is this man, Richard?" Tears streamed from Sadie's shocked face.

Richard recognized desperation in Sadie's cry. His body grew rigid with anticipation like a trapped animal. The severity of the ominous situation registered in his mind. This crisis had to be aborted without chaos. He could not allow this horrible man to harm the women. It was between the two of them.

"An old acquaintance." Deceptively calm, Richard spun his wheel chair toward the man.

"What do you want?" Sadie asked the brute bitterly.

"We're going to have a little chat." Rocco pointed his pistol at the women. "I need you ladies contained while Ice and I settle a little issue between us." Heartless eyes glared hatred. "You, Goth Girl, sit your ass in the chair."

"Let the women go, Rocco. This is between us."

He chuckled evilly. "Yeah, right?" Rocco shoved Sadie to sit at the table. Pulling duct tape from his belt he handed it to Becky. "Cover your mouth and the bitch's too." Becky calmly did as told. Rocco tossed her a handful of flex ties from his pocket. "Tie her hands behind her back." He glared bitterly daring her to defy.

Becky wrapped Sadie's wrists then pulled, not tight enough to hurt Sadie. Rocco grabbed the tie yanking it roughly. Sadie jerked and squealed in pain behind her duct taped mouth.

"Tie her hands to the chair." Becky approached her sister doing Rocco's bidding. She moved calmly, appearing ready to burst into tears. Apology written on her face, she attempted a weak smile for Sadie. Becky looped another tie between Sadie's bound hands, then around the chair rail securing it. Rocco grabbed Becky's hair yanking her against his chest.

"I'm so sorry Sadie. It'll be okay. I promise." She cooed to her sister. To Rocco she begged desperately, "Please, don't hurt my sister."

"Shut the hell up," Rocco snapped.

Ominous silence filled the room.

How would they survive? Becky and Sadie were defenseless. Richard confined to a wheel chair for the most part due with illness's gradually sapping of his strength. Thank goodness Justin took Evan with him. No one to save them, he must rely on his wits.

"How did you find me?" Richard spoke casually trying to defuse the situation. He had to distract and calm Rocco somehow. Richard resented the intrusion into his life. This wasn't the time to voice it.

Richard maintained composure, afraid to bungle the situation or panic. Too much at stake, he must maintain his cool in this crisis, and didn't dare risk the lives of the women he'd grown to love. He refused to surrender to panic in the volatile situation.

However, his voice depicted venom he tasted for Rocco. Horrified, the vicious man had seized control of his home and friends, he must avoid further violence.

Rocco shrugged. "Dumb luck, I guess. My daughter had gall bladder surgery. I visited her at the hospital. There you were. This little bitch wheeled you out to a car. You rolled right by me. You didn't notice. I got a look at your son's license plate and took it from there. I was shocked. I've searched for you since you conveniently disappeared years ago. When I didn't find you, I hoped you had died."

"I'm done with the life. I put it behind me. You have nothing to fear from me." Richard understood how reckless Rocco was. He needed to defuse the situation, so tried another tactic.

"You have a family. You've moved on as well." Richard hoped for distraction. "You've made a life for yourself." *Get him talking, maybe he'd regret this.*

"I have a family. I'm legit. I own a grocery in northern Kentucky. I'm a respected businessman." His declaration was soaked in irritation. Richard could end Rocco's legitimate life.

"Why drag this up now?" Richard struggled to disguise his fury. "Why look me up, after all these years? Let's both get on with our lives. I mean you no harm."

"Why?" Rocco's eyes opened wide, and his bulbous mouth flew open. "There's no statute of limitations on my crime. You're a loose end I can't afford. I tried finding you so I could end you years ago and became obsessed with searching since the seventies. Somehow you escaped unscathed. I won't sleep easy until you're out of the picture. You're a threat long as you live." Rocco spat pure venom.

"I'm out of the picture. I have nothing to prove and want nothing to do with you or the past," Richard tried maintaining composure. Haste might result in chaos.

"Easy for you to say, you could put me away for life if you change your mind." Rocco's searing eyes glared through his nemesis. Hatred dripped from every word. Cold hollow eyes glared at Richard. Rocco's soul hardened equally icy and empty.

"What's he talking about?" Tears filled Becky's eyes.

Ignoring her Richard locked on Rocco. "Listen Rocco, this is between you and me. The ladies aren't aware or involved. Keep it that way. Let them go. You and I can settle this once and for all, alone. Put them in the other room, and leave them be," Richard begged to no avail.

"We're going to settle it all right," Rocco grunted outraged. Piercing eyes glared contempt.

"It ends now. You end now, and your ladies with you. I'm leaving no loose ends this time. They go first. I want to watch you squirm when they die, the way I've squirmed these years wondering when you'd show up and confess. You little twerp, you had a conscience. Not a night goes by I don't dream of the electric chair. I've got to end you now."

"You've got nothing to fear from me, man.

You don't want to do this. If you kill us, you're deeper and deeper in the trench. You'll rot in prison for sure." Richard tried reasoning with the vicious animal.

"I won't be recognized or caught. You three die today. I'm home in an hour without a trace. No one will be the wiser. There's no way to connect us." Rocco laughed wickedly.

Harsh words sank in. He had worked out what he considered a fool-proof plan. There'd be no dissuading him.

He jerked Becky closer. The gun forced hard against her temple. He snickered at Richard evilly. "Say goodbye to this tasty, little piece. She's a cutie. Makes me wish I had time to play before I do her." Rocco spat brutally and slid a sickening tongue up the side of Becky's face. His slobbery, foul tongue emitted an obnoxious scent. She acted like she might puke.

He roughly slipped a flabby paw inside her shirt grabbing Becky's breast. He pinched her nipple.

She squealed.

The screech appeared to please him. He grinned as he withdrew his hand.

She breathed a startled gasp.

Releasing his grip slightly he brutally slapped Becky upside the head. It shot to the side as she blinked and struggled to maintain consciousness. Blood oozed from her nose and busted lip. Fury blazed in her eyes and she closed them.

Richard winced, observing helplessly

seeking an opportunity to defuse things. "Get away from her," he growled angrily shifting in his wheel chair.

"What you going to do, Old Man?" Rocco taunted. "Wish I had time to torture you. Fucking these bitches in front of you would be fun. Time is fleeting, and I must arrive home before supper. Don't want the old lady on my case. So I've got to get this done."

"Sorry Babe." His pouting lips taunted Becky melodramatically. "Rocco can't do you today. You die without the pleasure. You're missing out, Baby."

He glared at Richard. "Too bad you're a helpless, sick, old man and can't join me. We could do these two together. We acted as partners, maybe buddies. You became a part of it all." He laughed wickedly.

"We weren't buddies. You've always been a pig."

While his attention diverted from Becky to Richard, she spun in his arms until her face lay close to his chest. He groped for her neck unable to cut off her air supply. Urgently she slid to kneel before him. Making a fist she violently punched his groin with all her might, making contact.

He let out a loud yelp.

Becky retrieved the knife from her pocket. She slid sideways as he bent forward over her. She jabbed the knife to the hilt into Rocco's side. Blood squirted on both of them as she spun away from his reach, putting the counter between them.

Revealing his weapon concealed beneath the

blanket, Richard pointed the pistol at Rocco, writhing in pain and groping his side.

"What the hell?" Rocco grabbed his side smearing red goo oozing through his fingers. He yanked the small kitchen knife from his side. Scarlet flowed easily across his clothing.

"Bitch, you'll pay for this." He spat at Becky's fleeing figure, not realizing Richard pinned a weapon on him. Watching the direction of her glance, he eyed Richard. "You never had the guts to pull a trigger. You don't have it in you. You're weak. Look at you, gutless, helpless." Pure evil glowed in Rocco's eyes.

"I'm not a murderer like you, Rocco. You like it. I don't. I'll shoot if necessary."

"You're the same little twerp you always were. You aren't capable of pulling the trigger. You still don't have the guts." Venom dripped from Rocco's words. He lunged toward Richard. "You're dead."

No turning back. Death imminent. Richard stood. The wheel chair rolled backward. The blanket fell to his feet. The automatic pistol in his right hand fired three shots directly into Rocco's chest. He stared at Richard, a questioningly confused expression on his face. Rocco fell forward dropping his cocked pistol, yet unfired face first on the floor. A red pool seeped around him.

Richard flopped back defeated into his wheel chair. Leaning forward his face hid in his hands.

Becky rushed to untie Sadie and slit ties binding her with a kitchen knife. They pulled tape from their mouths and hugged each crying on her sister's shoulder.

CHAPTER 27

Evan asked permission to play with friends at the swings as Justin parked at the resort, so Justin sent him to the playground. Three gunshots rang. Justin rushed into the house and found a grizzly scene.

"What on earth happened? Dad, you okay?"

Richard nodded slumped in his mobile chair.

Sadie appeared unharmed. Swelling distorted Becky's jaw. Tears mingled with blood. "I look worse than I am." She grinned happily.

Justin held his arms out and Becky fell into them. Her head rested on his chest. Gently he lifted her chin surveying the damage. He tenderly wiped a tear away. Ever so carefully he kissed her swelling lips, cautious not to inflict more pain. Tears streamed unashamed from his eyes.

Sadie tried between crying and sniffing loudly, to explain. "The man came in here, tied us up and started arguing with Richard. He would've killed us if Richard hadn't shot him first."

"You know him, Dad?" Justin sat on the couch pulling a dazed Becky onto his lap. He reassuringly stroked her arm cradling her trembling body. Sadie settled in next to her leaning against them for support.

"Yes, this is the trigger man I told you about. He spotted me leaving the hospital and hunted me down. He meant to kill me and leave no witnesses. He wanted me to suffer though, so intended on shooting the gals in front of me first. He had a gun to Becky's head. You should've seen her. She's a quick thinking filly. She spun around and stabbed Rocco with a kitchen knife giving me time to pull my weapon and a clear shot without her in the way." Quivering in Richard's voice filtered with pride in Becky's tenacity and quick thinking.

Justin winced. Meeting Becky's smiling eyes, he snuggled her closer.

"I'm so proud of both these women. They kept level heads in a crisis. It's what you two train for." He acted like a proud papa, of more than Justin.

"Sure, Ricky, we're not used to men pulling guns on us." Sadie wiped sweat from her brow with a palm.

Justin had nearly lost all three of them. He was in awe it turned out this way. "Dad, I didn't realize you carried a handgun."

"I didn't normally. Sadie mentioned a stranger asking around. Between the vandalism around here and that, I suspected Rocco had found me. I asked Sadie to retrieve my pistol from the closet, and I've kept it at my side since. I hoped it would amount to nothing, but needed to err on the safe side."

"Ricky, he's the dude I told you about a couple weeks back asking about a guy with a strange nickname. Was he searching for you?" She exuded exhausted from the turmoil.

"Evidently he has been snooping around all this time. I assume he's responsible for the boat and cart damage. He tried to kill me in an accident."

"Why didn't you tell me you suspected he located you?" Justin was desperate to understand.

"I hoped to be wrong, or he'd leave well enough alone. If he learned, I'm dying or had too much to lose coming forward he'd forget about me. Bad judgment nearly cost these precious women their lives."

"Your life is precious too, Ricky." Sadie reached clasped his frail hand in hers, receiving a smile full of love in return.

"Thank you, Sweetie. But no, I can't apologize to you and Becky enough. I've put you in peril. It is inexcusable." Richard appeared more stricken by risk to the women than his own. "I'm so sorry, Son. Justin, Sadie, Becky will you ever forgive me?" Tears streaked across his pale withered cheeks.

Stroking Becky's face tears pooled in Justin's eyes. "Thank God you're all safe."

Becky sat erect in Justin's lap and glanced out the door. "Where's Evan?"

"At the playground with friends, I told him we'd call when dinner's ready."

She settled against his chest once more. "Thank God you didn't bring him in."

Sadie retrieved her phone from the kitchen table. "I'll call JJ." She spoke calmly explaining briefly what had occurred, giving JJ the barest of facts so he could figure out what assistance to bring. "Okay, thanks, Babe. See you in a few. I love you too." She clicked off and laid the phone on the coffee table. "He alerted the officer on duty and coroner." Sadie checked Rocco's vital signs making sure the immobile man was truly gone. She shook her head.

JJ arrived swiftly followed soon by another cruiser and an ambulance. Sadie waited for him at the door. His sympathetic expression caused her eyes to fill and tears she'd been holding at bay came with a gush. He buried her face in his shoulder as he held her close while her shoulders quaked and she sobbed loudly. He gently stroked her hair and kissed the crown of her head. Finally she calmed and pushed away gazing into his eyes sullenly smiling. Holding her hand they joined the others.

JJ checked Rocco's pulse. *Dead.* No chance in hell could the fellow be alive given the mass of blood puddled beneath him. Three rounds hit squarely around the heart. A bloody knife lay beside him.

The on-duty officer entered with the coroner who checked the body. After his examination, he brought the EMTs in and instructed them how to manage the body. The duty officer took individual statements with each witness separately and alone using Justin's bedroom while the others waited turns in the living room.

♥♥♥♥

Becky wept recounting the ordeal for the officer. Her voice quivered recalling the incident. The officer listened riveted to his chair while he recorded everything. He winced at the blood stain on Becky's chest. The young officer carefully proceeded with protocol, tough it was his first call where someone died other than by accident. "Extremely brave of you, Ma'am, you have a level head in a crisis."

"Thanks, Officer Brown. It comes from years as a cardio nurse, and I'm the mother of a young boy." She snickered, and the officer grinned.

Becky left the room and sent Sadie in. She spent time with the officer giving her statement, then sent Richard in for his turn. Lastly Justin gave his statement. By then EMT's and coroner had exited the premises, and a couple of deputies finished taking photos, drawing measurements and gathering evidence.

Evan attempted to run to the house when JJ arrived. An officer told him to play outside for a while longer. He obediently did so, but kept an eye on the cottage. After her statement, Becky watched him play from the deck. She waved casually, and he continued his game of Frisbee with his pals.

Justin came out when he finished with Officer Brown. Taking a chair beside her he stroked the damage to her forehead. "I've never felt so much rage as when I witnessed your blood and realized terror you experienced. I'd have killed the man with my bare hands if it turned out differently. I'm glad you weren't seriously hurt. The idea of the cold-blooded murderer's hands on you makes me crazy. The whole thing is a shock difficult to comprehend. It's a bitterness taste knowing I wasn't here to defend the people I love." Anguished tears filled his eyes.

"Richard made a daring rescue." She patted his hand. "Be proud of your Dad. If it weren't for him, we'd all be dead."

"I'm proud of him. I'm equally in awe of you. Dad swore your quick thinking and fighting spirit provided an edge he needed to be effective."

Sadie joined them overhearing their conversation. "Ricky's shrewd decisiveness and Becky catching the scumbag by surprise saved us. Not many men would've been ready for such an unexpected event or handled it so well." She took a chair beside Becky. Becky extended a hand. Sadie took it and squeezed as their eyes smiled mutual love the sisters shared.

The camp residents alerted something awful had happened by emergency responders mulling about, busily doing their jobs. They kept a distance attentively. Sitting on the deck with them watching was like being in a fishbowl.

Finally JJ finished giving a statement and joined them. He extended a hand, and Sadie took it. "Let's you and I walk to the playground to fetch Evan."

She nodded then reassured Becky, "We'll explain everything is fine and we'll keep him busy until you signal. It will give you time to usher the cops out and clean the kitchen floor."

Becky soberly nodded. "Thanks, Sis."

Finally the officers milled out and the last one stopped while his partner put their gear away.

♥♥♥♥

"I can't believe I nearly lost you today. I'm glad you're okay." JJ professed squeezing Sadie's hand lovingly as they walked toward the playground.

"Me too, I was terrified. I kept wishing for my phone. I wanted to hear your voice. I wanted to call you to come save us. I couldn't do anything to help. The brute tied me up before I realized what happened. Helpless, I prayed you'd show up early."

"I'm sorry I wasn't here to help. Thank God Richard prepared, and Becky helped him put the guy down."

"Man, Becky was amazing. She acted incredibly brave. I can't believe how well she kept her cool. She's been through a lot, been hurt in the past and viewed herself as a weak victim. She's anything but weak. She's strong inside. We might all be dead if it weren't for her and Ricky. Thank goodness he had a gun. I brought it from his closet shelf, thinking it was a pair of shoes, old photos or something. It never occurred to me it was a weapon." She started to shake and cry again. JJ held her tight and kissed the top of her head.

"You're alive and well. And yes, Becky was

brave. It angers me, I could've lost you. I don't want it to happen. I want you with me. Let's not waste a minute of our time together. I don't want you out of my sight. I want to hold you." He tipped her chin and gently kissed her. They clung together a long time, cherishing the closeness. Finally they broke away long enough for their eyes to meet. "I'm off duty. Go home with me. Let me take care of you." JJ's eyes pleaded.

"I'd like nothing better. Ricky has Justin, Becky and Evan here, so he'll be fine without me for the night."

Mrs. Braxton, a camp resident for the week with three boys around Evan's age walked to where they sat. "Miss, Watkins, the boys want Evan to come to our cabin for dinner. We're having mac n cheese. And they asked if they can have a sleepover. Would it be okay with you? It appears you have a lot going on at the main cabin tonight."

Sadie had met and liked the family during their stay at the resort. "It would be fine, if he wants to go." Evan nodded profusely in the background hovering with his pals. "Fine, I'll clear it with his mom, and she can drop his PJ's and toothbrush off later. Thank you Mrs. Braxton." Sadie extended a hand, which the lady shook.

"Great, come on you little rascals. We've got a cheesy delight to scarf down." She herded the boys toward her cabin.

Sadie grinned at JJ and led him to Ricky's cabin. Becky, Justin and Richard sat quietly talking in the kitchen. "Hey, everyone, I'm going to JJ's place for the night. Becky, you can help Richard with his meds and Justin can help him get ready for bed. You don't mind do you?"

"We're good. Go, rest. Sadie. We're immensely sorry about your harrowing experience tonight. I'm on top of the situation. I'll ensure this is finished once and for all." He and JJ exchanged knowing glances. JJ nodded.

"Thanks, Justin; I don't see why you feel responsible." Sadie clung to her man.

Becky smiled lovingly. "Of course. We understand. We're fine here."

Sadie grabbed her purse, walked to her cabin and threw a couple things in a bag. She and JJ left.

♥♥♥♥

Justin scrubbed the floor free of blood then put the kitchen back in order while Becky helped Richard prepare for bed and administered his meds. Richard resembled hell warmed over and needed a rest.

"Sadie needs space. I hope she doesn't hate me after what I put her through." Remorse filled Richard's eyes. "I hope you won't hold this against my boy. Justin cares deeply for you, Becky." His hand trembled as he laid it on her arm.

"Nonsense, Richard. You didn't cause this horrible thing to happen. You're as much a victim as Sadie and me. The only wrongdoer here is the maniac. Thank you for saving our lives." She kissed his forehead as he lay against the pillow then slipped from the room.

"How're you holding up, Dad?" Justin asked

stepping into the bedroom.

"Not bad, Son. It could've been much worse. I need to hit the sack though. It's been a tough day." He extended a hand. Justin clasped it in his.

"I love you, Dad." He kissed Richard's brow. "And, Dad, we'll make this right. No worries."

"Thank you, Son. I love you too, Justin. Never forget it. You're loved so very much." He emphasized his words each separately.

"I know, Dad. Thank you for everything. Now rest." He quietly shut the door.

Becky lay on the couch. Her sweet smile warmed his heart.

"How're you holding up?" He sat on the coffee table across from her and stroked her face.

"I'm exhausted. It's getting dark out. I took Evan's stuff to the Braxton's cabin. The boys had a blast. He's sleeping there for the night. Stay with me, Justin? Hold me tonight."

"Sure thing, I don't want to ever let you go." Becky wiped a tear from her cheek with the back of her arm. Justin wrapped his around her, and their eyes locked.

"I was terrified today. I had no choice. I struggled to not let fear take hold and to think clearly. I kept willing myself to breathe. Focusing on it kept me from tumbling off the deep end. I've had practice, and experience taught me the only way to survive is to remain calm." She wiped another tear away.

Understanding her past abuse, Justin's

stomach flip-flopped. *How could anyone hurt this precious woman?*

"Never again, never, do you hear me?" Tears welled in his eyes and his back stiffened. "No one will hurt you ever again. I swear it."

Becky smiled sweetly and touched the moisture with a delicate finger. She held his face and kissed him until he forgot his fears.

He scooped her into his arms and carried her to his bedroom. He quietly kicked the door quietly closed behind them. She fell with him onto the bed and giggled.

He brushed hair back from her face, holding it in his palms examining. He gently tasted her perfect lips. The tender, easy kiss tasted delicious and explored lovingly. Gradually hunger grew. Passion consumed them. Need grew with each gasping breath. She pulled him into her mouth and moaned. Indulging in her sweet taste, his hunger grew. She begged silently for more, and he didn't hesitate to meet her need.

Soon it wasn't enough. He explored her face memorizing every curve with his kiss. Debasing her ear, she shivered and clung desperately. He explored her neck, and a potent spark sizzled through his spine.

Heat spiked and settled between her legs. Anything but subtle, she tightened automatically jutting hips toward him shamelessly flirtatious. Insistently she kneaded his shoulders eagerly pushing beneath his shirt. She could not resist and would not deny herself touch of his firm chest. She rounded to examine sculptured muscle as his back flexed automatically beneath her palms. Lifting his arms, she pulled the shirt over his head briefly interrupting their kiss.

Justin cupped her buttocks and gently lifted her to him. She settled around his waist, crossing her feet against his firm behind. He groaned aloud as her hot crotch settle onto his erection. Kissing her deeply he laid her back on the bed. She welcomed his weight, clenching him tighter.

Justin raised himself balancing above her, hands on either side of her head. His smile said he was hers. Heady with passion she studied his expression.

"You're the most incredible woman I've ever met. You're exceedingly beautiful. I can't get enough of you."

Realizing power she had over this gorgeous, masculine man was sexy beyond belief. Her head spun, understanding her take-charge Justin stood strong against the world, yet vulnerable to her. How could she be so lucky to have found this amazing man? And he wanted her.

"Make me feel alive, Justin. I need you inside me." She squirmed against him mischievously.

Gazing into her eyes protectively, he communicated he would shield her against the world. "Make me yours."

Needing no assurance, he unbuttoned her shirt and removed it. Her eyes teased with a sultry lingering speaking of her longing and maintaining connection. Unhooking the slip of lacy white, he tossed it unleashing her breasts then slid her shorts away. All that remained was a simple white slip of lacy thong. Her eyes never left his taunt sexy body longing watching the desirable man undress. She became overwhelmed with anticipation.

Bending to kiss her lips, his fingers teased her taunt nipples. Slowly his lips explored her ears, her neck then downward. She shuddered with delightful abandon yielding with gratitude as her eager body arched for him shamelessly. Nipping satiny flesh torment forced a guttural moan of ecstasy. Racing pulses mingled with an agonizing desire taunting and teasing. They surrendered to desire, lost in a foggy cloud of lust clinging furiously together.

Nothing forbidden. Racing hearts and ragged breath dominated their world. Intense need drove an agonizing search for ecstasy oblivious to. Nothing existed in this state, only pure necessity to give and accept pleasure.

Hungrily he drew in her breast as though it was his last meal. She held him, eager hands tangled in his hair as he trailed kisses across her belly so slowly he appeared to memorize her body with his mouth and hands.

Her eyes locked on Justin's lingering gaze as he admired her body lying exposed, naked except for the tiny panties. "Mine." His guttural whisper sent pleasurable tingles though her.

"Yes." Completely surrendering felt heady, and he languished in trusting her with his soul.

Exploring, fingers skimmed breasts, tummy, hips, and inched along the inside of her thighs. He cupped her center with his palm gently parting her legs and followed suit with his mouth through filmy lace.

She emitted a tiny squeal of pleasure and clamped her hand across her mouth with wide eyes. "I'm sorry; I don't want to wake Richard."

Justin laughed. "No worries, Dad is out like a light. He'd never hear you scream at the top of your lungs."

"Still, I'd be embarrassed. I'll try to quiet down." He returned to the business of giving pleasure. Chewing gently until her panties soaked, and she grew ready to explode, his finger penetrated her being, and she gasped rocked against him. When her spasms slowed, he slid the lace off and tossed it aside.

Settling between licking a trail to her center, he gnawed as though starved for her while she twitched with abandonment and held him where he wanted to be. No inhibitions between them, she tightened again convulsing with a gasp and a muffled scream. Replacing his tongue with fingers he lifted himself to kiss her cry away. Needing him, she grasped his manhood tightly in her hand and pulled the strong shaft to her slick opening.

"Mine." Breathing hard, her legs circled his waist embracing his thrust lost in abandonment. She gasped for air against his kiss as he filled her with his being blissfully moaning.

Rhythm instinctive as though the dance practiced many times, together they rode the hard ride to ecstasy, higher and higher. This moment, this potent togetherness existed as their whole world.

"Justin," she uttered as she came, and Justin emptied himself into her completely. She gave herself completely to him, and he to her, neither having completely belonged to another before.

"We're meant to be." Justin stroked her forehead as he lay spent between her legs, still inside her.

She wiped a curl from his face and grinned. "Now I know I'm alive."

"I love you, Becky, and I want you."

The rich feeling of being in love prevailed. "Already?" She grinned teasingly. "I love you too, Justin."

"Are you sure? I'm not much of a catch." He grinned propping on an elbow with is head resting in a hand.

"You've got to be joking?" She screwed her mouth up.

"There's a lot about my past, about Dad's past you don't yet know. We'll rid ourselves of baggage. I'll do my damnedest to keep the blowback away from you. I don't only want to make love to you again—soon as I recover. I want you in my bed every night for the rest of my life."

She grinned wickedly as she stroked his limb, and he hardened in her hand. "I can tell. Let's take care of this first. We'll worry about problems later." She snickered as she rolled on top of him.

Later, once again spent, Justin lay next to her. Naked legs tangled in the sheets. Bodies glistened in moonlight shining from the window beside his bed.

"Becky, I've never felt like this. You make me a better man. I adore you. Marry me?"

"Are you certain? I come with a lot of baggage." She traced a finger along his nose.

"I'm not worried about your past. We'll take care of it."

"I'm talking about my two-legged baggage—the little guy." She cocked her head toward the cabin where her son slept with his friends.

He laughed heartily. "You can't possibly think it's a disadvantage. I love the boy with my whole heart. It would be an honor having him as a son. I'm sorry, Becky." His face showed regret.

"Sorry?" Her eyes widened woefully.

"Yep, I'm sorry. You see, it's a package. Either I get you both or the deal is off."

As the words registered her face grew a slow grin. "Absolutely, Justin, I love you, and I can't wait to be your wife. There're other matters too."

"Yes. Dad needs to give a statement to the Feds, so they can put the cold murder case to bed. And I had a talk this week with your ex. I told him he'd return to prison if he came near you again— you wouldn't hesitate to come after him. I didn't explain our involvement, so he assumed I contacted him as your attorney. He recently discovered you have a kid having finally located your address. He saw the swing set in back. The ass doesn't believe Evan is his child. He said, *The bitch ain't sticking me with no child support—not after sending me to the slammer."* I told him someone wants to adopt the child and will take full financial responsibility. Brent eagerly signed the papers giving you sole custody of the child. It began as a spur-of-the-moment idea when he started bitching about child support. I decided to get him legally out of the picture for you, so you no longer need to worry if he'll come back and cause problems later. He has no claim on your son."

"What about the adoption thing? Where did it come from?" She eyed him suspiciously holding the paperwork he handed her dumbfounded.

"It would be me. But I wanted to propose to you first then get your take on adoption. I never meant for the timing to go this way. Marry me and allow me to adopt your son?"

Becky listened wide-eyed. "Spur of the moment . . . so you've had time to reconsider. Sure you want to take it on?" She studied him as though trying to read his mind.

"Absolutely, it would be best for all of us, and I'd be over the moon having Evan as my son."

"Thanks for talking with Brent. I've worried he'd find my home, since he accosted me in the parking lot. I determined not to put up with his crap any longer. I'm not the meek victim I portrayed when he was sent to jail. He scares me. He's volatile, and I feared it might come to a bloody conclusion if he showed up in a temper. I promised myself he'd never hurt me again, and I won't let him hurt Evan."

"I know, baby. I figured if I approached him in a professional manner, it might work out without you needing to face him."

"Thank you. I don't know what to say."

"Say you're happy, and you love me." He brushed a curl from her eyes.

"I love you." She wiggled shamefully against him. "Think we can manage once more before we fall sleep?" She stroked him with urgency, electrifying his senses. He needed no more encouragement.

CHAPTER 28

Justin walked to the other cabin to retrieve Evan while Becky helped Richard and put breakfast on the table.

The boy eyed him suspiciously. "Justin, what happened last night?"

He couldn't dodge the boy's earnest concern. "A bad man came and tried to hurt Dad, your mom, and Sadie. I'm sorry if you were scared. Your mom and Aunt Sadie are fine. Everything is fine now."

"What happened to the bad man?" Fear filled his innocent eyes.

"You don't need to worry about him any longer. Dad fixed it. He'll never hurt anyone again." The boy's tiny hand took Justin's and felt right lying in his palm.

"Is Grandpa Richard fine too?"

"Dad's as good as he can be. You know his bad heart can't be fixed."

"Yeah, Mom told me about it. I hope he holds out a long, long time." Evan chewed his lower lip.

"Me too, Evan."

"Mom acted kind of shook up last night. Thanks for taking care of her." Evan gave him a tentative questioning glance.

"You bet, Evan. I care a lot for you and your mom, and being here for the two of you is my new, favorite job."

The boy grinned happily. "Really? I wish you were my dad."

"Seriously?" Justin kneeled, eye-to-eye with the boy.

"Yeah, sure. I love you and Grandpa Richard. I wish we lived here with you and didn't have to go back to the city."

"You know, little man. It might be arranged. Think we can talk your mom into it?"

"I don't know. She's pretty keen on her job at the hospital. I'm not sure she can be talked into it. I'm game if you are." Evan raised his hand.

Justin stood and slapped palms in a high-five. "Let's give it a shot." He led the boy into the cabin.

♥♥♥♥

"Good morning, Mom." Evan threw himself into her open arms.

"Morning, baby, ready for breakfast."

She scooped and whirled him around the room, landing him in a chair beside where Richard sat at the table. She'd worried how Evan might react after the episode played out the previous evening. He'd only heard the top line story, and there was no reason to reveal gory details to the child. He acted happy and unhindered—a good sign.

Evan screwed his lips. "I'm not a baby, Mom. I'm a little man. Justin said so."

Justin shrugged grinning at Becky with his palms toward the ceiling. She laughed.

"I must agree, Evan." She sat a glass of juice in front of him striving for an equal measure of calmness. He might have an adverse reaction from their experience, but had been told only the top line story. "How did you sleep?" She stroked his cheek. His soft skin warmed her soul. The boy as much a part of her as the hand she touched him with.

"Great, it was a fun sleepover, thanks for letting me stay. I'm starved. Can I make a peanut butter sandwich to go with my cereal?"

"If it is what you want. You sure you're okay?" She placed the jar, a dull knife and a loaf of bread in front of him, surprised it was all he said.

"Sure, Mom, Justin explained about the bad man. I'm fine, especially now you, Aunt Sadie and Grandpa Richard are safe."

"We're good, baby—I mean Evan."

Richard patted Evan's hand reassuringly, eagerly watching the exchange. Simple creatures, children needed basics, necessities, love, and security. Evan apparently had it all and was satisfied.

Becky faced Justin. She shrugged in confused. Justin snickered as Becky took her seat. "Evan and I have something to discuss."

A brow cocked, she eyed her favorite fellas. "And it would be?"

"Evan likes it here. He wants to live here. He and I want to be father and son. Dad's already his Grandpa. I want in on the action." He glanced at his dad who grinned like a fool. "We'd like to make the arrangement permanent."

Becky glared at the main men in her life with her arms crossed. Evan beamed anticipation on his adorable face. She ignored the urge to jump across the table and kiss his cherub cheeks.

"We want you and Evan to move here and live with me. Evan and I hoped you could transfer to the local hospital. You and I could get married. We could be a real family. What do you think, Becky? You game?" Justin obviously got off on splaying out this plan like a child would tell it—uncomplicated and extremely desirable.

"So, this is what the deep conversation was about the two of you had outside. I wondered what mischief you plotted." She continued to glare with a hint of laughter in her expression, trying to make them stew as long as possible. Evan wiggled adorably in his seat. Richard acted ready to bust a gut laughing. And Justin—the flirtatious smile made it hard not to rush into his arms and kiss every inch of his handsome face.

"Becky, I meant what I said." He reached for her hand, staring pleadingly into her eyes. "You never answered my proposal last night. Marry me?"

"Of course I will. I could never disappoint my men." She took Evan's and Justin's hands, tweaked Evan's nose, and pulled Justin's to her lips kissing him.

As they drew apart Justin winked.

"Possessiveness is endearing on you, Becky." They stood, and she walked into his waiting arms. Becky's head rested on Justin's shoulder and she contentedly sighed.

Glorious morning sun penetrated the room replacing the grisly scene witnessed the night before with blissful peace and warmth. Joy filled the air.

"Can we get married right away? Maybe today?" Evan was eager to settle things.

The adults laughed. "I'm not sure we could pull it off, Evan. There are details to manage." Becky stroked his head.

"It's not complicated. You want an elaborate wedding?" Richard asked Becky.

"No, I want you boys and Sadie there—nothing fancy."

"We might manage. You go to town for the license after breakfast. I'll phone my buddy. Judge Mike Stands owes me a favor, and would be happy to marry you if you want to do it here."

Justin appeared as enthusiastic as Evan. She shrugged. "Why not?"

"Are you sure, Becky? It would be amazing, and Dad's with us."

Her insides began doing their happy dance excited at the idea. "It's a marvelous idea. I can't think of a more perfect wedding."

"Son, wouldn't it be best if Becky waits to find a new job when you return to Nashville to live?" Richard eyed him curiously.

"No, Dad. I'm staying here. I quit my job and sold my condo. It's what I drove to town to sign yesterday in such a hurry. A substantial offer came in, and I jumped on it. I'm staying here. I'll manage the resort and keep working for the firm in town. Ben offered me a partnership." He beamed with satisfaction.

"It is great news, son. I suspected you might lean that direction, but didn't want to influence you one way or the other. I'm happy for you both. You're perfect for each other. This makes it official. I'm Evan's grandpa. Evan, you're going to enjoy living here."

Becky beamed. "He certainly will. He's always talking about this place."

After hugs and kisses, Richard reached for his phone. "Let's get this wedding going." A quick call and he grinned. "Judge Stands will be here at four."

Justin called JJ, and Becky rang Sadie who squealed loudly, thrilled. Sadie and JJ agreed to handle catering and inviting close friends. The plan set into action.

After breakfast, Garrett stayed with Richard while Becky and Justin drove to town. Richard, Evan and Garrett settled on the couch watching a fishing show on television.

At the courthouse, Justin and Becky purchased a license. They stopped by the florist and bought flowers. Justin checked in at the law office while Becky bought wedding attire for herself and Evan.

JJ and Sadie arrived. Everyone busily erected tables on the lawn for food and guests on a mission to make this happen. It fell together perfectly.

At four that afternoon Justin and JJ, dressed in their best suits, stood beneath a massive walnut tree in front of Richard's cabin. Richard proudly witnessed from his wheelchair wearing a navy suit. The men sported boutonnieres of tiny yellow and orange daisies. Judge Mike Stands faced the crowd of friends and resort patrons gathered to witness the nuptials.

An impressive banquet waited on a side table. Another held dozens of gaily wrapped gifts. Music flowed from Justin's music system speakers.

Richard had shown Evan how to knot his tie. The adorable boy wore it with a white shirt, navy slacks, and sport jacket, sporting a single yellow flower. Evan exited the cabin carrying a satin pillow with wedding rings tied in a bowed center. He grinned proudly as he walked toward Justin and stopped beside him.

Sadie emerged from her cabin carrying a bouquet of yellow and orange daisies with long, flowing sun-colored ribbons. Lovely in a strappy, turquoise sundress with a full skirt floating happily around her, she strolled toward the men and stood opposite JJ.

Becky appeared in the doorway in a lacy white tea-length sundress. She stood there a long moment taking it in.

Thin shoulder straps displayed the deep tan she'd gotten at the lake. A white rose pinned in her unruly hair, and she carried a bouquet of white roses intermingled with yellow and orange daisies, trailing white satin ribbons to her knees. Her petite feet had donned matching leather ballet flats.

At the sight of her Justin appeared to hold his breath. A gorgeous vision, he stood tall and strong. Her son stood with shoulders back proudly by Justin's side, grinning as though his fondest dream had come true.

Her smile radiated from within, and her heart over-flowed on the happiest day of her life.

This cheerful community of friends gathered eager to welcome her into their midst. These men and her sister stood waiting anxious to love and protect her. This, her family, adored her, as she did them. Her son finally had the clan he deserved, one to support and love them for as long as they lived.

Justin became the man of Becky's dreams. She hadn't been aware of her fantasies, but her dreams had come true. Justin would cherish her above all else. He'd never turn on her and would protect her with his life, as he would her son. Their home together would thrive and be happy.

Becky and Justin's eyes locked across the distance. Their gaze never faltered as she strolled toward him. He reached for her outstretched hand. His dwarfed hers and surrounded it with heat.

"Who gives this woman to this man in marriage?" Mike asked.

"We do." Evan and Richard answered simultaneously. Becky bent and kissed them each, then returned to Justin. After the quick ceremony Justin kissed his bride.

"Welcome home, Becky." Justin beamed with eyes filled with moisture.

"My love, always." Only he heard her low voice as she back-handed a tear from her cheek.

"Ladies and gentlemen, I present to you Mr. and Mrs. Justin Martin." The crowd cheered and clapped as Becky and Justin faced them, hand-in-hand.

Partiers mingled and festive air filled with chattering conversation as people helped themselves to the banquet and drinks. The bride and groom strolled among guests as they seated themselves to eat, speaking quietly with each person attending. Couples danced in a clearing.

During a long, slow-dance, Justin held his bride close as she flung the garter he'd stripped from her leg over her shoulder. A laughing group of single women dove for the possession.

"I cannot imagine a more perfect wedding." Becky smiled into Justin's eyes contentedly.

"It's perfect because of you." He kissed the tip of her nose, and she sighed happily.

Guests started driving off saying goodnights. JJ and Sadie began clearing the party remains while Evan and Richard played gin rummy on a table.

Becky and Justin sat leisurely soaking up the last of the sun's rays as it sank behind the tree line. Gold mingled with pink and orange blending a swirl of filmy clouds creating a spectacular show for avid observers.

"Wow, having faced tragedy, this place is the closed thing to heaven I've found." Becky's words came with a long, slow release of air.

"I can't disagree. I always loved this place. Now home means more than ever. This is where I belong—here with you." His arm slipped around her shoulders, and she shivered. "You cold?"

"Not with you around." She grinned. "I'd go anywhere with you, even Nashville. I'm happy you chose to stay here. It's lovely, and will be a perfect home for us. It's good you enjoy your new work and discovered what you want from life."

"I certainly have. Not just work and home. I found you."

Her head tilted to lie against his shoulder. "I still have tons of baggage to deal with."

"Me too. We'll work through it together. We've proved we can."

The End

Dear Reader,
If you enjoyed the read please leave me a review. Click one or all of these links. Thanks for taking the time to read my story and provide your feedback. It is appreciated and extremely important to me.
https://www.bookbub.com/profile/lynda-rees
Bookbub

https://www.goodreads.com/author/show/17187400.Lynda_Rees Goodreads

https://amazon.com/author/lyndarees Amazon

Dear Reader,

Thank you for reading God Father's Day. You may also be interested in reading my romantic suspense Madam Mom. Here's a few words about that book.

MADAM MOM

By Lynda Rees

Tisha McClain's attorney, Sam resents having a spoiled, rich-bitch heiress dropped onto his plate. The sexy, blonde male Tisha meets at the airport is an intrusive buttinski but appealing. Without revealing identities, they share an intimate fling.

Unraveling family's sordid past, Tisha discovers her prim, proper mother's involvement in shady mob business. Dad had associated with gangsters, and his brutal execution remains unsolved.

Recognizing misconceptions about each other, Tisha and Sam form a special bond. Tisha's been betrayed before. Can she get out of her unlawful predicament, evade a killer targeting her, and end the vicious McClain Curse to find love?

Find it here:
http://amazon.com/author/lyndarees

God Father's Day

About Lynda Rees

Lynda is a storyteller, an award-winning novelist, and a free-spirited dreamer with workaholic tendencies and a passion for writing romance. Her dreams come true, blessing her with a supportive family. Whatever crazy adventure Lynda congers up, her loving Mike is by her side. A diverse background, visits to exotic locations, and curiosity about history effects today's world fuel her writing. Born in the splendor of the Appalachian Mountains as a coal miner's daughter and part-Cherokee, she grew up in northern Kentucky when Newport prospered as a mecca for gambling and prostitution.

Published in romantic suspense, historical romance, children's middle grade, advertising copy, and freelance, Lynda is an active member of several professional writing organizations and judge of professional writing events.

Author's Note:

I hope you enjoy my work and we become life-long friends. ***Time for Romance.***

Lynda Rees

Love is a dangerous mystery

Get the latest book deals, exclusive content and FREE reads by subscribing to my newsletter.

Email: lyndareesauthor@gmail.com
Website: http://www.lyndareesauthor.com

Pinterest:
https://www.pinterest.com/lyndareesauthor/pins/

Goodreads:
https://www.goodreads.com/author/show/17187400.L
ynda_Rees

Twitter: https://twitter.com/LyndaReesauthor

Facebook:
https://www.facebook.com/lynda.rees.author/

ALSO BY LYNDA REES

Historical/Western: Gold Lust Conspiracy

The Bloodline Series:

Parsley, Sage, Rose, Mary & Wine

Leah's Story

Blood & Studs

Hot Blooded

Blood of Champions

Bloodlines & Lies

Horseshoes & Roses

The Bloodline Trail

Single Titles: God Father's Day

Madam Mom

Children Titles: Freckles & Blondie

Find information about these books at website:
http://www.lyndareesauthor.com

God Father's Day